The Bro

Book Four

Templar Fury

By

K. M. Ashman

Published by

SILVERBACK BOOKS LTD

Copyright K M Ashman - August 2020

All rights are reserved. No part of this publication may be reproduced, stored, or transmitted in any form or by any means, without prior written permission of the copyright owner.

All characters depicted within this publication are fictitious, and any resemblance to any real persons living or dead is entirely coincidental.

KMAshman.com

More books by K M Ashman

The India Summers Mysteries
The Vestal Conspiracy
The Treasures of Suleiman
The Mummies of the Reich
The Tomb Builders

The Roman Chronicles
The Fall of Britannia
The Rise of Caratacus
The Wrath of Boudicca

The Medieval Sagas
Blood of the Cross
In Shadows of Kings
Sword of Liberty
Ring of Steel

The Blood of Kings
A Land Divided
A Wounded Realm
Rebellion's Forge
Warrior Princess
The Blade Bearer

The Brotherhood
Templar Steel – The Battle of Montgisard
Templar Stone – The Siege of Jacob's Ford
Templar Blood – The Battle of Hattin
Templar Fury – The Siege of Acre
Templar Glory – The Road to Jerusalem

Standalone Novels
Savage Eden
The Last Citadel
Vampire
The Legacy Protocol
The Seventh God

Audio Books
Blood of the Cross
The Last Citadel
A Land Divided
A Wounded Realm
Rebellion's Forge
The Warrior Princess
The Vestal Conspiracies
The Tomb Builders

Map of the Holy-land

(Circa AD 1189)

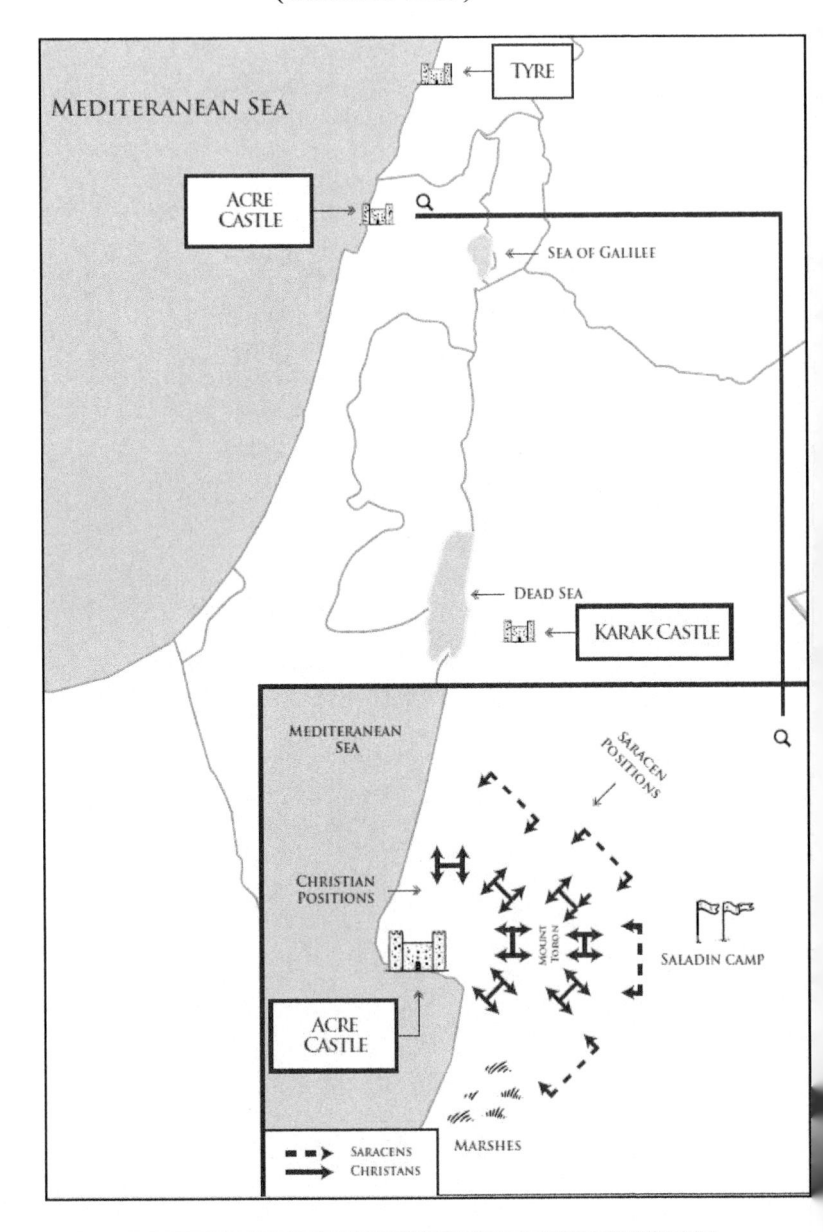

CHARACTER LIST

Main Christian Characters

Guy of Lusignan - King of Jerusalem from 1186
Sibylla of Jerusalem – Queen of Jerusalem from 1186
Richard the Lionheart – King of England
Conrad of Montferrat – Lord of Tyre
Sancho-martin – The Green Knight
Reginald of Sidon – Lord of Sidon
Balian of Ibelin – Lord of Nablus
Gerard of Ridefort - Grandmaster of the Knights Templar
Thomas Cronin - Sergeant at Arms
James Hunter – Scout
Arturas – Mercenary Leader
Sumeira – Healer
John-Loxley - Physician

Main Muslim Characters

Salah ad-Din (Saladin) – Sultan of Egypt and Syria
Muzaffar ad-Din Gökböri – Emir of Edessa
Al-Afdal ibn Salah ad-Din – Saladin's son
Fakhiri – Egyptian Cart-master
Prince Turan-Shah –Garrison commander in Acre
Barak el-Sayed – Jailer
Hassan Malouf - Bedouin Tribesman
Jahara – Hashashin disciple

Prologue

In AD 1187, Guy of Lusignan, King of Jerusalem, led a huge Christian army to lift a siege on the city of Tiberias. Having left the relative safety of the city of Sephorie only a day earlier, his underestimation of the rigours of the road meant the army struggled on the march, and by the time nightfall came, his men were already suffering great thirst and exhaustion.

Knowing that the only water-source large enough to serve his massive army was at the Springs of Kafr Hattin, Guy diverted off the road to Tiberias, and onto the plains of Hattin, a decision that was to change the course of history.

That night, Saladin's forces attacked Guy's army, maintaining the pressure without let-up. The Saracen army surrounded the Christians and kept them awake with chants, prayers, and continued arrow attacks. In the morning, they added to the despair by setting fire to the stubble on the plains, sending clouds of choking smoke throughout the Christian camps, and taunting them with their ample supply of water.

For many, it was too much, and thousands deserted, desperate to reach the life-giving springs. Others defected to the enemy, and some even begged to be killed quickly to end their suffering.

Guy and his commanders went on the offensive and made several attempts to take Saladin's camp, and though Raymond of Tripoli managed to escape with his army to the shores of the Tiberias sea, most of the Christian army was slaughtered or taken prisoner beneath the twin peaks of the ancient volcano that gives the plain its name.

Eventually, Guy had no other option than to surrender. Most of the surviving nobles were taken into captivity to be ransomed, but any common soldiers still alive were killed or taken as slaves. Many knights, including Templars and Hospitallers, were executed without mercy, as was the famous castellan of Karak Castle, Raynald of Chatillon. Guy himself was taken prisoner but treated cordially as befitted a king.

The consequences for the Holy-land were dire, and within months, Saladin had not only captured most of the castles and towns across the Outremer, but he had also conquered the heart of Christianity itself, Jerusalem.

In the west, the coastal city of Acre, crucial to any occupation of the Holy-land, was captured and occupied by Egyptian forces loyal to Saladin, and quickly fortified the already strong defences knowing that if a counter-offensive happened, then Acre would be the first target.

By late 1187, almost all of the Outremer was in Muslim hands. One or two smaller castles held out desperately including Belfort Castle, a fortress perched high on the rocks above the Litani River, but most had been captured or were under siege by Saladin's rampant forces.

Despite this, there remained one stronghold in the Outremer that continued to defy the Muslim onslaught, Tyre, the coastal city north of Acre. The population was at breaking point due to the constant arrival of Christian refugees from across the Holy-land, but its location meant at least it was able to receive supplies and reinforcements via its ports.

Even so, its temporary lord, Reginald of Sidon, knew they could not last much longer, and after hearing that Saladin was on his way to take the city, sent out envoys to negotiate a surrender.

Exhausted and hugely outnumbered, it seemed the Christians had no way back, but before any agreement was signed, the arrival of one man stopped the process in its tracks. That man's name was Conrad of Montferrat, and his arrival was pivotal in what came next.

Chapter One

Tyre

July - AD 1187

Reginald of Sidon sat on a chair, five hundred paces in front of the fortified walls of Tyre. A long line of crusader tents stretched away to either side, each flying the colours of Jerusalem and the city of Tyre. Before him was a table, laid out with a bowl of fresh dates, a pitcher of clean water, and four glass goblets, the best that could be found amongst the rich houses of the city.

At his side sat Edward of Gaza, the only Templar who had escaped the slaughter at Cresson. Across the table were two empty chairs, waiting for the Ayyubid envoys who would be negotiating the handover of the city to Saladin. The worst of the midday sun was held at bay by a giant canopy just above their heads, and a gentle sea breeze wafted in from the Mediterranean coast just half a league away to the east.

'They are late,' said Reginald, peering into the distance. 'They said they would be here by noon.'

'There must be a good reason,' said Edward, 'I have never known the sultan or his ambassadors to ever miss an agreed counsel. Perhaps they have had cause to reconsider our offer of surrender and rally their troops as we speak.'

'No,' said Reginald, 'Saladin is an astute man, and he would much rather gain control of Tyre by negotiation rather than fighting. His forces are spread out from as far south as Gaza right up to Damascus, and he fights on many fronts. He cannot afford another conflict.'

'I do not agree,' said Edward. 'Tyre is the last stronghold left in the Outremer, and you can be sure that his spies in the city will have reported our strengths and weaknesses.'

'We will see,' said Reginald. 'Either way, we cannot go on as we are. The city is full of refugees, and more appear by the day. We can only just about feed ourselves, and that is only because we still have control of our port. If Saladin were to cut us off, we would be starved out within days.'

'We will soon find out,' said Edward getting to his feet, 'here they come.'

Reginald stood up and gazed across the open plain. In the distance, a column of riders appeared in the south. A nearby knight bellowed his orders, and hundreds of men emerged from the tents to line up behind Reginald, a necessary show of force to any Saracens joining the negotiations.

Several minutes later, the Ayyubid column spread out into a line-abreast formation and slowed the pace to a walk. In the centre, Reginald could see several high-ranking officials, each accompanied by a flag bearer, and as they approached, the main body of warriors stopped as three riders continued right up to the negotiating table.

Reginald immediately recognised one of the men as Muzaffar ad-Din Gokbori, the Emir of Edessa, and one of Saladin's most trusted generals. The other was a black-clad Mamluk bodyguard, the slave warriors feared by men all across the Holy-land. The third was a flag bearer, carrying the yellow standard of the Ayyubid. The two envoys dismounted while the flag-bearer drove the yellow standard deep into the soft soil before turning to gallop back to the column.

'Muzaffar ad-Din Gokbori,' said Reginald with a slight bow of the head, 'we are honoured.'

'The respect is mutual,' said Gokbori, 'and I acknowledge that I am in the presence of men not afraid to fight yet are open to the words of peace.'

'Please,' said the Lord of Sidon, 'be seated and take refreshment.'

All four men sat and waited as a servant poured the water into the goblets. Each took a sip, cementing their promise that all present would negotiate in peace.

'So,' said Gokbori, placing his goblet upon the table, 'my master has told me that you sent envoys requesting terms to surrender the city.'

'Surrender is an emotive word,' said Reginald, 'but we did not invite you here to argue. I hope you will agree that the conflict between our people does not extend to civilians and if there is a handover, any who wish to leave will be allowed to do so in peace.'

Gokbori looked between the two men for a moment before taking another sip of water.

'Sir Reginald of Sidon,' he said, 'I have heard your name mentioned many times in our war counsels. I saw you fight at Hattin, and you have my respect. It is for that reason I will be straight and tell you no untruths. Many of your people were born here, and we recognise that they know no other home. They will be welcome to stay, but others came from foreign lands with no other intention than to rip the soil from beneath our feet. We have suffered the occupation of the Franks for almost one hundred years, and to them, there can be no forgiveness.'

Sir Reginald stared at the emir, his eyes narrowing with concern.

'I do not understand,' he said eventually, 'I invited you here to discuss the peaceful handover of the city. Are you now saying that your frustration will be taken out on the innocent?'

'Only those who cannot pay.'

'What do you mean?'

'Those who can speak the local language will be allowed to stay and live their lives as they did before. Those who came from foreign shores to seek fortune at our expense will be allowed to leave after paying the price to be agreed.'

'And those who cannot?'

'They will see out their days as slaves to the Ayyubid.'

'The price is too high,' said Reginald. 'The city is full of refugees from many other towns who fled your armies with only the clothes they wore. Most have nothing, and if I agree to these terms, those destined for slavery will number in the thousands.'

'This is not a situation of our making,' said Gokbori. 'They choose to come to our lands in the hope it would make them wealthy. That wager has not paid off, and now they will pay the price.'

Reginald glanced at Edward but received nothing in return.

'There has to be some room for negotiation,' he said eventually. 'This city enjoys a strategic position, second only to Acre. With both in your possession, you would control the supply routes from Tripoli to Egypt.'

'I agree,' said Gokbori, 'and we fully intend to claim it back in the name of Allah, but make no mistake, if that means we have to flood the streets with Christian blood, then that is what we will do. With regards to negotiation, my terms are clear and will not be altered. You are at a disadvantage here, Sir Reginald, as you well know. If I were to besiege your city, I do not think we would have to loose a single arrow in anger. All we would have to do is block off your supply lines on land and sea. With so many refugees in your city, they would soon tear down the gates from the inside to try to find food and water.'

'I must warn you, Gokbori,' said Reginald, 'I still have a powerful army at my command. It may not be as easy as you think.'

'Neither was Hattin,' said Gokbori.

Reginald stared at the emir. Hattin had been a disaster, and tens of thousands of men had lost their lives. The Christian army had been totally destroyed, and Reginald had been lucky to escape with his life.

'You have made it clear what it is you expect,' he said eventually, 'but you must now allow me time to consider.'

'Of course,' said Gokbori standing up. 'We will give you seven days.' He looked over at the flag. 'This standard will guarantee none of our people will attack while negotiations continue. I advise you to keep it visible until such time that an agreement is made, or not, as the case may be. On the eighth day, I will send a rider to retrieve the flag and to receive your answer. Think carefully, Reginald of Sidon, the lives of thousands are in your hands.'

Edward and Reginald watched as the two Saracens mounted their horses and returned to the Ayyubid line. When they had gone, Reginald slumped back into his chair and reached for his goblet of water.

'He has us over a cliff edge,' he said eventually, 'and he knows it.'

'We could call his bluff,' said Edward. 'Our men are angry and spoiling for a fight, so perhaps we should let him come. Don't forget, the Pope has called on all Christian nations to avenge Hattin. All we would have to do is hold out until they arrive.'

'That could take months,' said Reginald, 'years even. No, fighting will only water the soil with more blood, and I see no purpose in that.'

'So, what do you intend to do?'

'I am going to accept his proposition,' said Reginald, 'yet try to delay as much as possible.'

'To what end?'

'To get as many as the poor out of Tyre before the surrender is agreed. That way, those that can pay the price can still purchase their freedom, but fewer will suffer the fate of slavery.'

'There is no way we can get that many people out of Tyre without being seen. It is impossible.'

'Not if we use our supply ships,' said Reginald turning to look at Edward. 'As soon as they have been emptied, we can fill them with the poor, and send them back up the coast to Tripoli. If we start immediately, we can get thousands to safety before Gokbori returns.'

'It still won't be enough,' said Edward. 'There are just too many refugees.'

'I know, but at least we will have extra time to save even more souls.'

'I can't see it working,' said Edward, 'it won't take long before his spies realise what is happening and report back to the emir.'

'Then what do you suggest I do?' shouted Reginald, banging his fist on the table, *'just commit tens of thousands to slavery?* There is no way we can defeat him in battle, we would last less than two weeks if besieged, and there is not enough gold in Christendom to try to bribe him.'

'My lord,' said Edward, 'I only meant to add a second view to the consideration. I meant no insult, and I concur, it seems the best way to save as many lives as possible. I just fear that when Gokbori finds out we are depriving him of captives, as he will, he may not be so amenable to a peaceful handover.'

Reginald got to his feet.

'If that is his choice, then so be it. I cannot and will not just sign away the lives of thousands at the stroke of a quill.' He stood up and realised the guards were still standing in the afternoon sun, waiting for the command to stand down. 'Strike camp,' he said, 'and get our men back to the city. As soon as you get there, summon every captain of every ship in the harbour and tell them what we intend to do. I want to see the first of the refugees leave before nightfall. Is that clear?'

'It is, my lord,' said Edward. He stood up and looked over at the Ayyubid flag still fluttering in the coastal breeze. 'What do you want me to do about that?'

'Bring it with you,' said Reginald, 'you can guarantee he still has men watching our every move, and the last thing we need to be doing right now is giving him any cause to question our intentions. Place it on one of the gate towers to show good faith.'

'So, be it,' said Edward, and with a nod of respect, turned away to start dismantling the temporary camp.

Reginald of Sidon turned and walked back to his command tent. His squire was waiting at the entrance, and as he ducked inside, the young man followed him in.

'Help me with this,' he demanded, starting to undo the leather strap on his tabard, 'and then bring me my horse. We need to get back to the city immediately.'

'Yes, my lord,' said the squire, but little did they know that even as Reginald was formulating his plans for the mass evacuation of the city, a few leagues off the coast, a small fleet of ships were heading for Tyre, an intervention that would change everything.

Chapter Two

Tyre

July - AD 1187

Reginald stood atop one of the gate towers, peering across the narrow strip of land that connected Tyre to the mainland. It had been blocked with a timber palisade, and as it was the only landward approach to the city, it would slow down any attack, should the Saracens decide to go on the offensive. It had been three days since Gokbori had delivered Saladin's ultimatum, and already, Tyre had sent over a thousand refugees northward in a fleet of ships. But when the word got out, panic had ensued as each person desperately tried to gain passage, and the army had to be used to calm the situation. In the confusion, they lost valuable time, and it was clear that they would be unable to evacuate even a quarter of those who needed to go.

'My lord,' said a voice, and he turned to see Sir Edward standing behind him.

'Edward,' he said, 'I thought you were organising the next ships to leave for Tripoli.'

'I was, my lord,' said Edward, 'but I have news. A fleet of ten ships has appeared off the coast. They fly the flags of Genoa and request permission to dock. Obviously, I have granted their request, but I also received this note, sent from the commander of the fleet.' He handed a sealed parchment over and waited as Reginald tore it open to read the contents. A few minutes later, he turned to face Edward.

'It seems that Conrad of Montferrat is about to arrive,' he said.

'I have heard the name, but know not the man,' said Edward.

'He is a nobleman from Italy,' replied Reginald, 'and a powerful one at that.'

'What do you mean?'

'Well he is first-cousin to the Holy Roman Emperor, Frederick Barbarossa, and his wife is the sister of Leopold IV of Austria. Not only does he have powerful connections, but he has arrived with five hundred men at arms, including a hundred knights.'

'A considerable force,' said Edward. 'This changes everything.'

'It changes nothing,' snapped Reginald. 'Even if he had a thousand men, we could never defend Tyre from the Ayyubid. Saladin can muster an army ten times that size in days. As I said, the threat is not from arrows or swords, but from hunger and thirst should we be besieged.'

'What does he want?'

'Apparently, he intended to land at Acre, but the city has already fallen to Saladin so he seeks refuge here while he considers his options. More than that, I do not know. Go and meet him on my behalf at the dock, I will see about arranging suitable quarters for his men and horses.'

'As you wish, my lord,' said Edward, and left the tower.

Night was already closing in when the Conrad of Montferrat stepped from his ship. Tall in stature and elegantly dressed, he commanded immediate attention from everyone in the vicinity. His beard was trimmed short, and it swept up the side of his jowls to merge with his dark curly hair. As he stepped from the gangplank, Edward walked up to greet him.

'My Lord Conrad,' said Edward, with a nod of the head, 'welcome to Tyre.'

'And you are?' asked Conrad.

'I am Edward of Gaza,' came the reply, 'currently in the service of Reginald of Sidon until the grandmaster musters what is left of our order.'

'I have heard about Hattin,' said Conrad, 'were you there?'

'I was not,' said Edward. 'I fought at Cresson but was posted here by Gerard of Ridefort before the call to arms.'

'So, where do I find Reginald of Sidon?'

'He is waiting for you in the citadel, my lord. I have been sent to take you there as soon as you arrive.'

Conrad turned to stare at the lines of people waiting to board two ships on the far side of the harbour.

'Where are they going?'

'We are shipping them to Tripoli.'

'Why?'

'Because if they stay here, they might end up as slaves of the Ayyubid.'

'Why, are you under attack?'

'No, my lord, but negotiations are underway to hand over the city to Saladin, and any man, woman or child not born here, and who can't pay the toll, will be taken into slavery.'

'Hand over the city?' said Conrad turning to face Edward. 'Surely you are not going to surrender without a fight?'

'My lord,' said Edward, 'with the greatest respect, I feel you should be asking these questions of Sir Reginald.'

'Oh I will,' said Conrad, 'I came all the way here from Italy to fight the Saracens, not to cower like a beaten child. Where is he?'

'He is waiting for you in his quarters.'

'Then take me to him,' said Conrad, 'there is much to discuss.' He started to walk away, but before Edward could move, the newcomer turned his head and called out to one of the sergeants organising the lines of refugees. 'You there, send these people back into the city. Find them bread and water, and tell anyone with shelter to take them in.'

'My lord,' said the soldier, 'these people are being shipped to Tripoli.'

'They are going nowhere,' said Conrad. 'Get them fed and housed with those that have plenty. I don't care if they lodge with prince or peasant, I want every person with a roof over their heads by tomorrow night.'

'My lord,' said the sergeant, 'If people are forced to share what little they have, there will be much anger.'

'I care not. Crack skulls if you have to, but I need these people strong and available for work. Understood?'

'Yes, my lord,' said the sergeant, and as Conrad walked away, he turned to Edward.

'I am at a loss' he said, 'do I continue with Sir Reginald's orders, or does this new man outrank him?'

'Your guess is as good as mine,' said Edward. 'Just sit everyone down and find them water. I will see what is happening and send word as soon as I can.'

'Yes, my lord.'

Up in the citadel, Reginald was pacing the floor, wondering how to deal with the man who was only minutes away. He knew Conrad from old and knew he was a man of great strength and character. He was also a formidable fighter and was never happier than in the midst of battle. His arrival would certainly change the dynamic of the city and would probably alarm Gokbori as to the security of the proposed handover. But the situation was out of his hands and he had to deal with whatever came his way. He poured himself a glass of wine and walked over to stand at the window, peering out over the harbour to where the rest of the Genoese fleet was waiting to dock.

Moments later, Edward of Gaza entered the room.

'Sir Edward,' said Reginald, looking past the knight into the corridor, 'I thought you were going to greet Sir Conrad.'

'I did, my lord,' said Edward, 'and we were on our way here when he suddenly changed his mind and made a detour.'

'To where?'

'The gates, my lord. He demanded you meet him there, and he is not happy.'

'Why not?'

'Your guess is as good as mine,' said Edward, 'but tread carefully. He seems to be a man short on patience.'

'Oh, I know that,' said Reginald, 'his reputation precedes him like a desert storm.'

'Are you going to meet him?'

'Why wouldn't I?'

'Because you are the Lord of Tyre, and he is the visitor. You should not jump to the whims of such men.'

'If I was in my own castle, then I would agree, but I am only the Lord of Tyre as the role was empty when I arrived here from Hattin. The true successor must be decided by others, but for now, I only rule to keep the people alive until we can make other arrangements. Come, you will accompany me.'

The two men left the room and headed across the city towards the only gates leading into Tyre.

'Where is Lord Conrad?' asked Edward to one of the guards at the gate.

'Up there, my lord,' said the guard, pointing up to one of the gate towers, 'at least I think it is the man you seek.'

'Did you not challenge him?'

'We did, my lord,' said the guard, 'but he did not take kindly to the challenge.' He nodded towards one of his comrades who was sitting against a wall with blood pouring from his mouth. Sir Reginald sighed and pushed past the guard to enter the gate tower and climb the spiral stairway. At the top, he emerged onto the battlements to see the knight staring over the walls into the Outremer.

'Sir Conrad,' he said, walking towards him, 'welcome to the Holy-land.'

Conrad looked over his shoulder but did not turn.

'Sir Reginald,' he said, 'tell me, what is the purpose of that palisade on the spit of land before the gates?'

'Just another defensive wall,' said Reginald, 'Why?'

'It would last no more than a few minutes if it were to be attacked. I fail to see the purpose?'

'It will give us more time to call the city to arms.'

'So, it is the only approach?'

'Apart from the harbour, yes. The reason the city has remained undefeated for so long is because of its position. It is basically an island enclosed by impenetrable walls, as stout as any I have seen.'

'What about fresh water?'

'We have our own well though it has to be supplemented with supplies from Tripoli. The population has increased dramatically since Hattin, and we struggle to feed and water the people.'

'So I understand,' said Conrad, and turned to face Reginald square on. 'Your man there,' he said, nodding towards Edward, 'tells me that you are in negotiations with the Saracens to hand over the city within days. Why exactly is that?'

'I have no other option,' said Reginald, 'I have my own responsibilities elsewhere, and have to leave as soon as possible. If I leave the city without a lord, the Saracens could kill or enslave anyone at will. At least this way, many will survive.'

'What responsibilities are so important that you cannot stay and orchestrate the defence?'

'There are many, but the most pressing is my castle at Belfort. Its position is crucial to anyone wishing to press further into the Holy-land, and already Saladin has sent an army against it.

I need to get there to make sure we deny him the strategic advantage.'

Conrad walked to the other side of the tower and gazed along the city walls.

'I am impressed,' he said, 'with enough men and strong leadership, this could be a formidable stronghold.'

'Indeed, it could,' said Reginald. 'But alas, we have neither the men nor the necessary support.'

'Hmmm,' said Conrad, and looked over to a flagpole tied to a metal ring embedded into the wall. 'Tell me, why do we fly the colours of the Ayyubid upon our own ramparts?'

'It is a pledge from Gokbori not to attack, and an acknowledgement from us that we are committed to finding a peaceful agreement. As long as it is visible, the city is safe.'

'Is it?' said Conrad. 'Well there is a lot to discuss, but one thing is certain, we take a knee to no heathen no matter who he serves.' He strode over to the flag and wrenching it from its ties, threw it over the ramparts into the ditch to the front of the walls.

'My lord,' said Reginald, 'you don't know what you are doing.'

'Oh I know exactly what I am doing,' said Conrad, 'now take me to the citadel, there is much to discuss.'

Two days later, Conrad of Montferrat stood atop the gate tower again, this time watching as a small column of horsemen rode out of the city to head south. At their head was Reginald of Sidon, having handed over the control of Tyre to Conrad.

At Conrad's side was Edward of Gaza having sworn allegiance to the new lord during the negotiations.

'It is a grievous loss,' said Edward as the last of Reginald's foot-soldiers marched through the gate. 'After discarding Gokbori's standard, we are more at risk of attack than ever but are weaker without Reginald's army.'

'My men will more than make up for their absence,' said Conrad, 'and besides, we have an army bigger than any Saladin can muster.'

'Where?' asked Edward.

'I'm talking about the civilians within Tyre,' said Conrad. 'They number in their thousands, and with the right direction, can add greatly to the defence of the city.'

'My lord,' said the knight, 'I agree that some can bear arms if required, but they are untrained and small in number.'

'Then train them,' said Conrad. 'But first, I want every able man and woman to go out there and dig a ditch in front of that palisade.' He pointed towards the barrier. 'I want it as deep as three men, and wide enough that even the strongest of destriers would be unable to leap it. Fill it with spiked posts and human waste along with the rotting remains of any dead animals. Make it a barrier that any man would hesitate to cross.'

'My lord,' said Edward, 'that would take an age.'

'Why?' asked Conrad. 'By your count, there are almost ten thousand refugees in Tyre, each without the means of feeding themselves. If we engage them, we can strengthen this city within days. Instead of just handing out food as soon as the supply ships arrive, let them earn their bread by contributing to their own safety.'

'Of course,' said the knight.

'While some are digging the ditch,' continued Conrad, 'get others to reinforce the palisade. Use the spoil to build ramparts and create loading platforms for our archers. Load them with barrels of arrows and buckets of pitch. Keep fires kindled all along the defences and send women to aid the fletchers. We need to increase the production of arrows. Send word to Tripoli and request as many supplies as possible, I want more food, water, weapons and trained men at arms. And request more horses, we will be unable to counterattack with the number we have.'

'My lord,' said Edward, 'this is all well and good, but how will we pay for these supplies? The treasury is already empty, and the lords of Tripoli will demand payment.'

'Remind them that Pope Gregory himself has called for a combined war against the Saracens, and the Lord God himself expects every Christian to do what he can to secure the Holy-land. To do that, we need a secure seaport, and with Acre already in the hands of the Ayyubid, Tyre is the only option we have. In the meantime, I will send messages across Christendom rallying men to the cause. If Saladin wants full control of the Outremer, he will have to take Tyre, and when he comes, we will make him pay for every step he takes.'

Chapter Three

Tyre

November - AD 1187
Four months later

Conrad of Montferrat walked into the hall in the citadel at the heart of Tyre city. Waiting for him were several nobles as well as the Bishop of Tyre and Balian of Ibelin. Each was standing behind a chair at a large dining table.

'Your Grace,' said Conrad, taking his place, 'please continue.'

The bishop said a prayer in thanks for the food they were about to eat before everyone sat, and the room filled with conversation. Servants brought in the food, and though it was certainly no feast, the meat was ample and the bread freshly baked. Jugs of wine and ale passed along the table, and everyone filled their plates with enthusiasm.

Talk focussed on the continuing threat from Saladin. There had been several small probes against the city walls from Saracen patrols, but the threat from Gokbori still hadn't materialised. One man was strangely quiet, and after a while, the bishop turned to face him, determined to engage him in conversation.

'Sir Balian,' he said, 'I believe this is the first time you have dined with us in the citadel. Do you not appreciate fine fayre?'

'I do indeed, your Grace,' said Balian, 'but I have been through much with my men, and I prefer to share their company whenever I can.'

'There is no shame in sharing with the enlisted men,' said Conrad. 'It builds character and loyalty.'

'I hear you fought at Hattin,' said the bishop. 'Was it as bad as what they say?'

'It was worse than you can imagine,' said Balian. 'I have never seen so many dead men.'

'And what of Jerusalem, I hear you were instrumental in its surrender?'

The noise died away and all eyes turned to Balian.

'I was,' he sighed eventually, placing his tankard back on to the table, 'but it was the only solution open to us. The city was about to fall, and Saladin swore to kill or enslave any Christian not born in the city. By doing what we did, we saved countless lives. I have no regrets.'

'Perhaps not,' said the bishop, 'but the Holy-city now lays in the hands of the Muslims. With the greatest respect, under what authority did you act?'

'Everything we did was with the full authorisation of Queen Isabella,' said Balian. 'As I said, we had no other choice. If we had resisted, we would all now be dead, and Christendom's holiest place would be no more than a pile of blood-soaked rubble.'

'We don't know that for certain,' said the bishop.

'Your Grace,' intervened Conrad, 'where is this going? Surely you are not suggesting that Lord Balian surrendered Jerusalem without good reason?'

'All I am saying is that we will never know what would have happened. As far as we know, God may have intervened and prevented a defeat.'

'If you have any doubts as to the reality of the situation,' said Balian staring into his drink, 'ask the Bishop of Jerusalem, and all the other clerics who were there. They wasted no time in paying for their freedom and fleeing as fast as they could to Tripoli.'

'Oh, I will,' said the bishop. 'It's just a shame the population of Jerusalem did not share the same fortitude as those that now defend Tyre. If they had, perhaps we would now be dining in the Holy-city instead of Tyre.'

Balian looked up with anger in his eyes, but before he could speak, the doors burst open, and Edward of Gaza entered the hall.

'Sir Edward,' said Conrad getting to his feet. 'I thought you were out on patrol.'

'I was,' said Edward, 'but we spotted a Saracen army, not two leagues south of here, thousands of men supported by a supply caravan that stretches all the way back to Acre.'

'Are they are headed here?'

'They must be. There are no other towns or castles in the area that would necessitate such a force.'

The room burst into conversation again, and the men got to their feet. Conrad held up his hand to demand silence.

'Gentlemen,' he said, 'be seated. We will send messages to our people outside the city to come inside, but the Saracens are still many hours away. Finish your meals in comfort for it may be the last we enjoy in such circumstances for quite a while.' He turned to Edward. 'Double the guard,' he said, 'and pass the word to all our farmsteads outside the walls.'

'Yes, my lord,' said Edward, and turned to leave the room.

All eyes turned to Conrad as he picked up his tankard.

'Gentlemen,' he said, looking around the room. 'To us lies the task of teaching Saladin the strength of the Christian faith.' He lifted up the tankard and held it up to toast. 'To the struggle ahead and the retrieval of Jerusalem.' All the men got to their feet and followed suit, downing their tankards in one. All that is, except Balian. He alone had witnessed the slaughter at Hattin, and he alone could even imagine what was coming.

The following morning, Conrad and Edward of Gaza climbed the steps on the outer wall of the city, heading for the best vantage point. All around them, men at arms rushed to their positions, answering the call of the battle horns now echoing across the city.

They emerged onto the tower and gazed into the distance. Already they could see hundreds of Ayyubid cavalry, and thousands of foot-soldiers marching into position. Conrad looked down at the Christian civilians now rushing across the plain to reach the safety of the palisade before it was too late.

'Shall we raise the bridge?' asked Sir Edward.

'Not yet,' said Conrad. 'Unless their cavalry attacks, we will ensure as many people as possible get within the walls of Tyre. They are our responsibility and we will not cast them aside without good cause.'

For the next few hours, the two men watched as the Saracen army grew in size. In addition to the supply carts, teams of oxen drew heavy wagons piled high with partly assembled siege-engines in readiness for the assault.

Along the battlements, commanders organised their defences. Many of the preparations had already been made, and the ramparts were piled high with extra arrows, boulders and buckets of pitch. Down in the outer bailey, even more stores lay waiting to be transferred up to the ramparts by scores of civilian men, each now fully aware of what was expected.

'My lord, 'said a voice, and Conrad turned to see a messenger standing behind him.

'What is it?'

'My lord, this morning, three ships arrived from Genoa with men seeking to serve God's crusade. Their commander is on his way here, and he seeks audience.'

'Do you know his name?'

'I do. He is called Sancho-martin, and a stranger knight I have never seen.'

A smile played about Conrad's face as he recognised the name.

'Send him up,' he said eventually, 'and arrange quarters for his men. This day is one of many surprises.'

The servant turned away as Edward walked over to Conrad.

'I take it that you know this man,' he said.

'Not personally, but his reputation precedes him. He is one of Spain's foremost knights, and if the stories are true, the arrival of him and his vassals is probably one of the best things that could have happened to us.'

'What makes him so strange?'

'Again, my knowledge of him is based on rumours only, but if true, you are about to find out.'

Ten minutes later, the messenger returned to the tower, followed by the newly arrived knight. He was taller than most with a muscular build and an undoubtedly handsome face, but it was not his features that caused the men on the ramparts to stare, it was the fact that he was entirely clad in green.

'Sancho-martin,' said Conrad as the knight approached, 'your reputation precedes you. Welcome to Tyre.'

'My lord,' said the knight, 'I was serving my master in Spain when he read aloud your message seeking men at arms to defeat the Saracens. I begged leave to take the cross, and he allowed me to sail in his name with a hundred knights under my command. I hereby pledge fealty to you and to Jerusalem until such time that the Holy-city is back in the hands of Christendom.'

'Your master is a saint indeed,' said Conrad, 'and your pledge is both welcome and well-timed. As you can see, we are about to be placed under siege, and the city is woefully undermanned. Your men will make a huge difference.'

'I swear we will fight to the last man,' said the knight. 'Just tell us where to deploy.'

'I think we have a few days,' said Conrad looking out to the gathering Saracen army. 'For now, we will find your men and horses somewhere to bed down. Tomorrow, we will discuss tactics.'

'As you wish, my lord,' said Sancho-martin, and turned to face Edward. 'My apologies, Sir Knight, I did not mean to exclude you from my greeting. I see you are a Templar and I bow in deference.' He nodded his head slightly but did not lose eye contact with his fellow knight.

'I am Edward of Gaza,' said Edward, 'and your arrival is most opportune. We have a formidable fortress and thousands of willing hands, what we don't have, however, are enough trained men to take the battle to the Ayyubid.'

'Well now you do,' said Sancho-martin and turned to face Conrad. 'My lord, with your permission, I will return to my men and see they are well quartered. If you need me, just send a messenger and we will be at your side.'

Conrad nodded agreement, and both he and Edward watched the strange Spaniard depart.

'He seems a good man,' said Edward, 'though his choice of garb is a bit strange.'

'Let not his appearance fool you, Sir Edward,' said Conrad, 'he enjoys a reputation as one of the fiercest warriors in Christendom. Have you ever heard anyone speak of the Green knight?'

'Only in tales around campfires,' replied Edward. 'I paid them no heed, judging them to be folklore only.'

'Some may well be,' said Conrad, 'but most are based on truth, and you, my friend, have just met the man responsible.'

Nine leagues away to the south, another city had just received a fleet of ships into its well-defended harbour. Acre was one of the strongest cities on the coast, and its vast port enabled the city to maintain a supply chain without having to rely on the much slower overland routes. For years it had been in the hands of the Christians, but after the battle of Hattin, it had capitulated to the Saracens and was now completely in Muslim hands.

In the northwest corner of the city, the old Templar commandery had been turned into a jail for fifty or so prisoners, many of whom carried wounds of varying degrees. Any uninjured prisoners were spread throughout the city, pressed into hard labour by cruel overseers in the pay of their Ayyubid masters. High ranking officials were offered a purse of gold, elegant clothing and a magnificent horse in return for converting to Islam, but though there were few takers, the majority of Christian civilians had still been allowed to leave for Tripoli. Since then, supply ships from Egypt had been pouring supplies into the city, and Saladin himself had established a council in the citadel, a temporary base from which to continue his cleansing of the Holy-land.

Turan-Shah walked across the courtyard alongside two of his bodyguards. He had been summoned to an audience with the sultan himself, and though he was a Prince of Yemen in his own right, a meeting with Salah ad-Din was a huge honour and one which was not to be taken lightly. He entered the guarded doors and was taken to the audience chamber by a servant, passing through many narrow corridors along the way. Immediately he felt closed in and wondered how anyone could make this their permanent home when they could have the sky as their roof and olive groves for walls. Already he yearned to lead his men out of the gates and back into the openness of Palestine's fruitful plains, and he hoped that Saladin's summons would be the moment he had been waiting for.

They arrived at a closed set of doors, and Turan-Shah waited as the servant entered to announce his arrival. A few moments later, the doors opened and the Yemeni prince walked past a double line of Mamluk bodyguards into a room the likes of which he had never seen before.

Immediately he looked up at the vaulted ceiling, held in place by vast oaken timbers shipped from Europe by the Christian builders. Chained chandeliers hung from the beams containing hundreds of candles, and the walls had been repainted by Ayyubid artisans to reflect great scenes from Arabic history. Overall it was a very impressive setting, but already he was feeling the effects of being closed in between walls of stone instead of the lightweight tents preferred by his people.

Suddenly remembering why he was there, he re-focussed his attention on the main occupant of the room, Salah ad-Din.

Turan-Shah walked quickly over to the luxurious carpet placed before the sultan and lowered himself to his knees with his forehead touching the floor and his arms stretched wide.

'My lord, Salah ad-Din,' he said, 'Sultan of Syria and all Egypt, righteousness of the faith, please accept this humble servant into your presence.'

'Be upstanding, Turan-Shah,' said the sultan, 'and join the council. We have need of your services.' The prince got to his feet and sat on the waiting cushion already in place at the end of the half-circle of men.

'These people,' said Salah ad-Din, indicating the other attendees, 'are my trusted emirs. Most of them you know so I will not waste time with introductions.' He turned towards a man standing at the window. 'This is my son, Al-Afdal ibn Salah ad-Din.'

'I am blessed and honoured,' said Turan-Shah.

'Turan-Shah,' said Salah ad-Din, turning his attention back onto the prince, 'it has been brought to my attention that your courage and leadership was instrumental in bringing this city to its knees in so short a time. My emirs tell me that without your swift actions, we would probably still be manning siege-engines outside the city walls.'

'Your comments are gratefully received,' said the prince, 'but I am only one man, and it is the actions of my warriors that brought the campaign to a swift conclusion.'

'Nevertheless,' said Saladin, 'our warriors carry out the orders of their commanders, and you should accept the honour your achievements bring.'

'Thank you, my lord,' said Turan-Shah.

'As you know,' continued Salah ad-Din, 'we still have unfinished work to do. Several of the infidel castles hold out in the hope of a Christian army arriving from the west, and it is important we wrest them from their hands before any reinforcements arrive. By doing so, we will deny them a corridor into the east.'

Turan-Shah's heart beat a little faster, anticipating a campaign against one of the few remaining infidel strongholds.

'I stand ready and eager to carry out your whim,' he said, 'and welcome any task you set before me.'

'I have been told that your commitment is unwavering,' said the sultan, 'so, it is to you we turn to provide the most important task of all. Even as we speak, our armies besiege Karak, Tyre and the fortress the Franks call Belfort. Winter is coming, and many of the tribes are returning to their lands until the sun is hot again. This means we will not have enough men to fully garrison Acre, and that is why we turn to you.'

Turan-Shah stared at the sultan in shock. He had been hoping for a glorious campaign against one of the castles but instead faced the prospect of being cooped up within the stone walls of a Christian city, a place that stank of filth and the remains of rotting fish.

'I do not understand,' he said eventually. 'I thought I was to be given the task of delivering Karak into your hands?'

'There was discussion of such a move,' said Al-Afdal walking over from the window, 'and we have no doubt that you would be successful, but this is far more important.' He lowered himself to a cushion at the side of his father. 'Our spies have told us that the Christians are recruiting a huge army to retake our lands, and even as we speak, their commanders are mustering their men throughout the west. Their target is to retake Jerusalem but to gain a foothold, they have to have a seaport to land their supplies. Tyre will soon be in our hands, but it is here in Acre that we are most at risk. We want you and your men to ensure that this city never falls into the hands of the Christians again. You will be supplied with food, weapons, slaves and as many men as we can spare, but make no mistake, it is your courage and proven leadership that will ultimately ensure Acre stays in Muslim hands.'

Turan-Shah remained quiet. Despite his despair, he knew he could not question the role the sultan had lain before him. Any personal attention from the leader of the Ayyubid was a great honour, and he knew that if he refused, he might not live to see another day.

'My lords,' he said eventually, 'your trust is the greatest gift I have ever received, and I swear before Allah himself that I will do everything in my power to achieve what you desire.'

Saladin nodded, expecting nothing less and turned to his son.

'Make the necessary arrangements,' he said, 'and tell the emirs to prepare to leave. We will re-focus our attention against Belfort.'

'Yes, my lord,' said Al-Afdal. 'Is there anything else?'

'Not yet. We will meet again at the new camp to discuss our next move, but for now, just get me out of this place. I feel like the stone walls are crushing my very soul.'

The council got to their feet and walked backwards out of the sultan's presence. When they reached the doorway, they turned and headed down the corridor to make the arrangements for their men to leave the city. Turan-Shah was the last to leave, and as he walked, Al-Afdal caught up with him.

'Turan-Shah,' he said, 'we need to speak.'

The Yemeni prince stopped and turned to face the sultan's son.

'My lord?'

'Tell me,' said Al-Afdal, why do you not accept my father's request with a joyful heart?'

'But I do,' lied Turan-Shah. 'Did you not hear my words?'

'Your tongue said one thing,' said Al-Afdal, 'your face said another. It was as clear as the sun in a cloudless sky, this task is not what you wanted.'

'My lord,' said the prince, 'it is no secret that any man worth his salt wants to fight and if necessary, die in the name of Allah. I am no different and hoped to serve him by tearing down the walls of the Christian fortresses. If he now seeks my service in other ways, then I am not going to question my fate. If my reaction offended you then I humbly beg forgiveness, but I assure you, there is no other man alive who will defend this place better than I. This I swear before you and before Allah.'

'Make sure you do,' said Al-Afdal, *'Allah Akbar.'*

'Allah Akbar,' replied Turan-Shah and watched as the sultan's son followed the rest of the emirs out of the corridor. The task before him was not one he relished, but he meant to honour his pledge to the best of his ability.

Chapter Four

Tyre

January - AD 1188
Two months later

Balian of Ibelin sat on one of the outer castle ramparts, his head resting against a barrel of arrows. His sleep was shallow, and subconsciously he could hear everything that was going on around him. A nearby movement brought him instantly awake, but it was just a squire bring him a cloak.

'My lord,' said the boy, 'the night is cold so my master told me to bring you this.'

'Thank you,' said Balian as the squire placed the cloak over him. 'Your name is John-William, is it not?'

'It is, my lord.'

'And you served Sir Edward at Cresson?'

'I did, my lord, and it is my only regret that I did not die there alongside my comrades.'

'There is no shame in living,' said Balian. 'I understand Jakelin de Mailly ordered both you and your master from the field.'

'He did, but it was not my wish.'

'Were you not wounded?'

'I was, but so were many others. My place was alongside them.'

'Your life is a gift from God,' said Balian, 'he obviously has greater things planned for you. Where is Sir Edward now?'

'He commands the night watch on the eastern wall,' said the squire. 'He said I am to wake you the moment there is any danger.'

'Thank you,' said Balian, and as the boy walked away, pulled the cloak tighter around him.

The night was quiet, but the stink of Greek-fire and smouldering wood was a constant reminder of the dire situation they were in. Many timber buildings inside the walls had been completely destroyed, and the palisade defence was now nothing more than a ditch amongst a forest of burning timber.

The level of the seawater ensured there was no way the Saracen sappers could undermine the walls, but the constant barrage from the Ayyubid catapults meant that rubble lay scattered along the battlements and huge chunks of the wall were missing from the constant bombardment.

The siege had lasted over two months and the fighting had been hard, but the strengthened defensive walls and the commitment of everyone in the city had ensured the Saracens had been held at bay. Counterattacks led by Balian and Sancho-martin harried the attackers whenever possible, but their number was few and as soon as the Saracens rallied, they were forced back inside the city.

Dawn was already on the horizon when one of the guards woke Balian with a nudge of his foot.

'My lord, Conrad of Montferrat demands your attendance.'

Balian opened his eyes, momentarily confused as to where he was. It was the longest he had slept in days, and it took a moment to come to his senses.

'Why did you let me sleep so long?' he asked as he got to his feet.

'The night was quiet, my lord, so the guard commander allowed as many as possible to get some rest.'

'Thank you,' said Balian, 'I'll get someone to relieve you as soon as I can.' He walked down the steps and made his way through the smouldering remnants of the wooden houses along the outer perimeter of the city. As he neared the stone-built section, he passed hundreds of people sleeping in alleyways or already squatting on street corners, their hands extended in desperate need of alms simply to stay alive. Quickly he headed to the citadel and up to the campaign room. Conrad was already there as well as Sir Edward of Gaza and Sancho-martin.

'Sir Balian,' said Conrad as he entered the room. 'We have received worrying news. One of the supply ships from Cyprus reports that on their way here they saw ten Egyptian galleys laying offshore, each bearing many men at arms. He believes they may be waiting for orders before sailing to Tyre.'

'A seaborne assault,' said Balian, 'I wondered when that would occur to them.' He turned to Sir Edward. 'How many ships do we have?'

'Five at harbour,' said Edward, 'and another twelve somewhere between here and Tripoli.'

'What about the supply ships,' asked Balian removing his cloak, 'can we not press them into service?'

'Alas, that is not possible,' responded Edward, 'for they have already weighed anchor to return to Cyprus. They are merchantmen only and want to avoid any involvement.'

Balian gritted his teeth. Experienced captains with good ships would be essential if there was to be a naval battle.

'Our captains are good men,' said Balian, 'but we need to be careful they are not caught at anchor within the harbour. The passage is narrow, and the Saracen fleet would have no problem keeping them contained. Without those ships, we will run short of supplies in days.

'I have already instructed every ship to leave Tyre and head up the coast to await further orders,' said Conrad. 'Tell the harbour-master to raise the chain across the port entrance. Only ships loaded with supplies are to be allowed through until we see what Saladin is up to.'

'My lord,' said Balian, 'can I suggest we also send a message to Tripoli and tell them of the threat. They will have war galleys and men more suitable to fight at sea than any we have at our disposal.'

'Already done,' said Conrad, 'but I believe there is more to this than meets the eye.'

'In what way?' asked Edward.

'The Ayyubid cannot take this city from the sea alone,' said Conrad, 'even if they were to capture the harbour, their ships simply cannot hold enough men to make any sort of headway. This is either part of a long-term strategy to starve us out, in which case we can counter with our own ships, or an effort to turn our attention from his land army.'

'Do you think he intends to make another full-on assault?' asked Edward.

'I do. With the Ayyubid attacking on both sides, our resources will be stretched to their fullest. If I were him, I would have tried this a long time ago.'

'My lord, the main walls are barely standing as they are. Another full-scale attack will see them breached, and we simply do not have enough men to counter.'

'I agree,' said Conrad, 'at least in the scenario that you describe, but there is another strategy we could employ, one that Saladin will never suspect. It is daring and dangerous, but if we succeed, it has the capability of breaking this siege once and for all.'

The men in the room looked at each other nervously. Conrad had a reputation as a great leader, but he also had a history of foolish acts decided in the heat of the moment. Whatever he had in mind, they collectively hoped it wasn't the latter.

Two days later, Conrad joined Balian on the gate tower. Their suspicions had proved correct, and the full strength of the Ayyubid army now stretched along the shore to the front of Tyre, almost two thousand mounted warriors and over five thousand foot-soldiers. Amongst the front ranks, the defenders could see many men carrying siege ladders, as well as two long wooden bridges constructed to span the spike-filled ditch blocking the advance to the city.

To the west, the ten Egyptian galleys were now formed up offshore, blocking any access to the harbour and waiting for the command to attack from the sea. To a casual observer, it seemed that the city had no chance, and by the end of the day, Tyre would be in Muslim hands.

'Is everything ready?' asked Conrad quietly.

'It is,' said Balian looking along the wall. Instead of seeing his well-trained archers, the ramparts were now full of inexperienced civilians, each bearing a bow. They had been given intensive training, but Balian knew that decent bowmen were a special breed, and there was no way his makeshift defending force could repel a well-trained army.

'Have confidence, Balian,' said Conrad, 'victory or defeat is often decided by who has the element of surprise. Saladin has made intentions clear, now it is our turn to counter.'

'My lord,' said Balian, 'look.'

Conrad looked over the walls to where he could see a covered wagon emerge from the Saracen lines, accompanied by three Saracens, one of which was carrying the white flag of truce.

'It looks like they want to talk,' said Conrad. 'This will be interesting.'

'Do you want me to go out?' asked Balian.

'No, you stay here and stick to the plan. I'll go and see what he wants.'

He descended the stone stairs and ordered the guards to open the gate.

'Sir Edward,' he said, seeing the knight nearby, 'come with me.'

The knight followed Conrad out of the gates, taking a crossbow off one of the guards as he went. The two men walked over to the remains of the ramparts overlooking the ditch and climbed up to face the Saracen negotiating party on the far side. Conrad stared at all three before calling across the filth-filled ditch.

'I am Conrad of Montferrat,' he announced, 'lord of this city. To whom am I speaking?'

'I am Muzaffar ad-Din Gokbori, Emir of Edessa, loyal servant to Salah ad-Din, Sultan of Egypt and Syria, true lord of all you survey. I am here at his request to discuss terms for your surrender.'

'I have offered no such terms.'

'You have not, so my master, in his infinite mercy, makes you this offer. Cede the city and we will give you three things. The first is untold riches, enough to make you and your men wealthy beyond compare for the rest of your lives.'

'My family have riches enough, and my men fight in God's service, not for silver or gold.'

'I expected no less,' said Gokbori, 'so perhaps the second proposal is of more value.'

'Which is?'

'The lives of every man woman and child in the city. If you surrender, there will be no toll placed of any person, irrespective of wealth or status. All who wish to leave will be allowed to do so in peace, and we will even escort them to Tripoli to ensure they are safe while on Ayyubid lands.'

'Again, your master surprises me with his generosity,' said Conrad, 'but we have fought too long to cede now. On behalf of the people of Tyre, I refuse your offer and wait with anticipation to hear what could possibly better the first two.'

'I am disappointed at your refusal,' said Gokbori, 'for I thought a man such as you would put the lives of his people first. Alas, I now see you are not such a person, so I make our final proposal.' He nodded to the warrior at his side who dismounted and walked to the back of the cart.

'Even if that cart is filled with the best of Saladin's treasury, I will not be tempted,' taunted Conrad. 'We have already established that.'

'It is not silver or gold that I bear,' said Gokbori, 'but something far more valuable.' As he spoke, the Saracen returned from behind the cart, dragging a prisoner. The captive had his wrists tightly bound, and his head covered by a linen bag.

'What is this?' asked Conrad in confusion. 'That could be the King of Jerusalem himself, but even he knows that the safety of the Holy-land is greater than the life of one man.'

'It is not Guy of Lusignan, I offer,' said Gokbori, 'it is someone far more important.' He plucked the makeshift hood from the prisoner to reveal an elderly man, squinting against the sudden glare of the late morning sun.

Conrad stared in disbelief. One of the reasons he had left Italy to come to the Holy-land was to join this man on campaign, but after he had heard he had fought at Hattin, he had lost hope of ever seeing him alive again. It was his father, William V of Montferrat.

'This is your father, is it not?' asked Gokbori.

'It is,' said Conrad, 'and if you have an ounce of decency in that Saracen heart, you will hand him over to my keeping.'

'It would be my greatest pleasure,' said Gokbori. 'He can simply walk into your arms as a free man. All you have to do is hand over the city.'

'Don't do it, Conrad,' growled the old man, staring at his son. 'These people are nothing more than savages intent on bringing God's kingdom to its knees. Do what you came to do and serve the Lord by reclaiming Jerusalem in his name. I have already lived a full life, and if it is to come to an end, then I will die happy knowing that it was to further God's will.'

Conrad stared at his father. He had obviously suffered at the hands of his captors and was covered with filth and sores. There was nothing more he wanted in the world than to secure his release, but he knew his father was right. God's will was greater than any man, no matter who he was. He turned to the knight at his side.

'Sir Edward,' he said, 'give me your crossbow.'

'My lord?' said the knight, looking at his master.

'You heard me, give me your weapon.'

The knight handed over the ready loaded crossbow.

'Conrad of Montferrat,' said Gokbori as his hand went to the hilt of his own sword. 'Don't be foolish. Killing me will only bring down the wrath of Saladin upon your head. By defiling this flag of parley, every man, woman and child within those city walls will die a long and painful death. Think about what it is you are doing.'

'I know exactly what I am doing, Gokbori,' said Conrad lifting the weapon to his shoulder, but you should harness your self-importance. This bolt is not for you, it is for him.' He turned slightly and aimed the crossbow straight at his father's heart.

For a few seconds, there was a stunned silence as Conrad's finger rested on the trigger.

'My lord,' said Edward, 'don't do this. God will surely deny you access to the gates of heaven should you carry out such a heinous act.'

'God's judgement is between him, and me,' said Conrad, his finger tightening on the trigger.

'My lord,' snapped Edward. 'Please, don't do this.'

'Don't listen to him, Conrad,' shouted the old man. 'Left alive, I am a lever to be used against you and Christianity. I have made my peace with the lord and am ready to stand before him to account for my many failings. Jerusalem must take priority over one sinner's life. Pull the lever, my son. You have my blessing and my forgiveness.'

'Don't do it,' gasped Edward. 'My Lord, it is your father, you will never forgive yourself.'

Conrad didn't answer. Instead, he pulled the crossbow harder into his shoulder to steady his aim.

'Tell your master this, Gokbori,' he said eventually. 'The one true God is greater than any man, and we will be judged by him and him alone.' As he spoke the last word, he pulled the lever to send an iron-tipped crossbow bolt flying towards his father's heart.

Sir Edward gasped in shock as the bolt sped through the air towards. William had his eyes wide open, determined that his last sight in life would be that of his son.

'No,' shouted Gokbori, but as he turned toward his prisoner, the bolt passed through the outer flesh of the old man's upper arm and embedded itself into the ground behind him.

The wound caused William to spin to the left, but after a few seconds, realising it was a flesh wound only, he turned back to face his son with tears of pride in his eyes.

'You are a devil indeed,' roared Gokbori, struggling to control his horse. 'What sort of man tries to kill his own father? Shame upon your shoulders, Conrad of Montferrat, may Iblis himself be your master in the afterlife.'

'Begone from this place, Gokbori,' said Conrad, lowering the crossbow. 'I will not miss a second time.'

'You will pay for this,' shouted Gokbori, 'I swear we will tear down this city stone by stone. Stand to your defences, Christian, the wrath of Islam is about to descend upon you.'

'Do what you have to do, Gokbori,' replied Conrad, 'we are waiting.'

Gokbori turned and galloped away, struggling to accept the way he had just been humbled. The other two Saracens dragged William back to the cart and followed the emir back to the Ayyubid lines. Conrad and Edward turned to return to the castle as quickly as they could.

'As soon as we get back,' said Conrad, 'send the signal to the fleet. I suspect they will attack before this day is out.'

'I will, my lord,' said Edward, 'but I have a question. At that range, most men would have pierced the heart. Was the miss by design, or did the Lord guide its flight?'

The two men stopped and stared at each other beneath the damaged walls of the city.

'I believe I did what I had to do,' said Conrad. 'The outcome is that my father is still alive, but to answer your question, the reason that the bolt missed will remain between God and me. Now, the matter is closed, and we have a battle to fight. Come, the city awaits.'

He strode away towards the open gates, leaving Edward staring at his back with admiration.

Chapter Five

Tyre

January - AD 1188

As soon as he entered the city, Edward sent runners throughout Tyre warning of the imminent attack. Women ushered children into the safety of stone buildings while all available men rushed to the walls, ready to do what they could. Down in the harbour, the three ships untied from their mooring rings and headed out to sea past the lowered harbour chain.

On the northernmost wall, two men operated a large mirror, pivoted in a wooden frame. The beam of sunlight reflected from its polished copper surface shot away northward to the distant hills, a message that was relayed onward several times before it finally reached the fleet of ships lying at anchor halfway between Tyre and Tripoli.

Conrad stood upon one of the gate towers, now fully clad in his battle armour. Unlike the other men, he wore no chainmail hauberk upon his torso; instead, he wore a cuirass, two metal plates surrounding his upper body and fastened at the sides. In front of the city, the massed ranks of the Saracens were already manoeuvring into their attack formations, and the sound of drums and battle horns filled the air.

'Have the messages been sent?' asked Conrad.

'They have, my lord,' said Balian, 'and all have been acknowledged.'

'Then I hand the walls over to you, Sir Balian, defend them well.'

'With my life, my lord,' said Balian, and watched as Conrad descended the steps to join his men.

'Here they come,' roared a voice, and everybody turned to see the front ranks of the Saracen army marching towards the palisade. Behind them, half the massed catapults started launching pots of Greek-fire over the wall and into the city, filling the air with acrid black smoke. The rest launched boulders against the stone walls, smashing into the defences and causing many of the defenders to cower with fear.

'Steady,' shouted Balian, looking at the inexperienced archers along the wall. 'We do not loose a single arrow until they are in range.'

The barrage continued, and Balian peered over the parapet. The smoke burned his lungs and vision was difficult, but eventually it cleared enough to make out what was happening. The Saracens had bridged the ditch with the two makeshift platforms, and the archers were already lining up to begin their onslaught upon the defenders. This was the moment they had been waiting for.

Below the gate tower, Conrad sat upon his horse. Behind him, another five hundred lancers and knights waited, knowing that what they were about to do would probably end in many of their deaths.

'My lord,' shouted Balian, 'the time is upon us.'

Conrad drew his sword and turned to face his men.

'You know what we have to do,' he shouted, 'strike hard and strike fast.' He turned and faced the outer wall. *'God is with us,'* he roared, and with a dig of his heels, launched his horse into a gallop.

Out in the bay, the three ships sailed out of the harbour and straight at the Egyptian fleet. Sir Edward stood in the prow of the lead ship, wearing his white mantle emblazoned with the red cross. Each of the ships held a hundred of Conrad's best archers and was powered by an experienced crew of rowers.

'String your bows,' shouted Edward, seeing the Egyptians manoeuvring their ships to counter the threat. 'Remember, we do not stop to engage them at close hand, we will sail straight through to recover further out.'

The Christian ships gathered pace, and though the Egyptians had similar resources, they were slow to react, and by the time Edward and his fleet were in range, half were still unprepared.

'Archers,' shouted Edward as they approached the nearest ship, 'ready.'

Each archer dipped the end of an arrow into a brazier, setting the ends aflame with burning pitch.

'We will have moments only,' shouted Edward, 'so make every one count. Upon my command ... nock ... draw ... *loose!'*

The air filled with arrows, each leaving a smoky black trail in the clear morning sky. The effect was immediate, and as many thudded onto the deck, and amongst the rigging, the enemy crews raced to douse the flames. The unfortunate ship was soon ablaze, and Edward watched as dozens of men jumped overboard, desperate to escape the searing flames.

Behind him, the other two ships had a lesser impact, the element of surprise, lost. One of the Egyptian galleys managed to engage their deck-mounted mangonels and sent a series of granite boulders smashing through the last Christian ship. Immediately the ship listed, and it became obvious it would not survive. Men panicked and discarded their heavy armour before plunging into the sea.

'My lord,' shouted Edward's squire from mid-ship, 'they will never reach the shore. We have to go back.'

'We will do no such thing,' roared Edward, 'we will stick to the plan.' He turned to the captain. 'How is the wind?' he demanded, 'can you get us out of here?'

The captain looked up at the rigging.

'It seems that God is looking over us,' he said, 'it is picking up.'

'Then set the sails, captain' replied Edward, 'and get us further out to sea.'

The captain strode away along the deck, giving his commands to his crew. Within minutes, the sails were raised, and the ship lurched seaward. The other Christian vessel did the same, and they fled the battle leaving the damaged enemy ships behind them. Edward made his way to the stern, watching the Egyptians as they dealt with the aftermath of the unexpected attack.

'We did well,' said the captain joining him.' One has been sunk, and at least another two will have to return to port to fix the damage.'

'That still leaves seven,' said Edward, 'I had hoped for a better return.'

'Any success at sea is to be celebrated,' said the captain, 'all we can do now is hope they take the bait.' As they watched, four of the enemy ships raised their own sails and turned seaward as the remaining three closed in to rescue their comrades,

'Four against two,' said Edward. 'Now, we have a chance. Head north, captain, but keep the speed steady. We want to keep them interested.'

'As you wish, my lord,' said the captain and turned away to issue his commands.

Up at the city walls, Conrad led his men charging out of the gates, driving straight across the Saracen's own bridges towards the heart of the enemy. Behind them came hundreds of foot-soldiers, splitting into two separate forces to strike at the Ayyubid archers still rushing to get into formation.

The unexpected attack threw the Saracens into disarray, and despite being heavily outnumbered, the Christian soldiers fell upon them, cutting them down before they could react. Behind the trained soldiers came hundreds more men carrying whatever weapons they could find, civilians pressed into service by Conrad who were now fighting for their own existence. Up on the battlements, the inexperienced archers sent their arrows deep into the enemy archers' lines, taking advantage of their confusion to fill the air with iron-tipped willow.

Both sides committed everything they had to the fight. There were no organised formations, no lines of command and no overall strategy from either side, just thousands of men fighting to the death, each desperate to live.

The cries of the dying filled the air as men fell to the unforgiving attention of forged steel, and once again the soil of the Holy-land was drenched in the blood of men desperate to claim her as their own.

Beyond the ditch, Conrad led his men racing across the plain towards the main body of the Saracen cavalry. Again they were outnumbered, but as the Ayyubid horsemen spurred their horses to meet them head-on, his column split into two and headed in two different directions to attack the flanks.

'What is he doing?' asked Gokbori, from his vantage point on a nearby hill, 'he splits his force for no reason. He is inviting the death of himself and all his men.'

'His tactics are unexpected,' said the warrior at his side. 'We prepared for a siege, not for an attack such as this. Yet the man is foolish for he is outnumbered ten-fold.'

'Do not underestimate him,' said Gokbori, 'for he is the spawn of the devil himself and has the morals of a snake.'

Down below, a Saracen horn echoed across the battlefield, and the Ayyubid cavalry split in half to pursue the two Christian columns.

'My lord,' shouted one of the knights at the side of Conrad, 'they have taken the bait.'

Immediately Conrad reined in his horse and spun around to face the pursuing cavalry. His men followed and spread out into a line-abreast formation.

'God has done all he can to aid us,' he shouted, 'the rest is up to us. Men of Tyre, *advaaance!*'

His assembled knights lowered their lances and charged straight back at the approaching Ayyubid horsemen. On the other side of the plain, the rest of his knights did the same, and the ground rumbled to the sound of galloping hooves. Seconds later, cavalry on both sides crashed into their opponents at full gallop, and the screams of men and beast mingled into one deafening roar.

Up on the city walls, Balian watched as events unfolded. As expected, the enemy cavalry had veered to either side and was now engaged by Conrad and his knights. That meant that the main Saracen army, still waiting to be deployed at the centre of the field, were the only obstacle between the Christians and the Saracen's command tents.

Balian looked down and stared at the man waiting in the outer courtyard for just this moment. Sancho-martin sat upon his magnificent destrier, waiting for the command to advance. Bedecked in his usual green livery, and astride a horse with a similar coloured caparison, he struck an imposing figure. Behind him, the last remaining knights in the city waited upon their own mounts, two hundred men with only one focus, to drive through the Saracen lines and head for Gokbori himself. Each knew that their chances of success were minimal, but if they could cause doubt in the emir's heart, the chances were that he would flee the scene, and the enemy command-chain would crumble. Then, and only then, would they stand a chance.

'Sancho-martin,' called Balian from above, 'the road is paved for glory, my friend, the field is yours. May God go with you.'

Sancho-martin raised his sword in salute, and as the gates swung open, the Green Knight led his men in a fearless charge through a sea of bloodshed towards the waiting Ayyubid army. As soon as they had left, Balian turned to the men along the battlements.

'Men of Tyre,' he shouted, 'our work here is done. Look to your weapons and join me in defence of your families, your homes and of Christianity itself. Follow me, comrades, the future of the city is in our own hands.'

He ran down the steps to where every able-bodied man still in the city poured from the side-streets carrying anything they could get their hands on to serve as a weapon. The mood was of anger, fear and desperation, but knowing they faced certain death at the hands of the Ayyubid, the citizens of Tyre, led by Balian of Ibelin, poured out to defend their city.

Out at sea, the two remaining Christian vessels sailed northward, always keeping just out of reach of the pursuing Egyptians. Holding fewer men, and after stripping as much weight as possible from the decks, they were lighter than their counterparts and easier to manoeuvre. Despite being able to sail at a much faster speed, the captains were careful to remain close enough to encourage pursuit yet, far enough away to avoid the boulders and Greek-fire of the enemy mangonels.

'Where are they?' asked Edward, staring northward. 'They should be here by now.'

'The signals were acknowledged,' said the captain, 'but they are sailing into a headwind, so the journey is harder.'

'Nevertheless,' said Edward, 'if they don't appear soon, I fear the Egyptians will break off and return to Tyre. If they do that, the city will have nobody to defend the harbour.'

'My lord,' shouted John-William from his position perched on a higher deck, 'look there. I see ships.'

Edward and the captain peered forward, seeing the shapes of several vessels appearing on the horizon.

'It's them,' said Edward eventually, 'thank the Lord.'

As they watched, the fleet of Christian ships got closer and closer, each powered by dozens of strong oarsmen.

'Fourteen, my lord,' shouted the squire from above, 'I count fourteen galleys in all.'

'I had hoped for more,' said Edward, 'but it will have to be enough. Bring us around, captain, let's see what these Egyptians are made of.'

The crew raced to their stations, and as the two ships turned south to meet the enemy, Sir Edward climbed up onto the forecastle.

'The tables have turned, men,' he shouted, 'look to your weapons, but this time there will be no flight, we will sink every last ship or send them back to Egypt.

To the sounds of all the men roaring their approval, Edward jumped down to the main deck where his squire was waiting with his master's helmet.

'Let's get this done, John-William,' he said, 'and perhaps in some small way, it may ease the nightmares from Cresson.'

Conrad of Montferrat fought furiously, his sword scything through the leather protection of the lighter armoured Saracen cavalry. All around him, knights clad in heavy chainmail, their heads protected by full-faced helmets, ploughed into the enemy with unrivalled fury. Each swipe of a sword drew blood, each smash of a shield found flesh. Wide-eyed horses kicked out in fear, and many fell on both sides. One by one, the Saracens were cut down by superior strength and armament, but no sooner did one fall than another took his place. The battle raged on with many Christian knights now afoot, their steeds cut from beneath them, but still they fought, grouped to together in small pockets of unforgiving brutality.

Only a few knights remained horsed, and Conrad looked around desperately for reinforcements. On the far side of the field, he could see the rest of the cavalry had fared slightly better, but he knew they had their own problems and he could expect no relief from them.

'My lord,' called a voice, 'look.'

Conrad turned to face the city walls, and his heart missed a beat. At last, the rest of the knights had broken through, and led by Sancho-martin, were now driving directly at the main Ayyubid army. Almost immediately, Saracen horns filled the air, and Conrad sensed hesitancy in the enemy ranks. He jumped from his horse and ran to join his men.

'*Do not falter,*' he roared, 'the green Knight has broken through and is headed for their command tents. We have to keep up the pressure.'

Invigorated by their leader's example, the men surged forward into the remaining Ayyubid cavalry. The Arabian horses bore the brunt of the attack, their legs being cut clean from beneath them, a terrible sacrifice, but necessary to gain an advantage. Once unhorsed, the Saracen riders were no match for the knights, and the Christians marched relentlessly on, cutting a swathe through the battlefield.

Sancho-martin rode his horse hard, picking up speed as he neared the enemy lines. To either side, twenty other riders formed the arrowhead of the attack, a formation designed to thrust straight through the massed Saracen ranks. Behind him came the main body of the attack, a column of men intent on providing the main thrust once the way had been cleared. With a final roar of aggression, the Green knight dug in his spurs and crashed his horse into the front lines of the Saracens.

The impetus and sheer size of his horse drove him forward through row after row of Saracen warriors. Men lashed out wildly to try to kill him or his horse, but the ferocity of the attack had caused chaos, and few blades found their target. To either side, his fellow knights found similar success, and though some fell to Saracen blades, the thrust from those behind drove the attack even further towards the enemy camp. Saracens on the flanks watched on hopelessly for though they still vastly outnumbered the Christians, they could get nowhere near, such was the confusion amongst their own troops.

Suddenly, several riders broke through and headed for the Saracen tents. Immediately the rear ranks panicked, realising they could now be attacked from behind. Their lines broke, and with the enemy scattering in all directions, Sancho-martin leapt from his horse to wade into the fray with unbridled ferocity.

The colour of his armaments and his physical size made him stand out above all others, and he fought like a maniac, unrelenting and unforgiving. Over and over again, Saracen warriors poured forward to cut him down, but none could match his prowess, and he cut a path through all that came. To either side, the rest of his men followed his example and created chaos throughout the Saracen army.

On the hill overlooking the battle, Gokbori looked on in horror. The planned assault on the city had never fully materialised, and despite his overwhelming numerical advantage, he now found himself on the defensive against a smaller, but cleverer opponent. Despite the shock, he knew that the day was not yet lost, and he turned to the officer at his side.

'Send the signal for our cavalry to break contact and muster to the east of the valley,' he said. 'We will reorganise and send a fresh assault against their horsemen.'

'My lord,' said the officer, 'the signal has already been sounded, but many of our men have fled the field. Even if those that are left manage to free themselves, I fear there will not be enough to present a force strong enough against these devils.'

'Then rally our infantry,' demanded Gokbori, 'we still outnumber them ten to one, yet they stand off as if the Christians were riddled with the plague. Tell them to attack.'

'Of course, my lord,' said the officer.

Gokbori looked down on the continuing battle. The figure of the man in green stood out above all others, with he and his men cutting a huge path through the Ayyubid infantry. Several hundred paces away, Conrad and his men had changed direction and now made their way towards Green Knight, paving their own way with Saracen blood and Saracen flesh.

Suddenly the reality of the situation hit home and Gokbori could see that despite their superior numbers, his men had lost the fire needed to win any battle. Many were fleeing the field, and those that were left huddled together in defensive positions. The emir was furious and called for the rest of his commanders to attend.

'Who is responsible for this?' he roared, sweeping his hand out over the battlefield. 'Which of you assured me that the Christians were not strong enough to launch a counter-attack?'

One of the younger officers stepped forward and dropped to his knees.

'My lord,' he said, 'the task was mine. Our spies told me that Tyre was manned with few knights and relied on the people of the city to man their walls. Never did we expect to see so fierce a foe.'

'You were given a responsibility,' growled Gokbori drawing his scimitar, 'your failure has cost me this battle and the lives of many men.'

'I am shamed,' said the officer, bowing his head, 'and I accept your judgement.'

Gokbori stepped forward and lifted his sword high before swinging it down with full force to strike the head from the young man's body. For a few seconds, nobody moved until eventually, the blood-spattered emir looked up to face the rest of the officers.

'Let this be a lesson,' he said, 'I will suffer no incompetence within my ranks.' He turned to look over the battlefield once more. 'Sound the retreat and get our warriors out of there. They stand like scared sheep waiting for the wolves to attack.'

All the officers turned away, leaving only Gokbori and one of his Mamluk guards standing on the vantage point.

'The battle is lost,' said the emir, 'and will haunt my dreams.'

'They are a special breed,' said the Mamluk, staring down to where the Christian knights had now joined forces. Especially the one in green.'

'I agree,' said Gokbori, 'and when this is over, send envoys to find out his name. Now bring me my horse, this day is done.'

Two days later, Conrad of Montferrat, Balian of Ibelin, Edward of Gaza and Sancho-martin walked across the battlefield, surveying the results of the terrible battle. Hundreds of corpses still lay where they fell, and though there were dozens of funeral pyres already burning, the stench was unbearable.

'You did it, my lord,' said Balian, 'you have secured the safety of Tyre and provided Christendom with a secure port.'

'The job is not yet done, Sir Balian,' said Conrad, 'for our walls are severely damaged. We may have eased the threat, but now the hard work must begin. The city needs to be rebuilt. The walls need to be higher, the ditches deeper and our armouries re-stocked. We need to rebuild our fleet, but this time with ships armed with mangonels, but more importantly we need more men, knights that show the mettle of those that fought and died here today. With an army made from men such as these, Tyre will become truly invincible.'

Before Balian could answer, Sir Edward spoke up.

'My lord, look.'

Everyone looked to the south where a lone rider was approaching on a horse under the flag of the Ayyubid.

'I will go,' said Sancho-martin, his hand reaching for his sword.

'No,' said Conrad, 'he is one man. Let him come.

As the rider approached, some of the civilians gathered to watch him pass. He wore a hooded cloak, and the horse walked slowly, exhausted after a long ride.

'Who are you, stranger?' said Balian. 'Declare yourself.'

Slowly the man sat up straight and lifted his hand to remove his hood. As it fell away, Conrad of Montferrat gasped in surprise for facing him, alive, but exhausted was his father.

'My lord,' he gasped, walking over to the horse. 'How are you here? Did you escape?'

'I did not,' said William, looking down at his son. 'Gokbori was so impressed by your victory, he ordered me released.' He turned and looked back the way he had come. 'In fact, I think that at this very moment, he and his emirs are watching from that treeline.'

Conrad took a few steps towards the south and stared towards the forest.

'Do you think he is going to attack?' he asked.

'He is not going to attack, Conrad,' said William, 'this is his way of paying tribute to a fellow warrior. Take it for what it is, and enjoy your victory, my son, for it is one that may yet secure the fate of the Holy-land.'

Chapter Six

Tripoli

June - AD 1188
Five months later

Thomas Cronin walked through the streets of Tripoli on his way from the horse sales in the local market, thinking about the previous twelve months. The battle at Hattin had been devastating, and he had lost many fellow knights and sergeants to the Saracens. Many had been taken into slavery, but most had been killed, slaughtered by the overwhelming strength of the Saracen army.

He and many others had been captured when Guy of Lusignan, King of Jerusalem, had surrendered to Saladin and were certainly destined for slavery, but had fled in a daring escape from their captors. Many of his fellow escapees had been hunted down and killed, but he and four others had managed to reach Jerusalem after months living off the land and avoiding Saracen patrols. Since then, Jerusalem had fallen, and he had come with many others to the safety of Tripoli while the Holy-land adjusted to the new normality.

He headed back up the hill to the castle overlooking the city. As in most places, the Templars maintained a commandery within its walls, and it was to here that any survivors of Hattin, or indeed, any other places that Saladin had conquered, now fled. Their numbers had been decimated, but new Templar knights from across Europe had rallied to their comrade's call to arms, and over the months, their numbers increased dramatically.

He entered the gates of the commandery, but as he headed towards the treasury, one of the squires came running over.

'My lord,' he said, 'your presence is required by the grandmaster.'

'Tell him I will be there as soon as I have settled the account with the treasury,' he said.

'My lord,' said the squire, 'he said you must come immediately. There are matters that will not wait.'

With a sigh, Cronin followed the boy into the heart of the commandery and into the grandmaster's quarters. Brother Thierry stood at the far end of the room, and before him was a road-weary man with his back to the entrance.

'My lord,' said Cronin, 'you sent for me?'

The grandmaster looked up and bade him enter. Brother Thierry was not the order's leader in the truest sense, that role belonged to Gerard of Ridefort, but as Gerard was a prisoner of the Ayyubid, having been captured at Hattin, Brother Thierry had assumed the role until such time as he was released.

'Brother Cronin,' said Thierry as the sergeant approached, 'we have been blessed. Please greet and pay homage to our unexpected guest.' The man before the Templar knight turned slowly to face Cronin, and the sergeant stared in shock before falling to his knees. It was Guy of Lusignan, the King of Jerusalem.

'Your Grace,' gasped Cronin, 'I thought you were being held prisoner in Damascus.'

'I was,' said the king, 'but after vowing never to wage war against him, and after receiving countless letters from my wife pleading my case, he set me free just a few days since. Get to your feet, Thomas Cronin, it is good to see you again.'

Cronin stood up and stared at the king. He was a lot thinner than he had been at Hattin, but apart from that, seemed none the worse for his ordeal.

'Were you treated well, your Grace?' he asked.

'As well as can be expected,' said Guy. The worst thing was not being able to react as Saladin ran riot through the Outremer. I have since been told that almost all of our cities and castles have capitulated, and now lay in the hands of the Ayyubid.'

'Alas this is true,' said Cronin. 'However, Conrad of Montferrat successfully defended Tyre recently and has gone on to fortify the city against further attacks.'

'So I hear,' said Guy, 'and that is part of the reason I am here.' He turned to face the grandmaster. 'Brother Thierry,' he said, 'for reasons of security, the announcement of my release has been deliberately kept quiet. Some of my trusted barons were made aware and have mustered what men they could to my banner, however, it is not enough, and I need to recruit more.'

'Recruit more?' said Thierry, 'may I ask, to what end?'

'To attack Jerusalem, of course,' said Guy. 'Every moment the Holy-city lays in the hands of the Muslims is another dagger in my heart. I need to raise an army, and at the head of that army, I need a strong Templar force in the vanguard.'

'Your Grace,' said Thierry, 'with the greatest respect, you have been incarcerated for over a year, and may not be aware of the entire situation. Saladin controls the Outremer with a free hand. Except for Tyre, there is not one place that we can use as a secure base from which to launch a counter-campaign.'

'And that is why we will first go there,' said Guy. 'Tyre has secure seaports and is a perfect resupply point for a new crusade. As soon as the Holy-father learns of my release, he will issue a papal bull demanding my cause is supported by every monarch in Christendom. With that sort of support, we will raise an army larger than any these lands have ever seen, and march on Jerusalem before the year is out.'

'My lord,' said Cronin, 'with respect, did you not just say that you gave a vow to Saladin not to carry out such a campaign?'

'I did, but as soon as I leave here, I will seek out the Bishop of Tripoli and seek release from that vow. It was given to an unbeliever in the cause of furthering God's will, so can be broken without holy retribution.' He turned back to the knight. 'So, Brother Thierry, my needs are three-fold. First of all, I need an army to march under my banner. I believe Tripoli is full of men without employment, many of them men at arms who were forced from the castles and towns of Jerusalem. Set up a call to arms and have them muster before the walls of the city on the first day of next month.'

'Of course, your Grace,' said Thierry.

'My second need is a strong Templar force to be my vanguard. I have heard that your order's strength is growing due to new arrivals from the west. I witnessed many of your brothers being executed without trial with my own eyes, a heinous act that deserves retribution. This will be your chance to avenge their deaths.'

'We will embrace the opportunity with bursting hearts,' said Thierry.

'The third request is financial,' said the king. 'I will need a line of credit with which to service this army. As you are aware, King Henry had deposited a huge sum with the order to fund his campaign when he takes the cross. I will send word to Henry requesting this deposit to be used as surety against the credit. As

Jerusalem will be the prize, I am in no doubt that he will grant the request.'

Brother Thierry glanced at Brother Cronin momentarily before returning his gaze to the king. His demeanour had changed, and he looked uncomfortable.

'Is there a problem?' asked the king.

'Your Grace, perhaps we should discuss this in private.'

'Why?' asked the king, looking towards Cronin. 'I know this man well and am aware he is highly regarded amongst your order. Whatever you have to say can be said in front of him.'

'As you wish,' said Thierry. 'Regarding your request for funding, I am sure we can come to some arrangement, but alas, we will not be able to use King Henry's campaign money as surety.'

'Why not? Is the recapture of Jerusalem not a suitable cause?'

'Of course, it is,' said Brother Thierry, 'but the defeat at Hattin was costly, and it was these same funds that paid for your campaign.'

'I am aware of that fact,' said the king, 'but the dependency was not total. There must be at least half left, and that will be more than enough until I garrison Tyre and see about raising taxes.'

'I am only trying to help, your Grace,' said Brother Thierry. 'As you are aware, I hold this post in a temporary capacity until such time as the Holy-father decides who to back in the event that Brother Gerard does not return.'

'Ah,' interrupted the king. 'On that point I also have news. You will be glad to hear that your grandmaster has also been granted release. I believe he will be here within the month.'

Cronin turned to stare at the king. He had served Gerard of Ridefort at Hattin as his sergeant but had been unallocated a post since arriving at Tripoli in the hope that Gerard would return.

'What were the terms?' asked Brother Thierry. 'I don't seem to recall any ransom being demanded.'

'I know not the detail,' said the king, 'but rest assured, he will support any financial arrangement as soon as he arrives. His commitment to capturing Jerusalem is second only to mine. Now, I need quarters for myself and for my men. They are camped outside the city walls. Please arrange food and water as soon as you can.'

'I can take care of that, your Grace,' said Cronin.

'Excellent,' said Guy. 'Can you also summon the city barons to a meeting tomorrow evening at dusk, I will hold it here in the commandery?'

'Of course, your Grace,' said Cronin.

'Brother Cronin,' said Thierry. 'The seneschal has been taken ill, and the under-marshal is currently out on patrol. In their absence, I want you to undertake the recruitment for the king's army. The pay will be one silver penny a day for experienced men at arms, and twice that for lancers. A third for those who provide their own mounts.'

'What about knights, my lord?'

'No more than five pennies. Unskilled men will get one penny a week plus one meal a day. Any pickings from the battlefield will not be taxed.'

'The payments are low, my lord,' said Cronin. 'I fear the take up may be poor.'

'There are many hungry mouths in this city,' said Thierry. 'I believe your scepticism may be proved wrong.'

'Gentlemen,' said the king. 'Thank you for your attention. I now need to bathe and to have a hot meal. I also need to send notice of my arrival to the queen. Can this be arranged?'

'I will see to it,' said Thierry. 'Brother Cronin, you are dismissed.'

Outside, Cronin headed to the barracks where he and ten other sergeants shared a draughty room.

'Brother Cronin,' said a young sergeant, looking up from the single table at the centre of the room. 'You missed the evening meal, so I saved you a bowl of potage. It's cold but surprisingly flavoursome.'

'Thank you,' said Cronin, removing his cloak, and hanging it on a hook driven into the wall. He joined his fellow sergeant and set about the food. It was humble yet nutritious, and he was disappointed there was not more to enjoy.

'So,' said the young man, 'did you purchase any horses?'

'Alas, I did not,' said Cronin, 'good horses are as rare as the finest jewels.'

The young man stared at Cronin, struggling to find his words.

'Brother Cronin,' he said eventually, 'I need to ask you something, but request you keep the conversation between ourselves.'

Cronin looked at the man he had rescued at the Battle of Hattin. The slaughter had been Brother Martin's first taste of battle having arrived from England only a few weeks earlier, and the experience had affected him badly. His eyes were deep-set and dark from lack of sleep, his weight half what it should have been, and he was certainly in no shape to fight. The prolonged incarceration within the walls of Tripoli had not helped, but he had refused to see the physicians, fearing ridicule from his fellow sergeants.

'Is it about the bad dreams,' asked Cronin, 'for it is a burden we all share?'

'No,' said the young man, 'I mean yes, in a way. These past few months have been a nightmare, one from which I struggle to emerge. My body wastes away, and I am failing in my duties, both physical and spiritual. I fear I am becoming a burden to all, so I have made a decision.'

'Which is?'

'I am going to ask to leave the order,' said Martin, 'and seek passage back to England at the earliest opportunity.'

'I thought you had signed up for five years?' said Cronin.

'I did,' said Martin, 'but if I do not do something soon, I will be in my grave long before that.'

'You do realise,' said Cronin, 'that any chattels or money you donated to the order will not be returned. Nor will the order pay your passage unless you have fulfilled your full term.'

'I am aware of this,' said Martin, 'which is why I am turning to you. I do not have the means to pay for such a passage, nor the knowledge of how to raise such a sum. I am ashamed to ask, but I was wondering if you were able to forward me a loan towards my passage. I swear I will send the money back with interest as soon as I can, but at this moment, I am destitute with only my slow death upon the horizon.'

Cronin stared at the young man. Ordinarily, he would be annoyed at such a request, but they had grown close since Hattin, and he knew he would not have asked unless desperate.

'Brother Martin,' he said eventually. 'Alas, I have no such funds nor the means to acquire them. Perhaps there may be others I can ask, but in the meantime, you need to rest, and rebuild your strength.'

'Do you still have the purse meant to buy the horses?' asked Martin.

'I do,' said Cronin, 'why?'

'Perhaps you can let me have one of those gold coins. Just one will be enough to get me back home. You can say I attacked you and stole it, if you like, they will never know the truth.'

Cronin stared at the smaller man, knowing that nobody in their right mind would ever believe such a tale.

'Brother Martin,' he said eventually, 'you know full well that I cannot, and will not do such a thing. I will try to help you, I swear, but first, you need to get some rest and build up your strength. Go and see the physicians, and tell them of your plight, though I would not share your desire to leave the order, at least not yet.'

'Brother Cronin,' gasped the young man reaching across to grab his comrade's sleeve. 'I beg of you; one coin is all I need. Even if you tell them the truth, they will forgive you. You are the grandmaster's own sergeant and mix freely with royalty. Any punishment would be slight, and I swear I would make repayment.'

Cronin stood up and stared down at the young man.

'My friend,' he said, 'this conversation ends now. 'Yes, I will help, but I will not steal from the order. To do so compromises my own vows, and that I will not do. Now go and see the physicians. We will talk more of this in the morning when you have come to your senses.' He turned away and left the barracks, leaving the distraught young man behind him.

Cronin headed for the treasury to pay back the money he had been issued to buy the horses. Inside, he waited as one of the servants went to bring one of the brother knights from the vaults.

'Brother Cronin,' said a voice eventually, 'you have returned already. Have you heard the news? King Guy has returned from captivity.'

Cronin turned to see the Templar treasurer approach, a portly man who had served alongside him in Karak the previous year but had been reposted to Tripoli only weeks earlier.

'I know,' said Cronin, 'I shared an audience with him not an hour since.'

'An audience with the king?' said Sir Justin, his eyebrows raising with surprise. 'You are certainly making your way up in the world. How is he?'

'He seems well,' said Cronin, 'and is keen to get back on the campaign trail.'

'At last,' said Justin. 'War is so much more profitable than peace. So, was your task successful?'

'Alas not. There were plenty of horses, but nothing suitable for our needs.'

'Ah well,' said Sir Justin taking his seat at a table, 'we will just have to wait until the next shipment. We have ordered a hundred of the best money can buy, and they should be here within weeks.'

Cronin handed over the purse and waited as the treasurer counted the coins before making an entry into a journal.

'Everything is good,' he said at last, 'you are free to go.'

'Brother Justin,' said Cronin as the knight rose from his seat. 'Can I ask you a question?'

'Of course,' said the knight turning back to face the sergeant. 'What is it?'

'How much money do we hold in trust for King Henry's forthcoming campaign?'

Sir Justin stared at the sergeant. Both knew he could never divulge such information unless authorised by the grandmaster himself.

'You know I cannot tell you that,' he said eventually, 'why do you ask?'

'I'm just interested,' said Cronin. 'It seems the king is relying on it to fund his push to regain Jerusalem.'

'I fear such a task will demand much more funding than what is available,' said Sir Justin. 'Money is the lifeblood in the veins of any campaign and without it, any crusade, no matter how noble, is destined to fail.'

'So, how much is left ... half, less?'

'Master Cronin,' said Sir Justin sitting back down into his chair. 'Your interest exceeds your station. Where are you going with this?'

'I heard today that the grandmaster has been released,' said Cronin, 'yet apparently no ransom has been demanded or paid. Why would Saladin release such a valuable captive without reason, knowing full well he commands the one organisation that has the power to drive him back to Egypt?'

'You would have to ask him that,' said Sir Justin

'If only it were that simple,' said Cronin, getting to his feet. 'I just thought you may be able to hold a torch to such matters. Anyway, I have work to attend. Be aware that Sir Thierry has authorised the raising of an army for the king. I will be recruiting men from tomorrow and will be needing silver pennies to pay their signing fee.'

'As long as the necessary authorisations are in place,' said the knight, 'there will be no challenge from me.'

'Thank you, Sir Justin,' said Cronin, and left the treasurer alone with his thoughts.

For the next few days, Cronin, and two other sergeants sat at a table in the market square near the city gates. Word had been spread by the criers, and a long line of men snaked their way around the perimeter, each waiting to sign up to the forthcoming campaign. One by one, they approached to state their name and make their mark.

'Name?' said Cronin as the next man stepped up to the table.

'Edmond Fletcher,' said the man, 'and I make the finest arrows under God's sun.'

'That's quite a claim, Edward Fletcher,' said Cronin as he wrote the man's name onto the parchment. 'Have you seen battle?'

'I was in Jerusalem, my lord,' said Fletcher, 'I saw you there when I was delivering my arrows to the walls.'

Cronin nodded his approval. Good fletchers were always an asset in any army, and the fact that he had experienced warfare, albeit from behind the front line, meant he was no stranger to the stress and fear that warfare brought.

'Make your mark here,' said Cronin, pointing at the parchment.

'Yes, my lord,' said the man scraping an ineligible mark onto the parchment.

'Coin or food?' asked Cronin looking up.

'Sorry, my lord?'

'Do you want coin or food in return for your pledge? You have the choice of one penny or a hearty meal of potage, bread, cheese and wine.'

'I'll take the food,' said the fletcher. 'I haven't eaten for three days.'

'Join the men in that line,' said Cronin pointing across the square, 'and come back here in two weeks to meet your comrades. If you fail to turn up, the marshal will find you and remove your right hand for theft. Is that understood?'

'It is, my lord,' said the man, 'I'll be here, sure enough.'

'Good. Now begone.'

The man scurried away to be replaced by the next man in line.

'Name?' said Cronin without looking up.

'You know my name,' said a voice, 'and I want no stinking potage, I require silver so I can get blind drunk and bed as many women as I can before we march to war.'

Cronin looked up, and a huge grin spread across his face as he recognised the man before him.

'Arturas,' he said, getting to his feet and grabbing his friend's wrist in recognition. 'How are you, my friend, and how are you in Tripoli? I thought you would be digging salt for the sultan's table by now.'

'As did I,' said Arturas, 'but after Raynald was killed at Hattin, the new castellan knew it was only a matter of time before Saladin turned his attention on Karak. He fortified the castle but sent the contents of the treasury to Tyre for safekeeping and needed men to ensure it arrived here safely.'

'And you supplied those men?'

'I did, along with Hunter. We fully intended to return to Karak, but by the time we got here, the castle was already under siege, and well, here I am. Thirsty and unemployed.'

'Is Hunter here?' asked Cronin, looking along the line.

'He was, but I believe he headed south to collect his family.'

'And what news of Sumeira?'

'All I know is what Hunter told me. The last he heard of her, she had been sold into slavery and was serving Saladin's army outside of Damascus. I fear for her safety, but she is nothing if not strong, and if anyone can survive such an ordeal, it is she.'

'Anyway,' said Cronin, 'back to business. Why do you want to sign up? Have you not had enough of war?'

'Tripoli is a grand place,' said Arturas, 'and the ladies are very, shall we say, accommodating, but I am bored beyond compare, and fighting is the only thing I know.'

Cronin glanced down at his friend's leg.

'And your injury?'

'I have good days and bad days, but I got here from Karak on horseback so that should be proof enough I am capable of doing my job.'

'Do you have your own horse?'

'I do.'

'Then I suggest you ride with our scouts,' said Cronin, 'your knowledge of the Outremer will be invaluable. It pays three coins a day, two for you, and one to feed your horse.'

'Whatever you say, my lord.,' grinned Arturas, 'now show me where to sign and give me the king's silver. There's a pretty little thing waiting for me behind the church, and she grows impatient.'

Cronin laughed and shook his head. His friend was one of the best he had seen in battle, but his hunger for women and ale never seemed to diminish.

'Here,' he said, handing him three silver pennies, 'spend it wisely, my friend, and muster back here in two weeks.'

By the time dusk fell, Cronin and his comrades had signed up almost a thousand foot-soldiers, and a hundred knights. The tally was impressive and combined with those already camped outside the city gates, formed a sizeable army. However, everyone knew it was nowhere near enough, and if Guy were to be successful in his campaign to regain Jerusalem, they would need far, far more.

He made his way back up the hill to the citadel. The day had been long, but he knew many more such days lay before him.

He walked into the Treasury to return the unspent silver before heading back to the barracks. His mind was exhausted, and he craved hot food, but most of all, he needed his bed. He walked into the room and stopped dead in his tracks. Up above his head, suspended by a belt secured around his neck, swung the body of the young sergeant, Brother Martin.

Chapter Seven

Tyre

April - AD 1189

'My Lord,' said Balian of Ibelin, striding into the dining hall where Conrad of Montferrat was eating alongside his father, 'I have great news.'

'Sit,' said Conrad through a mouthful of bread, 'and grab some food while it is still hot.'

Balian sat and waited until one of the servants placed a bowlful of steaming pork soup before him. Conrad grabbed half a loaf of bread and threw it across the table, much to Balian's surprise.

'What's the matter?' asked Conrad, 'do you miss the niceties of Jerusalem's court? You are amongst men now, Balian, and unless there are visitors, I see no need to adhere to courtly protocol.'

His father laughed and beckoned one of the serving girls.

'More wine,' he said, 'and make sure there are plenty of pitchers available in the kitchen. I feel this night may be a long one.'

'Yes, my lord,' said the girl and ran from the room.

'So,' said the old man, 'what is this news that is so great?'

'My lords,' said Balian, wiping some soup from his mouth, 'I have received a message that Guy of Lusignan has been released, and is in the process of recruiting a great army.'

'I thought he was tucked up safely under the covers of his wife's bed in Tripoli.'

'He probably is,' said Balian, 'but has always stated that his intention was to free Jerusalem. Until now he has struggled to recruit an army, but apparently, William II of Sicily has sent a fleet with two hundred knights and the Bishop of Pisa arrived at Tripoli, not a few days since with fifty-two ships. Once he has recruited enough men, he intends to march here on the coastal road.'

'It will be good to meet him at last,' said Conrad. 'I hear he is a great king.'

'Then you have heard incorrectly,' snapped his father. 'The man is nothing but an incompetent fool enjoying the trappings of kingship only through right of marriage. You and I have a better claim to the throne than he.'

'I take it you are not an admirer,' said Balian coldly.

'I am not,' said William, 'and neither should you be. You fought at Hattin and saw the result of his incompetence. Our men were half-dead through thirst before a blade had been drawn. I lost many men that day, men who had become close friends. I hold that so-called king responsible for every single death, and if I were a younger man, would make him pay.'

'Be careful you are not overheard uttering such threats, my lord,' said Balian. 'He would not be best pleased with your dissent.'

'Would he not?' shouted William banging his tankard down on to the table. 'Well, I am not best pleased that within two years of cheating his way to the throne, that man is responsible for the defeat at Cresson, the slaughter at Hattin, the fall of Jerusalem, and the occupation of the whole of the Outremer. It was his decisions and his alone that have brought us to where we are today. The man is an imbecile and has no right to the throne.'

Conrad and Balian stared at each other, both surprised at the strength of the outburst.

'What does he want anyway?' continued the old man eventually, 'why is he coming here?'

'I believe he wants to base his kingship in Tyre to advance his push towards Jerusalem. With Acre already in Muslim hands, we are the only harbour outside of Tripoli with a harbour big enough to handle the sort of supply chain such an action demands.'

'You think he wants to command Tyre?' asked Conrad, placing his own tankard on the table.

'It is no secret,' said Balian. 'Tyre is in the county of Jerusalem, and Guy is its king. If he wants Tyre, then it is his to command.'

'Is it now?' said Conrad, 'well I may have something to say about that.'

The following evening, Guy's army approached Tyre from the north. Out at sea, the fleets from Pisa and Sicily matched their progress, and with eight thousand men at arms, and just under seven hundred knights marching along the coastal road, the force was one to be reckoned with.

At their head rode Guy of Lusignan alongside Gerard of Ridefort, the true Templar grandmaster, freshly released from Ayyubid captivity. Behind them came a hundred knights, and in their midst, the covered cart carrying Guy's wife, Sibylla, Queen of Jerusalem.

The column stretched back for several leagues, including hundreds of carts and camp followers. The journey had not been long, but the threat from the Ayyubid patrols was ever-present, and they yearned for the safety of the city walls.

'There it is,' said Gerard eventually as the massive battlements came into view. 'No wonder Gokbori found it so difficult to take, the whole island is a fortress.'

'A superb location,' said Guy, 'and with its deep harbour, an ideal base from which to launch the counter-offensive.'

'I agree,' said Gerard, and turned to Cronin riding just behind him.

'Brother Cronin, I expect we have been seen by now, but ride forward to announce our imminent arrival. I'm sure Lord Conrad will offer a welcome that befits a king, but it would be embarrassing for him if he were to be found wanting.'

'Yes, my lord,' said Cronin, and spurred his horse into a canter.

An hour later, the head of the column reached the open plain before the city walls where only months earlier, the people of the city had inflicted the terrible defeat on Gokbori's army. Night was falling, but the walls of Tyre were lit up with hundreds of burning torches.

'It looks like they are preparing a great reception,' said the king. 'I am humbled.'

'Brother Gerard,' called a voice, and Cronin appeared out of the gloom to ride up to the grandmaster.

'Brother Cronin,' replied Gerard, 'have the necessary arrangements been made?'

Cronin glanced towards the king, who was now in jovial conversation with one of his knights.

'My lord,' said Cronin, 'can I have a word in private?' He turned his horse away and rode out away from the column.

'What is it,' asked the Grandmaster, catching him up.

'My lord,' said Cronin, 'we have a problem. I rode to the city as you ordered, but the gate commander refused me entrance.'

'Did you explain you were there on behalf of the king?'

'I did, my lord, but the answer was the same. Apparently, the gates will remain locked until dawn, and only then will anyone be considered for entrance.'

'There must be some mistake,' said Gerard.

'There was no mistake, my lord,' said Cronin. 'The conversation was heated, and I left them under no illusion as to what they were doing, but they were adamant that we would not be let into the city.'

'I don't understand' said Ridefort. 'No man in his right mind would refuse entry to the king.'

'Don't forget, we are dealing with Conrad of Montferrat here,' said Cronin, 'and he has a reputation for doing things his own way in his own time.'

'Nevertheless, his actions are a snub, and the king will be embarrassed. Ride back to the city and demand an audience with Conrad at first light. I will make some excuse and arrange a camp to be set up out here.'

'As you wish, my lord,' said Conrad, and turned his horse to return to Tyre as Gerard of Ridefort rode back to the king.

'Your Grace,' said the grandmaster when he reached Guy, 'there has been a slight complication. I have received word that Conrad of Montferrat is indisposed and is unable to receive you before morning.'

'What is wrong with him?'

'I think he may be ill and is embarrassed he cannot receive you in person.'

'Nonsense,' said Guy, 'I expect little in the way of fanfare, and it may please him for me to visit his sickbed.'

'Your Grace,' said Ridefort, 'with respect, the man is about to lose command of his city. I suggest we smooth the transition by allowing him time to recover and greet you himself.'

'Perhaps you are right,' said Guy, 'one more night will make no difference. Set up camp before the city walls and arrange extra rations for the men. Tonight, alongside myself and my queen, they will dine one more time beneath the stars.'

'As you wish,' said Ridefort, and turned away to make the arrangements.

The following morning, the royal party approached the city walls along with the Templar grandmaster and Thomas Cronin. A dozen flag bearers flew the colours of Jerusalem, and behind them, a hundred of their finest knights provided the guard.

'The gates are still not open,' hissed the grandmaster to Cronin, 'what are they playing at?'

'I know not,' said Cronin, 'but upon my second visit last night, I received assurances that Conrad of Montferrat would receive him in person.'

'Then, where is he?'

The group came to a halt before the bridge that now spanned a much deeper and wider ditch.

'An impressive fortress,' said Guy looking up at the battlements. 'No wonder Gokbori was found wanting.' He looked across at Gerard of Ridefort. 'Grandmaster, are we early?'

Gerard searched for an excuse, but before he could answer, the gates creaked open, and a party of riders rode out from the city.

'Ah, here they are,' said Guy, 'and that looks like Balian of Ibelin in their midst.'

'Who's the knight in green?' asked Cronin.

Nobody answered, and they waited until the reception committee reined in their horses a few paces away.

'Your Grace,' announced Balian eventually, 'may I introduce Lord Conrad of Montferrat, master of the city of Tyre.'

Conrad dipped his head in acknowledgement but did not dismount.

'Lord Conrad,' said Guy, 'I have heard much about your recent defence of Tyre. You have my gratitude. It is certainly a formidable fortress.'

'Thank you, King Guy,' said Conrad, 'but in the interests of clear speaking, I have to be blunt, and say the defence of this city was done in the name of Christianity and not you.'

Guy stared at Conrad as the words sunk in. He maintained his composure, but inside he was shocked at the response.

'Lord Conrad,' interjected Gerard, 'If I may. There is no man that enjoys straight speaking more than I, but I feel your words may have been poorly chosen. Although the king was in captivity at the time, Tyre is part of Jerusalem and therefore, within his realm. By default, any defence would have been in his name.'

'My words conveyed the exact meaning I intended them to,' said Conrad. He turned to face Guy. 'King Guy,' he said, 'I mean you no offence, but if my understanding is correct, which the Bishop of Tyre assures me it is, the will of King Baldwin IV clearly stated that in the event of his successor dying before coming of age, then the kindship should be decided by a council consisting of Baldwin's kinsmen, the Kings of England and France, the Holy Roman Emperor, Frederick I and his holiness, Pope Urban III. As this arrangement was clearly ignored, I have no other option, but to declare that I do not recognise your claim to the throne and consequently, any claim to this city. I hasten to add that I wish you no ill, and we can open negotiations as to what we can do to support your campaign to reclaim Jerusalem in the name of Christianity, but it will be as allies only, not vassals.'

Gerard stared in horror, hardly believing what he was hearing.

'This is treachery,' he shouted, but Guy held up his hand to command silence.

'Lord Conrad,' he said calmly. 'I see that you are confused as to the situation, and that is understandable. Your stance is worrying, but nothing we can't overcome. Allow us into Tyre, and we will discuss the issues in detail. You have my word as king that there will be no animosity or recourse to violence, only constructive argument towards a mutually beneficial outcome.'

'Your Grace,' said Conrad. 'Your understanding is gratefully received, but alas, I cannot offer you the hospitality of Tyre. The political situation is confused at best, and until such time that it is sorted out, my stance is that Jerusalem has no true king. It is unfortunate, but that is the way it must be. You are welcome to maintain a camp outside the city, and I will allow your supply ships to dock in the harbour as required, but for now, that is all I can offer. Now if you will excuse me, I have things to attend.' He turned his horse and started riding back towards the gates. Hundreds of armed men watched the proceedings from the battlements, and the king looked upward, feeling their derision burning into his soul.

'Lord Conrad,' he called just before Conrad reached the gate. 'Your actions go in the face of God's will and are an insult to the throne of Jerusalem. They will never be forgotten, but today there are more important things to consider than the pettiness of a minor noble. Keep your city for with or without it, my destiny is to reclaim Jerusalem in the name of the Lord God. But before you go, know this. That is the last time you will ever turn your back on me.' Without another word, he turned his horse and headed back towards the tented camp.

Back at his tent, Guy threw his cloak at one of the servants and headed over to a cloth-covered trestle table to pour himself a goblet of wine.

'Is that wise?' said a voice, and he turned to see Sibylla standing behind him.

'Wise or not,' he replied, 'it is what the situation demands.'

'What the situation demands,' replied the queen, 'walking over to place her hand on his shoulder, is a clear mind and a cool head. I am just as embarrassed as you, but we must take a step back to consider all options. The last thing any of us should do is react without a clear plan.'

'The plan is clear,' said the king through gritted teeth, 'we attack that imposter and drag Tyre from beneath his feet. He may have stout walls, but what he does not have are the hearts of the people. Tyre is part of *my* kingdom, and many within that city are refugees from all across Jerusalem. If they knew their king had been snubbed like a common beggar, they would rally to my call.'

'*Our* kingdom,' said Sibylla, removing her hand from her husband's shoulder.

'What?'

'Jerusalem is *our* kingdom, not just yours.'

'Apologies,' said Guy, 'I meant no insult, but the fact remains he has disrespected us in full sight of those we rule, and we cannot let it go unpunished.'

'Put down the wine, Guy,' said Sibylla, 'and sit with me. Your heart is aflame with rage, and we need it icy cold before making decisions of such magnitude. Let us talk, and when we are thinking more clearly, only then will we decide what to do.'

Guy took a deep breath and placed the half-full goblet back on the table.

'You are right,' he said, 'these things should be dealt with by thought before deed.' He turned and looked at Sibylla. 'As usual, your counsel is sound. I will order the army to set up a permanent camp until such time as my decision is made.'

'It doesn't have to be here in full sight of that scoundrel,' said Sibylla, 'you should not give him that pleasure.'

'On the contrary,' said Guy. 'I want our presence to be a constant reminder that outside the gates lies an army capable of destroying the very city he saved, and besides, as it now seems I am a king without a kingdom, it has to be here. We have no other place to go.'

Chapter Eight

Acre

August - AD 1188

Deep in the heart of Acre, Sumeira of Greece carried two buckets of water from the well. Her hair was a tangled mess, and her clothing stank from the constant sweat of her forced labour. But she was alive, and at the moment, that was all that mattered.

Since being brought to the city just after it was taken by the Ayyubid, she had been forced to work in the prison building, formerly the Templar commandery. The work was hard and the days long, but the one saving grace of the guard commander was that he allowed no man to touch her on pain of death.

She walked through the gates, and placed down the buckets, struggling to regain her breath.

'Why do you stop,' asked a voice from the far side of the courtyard, 'did I say you could do so?'

Sumeira looked up and saw the familiar figure of the man who made life a daily hell for the Christian prisoners. Barak el-Sayed ruled the prison with an iron fist. His enormous frame suggested he would struggle with anything strenuous, but any prisoner on the wrong end of his wrath found out he was surprisingly agile, and more than able to administer a severe beating. Such punishments were not just reserved for the prisoners either, for any guard found failing in their duties would suffer a similar punishment, a situation that meant everyone was extra vigilant, and extra cruel.

Sumeira stared at the jailer. More than anything, she wanted to run over and lash out at the man who had inflicted so much misery on herself and the other prisoners. Even to scream at him would feel good, but to do so meant another beating, a price she had found out to her cost.

'No, my lord,' she said at last. 'You did not. I was just catching my breath.'

'You can rest when you sleep,' said Barak. 'Come here.'

With a deep sigh, Sumeira picked up the buckets and walked over to face him. He was sitting in a cushioned-chair and being fanned by two men with makeshift fans, each prisoner hardly able to stand, they were so emaciated. Behind them stood one of the armed guards, a vicious looking man with a scimitar tucked loosely in his waist belt.

She stopped just before the jailer and placed the buckets upon the floor. Barak stared at her, a faint smile of cruel enjoyment playing about his face.

'So,' he said eventually, 'you are a physician.'

'I have told you so on many occasions,' sighed Sumeira, 'and if you would just let me have access to the sick and the wounded, I know I could save at least some of their lives.'

'They do not deserve to live,' said Barak, 'they believe in the false God.'

'So, you keep telling me,' said Sumeira.

Again he stared, looking her up and down.

'Sumeira of Greece,' he continued, 'I have news that affects you. Salah ad-Din has left the city to rid Palestine of the remaining infidels that infest our lands. Now he has gone, the command of Acre falls to my master, Turan-Shah. That means he has little time to oversee the jail, which in turn, increases my responsibility and indeed, my power.'

Sumeira's heart sank. He already wielded total control over the prisoners, and many had already died at his whim.

'Unfortunately,' he continued, 'the departure of Salah ad-Din and his forces means we are short of healers, and we still have servants of Allah who need medical attention.'

Sumeira's eyes narrowed, realising where the conversation was going.

'So,' he continued, 'I have promised Turan-Shah that you will be only too happy to attend to our sick and wounded, though I suspect your methods are far too primitive to make any difference.'

'I have already told you,' said Sumeira, 'I will not care for any Saracen until I am allowed access to the Christian prisoners.'

'I know,' sighed Barak, 'and this is an argument I do not want to have so let me explain in a way you will understand.'

He flicked his hand, and before she could react, the guard drew his scimitar and sent it slicing through the air to connect with one of the prisoners' necks. The severed head hit the ground, and the falling body sent plumes of blood over Sumeira.

'No,' she cried, looking back up at the jailer. 'Why did you do that?'

'To add strength to my argument,' he said. 'Now, just so we understand each other, there are almost fifty prisoners within these walls, and I care not if any of them live or die.' He glanced over to the second prisoner, who had collapsed to his knees in fear. 'Each of us have a choice to make. Your choice is whether or not you agree to my request, my choice is whether or not I kill one of the prisoners. Do I make myself clear?'

Sumeira was still shocked and lifted her gaze to stare at the jailer.

'You say you believe in Allah,' she gasped, 'but you are no better than the lowest murdering filth that ever walked under the sun. That man did nothing to you, yet you killed him in cold blood.'

'His life was nothing to me,' said Barak, 'but now, you know the arrangement, so I will ask the question again. Will you treat our sick and wounded?'

Sumeira hesitated, but as the guard walked over to the cowering prisoner, she stepped forward.

'Wait,' she said, 'no more killing.'

'I thought you would agree,' said Barak.

'I will,' said Sumeira, 'on one condition.'

'You are in no position to demand any conditions, Sumeira of Greece.'

'My apologies, I meant I have a request.'

'Which is?'

'I will do as you ask, but I must also be allowed to treat the prisoners.'

'And if I refuse?'

'Then you may as well kill them all now, including me. Death would probably be a release for most of them anyway.'

'I like you, Sumeira,' said Barak eventually. 'You know how to fight. Perhaps if Acre had been defended with men as half as brave as you, then we would not be having this conversation.'

'So, you agree?'

'I do, but the Christians will not be allowed into the hospital, they will be treated in their cells only. Also, you will not use any supplies issued to treat my people.'

'But I will need herbs and clean bandages. How will I obtain them?'

'You are a resourceful woman, Sumeira,' said Barak, 'you will think of something.' He lifted his hand and used a finger to wipe some of the dead man's blood from his face. 'Now, I believe this negotiation is at an end. I will make the necessary arrangements and send word when we are ready.' As she stared, he placed his finger in his mouth and licked off the blood. Sumeira was horrified, but she did not react, desperate to keep his satisfaction to a minimum. She turned away but hadn't gone a few paces before he called out again.

'Sumeira, haven't you forgotten something?'

She walked back over and without taking her eyes from the jailer, picked up the two buckets of water.

'See,' said Barak, 'we are already helping each other.'

With hatred in her heart, Sumeira walked away, desperate to get as far away from him as possible.

The next few days were busy for Sumeira. The seats in the old chapel were stripped out and replaced with sleeping pallets. A line of prisoners spent all day ferrying buckets of water to fill two dedicated water barrels while others unloaded buckets of herbs and bandages from a cart, all essentials for anyone hoping to practice medicine.

'That's it,' she said eventually, looking around the chapel. 'It's not great, but it will do.' She turned to the Egyptian prisoner allocated to her as a helper. 'Shani, go to the kitchens and ask for a bucket of hot water.'

'Why?' asked Shani.

'Because we need to bathe. Infection is carried by filth, and we need to remain clean, or we will be wasting our time.'

Shani grimaced but hurried away to do as she asked. Sumeira turned to the guard watching from the doorway.

'You can tell your master that we will be ready from dawn tomorrow.'

The guard nodded but stayed where he was.

'You can leave,' she said, 'I am going nowhere. The gates are locked, and besides, where would I go?'

The guard looked around before walking over to stand before her. She expected the usual course comments, but instead, he rolled up his sleeve to reveal an infected cut on his arm.

'If you are a healer,' he said, looking around nervously, 'can you do something about this?'

Sumeira looked down and took his arm in her hands. The cut was no more than a graze but had become infected.

'Yes,' she said, 'I can. Come back later, and I will give you a poultice.'

'I cannot be seen,' said the guard. 'Barak will beat me for being weak.'

Sumeira thought for a moment. She would be sleeping in one of the back rooms of the hospital from now on so her rations would be brought by one of the kitchen servants.

'When they bring the food,' she said, looking around, 'take it off the servant and place it on my bed. I will leave a paste there for you to apply. Nobody will ever know we talked.'

The guard nodded before turning away to attend to his duties, leaving the healer to sweep the last of the rubbish from the chapel floor.

The following morning, she and Shani finished scrubbing the floors with hot water. No patients had arrived yet, so they took the opportunity to make the whole place as clean as they could. As she neared the door, she looked up to see Barak standing in the doorway. He looked around, obviously impressed, but careful not to offer any words of encouragement.

'So,' said Sumeira, 'where are all these sick and wounded that cost the life of that innocent man?'

'You will have patients soon enough,' he said. 'Do you have everything that you need?'

'I think so, but if you would just allow me one boon, my mind would be more focussed on the task in hand.'

'And that boon is?'

'If you allow me to attend the markets to purchase the things that I need, I can save you money and be far more effective.'

'How?'

'By being far more selective. Some of the items you have supplied will hardly be used. Others are far more useful, yet there is not enough.'

'You have been given what one of our physicians said you needed.'

'With respect, my lord, I use medicine from several cultures. If you restrict me to just that of Islam, then you may as well have one of your own physicians do the job. If you want me to save as many lives as I can, then I should be allowed to apply my own knowledge.'

'And if I do this, what is to stop you escaping the city?'

'I'm sure the gate guards would have something to say about that, and besides, if I escape, I suspect you will take your retribution out on the Christian prisoners.'

'You are learning fast,' said Barak. He stepped into the chapel to walk between the rows of sleeping-pallets. 'If you escape,' he continued, 'or even try to escape, I will torture every prisoner before hanging them from the city walls for all to see. Their deaths will be on your conscience, do you understand?'

'I do,' said Sumeira.

'In that case, you are free to do as you wish. However, I expect to see results.'

'I will do the best I can,' said Sumeira.

The jailer walked past her and out of the chapel, leaving Sumeira alone with Shani. The interaction had gone better than expected, and now she had an idea, one that could make a huge difference.

Outside the walls of Tyre in the north, Guys army had more than doubled in size. Days had turned into weeks and weeks into months, but despite constant negotiations between the two camps, Conrad of Montferrat still refused him access to the city. Frustrated at the lack of cooperation, and with an army growing impatient to go to war, Guy of Lusignan summoned all his commanders to the campaign tent situated right in the heart of his makeshift camp.

Ever since the first rebuff by Conrad, he and his nobles had been in intense discussions as to their next move. Opinions were divided and often heated, but eventually, they had come up with a plan. It was audacious, and some would say foolhardy, but deep inside, Guy knew it was the only real option they had, and the time had come to inform the army commanders.

Men shuffled for space until each faced the king. Alongside Guy stood the Master of the Temple, Gerard of

Ridefort, and he held up his hand for silence. The tent fell quiet, and the king climbed up onto a wooden box to be seen by all.

'Men of Jerusalem,' he said, 'fellow soldiers of Christ. Each of you are fully aware of our current situation and will accept that things cannot stay as they are. We are fighting men, and our pledge is to free Jerusalem from the hands of the unbelievers. Our army is strong and will be a match for anything Saladin can bring against us, but it is not enough. Before we can march on the Holy-city, we need a secure harbour, one which we can control ourselves and not be reliant on those who see themselves above God's law.'

A murmur of anger rippled around the room; each man equally annoyed at the power that still lay in Conrad's grasp.

'We should attack Tyre immediately,' growled one of the older knights, 'and wrest the city from his hands.'

'I have no doubt you would be successful,' said the king, 'but that pits Christian against Christian, and I will not shed the blood of those who worship the same God as us.' He looked around the room as every set of eyes stared back. 'So,' he continued, 'we have to look elsewhere. We already know that many ships are already on their way to support our crusade, and we have to establish a secure place for them to dock. That place, my fellows is Acre, the greatest seaport in the Outremer.'

'But Acre is in the hands of Saladin,' said one of the officers,' and has some of the greatest defences of any fortress. We will need an army ten times our size.'

'Do not underestimate our own strength,' said Guy, 'but you are correct in one sense, we will need more men. I am aware that tens of thousands are already on their way to the Holy-land, so we will not be short of numbers, but in the meantime, Conrad has agreed to supply us with men and supplies from Tyre in return for us not attacking the city.

Gerard glanced towards Guy knowing the statement was a lie and the king's envoys had to almost beg Conrad for his support.

'So,' continued Guy, 'our path is clear once again. Rally your troops and prepare to strike camp. We will stay here one more night, but tomorrow as the sun rises in the east, we march on Acre.

The following morning, with almost ten thousand men at arms including seven hundred knights, Guy marched south towards Acre. Behind them came a long line of carts and pack animals, the necessary supply caravan needed to sustain any campaign. For leagues inland, foraging parties were already sweeping the countryside to find whatever they could to supplement their supplies.

'How far to Acre?' asked the king as he rode.

'Another few hours,' said Gerard of Ridefort at his side. 'I suspect their scouts have seen us by now and have already sent word to the city.'

'It was to be expected,' said Guy. 'Are our men ready?'

'They are. Do you still want us to attack straight away? I suspect it would be better to establish a camp first before we unveil any of our strength.'

'I agree to a certain extent,' said Guy, 'but I want to send a message to Acre's castellan, whoever that may be, that we mean business. As soon as we are in place, get the cart-mounted mangonels to open a barrage.'

'With respect, your Grace,' said Gerard, 'I have seen the walls of Acre, and mangonels will have little impact.'

'Maybe not, but Greek-fire will. Have them launch pots over the walls, and into the heart of the city. I want to cause as much damage and disruption as we can before we commit a single man to the assault.'

In Acre, bells that had once summoned Christians to prayers now rang as an alarm, warning the city that they were in danger. People ran in confusion, not knowing what was happening, and hundreds of traders who had set up a market outside the city gates hastily disassembled their stalls and piled them onto their carts and donkeys.

The noise was deafening, and the streets rammed with people as they sought safety within the city walls, but up above on the northern battlements, one man stayed icy calm as he stared northward. Turan-Shah had been warned just over an hour earlier that an army was on its way. He hated living within Acre's cold walls, but he knew the fortress was strong and would be relatively simple to defend.

'Malik,' he said eventually, turning to the guard commander at his side. 'Muster our forces. Spread them out along all the walls, but I want double the amount on the landward side.'

'Yes, my lord,' said the soldier.

'And send messages to Salah ad-Din. Tell him we are about to come under attack and request he sends his warriors to swipe this annoyance from the soil.'

'As you wish, my lord,' said Malik, and hurried away.

Down by the gates, the guards struggled to control the throng trying to get into the city. Rich and poor alike pushed their way through the crowd and amongst them, a small Egyptian posing as a beggar to draw as little attention as possible.

Fakhiri was a former cart-master who had befriended Sumeira the previous year in her quest to find her son in the town of Segor, but shortly after they had split up, a slave-trader betrayed Sumeira and took her into captivity.

At the same time, the slave-trader sent his men to rob and kill Fakhiri, but they identified the wrong man and murdered his brother instead. The Egyptian had killed the slave-trader in retribution but had sworn to find Sumeira and set her free. Now, after months of searching, he had found out that there was a Christian woman confined in Acre, one who was reputed to be a physician.

Taking advantage of the crowds, he walked deeper into the maze of streets. He knew he had to find her as soon as he could, but first, he had to find a way to survive. With a siege imminent, food would soon be hard to find, but as a child, he and his brothers had lived on the streets of Cairo, so living off his wits was nothing new.

He walked on until he found the central square. Many traders still had their carts on display, especially those with vegetables and meat, each keen to sell their wares before it rotted. Fakhiri sat back against a wall in the shade, his begging bowl between his feet. He had little hope of getting much, but from his position he could see the comings and goings of everyone who had any involvement in the square, and in the game of survival, that was essential information.

Chapter Nine

Acre

August - AD 1189

'Pick up the rate,' roared the siege-master, 'or I'll have your scabby hides launched over the walls on the next volley.'

The men operating the mangonels doubled down to work as hard as they could. Their siege-engines had been launching pots of Greek-fire and head-sized boulders into Acre for the past few days without respite. Behind them, cart after cart brought a steady supply of rocks from nearby quarries, hewn from the bedrock by hundreds of Ayyubid slaves bought in the markets of Tripoli.

To the rear, a team of alchemists mixed the ingredients needed to create Greek-fire, a carefully guarded formula known to few, yet feared by all. Its flammable, glutinous consistency meant that it spread on everything it touched and was almost impossible to extinguish once lit. Even water seemed to spread the flames, and it was usual to let them die down of their own accord.

Several times a day, ranks of archers marched as close as they dared, and sent volley after volley of flaming arrows over the walls and into the city. The effect on human life was minimal, but the damage caused was horrific. Hundreds of wooden buildings burnt to the ground and a permanent haze of dust and smoke hung over acre like its own thunderstorm. Inside the walls, day to day life was hard, but they knew the worst was yet to come.

Up in the jail, Sumeira's empty hospital quickly filled up. Some people had been hit by the thousands of arrows pouring from the sky while others had suffered burns while trying to extinguish the many fires still burning around the city.

As soon as she had heard the news of an advancing army, her heart raced with relief, but knowing there was no chance to escape, her thoughts had turned to her new role, and in particular, the continuing despair of the Christian prisoners. Taking advantage of her new-found trust, she had left Shani in charge before scouring the markets, and with a letter of authorisation from the jailer, quickly found what she needed. Having spent many years living in Segor, she was no stranger to barter and managed to strike good deals, offering guarantees of further purchases in return for a little extra product. That surplus was quickly hidden away beneath her thawb, destined for use amongst the Christian prisoners. It was a risky ploy, but her hope was that Barak would have too much on his mind to notice a few leaves missing from each purchase.

Now, with the siege well and truly underway, the supply had finally run dry, and for the first time in a week, she returned to the jail empty-handed. As she entered the gates, she was greeted once more by the obese jailer.

'Sumeira,' he called from a balcony outside one of the upper windows. 'You seem to spend more time in the markets than in the hospital. I'm beginning to think you don't like it here.'

'I am only making sure we are well stocked, my lord,' she said. 'When the assault comes, the hospital will likely be full to the rafters, and if that happens, we will need everything we can get our hands on.'

'So, now there is no more reason to leave this place?'

'No, my lord, unless the city receives any supply ships. We still need more willow bark and poppy seeds.'

'Christian remedies,' said Barak.

'Yet effective and recognised by all physicians as great killers of pain.'

'You should get to work. Your servant is no physician, and I do not have to remind you that there will be consequences if you fall short on my expectations.'

'I'm on my way,' said Sumeira and headed for the chapel.

Outside the city, King Guy was in his campaign tent briefing his commanders. For the past week, they had kept up a constant barrage against the eastern wall, an approach designed to keep the enemy busy while they made their preparations for the main assault. Now the time was approaching, and the king had called one last council. He pointed at the large map spread out on the table before him.

'We have had a message from one of our spies within Acre,' he said. 'The city is defended by Egyptians and has a garrison of about six thousand men at arms. The civilians number five times that amount, and they are struggling for food. Despite this, there seems to be no sign of any great suffering amongst the defenders for they are given first call on any food being delivered to the harbour by the Egyptian fleet.'

'Are their ships still getting through?' asked Cronin.

'They are,' said the king, 'for our own are outnumbered, but I have it on good authority that there are two Christian fleets just a day or so away. When they arrive, I will task them with creating a blockade to starve the city.'

'Perhaps we should wait until they arrive,' said Cronin. 'A hungry foe is a far easier one to defeat.'

'We have already wasted too much time,' said Guy.' If we break through now, when these new fleets arrive, they will see who the true King of Jerusalem is and will pledge their allegiance.' He looked around at the gathered commanders. 'Tonight, I want every mangonel we have to focus on the gate towers. Use boulders to smash the castellations while our men approach the city walls. At first light, the catapults are to change their loads and cover the parapets with Greek-fire. Tell them to use extra pitch, I want as much smoke as possible. At my command, the front ranks will assault the gate wall with siege ladders. Their approach will be covered by a thousand crossbows so they should encounter little resistance.' He turned to face the Templar grandmaster. 'Sir Gerard, at the same time, I want you and your men to create a diversion at the northern gate. Hopefully, this will keep their defenders split while we force a breach.'

'As you wish, your Grace.' said Gerard.

'Your Grace,' said Cronin, 'if I may.'

'Speak freely, Brother Cronin,' said the king, 'your input is always welcome.'

'Your Grace,' said Cronin. 'Over the past few years, I have spent a lot of time in Acre. While there, I realised that one day I may have to defend it against the Saracens so made it my business to learn its defences in detail. Never did I think that I would be part of an assault.'

'And your point is?' interjected Gerard of Ridefort.

'My lord, the point is that there are not many cities with better defences than Acre. Most are larger or enjoy better locations, but the core of their outer walls are mainly formed with loose spoil. Here in Acre, the walls are not only made from the strongest stone the builders could quarry but are mostly built on solid bedrock denying us any chance to tunnel beneath. Our mangonels will have little effect, and the entrance has three gates, each as stout as the other. I fear a frontal assault is doomed to fail so we should learn a lesson from Saladin and focus all our energy on any point of weakness.'

'And is there one?' asked the king.

'There is,' said Cronin, 'here.' He pointed at the map indicating one of the crudely drawn towers on the north-east corner of the city walls. 'The Accursed-Tower.'

For a few seconds, there was silence before several of the men burst into laughter.

'Your mind has been poisoned,' said one, 'that is one of the largest and strongest towers I have ever seen. We would lose a thousand men before we got anywhere near it.'

'I am not suggesting we attack it,' said Cronin, 'I am suggesting we collapse it.'

'By mining?' suggested Gerard.

'Yes, my lord. Saladin used the strategy at Jacob's Ford, Tiberias and again at Jerusalem. Perhaps it is time to use it against them.'

'Wait a moment,' said the king. 'Did you not just say the walls of Acre are all built upon bedrock.'

'I said mostly, your Grace,' said Cronin. 'The one place where they had to build deeper foundations was in the north-east corner, and I believe if we go deep enough, we can undermine the walls.'

'The man is an imbecile,' said one of the officers, pushing through to the front, 'why do we allow sergeants in our midst. He should be organising the men, not discussing strategy with his betters.'

'Sir Geraint,' said the king, 'Brother Cronin has proved his worth time and time again and I will hear no challenge to his presence. Feel free to provide argument against any opinion but keep your insults to yourself. Now, do you have comment on his suggestion?'

'Aye, I do,' said Geraint. 'Even if this plan had merit, which it does not, we would have to start mining too far out and if we hit rock on the way, who knows how thick it would be? It could take months, if not years.'

'All the more reason to start now,' said Cronin. 'There is no reason for this to affect any other plans, but if it is something we need to consider, then we should be recruiting sappers.'

'You may have time to undertake such a task,' said the knight, 'but I came here to fight. Dig holes if you wish, but my men stand ready and able to face whatever waits for them behind those walls.'

Murmurs of approval rippled throughout the command tent until eventually, all eyes turned to the king.

'Brother Cronin,' said Guy eventually. 'As usual, your counsel is informative and wise. Such a move would indeed be beneficial, but alas we cannot afford the time. With the might of Christendom answering our call, we need this city within weeks not months. When it falls, as it will, I will lead a crusade against the defilers of the Holy-city, the likes of which has never been seen before. But to achieve that, every man at my disposal has to be deployed where they will be needed most, and at this moment, that is on a frontal assault.'

'As you wish, your Grace,' said Cronin with a slight nod of deference and retreated from the table to stand alongside the grandmaster.

'At last,' said Geraint, 'perhaps we can now agree the detail.'

For the next hour, everyone in the tent discussed the plans until each knew them by heart. They left to brief their men, and by the time darkness fell, every mangonel in the front line were sending their devastating payloads against the walls of Acre. The first assault had begun.

The following morning, the light from the dawning sun struggled to break through the heavy fog of thick, oily smoke swirling around the eastern wall. For the past two hours, assault troops had crawled into position just out of the defenders' arrow range. Behind them came over a thousand arbalists bearing powerful crossbows. Visibility was minimal, and the choking fog filled the lungs of men on both sides, but they knew, much worse was to come.

'Are we ready?' asked the king.
'We are,' said Sir Geraint at his side.

'Then give the signal, Sir Knight, and let us take the first step back to Jerusalem.'

Chapter Ten

Karak Castle

August - AD 1189

John-Loxley sat in a chair in the room he had shared with Sumeira two years earlier, staring at the two children now fast asleep beneath heavy woollen blankets. The children were not his by blood, but as Sumeira's partner, he had sworn to take care of them, defending them with his life if necessary.

Before she had headed south to Segor to find her son, Sumeira had made him promise that if anything happened to her, he would take her daughter back to Greece to live with her family. Since then, she had been betrayed by a slave-trader and sold into slavery, though not before securing freedom for her son.

Outside, the night was strangely quiet. For the past few weeks, Karak had been under siege and had suffered heavy bombardment from the Saracen trebuchets. Death and destruction filled the lower reaches of the fortress, and the outer walls had already fallen, but the castle was immense, and the garrison had fought desperately to deny the attackers any further ground.

Many people had taken the risk of fleeing the castle under cover of darkness, but with so many Saracen troops flooding the surrounding area, the risk of being captured and taken into slavery was high, and John-Loxley was unwilling to take such a risk with the children. Despite this, he knew he had to do something for with food running out, and many of the defenders either dead or wounded, it was only a matter of time before the city fell.

Slowly his eyelids lowered, his exhaustion taking over. He hadn't slept properly in days, and the silence was an unexpected gift.

Just over an hour later, he awoke with a start, momentarily confused about what was happening. Both children sat up, equally startled.

'Father,' said Emani, 'what's that?'

'I'm not sure,' said John-Loxley, getting to his feet.

'Someone is knocking the door,' said Jamal. 'I heard it.'

The physician stared at the door, unsure what to do. The shortage of food in the castle meant there were many scoundrels willing to hurt or even kill innocent people in return for a crust of bread, and he had to be careful. The knock came again, but this time it was accompanied by a demand.

'John-Loxley' said a man's voice, 'open the door, it's me, Hunter.'

John sighed with relief and walked across to the door to throw back the bolt.

'Hunter,' he said as the scout pushed himself into the room, 'I thought you had left Karak. What are you doing here?'

'I've come to get you out,' said Hunter looking over at the children. 'Karak will fall within days, and Saladin's generals are in no mood to take prisoners.'

'Why do you say that?'

'Because Tyre stood strong against them and they lost many men. Now they seek retribution, and I fear it will be taken out on the people of Karak'

'But we can't just walk out of here, we'll walk straight into the arms of the Saracens. It's just too dangerous.'

'We'll use the sally-gate in the western wall,' said Hunter. 'Others have already used it so we will do the same.'

'I know about the gate,' said the physician, 'and it is said that the Saracens watch it like hawks. We would never get past.'

'John,' snapped Hunter, 'listen to me. I came into Karak that way just an hour since. Yes, the main route is guarded, and of course there are risks, but if you stay here, you will all probably die.' He glanced at Emani. 'Or worse.'

He looked back at the physician, a look of urgency on his face. When he had been forced to leave Sumeira in the hands of the slave-trader, he had sworn to do whatever he could to protect her family, and he was determined to carry out that oath to the best of his ability.

John-Loxley stared back at Hunter, his mind spinning.

'I'm not sure, Hunter,' he said eventually, 'our chances may be greater if we stay here.'

'John,' said Hunter, 'have you noticed the barrage has stopped.'

'I have.'

'That is because the Saracens are moving their trebuchets closer to gain maximum effect. That means they are going to launch a massive attack and make no mistake, Karak is in no state to defend itself.'

'But these walls are enormous. It would take months to break through.'

'The garrison is on its last legs,' said Hunter. 'The dead already pile up, and disease is spreading like fire. Food is running out, and unless the castle can get reinforcements, the castellan will have no other option than to surrender within days.'

'Are reinforcements on the way?'

'It is unlikely. Karak is the only fortress left in Christian hands, even Jerusalem has fallen.'

John-Loxley was shocked. Up until now, they had been told that the Christian forces had suffered a terrible defeat at Hattin but had reorganised and were fighting back. Nobody had said Jerusalem had fallen.

'What do you want us to do?' he asked with a sigh.

'Do you have any food?'

'A little, yes.'

'Gather it together as well as enough water to last for two days. Bring nothing else, we need to travel as lightly as possible.'

'But we have a horse and a mule?'

'Leave them behind.'

'We are travelling on foot?'

'The way we are going will be hard enough for us. No horse would ever pass.'

'But...'

'John, we don't have time for this,' said Hunter. 'These children's lives are at risk, so you need to make a decision now. Are you coming or not because if you are, we need to leave as soon as possible?'

'Sorry,' said John. 'You are right. I'll gather what we need.'

'Good,' said Hunter. 'I have some things to do but will be back as soon as I can. Be ready.'

'We will' said John.

Hunter left the room, and Jamal locked the door behind him.

'Get dressed,' said John, turning to the children. 'Wear daytime clothes but carry your heavy cloaks, it will be cold at night. Emani, empty the food box onto the bed, let's see what we have. Jamal, I want you to fill the water flasks from the barrel.'

The two children rushed away while John-Loxley retrieved his medical chest. There was no way he could carry it all, but he wanted to select whatever he could in case of an emergency.'

Half an hour later they were ready, each with two water flasks attached to their waist-belts. In addition, three hastily assembled packs lay on the bed, thin blankets tied around extra food and water flasks. John's pack was heavy, but he knew there was nothing inside that he could leave behind.

A few minutes later, Hunter returned, and after donning their cloaks, all three followed him outside. To John-Loxley's surprise, there were three more people waiting, a woman and two young boys. Each similarly loaded with makeshift packs.'

'Who are these?' he asked quietly.

'This is my family,' said Hunter, 'my wife, Aleena, and my sons, Adam, and Rashid.'

John-Loxley smiled at the woman. He had no idea that Hunter was married, let alone to an Arab woman.

'Ready?' asked Hunter.

Everyone nodded in reply.

'Good. I have already bribed the guards to let us out of the sally-gate, but the less attention we draw to ourselves, the better.' He leaned down and picked up a coil of rope from the floor. 'Here,' he said, handing it to John. 'Carry this.'

'What is it for?' asked John.

'You'll find out soon enough,' said Hunter, 'now follow me.'

They made their way up towards the gated walls of the upper bailey, staying in the shadows as much as possible. As they approached, Hunter held his hand up, causing the others to stop before walking up to talk to the men guarding the inner gates. A few moments later, they were ushered into the upper bailey before Hunter led them across the courtyard and past the barracks. John-Loxley was shocked to see almost a hundred people already there, along with dozens of pack horses and mules. Hunter called his group to one side, away from the crowd.

'What's going on?' he asked. 'You said we were not to bring our animals for the path was too difficult.'

'And it is,' said Hunter. 'Those people are going to take the main path down onto the plain and take their chances with the Saracen patrols. We, on the other hand, are going a different route.'

'What route?'

'You will see,' said Hunter, 'just be patient.'

A guard emerged from one of the huts and walked over to a heavy gate set into the outer wall. He looked around the crowd, knowing that most if not all would be prisoners of the Ayyubid before dawn.

'When I open this gate,' he said, 'you will head through as quickly as you can and turn to your right. Be careful as the castle walls are built atop a cliff, and there is a steep drop to the left. The path is narrow but passable and descends the mountain to the plains below. Once there, I suggest you split up and use the rest of the night to get as far away as you can. Those that manage to avoid the Saracens, head north-east and try to reach Tyre or Tripoli. You will be safe there.'

'Has anyone made it yet?' asked a voice in the dark.

'I don't know,' said the guard, 'but if God is on your side, I see no reason why you cannot. Travel by night and hide by day, at least that way you will be harder to find.' He looked around the group. 'When you leave these gates there will be no coming back so move quickly.' He turned towards the two guards standing near the gateway. 'Open the sally-gate.'

Moments later, the crowd surged forward. John-Loxley stepped forward to join them, but Hunter grabbed his shoulder.

'Wait,' he said and watched as everyone headed out through the walls. As the last people passed, he released John-Loxley's shoulder and turned to the smaller group. 'When we leave the gate, we will turn left and keep tight to the castle walls.'

'He said to turn right,' said John-Loxley.

'Aye, he did, but I am saying left, now follow me.' They followed the last of the refugees out through the gate before following Hunter along a tiny path. The gates slammed shut behind them, and they walked nervously, fully aware of the huge drop to one side.

'This is as far as we can go on this path,' he said eventually. 'Now we need to take a different route.'

'Which way?' asked John-Loxley. 'There's nowhere left to go.'

'There is one way,' said Hunter, 'straight down.'

John-Loxley looked over the cliff edge into the darkness before turning back to Hunter.

'Are you sure about this?' he asked.

'John, I have my family with me. Do you think I would put them at risk if I were not sure? What I need you to do is to help me lower everyone down to another ledge halfway down the cliff. That ledge leads to a path that takes us to the western side of the mountain. There are fewer patrols that way, and our chances of success are greater.'

'How do you know?'

'Because this is the way I came.'

'You climbed this?' asked John looking over the cliff edge again.

'I did, but it is easier to climb than to descend, that is why we need the ropes.'

John nodded and looked at the rest of the group.

'I'll go first,' said Aleena, stepping forward, 'that way I can look after the children as they come down.'

Hunter nodded and tied one end of the rope under her arms.

'Don't look down,' he said, 'and when you get to the ledge, stay tight against the wall. There will still be a big drop below you, so be careful.'

Before Aleena could answer, a huge fireball flew over the castle walls above their heads, and into the void below them, momentarily illuminating the huge drop to the valley floor.

'What's that?' gasped Jamal.

'An overshot from the Saracen trebuchets,' said Hunter. 'It looks like the final assault is starting.' Within seconds, the sounds of huge boulders smashing amongst the stone buildings of the castle filled the air, and they could hear the muffled screams of those still within the castle walls.

'Come,' said Hunter, tightening the knot, 'we have no time to waste. '

Aleena walked to the edge and sat down with her feet dangling into space.

'Ready?' asked Hunter.

'I trust you,' she said, and as both her husband and John-Loxley took the strain, she eased herself over the edge. For a few seconds she dangled in space with the rope cutting in beneath her arms, but she soon found herself in touch with the cliff face and started to steady her descent with her hands and feet. A minute or so later, her feet hit solid ground, and she breathed a sigh of relief before slackening the rope and lifting it over her head.

The noise from the castle now echoed across the valley. The screams of the initial victims had been replaced with the unmistakable roar of thousands of men attacking the castle walls, and the Saracen siege-engines found their range as boulder after boulder crashed into the upper bailey. Hunter and John-Loxley men quickly pulled up the rope before repeating the operation with the four children. When all had descended safely, Hunter tied one end of the rope to a boulder before throwing the rest over the edge.

'You and I are on our own,' he said. 'Wrap the rope around your arm like this and under your shoulders. Use your feet to climb down the rock and allow the rope to slide across your sleeve as you go.'

'If I fall to my death,' mumbled the physician picking up the rope, 'I will hold you entirely responsible.' Without another word, he lowered himself over the edge and disappeared from sight.

A few minutes later, Hunter followed him and joined the others on the ledge below.

'Is everyone alright?' he asked.

'My hands are a bit burned,' said John, 'but I'll survive. What now?'

'Now,' said Hunter, looking up at the dawning sky, 'we find somewhere to hide.'

Chapter Eleven

Acre

August - AD 1189

The noise from the battle was already deafening. Boulders from the mangonels smashed into walls, and men screamed in agony as they were cut down by the arrows of the Saracen archers defending Acre. The strength of the response had taken everyone by surprise, but Guy's men were committed, and hundreds pushed forward towards the walls. Behind them, war drums and horns added to the cacophony and their own arbalists sent volleys of arrows towards those standing atop Acre's defences.

The smoke was choking, but still they pushed until the first of the ladder-bearers reached the base of the wall. Well-practised drills fell into place, and as some men held the bases, others pivoted the ladders upward until they rested against the parapets. Immediately, the assault troops climbed as fast as they could knowing that the more men they could get on the ladders, the harder it would be for the defenders to push them away.

Using one hand to hold their shields up as protection, they climbed as fast as they could. Those in the front were immediately attacked, and many fell before they could even get a handhold on the battlements, but still their comrades pushed on from below.

'*Keep going,*' roared the sergeants, knowing that if even one man could get onto the wall, they would create enough of a problem for his comrades to follow, and when that happened, they had a real chance.

Desperately the attackers fought and died trying to gain a foothold, but despite there being dozens of ladders successfully in place, there were just too many defenders waiting for them, and they died by the dozen.

Guy looked on from a nearby knoll, his heart in his mouth. The initial assault had caught the Saracens by surprise, and the ladders had gone up quicker than he had expected, but now they were paying the price, and his men were dying in droves.

'My lord,' said Sir Geraint, 'they are getting nowhere. We should sound the retreat.'

'Wait,' said the king, desperate for success, 'look there, those men are almost up.' He pointed to one side, but as they watched, one of the defenders sent the ladder backwards with a long pole, sending dozens of men plummeting to the ground below.

'My lord,' said Sir Geraint, 'with respect, we are losing men for no reason. We had no idea their garrison was so strong, and we have used the wrong tactics. Call them back to fight another day else we are doomed to lose half of our army on the first assault.'

The king stared, but when another two ladders were pushed backwards, sending the men at the top to their deaths, he knew the knight was right. They had come close, but there was no way they were going to cause a breach with this assault. He turned to the signaller at his side.

'Sound the withdrawal,' he sighed and turned his horse away to return to the camp.

In front of the city walls, the Christian archers ran forward to cover the foot-soldiers' retreat, sending volley after volley up at the parapets as their comrades ran back to cover. Ladders were abandoned, and men grabbed their wounded comrades to drag them back to safety.

Some of the defending Saracens responded with their own arrows, but most just lowered themselves behind the castellations, knowing that their job was done, the first assault had been repulsed.

Up on one of the nearby towers, Turan-Shah watched as the Christians fled back to the safety of their own lines. He was tempted to send his own cavalry through the gates in pursuit, but soon realised it would be a futile act. The Christians had lost a lot of men in the attack, but they were foot-soldiers only, and their cavalry was still untested. He turned to the man at his side.

'Withdraw the men on the walls,' he said, 'and replace them with fresh warriors. Replenish the stocks of arrows and stay alert, I suspect that will be the first assault of many.'

'Yes, my lord,' said the warrior.

'And send for news from the harbour. A fleet arrived from Egypt this morning. I want it unloaded and sent back for more supplies before dusk tomorrow. If the Christians tighten the noose, we are going to need all the supplies we can get.'

The warrior nodded and headed down the steps of the tower. Turan-Shah stayed where he was, watching the retreating Christians. It had been a good victory, but he knew it was only the beginning of what could be a very long siege.

Over in the Christian camp, the various commanders were already arriving for a debriefing in the king's campaign tent. Gerard of Ridefort entered followed by Cronin and made their way to the table.

'We received a message to withdraw from the north wall,' said the grandmaster, 'what happened?'

'Our men were found wanting,' said the king. 'The city is far better defended than we first thought.'

'How many did we lose?'

'About a hundred dead,' said Sir Geraint, 'twice that wounded or injured.'

'How much damage did the mangonels cause?'

'Some, but not enough to cause a breach.'

'We need trebuchets,' said Cronin. 'Without those, we may as well just hurl stones with our bare hands.'

'And we will have them,' said the king, 'but at the moment we do not have any timber.'

'So, what next?' asked Gerard.

'We have tested their resolve in a fight,' said the king, 'but behind those walls, they present a formidable foe. However, at the moment they are well supplied by sea as well as the southern coastal road. What we need to do is deny them that luxury.'

'We do not have enough men or ships,' said Gerard.

'Not yet,' said the king, 'but we will have reinforcements any day soon. What I propose is that we withdraw to the hill of Toron here,' he pointed at the feature indicated on the map less than half a league east of Acre, 'and await the arrival of the reinforcements. When they arrive, we will encircle Acre, and deny the enemy the sea routes. If the bite of our arrows failed to have any effect, let them try the pain of hunger.' He looked around the room. 'Any questions?'

When there was no answer, he stood up straight and addressed the tent. 'See to the wounded and strike camp. I want us to be in position along the base of Mount Toron by tomorrow.' He turned to the Templar grandmaster. 'Brother Gerard, I want you and your men to watch our backs during the relocation. Make no mistake, this is a strategic move and not a retreat, but we will be at risk of a counterattack until our lines are reformed.'

'As you wish, your Grace,' said Gerard.

'Good,' said the king, 'now let's get this done.'

Several leagues away, Salah ad-Din sat in his own tent, attended by his generals.

'So, the Christians failed,' said the sultan.

'They did, my lord,' said one of the scouts. 'Many fell to our arrows, and they fled back to their lines like frightened children.'

'Turan-Shah is a good man,' said Saladin's son. 'He will not let us down.'

'His heart is not in doubt, nor his ability,' said Gokbori, 'but his numbers are few and Acre's walls long. This time they assaulted only the eastern section along with a cursory attack in the north. If the strike had been wider spread, we might not have been so lucky.'

'They do not have the numbers for such an assault,' said Al-Afdal.

'Not yet,' interjected Salah ad-Din, 'my spies tell of a great crusader army being prepared in the west, led by a fierce Christian warrior called Barbarossa. I have already sent a call to our brothers in the north to hinder his advance, but such an army will be difficult to stop.'

'With respect, my lord, it could take months for him to get here. Our worries are more immediate.'

'I agree,' said Salah ad-Din, 'but there is already news that the sea of the west is full of Christian sails. If they are allowed to join King Guy, their numbers will be overwhelming.'

'My lord,' said Al-Afdal, 'perhaps we can take the pressure off Acre with a siege of our own.' Al-Afdal leaned forward and pointed at the beautifully crafted map between them. 'The Christians are here,' he said, 'and are focussed inward on Acre. If we deploy our armies further out, they will be forced to turn their heads eastward to defend those positions. This will not only weaken their ability to attack the city but would stop any supplies reaching them overland. They would be forced to rely on their ships, but if their army is going to be as big as you say, they will struggle to feed it.'

Salah ad-Din stared at the map before reaching out with his knife and drawing it across the map in a semi-circle further to the east of the Christian positions.

'We have enough men to form lines here,' he said, 'denying Guy's army the road north to Tyre and Tripoli. If we move our main camp here to the hills of El-Aiyadia with a secondary camp further south in the hills of Tel-el-Nahl, we cut off any possibility of them breaking out to the east or the south. That leaves them with only the sea as a supply route, but no port in which they can land their supplies.'

'Will they not just use the shore?'

'Perhaps, but the task is more arduous, and our warriors can make sure they have no respite. In the meantime, I will summon all the tribal elders and call for a Jihad against the invaders. The Christians may have great numbers, but our people are like ants upon the desert. Worry not, my brothers, these people are often blinded by plunder and the need for glory in battle, but Acre will be the pit of defeat into which they will fall. Now send out the message to all our men, we will form our own walls to withstand their advance. Not one made of wood or stone, but one of flesh, bravery and prayer. *Allah Akbar.*'

The following day, Cronin stood on top of the small hill called Mount Toron. Several lookouts stood amongst the rocks, looking eastward for any sign of Saracen movement. Behind him, at the base of the hill, the Christian camp was already taking shape as thousands of men pitched their tents.

'Brother Cronin,' called a voice, and he turned to see Gerard of Ridefort climbing up the slope to join him.

'Grandmaster,' said Cronin. 'I did not expect you.'

Gerard reached the top and stared back towards Acre in the distance. On the far side, the Mediterranean Sea glistened like a belt of diamonds, interrupted only by the plumes of smoke still rising from the city.

'It is a formidable task,' said Gerard, looking at huge walls.

'It is, said Cronin, 'and I fear the king may be underestimating the effort it will take to bring it down.'

'I fear you are correct,' said Gerard, 'but his mind is set, and he is blinded by the prize. All we can do is hope that the arrival of others will make him think again his tactics.'

'Do you believe there are truly more on the way?' asked Cronin turning towards the grandmaster.

'Indeed I do,' said Gerard, 'and that is why I came up here. I have received a message that Louis of Thuringia has already resupplied his ships in Cyprus and will be here the day after tomorrow. In addition, I have been told that Emperor Frederick Barbarossa of Germany took the cross only a few months ago and plans to march here with over two hundred thousand men under his command.'

'Why is he marching, could he not rent passage from the Genoese fleet?'

'Frederick is known to fear water,' said Gerard. 'It is said he foresaw his own death by drowning in a dream. Since then he refuses to set foot on any ship.'

'The journey is arduous,' said Cronin. 'It will take months and cost the lives of many men.'

'Perhaps so, but when he gets here, we will have more than enough men to take Jerusalem. That is why we need to take Acre first, to feed such an army will be a task like none we have ever seen, and we need as many ports as we can get.'

'What about the kings of England and France?'

'They have committed to sending armies,' said Gerard, 'but both are too busy fighting each other to fulfil their oath. Hopefully, that will end soon, but until it does, we have to rely on the lesser nobles across Christendom.'

'Kingship must be a disease of the mind,' murmured Cronin turning around to gaze eastward over the Plains of Jawarneh.

'My lord, look,' he said.

Gerard turned around and stared eastward. For a few seconds he could see nothing, but then his eyes were drawn to a line of dust on the horizon.

'Saracen warriors?' he asked.

'It has to be,' said Cronin, 'and they look to be getting closer.' He turned to one of the lookouts who were now all on their feet. 'Sound the alarm,' he shouted, 'alert the camp.'

Within moments, the sound of the warning horns filled the air, and down below, men ran to collect their arms. Cronin and Gerard ran down the slope as fast as they could, heading towards their horses.

'You gather the sergeants,' shouted Gerard, 'I'll bring the knights. Meet on the far side of the hill. We'll try to hold them off until the army can muster.'

Cronin mounted his horse and galloped away to where the Templar camp was still being erected half a league to the north. By the time he got there, the men had already been alerted, and most were already on horseback.

'There's a Saracen army headed this way,' he shouted, 'and Guy's army is in disarray. We need to slow them down. Follow me.'

He turned his horse and galloped towards the northern slope of the hill, skirting around the edge until they were on the far side. To the south, he could see a column of Templar knights riding towards them, and within minutes, they joined forces to create a defensive line. The knights formed a line-abreast formation, each tight to the man next to him. Behind them came three lines of Templar sergeants, ready to add the impetus behind any charge while hired turcopole lancers formed the flanks.

Up in front, they could see many thousands of riders stretched out as far as the eye could see, and Gerard knew that without the support of Guy's army, there was no way they could defeat such a foe.

'If we meet them in battle,' shouted Gerard, 'our role is to disrupt only. We will strike fast and hard, but then peel off to regroup before hitting them again. The longer we can delay them, the more chance of the army getting here. Templars, *advance*.'

As one, the Templar command walked their horses forward, their banners flying high above their heads. As they neared, they could see the depth of the enemy lines and Gerard knew that even if they managed to slow them up, Guy's army would have little chance against such a force.

Closer and closer they rode, hearts racing at the thought of the forthcoming battle. The chances of victory were virtually nil, but Gerard knew that before the day was done, there would be far more Saracen dead than Christians.

'My lord,' shouted a voice, 'they've stopped.'

Gerard held up his hand, and the advance came to a halt.

'What are they up to,' he asked, 'why are they stopping?'

'I think they may just be preparing to attack,' said one of the knights at his side.

'I don't think, so,' said Cronin, 'look.'

As they watched, dozens of horsemen rode forward, each bearing a yellow Ayyubid banner. Once they were only a few hundred paces away, they reined in their horses and drove the flagpoles into the ground, creating a line of flags all the way across the plain.

'They're declaring a boundary,' said Gerard, 'a line beyond which they will not allow us to pass.'

'It's more than that,' said Cronin, looking into the distance, 'that army is supported by a huge supply caravan. It looks like they are going to set up a camp.'

'To what end?' asked one of the knights.

'To cut off any hope we have of getting supplies from inland,' said Gerard, 'which means, if I'm not mistaken, the besiegers have just become the besieged.'

Chapter Twelve

East of the Salt-sea

August - AD 1189

John-Loxley slept fitfully. The ground beneath him was hard, and despite the heavy cloak wrapped around him, the cold seeped into his bones. Beside him, Emani and Jamal also lay shivering in their own cloaks, each exhausted after their long walk through the foothills since fleeing Karak Castle. It had been a hard few days, but against all odds, they had managed to escape the siege and had headed west towards the Salt-sea, a route that provided a far better chance of avoiding discovery.

During the hours of daylight, they had all hidden in the depths of any thicket that offered them protection, only travelling at night to reduce the risk of discovery. Now they were hidden in a sandy cave only half a league away from the Salt-sea, an area that according to Hunter, had far fewer Saracen patrols.

John-Loxley opened his eyes and saw that Hunter's family were still asleep on the opposite side of the cave, but the scout was absent. He got to his feet and walked towards the entrance of the cave. Hunter was sat just inside, peering over the fields towards the sea.

'Checking the lay of the land?' asked John-Loxley, sitting down beside him.

'I am,' said Hunter. 'The sun will be going down soon, and I just want to be sure there are no surprises waiting for us out there.'

'I thought you said there were no Saracens around here.'

'I said there were fewer,' said Hunter, 'that doesn't mean they don't come this way.'

'Can I ask you something?' asked John-Loxley.

Hunter glanced over at the physician.

'What do you want to know?'

'What were the real chances of those other people escaping back at Karak?'

'Some may have made it through,' said Hunter, 'if they were lucky, but most are probably already in chains and on their way to Damascus.'

'And you knew they had little chance of success?'

'Nobody could know for sure, but I had my suspicions. That is why I chose a different route.'

'So, why did you not bring more people with us?'

Hunter turned and stared at the physician.

'Listen to me, John-Loxley,' he said eventually, 'I have made many mistakes in my life, one of which is allowing Sumeira to be taken prisoner. My conscience allows no respite, and though I cannot do anything to change that fact, I will do everything in my power to fulfil my pledge to look after her family. You saw how dangerous that route was, and even with us few, the sun was already coming up by the time we got down to the second ledge. If we had brought any more with us, we would have still been lowering them down at sunrise and would have been seen by any Saracen within five leagues. I hope and pray that those other people managed to escape, but their responsibility does not lie with me. These are dangerous times, and I owe it to my own family, as well as yours, to do what I can to keep them alive. That is my vow, and I will answer to no man who expects otherwise.'

He turned away and stared out towards the sea once again.

'I meant no insult,' said John-Loxley eventually, 'and you have my gratitude.'

'I don't need your gratitude,' said Hunter, 'just make sure you, and your children do exactly as I say.'

'Of course. So what now, do we head north?'

'No,' said Hunter, 'we head west.'

'But that way lies the sea,' said the physician. 'Why do we go there?'

'Because the sea is far lower than the surrounding countryside, and by following the water's edge, we can remain unseen from anyone except those who come near. Once we reach the northernmost point, we will head across country towards Tripoli.'

'So, be it,' said John-Loxley getting to his feet. 'I'll wake everyone up.'

In Acre, Sumeira was busy trying to find space for all the injured being brought to the hospital from the outer walls. Some had arrow wounds while others had burns, and by the end of the day, all the beds were full. She brushed the hair from her face and walked outside to get some fresh air. Shani followed carrying a tankard of water.

'Would you like a drink?' he asked.

Sumeira drank it down in one before handing it back to the orderly.

'Shani,' she said, 'we have to make some changes. From now on, we will treat and dress every wound that we see, but once that is done, any man able to walk must be asked to leave. We can supply poultices and instructions on the need to keep clean, but there is no need for anyone to stay who can help themselves.'

'Understood,' said Shani, 'I will start straight away.'

Sumeira looked over to the block that used to house the Templar knights. Outside the main entrance stood the guard that she had treated for an infected arm.

'Shani,' she said, 'bring me the poultice pot.'

A few minutes later, Sumeira walked across the courtyard from the chapel, expecting to hear Barak's evil voice at any time.

'Hello again,' she said as she neared the guard. 'How is your affliction?'

'It is healing well,' said the guard. 'You have my gratitude.'

'There is no need for gratitude,' said Sumeira. 'My role is to heal people no matter what god they worship. What is your name?'

'I am called Ragesh,' said the guard.

'Ragesh,' she said, 'I have a boon to ask. I understand if you cannot allow it but will ask anyway.'

'You wish to go inside to visit the Christian prisoners?'

'Yes, and your master allows that, but this time, I want to take this.' She produced the small pot of balm from beneath her cloak.

'What is it?'

'Just some ointment similar to what I gave you. One of the men inside has an infection that needs treating.'

'But you are not allowed to waste medicines on the prisoners.'

'I know, but this does not come from your master's stock. I managed to get extra from the market. Believe me when I say not a single one of your comrades will suffer by me bringing this to my fellows. Please, it is just an ointment, and nobody will ever know.'

Ragesh hesitated but was growing fond of the Christian Physician and eventually stepped aside.

'Thank you,' said Sumeira and stepped through the door. The candlelit corridor led to a doorway into a hall once used as a dining room for the Templars. Another guard watched her approach and unbolted the door to let her in.

Inside the stench was overpowering, and she could smell the unmistakable odour of infected flesh.

'Sumeira,' said one of the men sitting in the corner, 'we thought you had forgotten about us.'

'I have had to do the jailers' bidding,' she said, 'but should now be able to attend more often. I have brought something with me.'

'I hope it's food,' said one of the men, 'We haven't eaten in days.'

'Alas no,' said Sumeira, 'it's ointment for your friend.' She nodded towards a man laying on one of the tables being used as bunks. 'The last time I was here, I saw his wound needed treating, but it has taken this long to be able to get something that may be of any use.' She walked over and stood alongside the sick man, her breathing shallow to avoid the stench.

'What's his name?' she asked.

'Dafydd,' said one of the men, 'but he is beyond help.'

She lifted his shirt to see a deeply infected wound crawling with maggots.

'I told you,' said the first prisoner again, 'he's as good as dead.'

'Not necessarily,' said Sumeira, 'the maggots have kept most of the infection from spreading. Do you have any water?'

'Water,' laughed one of the men, 'what we get hardly keeps us alive as it is.'

Sumeira reached beneath her cloak and retrieved her own waterskin before using the contents to wash the injury. Once done, she dipped her finger into the pot of ointment and pushed it liberally into the wound before stitching the edges of the swollen flesh together.

'A neat job,' said one of the men.

'It may work, it may not,' said Sumeira turning around, 'but it is the best I can do.' She held out the pot. 'Apply the last of this balm at last light, and again at dawn until the infection has gone.'

'What is happening out there?' asked another of the prisoners, a blacksmith called Robin. 'We heard a barrage, but nobody has told us anything.'

'I believe King Guy attacked the walls,' said Sumeira, 'but was unsuccessful. Now his army has retreated eastward and set up a camp. More than that, I do not know.'

'They're going to start a siege,' said one of the men, 'and you know what that means, even less food for us. We have to get out of here. He headed towards the door, but Sumeira stepped in front of him, blocking his way.

'Wait,' she said, 'if you try to leave now, you will be dead before you reach the gates.'

'I'm not staying in here to starve to death,' said the prisoner. 'I'd rather take my chances out there. If I can get out of this place, I can hide in the city.'

'She's right,' said the blacksmith stepping forward. 'At the moment we are at least alive and having some food and water. Let us first see what happens before doing anything rash.' He turned to Sumeira. 'I know this is a lot to ask, but do you think you can get us any weapons? Knives, spikes, anything you can secret about your person?'

'I don't know,' said Sumeira, 'I suppose I can try but to what purpose? You will never be able to overpower so many guards.'

'I accept that,' said Robin, 'but if the city falls and the Muslims come to kill us, at least we will be able to take some of them with us.'

Sumeira nodded and looked around the room.

'I promise I will do what I can,' she said, 'but be careful. At the moment, this place is full of well-armed men.' She turned and knocked on the door, signalling she was ready to leave. The guard let her out, and she headed back across the courtyard to the chapel. Her life inside Acre was difficult enough as it was, but it had just got a lot more dangerous.

Out on the plains to the east, Guy of Lusignan had wasted no time in responding to the manoeuvres of Saladin's army. Splitting his force in half, he spread them out in two defensive lines, the first facing the city on the western side of Mount Toron, the second on the eastern side, facing the newly formed Saracen positions. He knew that his resources were spread thinly, but with a threat from both directions, he had little other option.

Every man available from foot-soldiers to lancers were tasked with digging defensive trenches. Templars and Hospitallers guarded both positions, ready to react at any sign of enemy approach, and over a space of a few days, the Christian positions started to take shape.

On the far side of the plain, similar preparations were being undertaken by the Saracens as both sides prepared for a long campaign.

On the top of the hill, Guy stood alongside Gerard of Ridefort, assessing the strengths and weaknesses of their positions.

'They outnumber us hugely,' said Gerard, staring at the vast camp in the distance, 'I'm surprised he hasn't attacked already.'

'As am I,' said the king, 'but I suspect the presence of your knights gives him reason to pause. Out there on the plain, they would be as effective as any army.'

'We have a bloody debt to pay,' said Gerard coldly. 'Hattin is in our hearts and prayers every day, and I swear that we will avenge every single one of our brothers who was murdered in cold blood after the battle.'

'One thing is certain,' said the king, 'over the next few months, I suspect there will be more than enough opportunity.' He looked to one side as a messenger rode up the slopes towards them.

'Your Grace,' said the messenger, 'I have news. A great Christian fleet has anchored offshore to the south and are unloading men as we speak. Never have I seen so many ships.'

'At last,' said Guy, 'do you know who it is?'

'Not yet, my lord, but there is more. Our scouts have reported a huge army is on the march from Tyre under the command of Louis of Thuringia. They docked a few days ago and are headed here with all speed.'

'Send an envoy to welcome him,' said the king, 'and find out who it is that leads the fleet.'

'Yes, your Grace,' said the messenger, and turned his horse around to gallop back down the hill.

'We should go and prepare to receive them,' said the king, 'our hospitality will not be found wanting.'

'Your Grace,' said Gerard, 'can I make a suggestion?'

'Your views are always welcome,' said Guy.

'Then I suggest you meet them up here on the hill. From this position, you can see for leagues in every direction, a massive tactical advantage over Saladin. It also has the advantage of placing you physically above all those who may sail here convinced of their own importance.'

King Guy stared at the grandmaster with respect. The suggestion would not only gain a military advantage over his enemies, but also a psychological one over his allies.

'Excellent idea,' he said. 'I'll have my command tent brought up and we will fortify the lower slopes.'

'Leave that to me,' said Gerard. 'I'll pass on the orders.'

The following evening, the hill was full of the king's tents, each bedecked with the banners of Jerusalem. All around the slopes, men dug trenches and erected archers' palisades as a defence against any attack.

Louis of Thuringia had camped his army just north of Acre and had arrived to meet the king in person hours earlier. Now, after having dined with Guy, both men stood at the highest point as the king pointed out the landscape.

'As you can see,' he said, pointing to the distant Saracen camp, 'their numbers are substantial, and before you arrived, we were at a significant disadvantage. Now, including your men and those disembarking to the south, we have more than enough to fortify both lines as well as continuing our siege positions all the way around to the sea. In a matter of days, the city will be fully isolated, and with the Italian fleet blockading the harbour, I have no doubt they will soon succumb to hunger.'

'How many men do we now have?' asked the count.

'Including yours, over twenty thousand, a force that even Saladin himself will fear to engage.'

'It is also a lot of men to feed,' said Louis.

'I am aware of the logistical problems,' said Guy,' and have already sent messages throughout Christendom requesting supplies. Once the ships have been emptied, they will ferry stores from Cyprus and the other Christian countries around the coastline, but for that to have any effect, I need the ports of Tyre.'

'You already have them,' said Louis turning to face the king. 'Conrad of Montferrat is my nephew, and before I left Tyre, I convinced him to rally to your cause.'

'Why would he do that?' asked Guy. 'He has already made it plain to me that he does not support my rightful claim to the throne.'

'The argument is nothing but politics,' said Louis, 'and as such, must be put aside for another day. The important thing is, Conrad has pledged his support by once more opening up his harbours, and what is more, he is raising an army to strengthen the assault on Acre. He will be here within days.'

'This is great news,' said Guy, 'and at last, I feel that Jerusalem is almost within our grasp.'

'Let us not get carried away,' said Louis, turning to face Acre in the distance, 'for first, we have to deal with that.'

Chapter Thirteen

East of the Salt-sea

September - AD 1189

Hunter hurried back to where the rest of the group were hiding in one of the hundreds of caves overlooking the north-eastern edge of the Salt-sea. For the last two days they had stayed hidden due to Emani falling and badly twisting her foot, but they had run out of water so he had left them hidden away while he filled the water-skins from a nearby stream.

The sun was already rising in the east, and he increased the pace as much as he dared, keen to be out of sight before the inevitable Saracen patrols had any chance to find his tracks.

In the cave, John-Loxley and Emani were fast asleep as was Hunter's wife, Aleena, while the three boys, all of a similar age, sat at the entrance watching the morning sun ripple across the water.

Emani opened her eyes and looked across at the three boys. It was warming to see her half-brother interacting with Hunter's sons, especially in the difficult circumstances they now found themselves. Jamal's life so far had been hard, especially the few months leading up to the time when his surrogate family had sold him into slavery.

When he was a baby, Sumeira's husband had forced her to give the child away, suspicious that he may not be the father, but after running away from him a year or so later, Sumeira had vowed that one day she would return to find her son. Despite succeeding, the quest took a terrible turn when Sumeira herself had been taken into slavery, leaving John-Loxley, Emani and Jamal to fend for themselves. Despite the setback, they had not given up hope on Sumeira and knew that people were already trying to find her.

Emani looked at Jamal. He was far too thin and very withdrawn, but with plenty of love and affection from her and John-Loxley, he was getting stronger by the day. She smiled gently and knowing they were safe, at least for the time being, fell back asleep.

Half an hour later, the sound of John-Loxley's voice dragged echoed around the cave.

'Emani, wake up, we have a problem.'

Emani sat up to see him pacing the cave, his face etched with worry. Aleena sat on the floor, pulling on her boots as fast as she could.

'What's wrong?' asked Emani, rubbing her eyes. 'What's happened?'

'It's the boys,' said John-Loxley, 'they've gone.'

'*What?*' gasped Emani, looking around the cave, 'they were here just a few minutes ago.'

'You've been fast asleep,' said the Physician, 'we all have. For all we know they could have been gone for hours.'

Emani jumped to her feet and ran to the cave entrance to peer outside.

'The sun is still low,' she said, 'and was already up when I saw them last. They can't have gone far.'

'I have to go and find them,' said Aleena getting to her feet.

'I'll go with you,' said John-Loxley.

'Wait for me,' said Emani, 'I'll get my boots.'

'No,' said John-Loxley sharply, 'it's pointless all of us being at risk. You have to stay here in case they come back while we are gone. Otherwise, they will think we have left without them.'

'But...'

'Emani, Hunter will be back soon and will need to know what has happened. Stay here and if he returns before we do, tell him everything that happened.'

All three walked to the entrance of the cave and looked out in all directions. The shore was empty as far as they could see though outcrops of rock meant much of the ground was blocked from view.

'You go north,' said John-Loxley to Aleena. 'I'll go south. If there's no sign of them, meet back here in about an hour, and we'll search inland.'

Emani watched them go before running back into the cave to put on her boots and pack their things. When Hunter returned, she had to be ready to move as quickly as possible.

John-Loxley walked as fast as he could along the shore. The ground beneath his feet was rocky, and he had little hope of finding any footprints, but he had to check at least as far as the next headland just a few hundred paces to his front. His heart raced, fearing the worst. He had already lost one person he loved to slavery and could not even imagine losing a second, especially as Jamal had only recently been freed. He reached the headland and climbed up the slope. On the other side, the shore flattened out and stretched away uninterrupted for leagues. Immediately he realised there was no way they could have come this way and turned around to face north. Aleena was already searching that way so as he was headed back to the cave anyway, he turned inland to check the coastal paths on top of the sandy cliffs above the sea.

Half a league northward, Aleena was also making as much speed as she could, half walking and half running towards a spit of land heading out into the sea. The outcrop was topped with the ruins of an ancient building, and she had no doubt that it would have attracted the attention of any child heading that way. After a few minutes she had to stop to catch her breath, but as she looked up, she saw one of her sons disappearing in amongst the ruins and she gasped in relief.

'Allah be praised,' she said to herself and doubled her efforts. Within minutes she reached the outcrop and climbed as quickly as she dared. 'Rashid,' she called, 'where are you?'

She scrambled around the ruins of a doorway and stopped in her tracks when she saw all three boys standing alongside each other, staring down onto the sandy beach on the far side.

'What are you doing here?' she shouted. 'I told you not to leave the cave.'

One of her sons turned to glance at her before returning his gaze to whatever had caught their attention down below.

'Why are you not listening to me?' she demanded, and stamped over to join them, but as soon as she reached the three boys, her anger was replaced by fear. Just below them, staring back up at her, was a mounted Saracen warrior, and behind him, a hundred horsemen.

John-Loxley ran along the path, his eyes scanning the open spaces all around him. The trees were sparse with few areas to hide, and his heart sunk as he realised there was no way any of the boys had come this way. He headed back towards the coast to find the cave when a voice called out, and he saw Hunter running down a hill towards him.

'Hunter,' he shouted, 'thank God. The Children have gone, we can't find them.'

'What do you mean, gone?' asked Hunter. 'Were you not watching them?'

'We were, but I think the boys must have left when we all fell asleep. '

'What about Emani?'

'She's fine, she's waiting in the cave until Aleena and I return.'

'Where is Aleena?'

She went north to look for them along the shore while I went south, but they did not go that way.'

'Are you sure?'

'As certain as I can be. There is no sign of them anywhere.'

'Then let's hope Aleena has had more luck,' said Hunter, 'here, carry these.' He gave John-Loxley two of the water-skins and turned north-east to head for the sea. John-Loxley removed the stopper from one of the skins and drank deeply before hanging it over his shoulder and running to catch up with the scout.

'We had no idea,' he gasped as he walked alongside Hunter, 'I mean, why would they leave the cave? I think they may have been looking for water.'

'They are children, Loxley,' said Hunter, 'and know no better. All we can do now is find them as soon as we can and hope no harm has come to them.'

They pushed hard until they reached the coast halfway between the cave and the outcrop. Both turned northward and a few minutes later, walked amongst the ruins where Aleena had found the boys.

They stared along the coast, seeing nothing, and was about to turn away when Hunter saw something down on the rocky shore. Quickly he climbed down and ran across to where a headscarf was floating in a rockpool. Hunter fished it out and looked further along the beach.

'What is it?' asked John-Loxley, catching him up.

'It's Aleena's headscarf,' said Hunter. 'She must have left it for me to find.'

'Are you sure,' asked the physician, 'because if so, where is she?'

'Look around you,' said Hunter, 'what do you see?'

John looked around, but suddenly he saw what Hunter was referring to. Horse droppings, and plenty of them.

'Oh dear God in heaven,' he gasped, looking up at Hunter. 'There were horsemen here.'

'There were,' said Hunter, 'and it looks like they have taken Aleena and the boys with them.'

'No,' said John-Loxley, 'you don't know that. Perhaps they are hiding. Come on, we should keep trying.'

'No,' said Hunter. 'If they were hiding, they would have come out by now, and they certainly are not on the higher ground for I would have seen them.' He held up the scarf. 'Aleena knows what she is doing and left this as a sign. They were definitely here and are now in the hands of the Ayyubid.'

All of John-Loxley's strength left his body, and he fell to his knees.

'Oh no,' he said, 'those poor children.'

'And my wife,' said Hunter.

'Of course, I meant…'

'I know what you meant,' said Hunter turning to face the physician, 'but we have no time to waste. Get to your feet and bring your daughter. We need to keep going.'

'Keep going?' responded John-Loxley, 'to where?'

'To Tyre as we originally planned.'

'But shouldn't we go after them?'

'And do what?' asked Hunter. 'They are on horseback so we would never catch them and even if we did, there are signs that there were more than a hundred riders. How do you propose we fight an entire patrol of battle-hardened Saracen Warriors?'

'I don't know,' stuttered John-Loxley, 'but surely we must be able to do something. We can't just leave them to die.'

'They are not going to die,' said Hunter.

'How can you be so sure?'

'Listen,' said Hunter, 'my wife is Arabic and knows what to do. My two boys were born and bred here, and Jamal was raised in Segor. Aleena will try to convince the Saracens that they are no more than refugees fleeing the war. If that works, the patrol may have just taken them back to wherever they originated.'

'And where may that be,' asked John-Loxley, 'it could be anywhere?'

'No,' said Hunter. 'They are heading back around the northern end of the Salt-sea, and there is only one city that in that direction that warrants sending such a strong force out on patrol.'

'And that is?'

'The new Saracen capital,' said Hunter, looking westward across the sea, 'they are taking them to Jerusalem.'

Less than an hour later, Hunter, John-Loxley and Emani walked as fast as they could towards the northern end of the sea. Once there they turned to follow the river Jordan upstream before stopping to rest amongst a thicket of trees.

Hunter dipped his head into the clear water and drank deeply before sitting back on his haunches and staring into nowhere. Emani walked over and knelt at his side.

'Will they be alright?' she asked eventually.

'I don't know,' said Hunter with a sigh. 'But if those warriors had wanted them dead, we would have found their bodies on the rocks.'

'So why would they take them?'

'Compassion at best, slavery at worst.'

'Compassion?' said Emani, looking over at the scout. 'Since when has any Saracen shown any sign of compassion?'

'Many of the best men I have ever met have been Saracens,' said Hunter, 'and most have more honour than many of the Christians who claim to fight in the name of God.'

'I do not believe you,' said Emani. 'Every Saracen I have ever seen has been trying to kill us.'

'That's because you have only ever seen them in battle, and that is what warriors do on both sides, they kill.'

'But they don't believe in God?'

'Oh they believe in God,' said Hunter, 'the same God as us, but they believe Jesus was just a messenger and not God's son.'

'But if that is the case, why do so many men die fighting each other to own the same country, the same places, the same cities? Why can't we just share them in peace?'

'If we knew the answer to that,' said Hunter with a sigh, 'then this would truly be a paradise on earth.'
They fell silent for a few minutes.
'So, what now?' asked Emani. 'Are we truly going to let your family and Jamal go to Jerusalem?'
'We have no other choice,' said Hunter. 'Somehow I will get them back, but first I have to get the both of you to Tyre.'
'Why?'
'Because as far as I know, it is the only Christian stronghold in the whole of the Outremer. You will be safe there.'
'And how do we get there?'
'We have to follow this river upstream to the Sea of Tiberias,' said Hunter, 'and walk to its northern-most edge. After that, we will head north-east until we reach Tyre. Once I've made sure you are safe, I will do whatever I have to do to get Jamal and my family back.'
'You said that about my mother,' said Emani, 'and she is still a slave somewhere. Either that or dead.'
Hunter turned to look at the girl.
'I know I've let you down,' he said, 'but I swear, if it is the last thing I do, I will see you all reunited as a family.'
'I know you mean well,' said Emani, 'but don't promise what you can't achieve.' She stood up and walked over to where John-Loxley was sitting with his back against a tree.
'Ready?' she asked
'For what?' he replied.
'We have a long way to go,' she said, 'and the quicker we get to Tyre, the quicker Hunter can see about rescuing Jamal.' She turned to give Hunter a withering glance. 'That is if he is able.' Without another word, she turned and followed the river upstream. Hunter got to his feet and walked over to stand alongside John-Loxley.
'Well,' he said eventually, 'you heard the girl. Let's get going.'

Chapter Fourteen

The Christian Siege Camp

September 15 - AD 1189

The king rode along the Christian positions, inspecting the defences. Alongside him was Gerard of Ridefort, Thomas Cronin and Sir Geraint, and behind them, a contingent of ten knights acting as the king's bodyguard.

On the outer ring of defences to the east of Mount Toron, men were busy erecting hundreds of small palisades, each big enough for ten archers to stand behind in case of a frontal attack. Every palisade was connected to the next with a line of outwardly facing wooden stakes, pointed at the end to deter any cavalry charge. Behind the barricades, more men were digging deep trenches, not just as a place to sleep and eat, but also as a lethal barrier to any cavalry that decided to leap the palisades.

On the inward-facing lines a few hundred paces away, the preparations also included palisades and trenches, but the likelihood of an attack coming from the castle was deemed far less likely.

Between the two lines, the inevitable camp-followers had already started making their own camp with rows of tents and carts stretching in both directions. Guy looked at the growing camp with distaste. He knew the whores and ale-carts would become a distraction for many of his men, but despite his revulsion, he also knew it would become a necessary resource when it came to feeding his growing army.

The emerging village was not just the result of the needy trying to earn a living, it also contained many families of the men who had signed up to fight. With nowhere else to go and unable to support themselves, they had followed their men to battle knowing that despite the danger, at least the soldiers would get paid and be able to buy food.

'Do we have the city fully isolated?' asked Guy, turning to Gerard as he rode.

'Not quite, your Grace, they are still managing to get ships through the Italian blockade, but we hope to increase the size of our fleet within days.'

'What about landward?'

'We have created lines surrounding the city in a half-circle. Those lines have been split into four positions. My own order has set up camp in the northernmost quadrant covering the road from Tyre. Count Louis of Thuringia covers the next quarter between the hills of Hisrel-Hammar down to Mount Toron where his men link up with those of Conrad of Montferrat. His lines then stretch south to your own army who straddle the road to Saffaria and extends as far as the southern marshes.'

'Any more news of Barbarossa?'

'Only that he is still trying to negotiate with Bulgaria and Hungary to allow him safe passage.'

The men continued riding along the lines, picking out areas of weakness and instructing the local commanders where they needed reinforcing. In the distance they could see hundreds of Saracens on the city walls, doing what they could to repair the damage done by the assault a few days earlier.

'Do you want us to continue the barrage?' asked Sir Geraint, seeing the king's gaze.

'Not yet, 'replied Guy. 'Let us first finish our positions and allow the reinforcements to disembark.'

The grandmaster was about to reply when a warning horn echoed from the top of Mount Toron. Immediately, the signal was repeated all along the lines, calling every man to arms, and the king's first reaction was to stare towards Acre. Seeing no sign of any enemy activity, he spun his horse around.

'The threat must be from the east,' he said. 'Re-join your commands and prepare for battle.' Before anyone could answer, Guy spurred his horse and galloped south to where his own army was waiting, closely followed by Sir Geraint.

Gerard and Cronin turned north and galloped towards their own lines in the northern quarter, dodging the men now rushing to their defensive positions.

On the other side of the hill, digging tools were discarded, and archers ran to the palisades. Buckets of crossbow bolts were already in place, and men loaded their weapons, knowing that the range on the crossbows far outreached those of the Saracen bows.

On the other side of the plain, hundreds of Saracen horsemen manoeuvred into position behind massed ranks of archers. Behind them, thousands of Ayyubid warriors formed up below a sea of Ayyubid banners. The inevitable drums and horns of battle filled the air, and within moments the massed Saracen lines started marching forward.

In the Christian lines, foot soldiers rushed to their positions as horses and carts were led to the rear. Normally the army would confront any enemy head-on, but the defensive fortifications gave them an advantage and their commanders were determined to use them to their fullest.

Guy galloped his horse to the top of Mount Toron and walked to a promontory looking over the plain. Messengers gathered around ready to convey his orders to his various commanders, and as his squire hurried over with his armour, Balian of Ibelin appeared from the southern slopes, sent by Conrad of Montferrat.

'Balian,' said the king as his squire tightened the leather fastenings on the side of his hauberk, 'it has been a while.'

'It has, your Grace,' replied Balian, 'and it is pleasing to see you emerged safely from your imprisonment.'

'So are you now sworn to Conrad?' asked the king, fastening his sword belt.

'With you gone,' said Balian, 'I had nowhere else to go. Conrad was offering a chance to strike back at Saladin, and I took the oath. I am his man until Jerusalem falls, or one of us dies. My apologies if the situation offends you.'

'On the contrary,' said the king picking up his helmet. 'I could use a good contact within Conrad's ranks. I do not trust him, yet you are an honourable man. If he is willing, ask him if you could be stationed at my side as a permanent liaison between the two camps.'

'Of course,' said Balian with the slightest of bows.

'Good,' said the king, and turned to stare down at his eastward facing positions. 'We need more men on the right flank,' he said, 'summon the Turcopoles from the rear.'

'Yes, my lord,' said one of the messengers and ran to his horse.

'Where are the Templars?' asked one of the knights. 'They should be here.'

'I've told them to hold their position,' said Guy, 'a charge at this time would see little effect.'

The Saracen army marched closer, and one of the Christian commanders on the lower slopes issued the first order of the battle, his voice echoing up the hill.

'Crossbows ready,' he roared.

Over a thousand men got to their knees behind the palisades and lifted their weapons into their shoulders.

'Upon my command,' shouted the commander, 'we will unleash in rank order. Front, centre and rear, just as we practised. *Is that clear?'*

'Aye, my lord,' shouted the archers and stared nervously at the approaching army. The noise grew louder, and as they neared the limits of the Christian archers, the Ayyubid warriors broke into a charge.

'Ready,' roared the Christian commander, 'front rank, aim, steady *loose!'*

Hundreds of iron-tipped bolts flew through the air, smashing through the wooden shields and deep into human flesh. Men fell by the dozen but had hardly hit the floor when a second volley followed the first, the impact no less devastating.

Despite the casualties, the enemy roared their defiance and leapt the fallen to continue the charge.

With the enemy only moments away, Guy ordered the attack and thousands of Christian soldiers poured through their own defences to smash into the front of the Saracen army. The initial clash was devastating as spears and swords cut through armour and flesh alike. Those in the front ranks had no chance, and as they fell, their own comrades trampled them underfoot, the impetus of the tightly packed charge allowing no let-up of pace or power.

Up on the hill, Guy looked down on the battle, mesmerised by the sun glistening off the blades of both sides. Even up there, the noise was loud, and he had to shout to get his voice heard.

'Withdraw the archers,' he shouted to one of the messengers, 'tell them to form up a hundred paces to the rear.'

One of Guy's entourage pointed across the battlefield

'My lord, their cavalry are making a move.'

Guy stared and saw hundreds of horsemen veer northward towards the gap between the two hills.

'Send a signal to the Templars,' shouted Guy. 'Tell him to slam the door.'

'Aye, your Grace,' said the knight, and turned to a flag bearer standing on a rock.

'*Send the signal,*' he roared, and the flag bearer turned northward to wave a Templar banner back and forth. On the next hill, another flag-bearer repeated the signal, and down below, Gerard of Ridefort turned to his fellow Templars.

'There's the signal,' he shouted, 'double file behind me. *Advaaance.*'

The column of knights spurred their horses and snaked between the two hills out onto the plain. Immediately the Ayyubid horsemen reacted to their arrival and spread out to form a broad front. The Templars did the same, forming up tightly alongside each other to form an impenetrable barrier. Behind them came the sergeants, and to either side, the Turcopole light cavalry.

The entire force formed up in a blunt wedge formation with the Templars to the fore. Gerard rode along the front line of his men. Many had only recently arrived in the Outremer so had not yet experienced battle against the Saracens, but they were well trained and eager to serve.

'Many of you,' he shouted, 'have come here to avenge the deaths of hundreds of our brothers, mercilessly executed at Hattin.' He reined in his horse and looked along the line. 'Those men before you are the ones responsible. They are well-armed but make no mistake, they are no match for Templar Steel.' His hand went unconsciously to his sword. 'During the advance, they will use their archers to try to cut us down, but if you stay focussed and keep a tight formation, your shields and armour will prevent most from getting through. If a brother falls, keep going and close the gap. We will look to him when the battle is won. Are you ready?'

'*Aye,*' roared the knights.

Gerard rode to the centre of the line and took his place amongst his men. The enemy had also formed up, but despite him wanting to charge with every fibre of his body, he knew that to commit too early would play right into Saladin's hands. They had to wait.

At the base of Mount Toron, the battle raged on. Men fought and died on both sides, and the air was filled with the screams of the wounded from as they fell in their hundreds. Out on the plain, thousands more Saracens lined up, waiting patiently for the command they knew would come.

The incessant beat of the naqqara filled the air, the war drums used by the Ayyubid to instil fear into their enemies. Battle horns and trumpets added to the cacophony, and the Christians found it hard to communicate.

Many in the Christian army were civilians with little experience of fighting, and most bore only the makeshift weapons they had brought with them from Tripoli. Every blacksmith in the camp had already been pressed into converting them into usable weapons, but many still only bore the blades and tools they had brought from home. Despite this, their bravery and aggression bore dividends, and supported by the better-trained soldiers, they kept out the surging Saracens, forming tight lines and counter-attacking as ordered by their sergeants and officers.

On a hill on the far side of the valley, Salah ad-Din watched the situation unfold. His men had made little impression on the deep Christian lines, and those who managed to break through were quickly cut down by the strategically positioned crossbows. He looked at the rest of his army waiting at the centre of the plain. His numbers were huge, but the Christian defences were stronger than he had envisaged and well thought out. If he committed his full force, the chances were that they would take the hill, but he knew there were far more Christians on both flanks, and they would immediately launch a counter-attack.

He looked towards the massed ranks of cavalry, now facing each across the plain, and knew that any engagement would be costly. He remembered Montgisard where, despite being massively outnumbered, the Christian army had inflicted a huge defeat on his forces, mainly due to the eighty or so Templar knights who had led them into battle. Their fearsome reputation was known across the east, but he defeated them at Cresson and at Hattin and knew they were nothing more than well-trained men.

'My lord,' said Gokbori, 'our cavalry are ready. What are your orders?'

Saladin looked back towards the main battle spreading across the eastern slopes of Mount Toron. Advantage ebbed and flowed with no clear outcome in sight. His aim had been to temporarily breach the Christian lines allowing Ayyubid reinforcements to reach the city, but he had underestimated the enemy's resolve. The advantage of surprise had been lost, and he had no doubt that every Christian capable of holding a weapon now waited for his warriors.

'Give the signal to withdraw,' he said eventually, 'there is no point in losing more men.'

'But my lord,' said Gokbori. 'They have deployed their full Templar force on the open plain. Remember what we did to them at Hattin. Surely this is an opportunity to do a similar thing?'

'At Hattin they were weary and crippled by thirst. The ground also favoured us, but out there, they are fresh, strong with the open plain in which to manoeuvre. We will face them soon enough, but this is not the time.'

'As you wish, my lord,' said Gokbori and nodded to one of the servants who ran off to pass the message to the signallers.

Within minutes, Ayyubid horns echoed from the hilltops. Hundreds of Saracen warriors heard the command and started a fighting withdrawal.

Encouraged by the victory, many Christians pushed forward, making the enemy fight every step of the way, but eventually they pulled up, and as the two forces disengaged, the Saracens turned to run back to safety.

Cheers erupted throughout the Christian army and King Guy looked down with relief. This had been the first major battle since Hattin, and he knew the victory would be a massive boost, not just to the morale of his men, but to his standing as King of Jerusalem. He looked to the north and saw the Ayyubid cavalry was also withdrawing from the standoff with the Templars. It was a better result than he could have hoped for but knew it could have been far, far worse.

'Send a message to the other positions,' he said to the messenger at his side. 'Saladin is retreating, the day is ours.'

'Yes, your Grace,' said the messenger with a grin.

Guy turned away and headed towards his command tent to remove his armour. Should the day have turned out differently, he would have led a squadron of experienced knights in relief, but his intervention had not been needed. Twenty minutes later, Balian of Ibelin returned and walked into the tent.

'Your Grace,' he said, 'you are to be congratulated on a great victory.'

'Thank you,' said the king, 'but it was a skirmish only. I have no doubt that Saladin was just testing our lines, and next time, the task will be far harder.'

'Nevertheless,' said Balian, 'the men are celebrating and speak in glowing terms. Take the victory for what it is.'

Guy nodded and poured two tankards of watered wine before offering one to Balian.

'Served by a king,' said Balian with a smile, 'there are not many men who can claim such a thing.'

'Am I not already a servant of the people?' asked Guy.

'And of God,' said Balian taking the tankard, 'and I salute your victory.' He held up the tankard before downing the contents in one. Guy did the same before walking over to the map on the table in the centre of the tent.

'So what now?' asked Balian, joining him.

'Now we fortify the positions,' said the king, 'and prepare for winter. This campaign has only just begun, Balian, now it gets serious.'

Chapter Fifteen

Acre

October - AD 1189

Fakhiri waited in the darkest shadows waiting for his next victim to pass. For weeks he had managed to beg or steal enough food to survive, for though Egyptian supply ships were still getting through, most of the food was being commandeered by the garrison commander for his men. Throughout the city, people were turning to crime just to survive, and Fakhiri was no different. For days he would watch and follow anyone who seemed to have access to money or food just to learn their routine and assess their strengths and weaknesses. Then, when circumstances allowed, he would strike from the shadows, robbing them of anything they had of value before disappearing into the warren of side streets.

One such target was a fat man by the name of Kareem, a trader who had family working in the docks. He always managed to have something to sell to the desperate. Sometimes it was flour or dried meat, but usually it was dried fish, a cheap food sent to him in barrels from his contacts in Egypt. The garrison commander always took a share, but that still left Kareem with enough to make a healthy profit from the starving. Fakhiri had been watching him the trader for days and knew he had a weakness, a whorehouse near the docks where he visited his favourite girl every seven days.

With hunger clawing at his insides, the Egyptian knew he could wait no longer and hid in an alleyway leading to the docks. He didn't want to hurt the man any more than he had to, but he needed food, and the trader would have a purse about him to pay the whores. The night grew darker, and eventually, Fakhiri could hear the laboured breathing of the fat man as he descended the steep steps from the city.

His hand crept to his knife, and he was about to step out of his hiding place when something moved further up the alley. He pushed himself back into the doorway as two figures moved towards the trader, and before he could do a thing, they pounced on the fat man, knocking him to the floor. For a few seconds, he watched as the two attackers laid into him with their boots before dropping to their knees to search the whimpering man for anything of value. At first, Fakhiri was frustrated at losing his victim, but very quickly became angry as one of the men kept hitting the trader for no other reason except for pleasure. Before he had time to consider the consequences, Fakhiri ran from the doorway and launched a punch at the first man's face, sending him backwards onto the floor. He followed it up with a kick to his ribs before producing his knife and spinning around to face the second attacker who was now on his feet and staring at Fakhiri's knife with fear written across his face.

'There's no need for that,' said the man, 'there's enough here for all of us.' He held up a leather purse into the light from the moon. 'See,' he said, 'we'll share it three ways. No harm done.'

'Throw it here,' snarled Fakhiri.

The man tossed over the purse, but as Fakhiri reached out to catch it, the man on the floor kicked his feet from under him, and he fell to the stone path, knocking his head on the stone paving.

'Stick him,' roared the first man, 'cut his throat.'

Fakhiri was dazed, but his instincts took over, and he rolled to one side before scrambling to his knees. The first attacker came back at him, but he was no knife-fighter, and Fakhiri knocked his attacker's arm away before plunging his blade into the man's side. His victim cried out and dropped to his knees as his comrade backed against a wall.

'Enough,' he said, 'take the purse. 'Just let us go.'

'Take your friend and get out of here,' hissed the Egyptian, 'before I kill you both.'

The man helped his comrade to his feet and headed out of the alley. When they had gone, Fakhiri turned to pick up the purse, knowing he had to get from there before the alarm was raised. To his dismay, the trader was now conscious and sitting against the far wall.

'Thank you,' gasped the trader, 'you saved my life.'

Fakhiri stared, not sure what to do. The trader had retrieved his purse, and it now sat in his lap.

'I know you,' said the fat man before Fakhiri could respond. 'You are the beggar from the market. Your name is Fakhiri?'

The Egyptian cursed silently. Not only did the trader recognise him, but also knew his name. That meant that if he wanted to relieve him of his purse, he would have to kill him.

'I have been watching you,' said Kareem, 'from a window high above the square. Sometimes you steal from those who have plenty, but never have I seen you steal from the poor.'

'I take what I need from those who have the most,' said Fakhiri. 'There is no shame in living.'

'I do not judge you,' said Kareem, 'besides, you just saved my life.'

'I did not do so out of compassion.'

'Oh, I am under no false illusions,' said Kareem, 'I realise that you would probably have taken my purse from me if they had not gotten to me first. Yet that does not change the fact that they would have killed me, whilst you, my friend, will probably not.'

'I have killed many men.'

'I'm sure you have,' said Kareem, 'yet I will not be one of them.'

'Don't be so sure, I still want that purse.'

Kareem looked down at the purse in his lap before looking back up at Fakhiri.

'Here,' he said, 'take it,' and tossed it across the alley.

Fakhiri caught the purse and tucked it inside his clothing.

'So, what are you going to do now,' said Kareem, 'kill me so I cannot report you to the guards?'

'Do you have a better suggestion?'

'As it happens, I do,' said Kareem. 'These streets are getting more dangerous, especially at night. People like me are becoming more vulnerable through no fault of our own. All I have done is work hard to build my business, and now people like you want to take it all away.'

'All we want to do is eat,' said Fakhiri, 'so perhaps if you shared some of your fortune, not so many people would be hungry.'

'I do what I can,' said Kareem, 'but business is business.'

'I've heard enough,' said Fakhiri, 'I'll let you live, but if I ever hear my name mentioned in connection with this, I'll know it came from you and will slit your throat.'

'Of that, I'm sure,' said Kareem, 'but hear me out. I am in need of someone like you to help in my business. Why not work for me? I offer a wage, food and a place to sleep. All you have to do is say yes, and you will never be hungry again.'

'Work for you?' said Fakhiri. 'Doing what?'

'Numerous things,' said the trader, 'but chief amongst them is keeping me safe from people like yourself.'

'A bodyguard?'

'If you say so. I need protection and would rather have a man who knows how to fight dirty rather than someone who talks a good fight but will let me down when the odds are against him.'

Fakhiri stared at the trader. Times were getting harder, and he had still not managed to contact Sumeira.

'How do I know you won't turn me in at the first opportunity?'

'You don't, but I like my head attached to my neck, and somehow, I think you will separate them if I betray you. Do what you like, Fakhiri, the purse is yours for saving my life, but there is plenty more where that came from. What do you say?'

Again Fakhiri paused while he considered the situation, but he knew he might never have the chance again.

'We have an agreement,' he said eventually.

'Good,' said the trader, getting to his feet. 'Come to my house at dawn to discuss the details.' He started walking down the hill, away from the Egyptian.

'Your house is the other direction,' said Fakhiri.

'Aye, it is,' said the trader over his shoulder, 'but I have unfinished business in the whorehouse. See me at dawn.'

Over in the commandery, Sumeira walked through the chapel, checking on those confined to the beds. Many of the men who had been wounded during the initial assault had moved on, their wounds now dressed and healing. Some hadn't been so lucky and had succumbed to infection, but overall the death rate had been low, and the pressure was easing.

Every day, she and Shani worked hard to keep the patients and surroundings clean. Food was limited and usually consisted of fish and dried dates, a monotonous fayre, but the only one available from the garrison commander.

The Christian prisoners were even worse off, often going days without anything and Sumeira scavenged whatever she could find to provide a broth. Her growing reputation meant that people sometimes came to the gates to seek medicine and in return would pay with whatever they could, fish bones, the entrails of dead animals and even the occasional rat caught from the thousands infesting the city. It wasn't ideal, but she used whatever she could get, boiling everything into a watery soup before issuing it to the prisoners. She finished checking her patients and turned to see Shani standing at the doorway.

'My lady,' he said, 'it is ready.'

She turned back and walked out of the chapel to join her assistant outside. At his feet, he had a bucket of fresh water and another of hot soup.

'It looks thicker than usual,' said Sumeira, leaning down to stir the soup with a ladle. 'What's in it?'

'The usual scraps of meat,' said Shani, 'but I managed to steal some flour from the storeroom. The rats had torn open a sack and spilt it on the floor. I put the last few scoops into the buckets.'

'And nobody saw you?'

'No,' said Shani, 'they are all fast asleep in their quarters.'

'Wait,' said Sumeira, 'there is something I need to get.' She hurried away but was back within moments before adding something to the bucket of soup. Shani looked up at her with inquisitive eyes but said nothing.

They crossed the courtyard and into the torchlit corridor of the commandery, each carrying a bucket. The guard searched them both before opening the door and allowing them through.

Inside, all the men were asleep or sitting against the walls, their bodies emaciated and covered with filth. Robin the blacksmith looked up as the door slammed behind her.

'Sumeira,' he said, 'have you brought food?'

'I have,' she said, 'it's not much but should fortify you.'

The men around the room struggled to their feet and staggered over with their mugs, the only utensils they had.

'Take your time,' said Sumeira as they crowded around her, 'there's enough for all.'

'Form a line,' shouted the Blacksmith, 'we are men, not animals.'

The prisoners limped into position, and as Shani filled each mug, Sumeira took Robin to one side.

'The food situation is getting worse,' she said, 'we are doing what we can, but the jailer has eyes everywhere.'

'We appreciate what you do for us,' said Robin. 'What news of the siege?'

'The attacks have fallen away,' said Sumeira, 'but I have befriended one of the guards, and he says that Guy's army has dug in half a league to the east. Beyond that, Saladin has amassed his own armies to stop them from being resupplied by land.'

'There were rumours of a great Christian army coming to help the king,' said the blacksmith, 'is that true?'

'If it is, I have not heard of it,' said Sumeira and looked over at the diminishing line of men at the soup bucket.

'I have to go,' she said, 'but I will leave the soup here. Once everyone has been fed, share what is left but first dredge the bottom with your mug. There is something there you may want.'

Robin nodded and waited until she left the cell. Once the door had been locked by the guard, he grabbed his own mug and dragged it across the bottom of the bucket. Feeling something pushed up against the side, he retrieved his mug and put his fingers into the soup before withdrawing a short, but very sharp knife.

'Sumeira,' he said to himself, 'you are an extraordinary woman.'

Several leagues away, Al-Afdal stood talking to Gokbori outside his tent. The latest patrols had returned with bad news. Every approach road to acre was blocked by Christian positions, and there was no way to get a supply caravan through.

'How bad is the situation in the city?' asked Al-Afdal.

'Some messengers managed to get through,' said Gokbori, 'and they tell of increasing hardship. Some ships have managed to break the blockade, but not enough to make a huge difference. What worries me more is the number of reinforcements landing every day by the Franks. Their numbers are almost as great as ours, and it can't be long before they try another assault. If they do, I can't see how Turan-Shah's forces can hold them out. He needs reinforcements quickly.'

'Without a land-route, there is nothing we can do,' said Al-Afdal.

'My lord,' said one of the scouts, 'with your permission, may I suggest something?'

'Approach,' said Saladin's son, and the scout dismounted to approach the two men, bowing deeply as he came to a halt.

'You are a Bedouin,' said Gokbori.

'I am, my lord,' said the scout.

'Oh he is more than that,' said Al-Afdal, recognising the young man, 'he is also a Christian, or at least he was.'

'A Christian serving amongst those we trust the most,' said Gokbori. 'I hope you know what you are doing.'

'Trust me,' said Al-Afdal, 'he has more than proven his worth since Hattin, and I trust him with my life.' He turned to the scout. 'Hassan Malouf, what is it you want to say?'

'My lord,' said Hassan, 'as a boy, I spent many years living on the streets of Acre, but I also wandered beyond the walls and learned the land outside the city.'

'And?' asked Gokbori.

Hassan turned to face the emir.

'With respect, my lord,' he said, 'I do not agree there is no route into Acre. The Christians have all the roads and tracks covered, but they do not have anyone on the shore to the south of the city.'

'That is because there is no need,' said Gokbori. 'The marshlands create a natural barrier, and any column trying to get through that way would get bogged down in minutes.'

'You are correct,' said Hassan, 'unless of course, there was a path known only to the fishermen and shepherds.'

The two Saracen officers stared at Hassan, realising what he was getting at.

'Do you know of such a path?' asked Al-Afdal.

'I do, my lord. It is narrow and easily lost in the dark, but it is big enough for two men to pass side by side. I think that if we take a column after dark, we could get a few hundred to the city walls by dawn.'

Al-Afdal turned to Gokbori.

'Will a few hundred men make a difference?'

'It would,' said Gokbori, 'but how do we get in? The gates are in the eastern and northern walls.'

'There is an old sally-gate near the water's edge,' said Hassan. 'Not many knew about it except those who stole from the many ships which landed at Acre. Inside it is hard to find, but I know where it is. If I can get inside the walls, I can open the gate from the inside and let our warriors through.'

'And how do you intend to get inside? Any group of men approaching the walls in darkness will be assumed to be the enemy and treated as such, but if you call out, you will alert the Christian lines.'

'There is a way,' said Hassan, 'all I need to do is to get there.'

Al-Afdal stared for a moment before grabbing Hassan's shoulder.

'The more I get to know you, Hassan,' he said, 'the more I get to like you. When do you think we should go?'

'Tomorrow it is the last night of the new moon,' said Hassan, 'so, it has to be then. After that, we will be too easily seen and will have to wait another month.'

'Then tomorrow it will be,' said Al-Afdal. 'Now go and get some rest. You have done well.'

The following night, Hassan led two hundred warriors through the marshlands, each staying close to the man in front so as not to lose the path. Everyone carried a heavy pack containing as much grain as they could carry, as well as their personal weapons. A few hours before dawn, they reached the sand dunes to the south of the city and disappeared into the shadows to wait as Hassan looked up at the looming walls.

'Where's the doorway?' whispered Salman, the Saracen in charge of the column.

'Where the wall meets the water,' said Hassan. 'Tucked into the corner next to the tower.'

The Saracen warrior looked to the wall of the city stretching out into the sea to form a harbour wall.

'How are you going to get inside?' he asked.

'It's simple,' said Hassan, dropping his pack and removing his thawb, 'I'm going to swim out around the wall and into the harbour. Once there, it will take minutes to find the door. Keep the men hidden until I come for you.'

The warrior stared at Hassan with admiration.

'You are a strange one, Bedouin,' he said, 'but if you say it can be done, then may Allah go with you.'

'If I'm not back by dawn,' said Hassan, removing the last of his clothing, 'keep the men hidden along the cliffs. Hopefully, there will be no Christian patrols, but we can't be sure.'

'Do not worry about us, Hassan,' said Salman, 'just do what you have to do.'

Hassan nodded and turned to walk into the sea. The temperature took his breath away, but as soon as he started swimming, his body warmed up, and he headed out towards the end of the wall.

A few minutes later, he rounded the tower and headed into the harbour. His limbs were aching, and his breath came in shorter gasps as his inexperience began to tell. He reached the side of a ship tied to a ring on the harbour wall and climbed up the rope before falling onto the deck. He lay there shivering, trying to regain his breath, but seeing a slight glow in the morning sky, realised he had little time to waste. He got to his feet and ran across the gangplank to the dock before heading towards the tower he had been outside only a few minutes earlier.

He ran ducked in through the unlocked door to a tiny corridor. To his right, the light of a fire illuminated a tiny room containing two sleeping guards. For a moment, he considered waking them up but realising he may be mistaken for a Christian spy, decided to carry on alone, and walked over to where a staircase spiralled down to a basement.

He headed down, using his hands to steady his descent in the dark. At the bottom, he followed the wall around until he found a pile of rubble and old timber left there by the builders of the tower many years earlier. He pulled away the timber and created a gap before pulling his way through and into a waist-high opening cut deep into the wall. He crawled forwards on his hands and knees before reaching a doorway and sat back against the wall to catch his breath. Removing the two locking bars from their cradles, he pulled the door inward, gasping at the sudden rush of fresh air. Outside, the Saracen officer was waiting for him and pulled him through.

'You did it,' he said, looking at Hassan. 'You have my respect.'

'We need to hurry,' said Hassan, 'it is getting light. Somebody needs to go in and tell the guards what is happening to avoid confusion. '

'I will lead the way,' said the officer, 'you get dressed and bring our men.'

'The passage is low but passable,' said Hassan. 'On the other side, there is a stairway that leads up to a corridor and a guard room. There are only two men there, but they need to know what is happening.'

'Leave it to me,' said Salman, and ducked down to crawl through the sally-port.

Hassan hurried over to where he had left his clothes and got dressed before crouching low and running to where the first of the men were hiding.

The way is clear,' he whispered, 'head for that tower and into the doorway at its base. Hurry, it's almost light.'

The Saracen warrior did as he was bid, followed by the rest of the men. Hassan looked up at the sky with concern. In a few minutes it would be light, and anyone still outside would be exposed to the Christians and city guards alike.

'*Hurry,*' he hissed as the men shuffled past him. 'There is no time to waste. '

He ran over to the doorway to help as each man dropped to his knees and dragged their packs in behind them. Almost three quarters had managed to get in before a horn rent the air and the sound of Christian voices echoed across the dunes.

'*Alarm, stand to your weapons.*'

'*They've seen us,*' shouted Hassan, 'drop the bags and form a line of defence.'

Fifty men threw the food bags towards the wall and strung their bows to face the nearby Christian lines. Others passed the bags hand to hand through the opening, piling them up on the inside.

A few hundred paces away, Christian foot-soldiers appeared on the top of the dunes, each heavily armed and heading for the stranded Saracens. In the distance, Hassan could see dozens of lancers riding down a path onto the shore, and he knew there was no way they could fight off any cavalry attack. Moments later, the sound of hundreds of arrows filled the air, and Hassan looked up with relief. They were coming from the city walls and aimed at the horsemen.

'Hassan Malouf,' called Salman from above, 'leave what remains of the bags and get our men inside. We can hold them for moments only.'

Hassan turned to the defensive line.

'You heard him,' he shouted, 'get inside the walls. '

The remaining men ran to the sally-port leaving the last of the food bags outside. Hassan followed them in and barred the door behind him. Everyone made their way up the spiral stairway and out onto the courtyard alongside the harbour.

Guards ran from all directions and forced the newcomers against the walls, not sure of what was happening. Salman ran down the steps to explain to the guard commander, and when the situation became clearer, the reinforcements were led away to a nearby barracks to get some food and rest. Salman and Hassan were led deeper into the heart of the city and within fifteen minutes, stood in an ante-chamber waiting for an audience with Turan-Shah.

'My lord,' said one of the officers as the prince entered, 'these are the men who led Salah ad-Din's warriors here.'

Turan-Shah stared at the two men. He had only just heard what had happened and was still not sure what to make of it.

'You,' he said eventually, staring at Hassan, 'you are a Bedouin?'

'I am, my lord,' said Hassan with a bow, 'but serve Allah and Salah ad-Din in the fight against the Christians.'

'Your people are usually loyal to the infidels,' said Turan-Shah, 'why do you choose us over them?'

'They slaughtered my family,' said Hassan. 'This is my way of seeking retribution.'

'Do you trust this man,' asked Turan-Shah, turning to Salman.

'I do,' said Salman, 'as does 'Al-Afdal ibn Salah ad-Din. Without him, we would not be here.'

Turan-Shah nodded silently before turning to one of his servants.

'Find quarters for these men and see that they are fed. Bring them back to me at noon so I can learn more of what is happening outside the city.'

'Yes, my lord,' said the servant and bowed before leading the newcomers from the audience chamber.

One of Turan-Shah's officers turned to face his commander.

'They say they have almost two hundred men,' he said, 'a useful addition to our garrison.'

'It is,' said Turan-Shah, 'but still nowhere near enough. We need more men, and soon.'

Chapter Sixteen

Acre

October 4th - AD 1189

Gerard of Ridefort emerged from his tent into the pre-dawn gloom. The chill of the night air caught his breath, and he pulled his cloak tighter about him as he walked over to the nearest campfire. Several men were already enjoying the warmth including Thomas Cronin, Robert of Hastings and one of the Turcopoles who had led the night patrol along the outer boundaries of their positions. As the grandmaster approached, the conversation died away, and all the men turned to face him.

'You called for me,' said Gerard, coming to a halt. 'Is there a problem?'

'On the contrary, my lord,' said Robert, 'we believe we may have an opportunity, but we must move quickly.'

'What sort of opportunity,' asked Gerard.

'My lord,' said Robert, 'this is Amman, captain of the Turcopole lancers. Tonight he was on patrol along the forward lines and saw many of the Saracens withdrawing to the rear, leaving only a few to protect Saladin's right flank.'

'Withdrawing?' asked Gerard. 'Why would they do that?'

'I think,' said Cronin, 'that withdrawing is too strong a word, and they may just be making way for a relief force. However, the fact that they have retired before the reinforcements arrive leaves them vulnerable.'

'I agree,' said Sir Robert, 'and even if the new force is on their way, there will be some confusion while they get to know the strengths and weaknesses of their positions. The chances are that Saladin's right flank will never be as vulnerable as it is right now.'

'Suggestions?' asked Gerard.

'My lord,' said Robert, 'the way is clear. If we attack before they have a chance to organise, we could break through the lines and potentially reach Saladin himself. This is an opportunity too good to miss.'

Gerard turned to Cronin.

'What about you, Brother Cronin, what is your feeling?'

'I don't think it will be as simple as Brother Robert suggests,' said Cronin, 'but I agree this is a unique opportunity. With the support of our fellows in the centre to guard our right flank, there is certainly a chance we could break through, especially if we use crossbows in the vanguard.'

'My lord,' interjected Robert of Hastings, 'I agree regarding the arbalists, but we have no time to arrange a coordinated attack with Guy or those on the outer flanks. If we are to succeed, we have to act now.'

Gerard looked around the men, each now silent and waiting for his decision.

'I agree,' he said eventually. 'Sir Robert, muster our knights and sergeants for an immediate advance. Brother Cronin, assemble the arbalists and have them form up, line abreast and three men deep.' He turned to the Turcopole. 'Amman, you will ride to the king and to Conrad of Montferrat. Inform them of our intentions, and request they protect our right flank as soon as they are able.'

'As you wish, my lord,' said the Turcopole and turned away to mount his horse.

'Rouse the men,' said Gerard, turning back to those that remained, 'and have them make ready, but keep the noise down, let's not give the enemy any advance warning of what is about to fall upon them.'

All the men ran to their duties, and as the Templar lines came to life, Gerard returned to his tent to don his armour. This was the chance he had been waiting for, an opportunity to truly repay the Saracens for the slaughter of his brothers at Hattin.

Less than half an hour later, Thomas Cronin sat upon his horse and looked towards the first slivers of light appearing over the eastern mountains. To either side and to his rear, hundreds of fellow sergeants did the same, ready to ride into battle. Behind them, two thousand foot-soldiers waited nervously, recently dragged from their sleep to support the advance, a prospect none had anticipated only hours earlier.

In front of the sergeants, a solid line of Templar knights sat upon their own chargers, each tight to the one alongside him, a solid wall of experienced, battle-hardened warrior monks waiting to lead the charge. They feared nothing and were more than willing to die in the service of God.

As the sky lightened, the first of the arbalists made their way through the cavalry lines and formed up to the fore with their crossbows. Each was protected by heavily quilted gambesons and had a packed quiver of bolts hanging from their belts. When they were ready, Gerard of Ridefort rode forward to join Robert of Hastings.

'Ready?' he asked, turning to the knight.

'Ready,' confirmed Robert.

'In that case,' said Gerard, 'let us waste no more time. Start the advance, Brother Robert, lead us into battle.'

The knight rode to the front of the arbalists' lines and turned to face them.

'We will keep as quiet as we can for as long as we can,' he said, 'but as soon as we are seen, I want you to unleash hell. Their numbers are few, but their positions are strong and they have dug in well. If we keep them pinned down, our foot soldiers will drive them from their holes and out onto the plains. From there, our knights will take over.'

He rode forward a few paces and drew his sword, holding it up into the morning air. He waited to make sure the message had been shared before bringing the sword sharply down, and as one, over five hundred arbalists marched forward to attack Saladin's right flank.

Within minutes, an alarm horn echoed across the plain as a Saracen sentry saw the threat. Immediately the sound was repeated by other guards, and all along the Saracen lines, men ran to their weapons.

'Keep going,' shouted Sir Robert, all attempts at silence now abandoned, 'front rank get ready, loose on my command.'

The arbalists raised the stocks of their crossbows into their shoulders, anticipating the command. Within moments a volley of Saracen arrows sped through the air towards them but fell well short.

'Arbalists hold, 'shouted Robert and waited as the ranks came to a standstill. 'Front rank present, aim, *release!*'

A volley of crossbow bolts shot across the open space between the Christians and the Saracen defences. The power of the crossbows meant the missiles easily reached the enemy lines and steel-tipped quarrels tore into wood and flesh alike, sending shockwaves of fear through the Saracen defenders.

'*Second rank advance,*' roared Robert, and the next row of men marched through the first, stopping five paces to their front.

'*Present, aim, release,*' shouted Robert, and again the morning air filled with bolts, devastating the Saracen forward lines. Over and over again the Templar knight repeated the commands, each time getting closer to the enemy positions until they were no more than fifty paces away.

'*Arbalists hold',* roared a voice from behind, and as they waited, two thousand foot-soldiers ran through their lines to form up to their front.

'*Men at arms,*' roared their commander, '*advaaance.*'

Immediately the foot-soldiers started running towards the enemy positions. Behind them, the arbalists slung their crossbows over their backs and followed them into the charge.

Hundreds of Saracens emerged from behind their defences to meet the Christians head-on, but many more knew they were doomed and turned to flee.

The first of the Christians smashed into the weaker Saracen forces, ploughing through them like a sharp sword through flesh. The impact was overwhelming, and it was obvious there could be only one victor in the unexpected battle. Deeper into the enemy position, more Saracens knew they had no chance, and turned to join the many others now fleeing the battle. Any organised formations broke apart, and men fought individually using anything to hand to kill their opponents. Once again, the sand sucked at the free-flowing blood and the morning air echoed to the sound of mans' brutality.

On the hill to the south, King Guy watched the battle unfold with fascination. The swift action had yielded unexpected results, but he could see that further back, the main Saracen camp was already responding.

'It looks like they are mobilising their central cavalry,' said Balian. 'They must be intending to support their right flank.'

'My thoughts exactly,' said Guy, 'and if they do, that will weaken the defence of their main positions.'

'It will,' said Balian glancing at the king. 'What are you thinking?'

'I think this is too good an opportunity to miss,' replied the king. 'Are our men ready?'

'They are, your Grace.'

'In that case, prepare to advance, Balian, let us give Saladin something else to worry about.'

On the left flank, the Christians had overwhelmed the Saracen forward lines and now continued after those who had fled. With few obstacles to overcome, Gerard deployed his mounted Templar knights and gave chase to the hundreds of men now spreading out over the plain.

'My lord,' shouted the seneschal to Gerard's side, 'look.'

The grandmaster glanced over his shoulder to see Guy's cavalry thundering from the king's positions. Enthused by the support, he encouraged his men to greater efforts, and their swords sought out fresh victims, cutting down hundreds without mercy.

'Keep going,' roared Gerard, his blood lust raging through him like a fire, 'kill them all.'

The Templar-led army rampaged forward, soaked in the blood of their enemies. Foot-soldiers fought like demons, releasing pent-up fury upon anyone they could reach. Screams for mercy were ignored, and the Christian wave overwhelmed the Saracens with ease.

To their right, Guy's cavalry enjoyed similar success, the huge numbers overwhelming the Saracen central lines. Again, thousands of foot-soldiers followed up and tore into any warriors trying to defend their positions, and it was soon clear the unexpected attack had reaped huge rewards.

As the last of the defenders were killed or disappeared into the distance, the foot-soldiers took the opportunity to catch their breath, and many looked around the destroyed enemy camp, their fury dissipating after the rage of battle.

'In the name of God,' shouted a voice, 'look at all this.'

Due to the suddenness of the attack, the Saracens had had no time to pick up their belongings, and the camp was still full of food and possessions. The Christian army stared in disbelief. Carts of food, water and wine lay untouched, and in the commanders' tents, luxurious rugs still lay where they had been abandoned. One of the Christian bloodied soldiers emerged from one bearing a golden candlestick and a silver platter.

'Gold,' he roared across the battlefield, *'we're rich.'*

Within moments, men broke ranks to plunder the enemy positions. Tents were torn down, and bodies searched for anything of value. Some just settled for food and tore at the carcasses of goats still roasting above the fires. Others searched for anything of value and fights broke out throughout the ranks as men tried to rob their own comrades of their ill-gotten gains. All discipline completely disappeared, and the advance descended into chaos.

In the distance, Salah ad-Din sat upon his own horse, watching events unfold. The attack had caught the front lines unprepared, but most of the Muslim army was based far to the rear and were now mobilising to counterattack the rampaging Christians.

Behind him were almost five thousand horsemen jostling into position, and behind them, another five thousand warriors, each armed with fearsome scimitars hanging from their belts. Another two thousand mounted archers lined up on the lower slopes of a hill to the south to await their orders, skilled bowmen renowned for their horsemanship and accuracy in the heat of battle.

Salah ad-Din looked across the battlefield. The initial devastating thrusts had petered out, and the enemy was now focussed on looting the Saracen positions. The feared Templar knights were still fighting, but spread out and disorganised, a rare opportunity for any defender of Islam.

To the south, the army from Tyre had also ventured out of their strong positions, keen to be part of such an overwhelming victory, but they were low in number with few foot soldiers. The sultan quickly made his plans and turned to the men at his side.

'Muzaffar ad-Din Gokbori,' he said. 'Take the archers and attack the Christians in the south. It is imperative they are not allowed to join up with those in the centre.'

'Understood,' said Gokbori, and turned his horse away as Salah ad-Din turned to his son.

'Al-Afdal, to you lies the greater honour. You will lead my main army against those who think they have won a victory. Drive them back to whence they came but do unto them as they have done to our people. Show no mercy.'

'I am honoured, father,' said Al-Afdal, and turned away to race his horse back to the waiting army. Salah ad-Din waited patiently, watching as the enemy ranks dispersed to plunder. Behind him, the Saracen cavalry moved closer until eventually, his son reappeared beside him.

'We are ready,' he said.

The sultan nodded to one of his officers, and a few seconds later, a solitary arrow soared through the air, leaving a trail of black smoke behind it. A few hundred paces away, Gokbori's battle horns sounded, and his mounted archers galloped towards the approaching army of Tyre. More horns sounded, and as Salah ad-Din watched, thousands of Ayyubid mounted warriors galloped past him. The fightback had begun.

Up on Mount Toron, Guy of Lusignan watched with growing concern. A few minutes earlier, his heart had raced at the thought of an overwhelming victory, but his men now focussed on plunder instead of driving the advantage home.'

On the battlements of Acre castle, Turan-Shah stood alongside his own commanders watching the battle unfold. At first, the garrison commander had been horrified at the unstoppable advance of the Christian forces on the left flank, but now he could see that the Sultan was responding, and in the distance, could see a huge force of Ayyubid horsemen racing into position.

'The tide is about to turn,' he said eventually, 'the Christians will not be able to withstand what the sultan is about to unleash.'

'Allah Akbar,' said one of the officers at his side, his gaze fixed on the distant battlefield, but Hassan Malouf was looking elsewhere, down into the nearby Templar lines.

'My lord,' he said eventually, turning towards Turan-Shah. 'May I speak?'

The Yemeni prince nodded.

'My lord,' said Hassan, 'the sultan fields a great army, but the Templars are strong and great in number. They present a huge risk to our people and should not be dismissed.'

'They number in the hundreds,' said Turan-Shah, 'while Salah ad-Din's men are in their thousands. Our warriors will sweep the men of the blood-cross before them.'

'With respect, my lord,' said Hassan. 'I have seen these men in battle. Their strengths are on the open fields, and there are none that can withstand them in such situations.' He looked out over the walls. 'Out there, they have the perfect conditions to deploy their tactics, and even if they are ultimately defeated, they will kill thousands of our people before the day is done.'

'I agree,' said one of the officers, 'this battle is not yet won, and the knights of the blood-cross will have a huge say in the outcome.'

'I am aware of such claims,' said Turan-Shah, 'but it is out of our hands. Even if we could reach them, our numbers are few and would have little impact. We cannot influence what is about to befall.'

'I think we can,' said Hassan. 'The commander of the Templars has committed most of his men to the attack which leaves their own lines poorly defended. If we were to attack their positions from the rear, the knights would be forced to respond lest they lose the northern road to us.'

'Even if we are successful,' said Turan-Shah, 'we could not defend our gains from a counterattack.'

'We do not have to,' said Hassan. 'All we need to do is plant the fear in their minds, and their foot-soldiers will turn their attention inward to save their families. They will stream back in their hundreds, leaving the Christian army in disarray and when they do, Salah ad-Din will find the opposition much easier to deal with.'

'And the Templars?'

'As I said, their preference is for open battle, but even they cannot ignore an attack on their camp. There are women and children there, and they will not stand by to see the innocent killed.'

Turan-Shah turned to his officers.

'What say you?'

'The Bedouin talks sense,' said one of the officers, 'but I am told he once served under the knights of the blood-cross. This could be a trick.'

'It is no trick,' said Hassan. 'I want them dead as much as you. I have shared my thoughts; the decision is now for others.'

'My lord,' interjected Salman. 'Hassan has the ear of Al-Afdal himself. The boy can be trusted.'

Turan-Shah walked to the battlements and stared over into the Templar positions, an encampment stretching several hundreds of paces in all directions and protected by a series of palisades and trenches.

'I agree the plan has merit,' he said, 'but I also worry about the word of a man who once worshipped the Christian God.' He turned to Hassan. 'I respect that the sultan's son trusts you,' he said, 'but I do not yet share that belief. How do I know you are not still an infidel at heart?'

'The one I call God is irrelevant,' said Hassan,' all you need to know is I want to kill Christians as much as you. If there is doubt, then allow me to join your men on the assault. I swear I will shed Templar blood, but if I falter, have your men cut me down.'

Turan-Shah looked at his officers before turning back to Hassan.

'So be it, he said. We will muster what cavalry we have and lead an attack on the Templar camp. Prove yourself today, Hassan Malouf, and I will send word to the sultan himself about your loyalty.'

Hassan bowed before turning away and headed down to the stables.

'He will not let you down, my lord,' said Salman as he left. 'He is an extraordinary young man.'

'He may be,' said Turan-Shah, 'but if he hesitates for even a moment, then his body will rot amongst the Christians.'

Ten minutes later, Hassan sat astride a horse just inside the northern gate of the city. Behind him, two hundred Saracen knights waited on their own horses, each man handpicked for his prowess in battle.

'Open the gates,' said Hassan, and after one last glance at the men behind him, urged his horse forward. Outside, the Saracen cavalry quickly spread out into one long line and trotted their horses towards the enemy positions. Within moments, an alarm cry arose from the Christian positions, and Hassan knew the time had come.

One of the Egyptian officers at his side drew his scimitar, and holding it high in the air, called out his rallying call.

'Allah Akbar,' he roared and with a dig of his heels, drove his horse into a gallop. The rest of the men followed his example

and raced their horses straight at the sparsely defended Templar defences, striking down anyone they could reach.

Using every skill he had learned from Thomas Cronin, Hassan joined the slaughter, his scimitar no less bloody, his heart still black from the memory of what had happened to his wife and unborn child.

A figure tried to escape by fleeing towards the palisades and Hassan rode his horse to block off their escape, but as he raised his scimitar, his intended victim turned to look up at him, a desperate plea for mercy upon her face.

'Please,' begged the woman, 'mercy I beseech thee.'

Hassan paused, unsure what to do. The escapee was holding a baby, and he could not help but wonder if his own wife had made such a plea when facing her own death.

'Kill her,' roared a voice, but Hassan hesitated, looking into the woman's tearful eyes.

'Go,' said Hassan lowering his blade, 'before I change my mind.'

The woman staggered towards a line of palisades and was dragged to safety by willing hands.

'Sound the alarm,' roared a voice behind the Christian defences, and a series of horns echoed throughout the camp, warning anyone in earshot of the danger.

Further out on the battlefield, the Templar knights focussed on slaughtering any fleeing Saracens, but as the alarm signal reached their ears, many turned to stare back in horror towards their own lines.

'The camp is being attacked,' shouted one, 'we have to return.'

'We will do no such thing,' roared Gerard, 'muster to the flag and reform the line.'

Many of the knights heeded the command, but while they had been busy killing, Al-Afdal had brought his own cavalry within striking distance, and now drove into them, motivated by revenge.

The two forces clashed in a fury of steel and blood, but with surprise on their side, the thrust by the Saracens paid dividends, and the Templar formation fell apart. Horses and men died alongside each other, their screams of pain mingling as both sides fought for dominance.

The battle expanded across the plain as men fought desperately. The Christian army, who had only minutes earlier had been in the ascendancy, now found itself under extreme pressure as Saladin directed his reserve forces against them. Numbers were equal, but the Saracens were better organised, and far more disciplined.

Laden with the spoils of war, many Christian soldiers fled back to the safety of Mount Toron, but many were ridden down and killed by Ayyubid cavalry. On the southern edge of the battlefield, Conrad of Montferrat's men had been surrounded by Gokbori's archers and were being slaughtered without a chance of retribution. Desperately he ordered the retreat and headed back to his own lines with what remained of his men.

Up on Mount Toron, the king watched with growing horror as the tide turned against them. His main army was now in headlong retreat back to their positions while on the left, the Templars had managed to extract themselves, and were fighting an organised withdrawal back to their own lines. On the right, Conrad of Montferrat's men had been reinforced by a column of Guy's own knights and were now heading back to their own positions.

Guy stared at the unfolding disaster. What had seemed an unlikely but welcome victory only hours earlier, had somehow turned into a defeat, costing the lives of hundreds.

'How did this happen?' he growled as lines of weary men made their way back through the palisades below.

'It seems we underestimated Saladin's reserves,' said Balian, 'and when our men broke ranks to loot the Saracen camps, the sultan made them pay a terrible price.'

'And the Templars?'

'The grandmaster would not have led such an attack if he did not believe it was worthwhile,' said Balian. 'He must have been in possession of information that made the risk justifiable.'

'Either that or his judgement was clouded by the thought of revenge,' replied the king. 'Either way, he owes me an explanation. Send a message, I want him here at dusk.'

'As you wish, your Grace,' said Balian.

'And find out who first broke the lines to start the looting,' added the king, 'I want to make an example of them. Without their greed and cowardice, this day may have turned out differently.'

Balian nodded and turned away as the king watched the last of the Christian army arrive back from the battle.

A few hours later, as the sun lowered over the distant sea, Guy stood amongst several of his commanders in his campaign tent, listening to their reports. Across the tent, the flap opened and Balian walked up to the map-table.

'Balian,' said the king, 'you have returned at last. Have you brought the grandmaster with you?'

'I have not, your Grace, for I have grave news.'

The king stared at Balian, suspecting the worst. He may be annoyed with the grandmaster, but he certainly wished him no ill.

'Is he dead?' he asked eventually.

'No, your Grace,' said Balian, 'the grandmaster has been captured.'

'But he is alive?'

'As far as we know, but as you are aware, he was recently released from captivity by Saladin in return for a pledge not to raise a sword against the Ayyubid. I worry that his involvement will anger the Sultan, and he may be seen as not worthy of a ransom.'

'Nonsense,' said Guy. 'Saladin is an astute man and knows the grandmaster's worth. Send an envoy immediately to open negotiations.'

'I will go myself,' said Balian.

'Good,' said the king, 'now join us for there is much to discuss.'

The men around the table returned their attention to the map and as the last of the sun disappeared below the horizon, the silence of the night was broken only by the moans of the wounded and the crying of the women whose men would never return.

In Acre castle, most of the Saracens who had launched the surprise attack on the Templar lines had returned safely with few casualties. Hassan now stood in a hall alongside those who had survived and faced Turan-Shah standing on a dais.

'You did well,' announced Turan-Shah, 'and I will ensure the sultan himself hears of your bravery. To celebrate, I have had refreshments prepared in your name, but first, we should acknowledge our Bedouin friend here who suggested the attack.' He turned to look at Hassan. 'I hear his blade was no less bloody than anyone else's today and henceforth I will hear no more words of doubt against his name.'

A great cheer echoed around the hall, and some of the men slapped him on the back as they headed towards the trestle tables containing platters of meat and wine. Hassan watched them go but had little appetite. His mind was still tortured with the sight of the fear he had seen on the young Christian woman's face only hours later.

'Are you not eating?' asked a voice, and he turned to see Salman coming towards him.

'I'm not hungry,' replied Hassan with a thin-lipped smile.

'Hassan,' said Salman, 'food is scarce enough in the city as it is. You should eat while you can.'

'I'll take something with me,' said Hassan, his hand pressing against his side.

'Why, where are you going?'

'Back to my quarters, I need to sleep.'

'Hassan,' said Salman, 'you have the colour of a westerner.' He looked down at Hassan's hand and saw blood seeping through the Bedouin's fingers. 'You have been wounded,' he gasped, looking up. 'Why didn't you say?'

'A scratch only,' said Hassan, but before he could say anymore, his eyes rolled backwards, and he collapsed unconscious onto the floor.

Five days later, Hassan opened his eyes and stared at the ceiling. His vision was blurred, but he could see movement and could hear the murmurings of other men in the room. For a few seconds, he lay there, waiting until his sight cleared before turning his head to look around. He soon realised he was laying on a cot, and as his most recent memories came flooding back, his hand crept to his side to feel for the wound.

His touch was like a dagger, and he winced in pain as he found his whole torso had been tightly wrapped in bandages.

'You are awake,' said a voice, and Hassan turned his head to see Salman standing above him.

'Salman,' said Hassan, 'where am I?'

'Do you not recognise these halls?' asked Salman. 'I believe you once walked amongst them.'

'I do not understand,' said Hassan.

'You are in the Templar quarter of Acre,' said Salman, 'Turan-Shah has designated it as a hospital.'

'How long have I been here?'

'A few days. Your wound became infected, and you had a fever as hot as the desert. But it has broken, and your friend has told me that you will be back on your feet before the next moon.'

'What friend?'

Salman took a step to the side, and another person stepped into view.

'Hello Hassan,' said Sumeira, 'we meet again.'

A league to the east, Balian of Ibelin and Thomas Cronin rode slowly between two lines of Saracen warriors. Eventually, they reached a clearing where the Ayyubid had set up a canopy to provide shelter from the sun. Beneath the shelter sat Al-Afdal, and Gokbori, both waiting in silence as the Christians approached. Cronin and Balian dismounted and walked over to the tent.

'Al-Afdal ibn Salah ad-Din,' said Balian, 'Muzaffar ad-Din Gökböri, thank you for granting us an audience. We come in peace and are unarmed.'

'You are welcome,' said Al-Afdal, 'and whilst in my company, I grant you the protection of my father.' He indicated the two cushions opposite him. 'Please be seated.'

Balian glanced at Cronin before the two men lowered themselves to the ground.

'Is your father not coming?' asked Balian.

'He sends greetings but has other business to attend,' said Al-Afdal, 'but you can rest assured, I speak with his voice.'

'We appreciate the gesture,' said Balian, 'but what I have to say will need the approval of the sultan himself.'

Al-Afdal smiled without warmth.

'I think you overestimate your importance, Balian of Ibelin,' he said, 'you are a minor lord in an army of infidels. My father talks only to kings and emperors.

'Yet he talked to both of us at the surrender of Jerusalem,' said Cronin.

'Indeed he did,' interjected Gokbori, 'but if I recall, Guy of Lusignan was already languishing in chains in Damascus, and the Lord of Nablus was the commander of the Holy-city. Today is different as your king hides himself upon the Mount Toron like a frightened child. Had he the nerve to ride here himself, perhaps the sultan would have graced us with his presence. Say what you have to say, Christians, and be thankful that we have been instructed to let you live.'

Balian glanced at Cronin again before turning back to Saladin's son.

'Al-Afdal ibn Salah ad-Din,' he said eventually, 'as you know, a great many men died a few days ago, on both sides.'

'More Christians than Ayyubid,' interjected Gokbori.

'Perhaps,' said Balian, 'but there were also many captives taken, and we have many Ayyubid prisoners. We are here to offer you a trade, a prisoner exchange between both sides.'

Both Saracens stared at the Christians before Al-Afdal summoned one of the servants with a wave of his hand. The slave walked over and poured four goblets of water before walking backwards away from the meeting.

'Drink,' said Al-Afdal, picking up his goblet.

All four men sipped at the iced water before placing their goblets on the low table before them.

'Balian of Ibelin,' said Al-Afdal eventually, 'you are well known to us as a man of honour. You also have the respect of my father, and it is for that reason you are welcomed here. Yet you sit before me now and offer me a proposition designed to cloud my eyes to the real reason you are here.'

'What do you mean?' asked Balian nervously.

'I do not believe you are here to exchange prisoners,' said Al-Afdal, 'for their sacrifice will not affect the outcome of this war. I think you are using the opportunity to retrieve one man in particular.' He turned to stare at Cronin. 'I think you are here to gain the freedom of Gerard of Ridefort, lord and master of the knights of the blood cross.'

'I can assure you…' started Balian, but Cronin's hand shot out and grabbed him by the arm. Silence fell around the table until Cronin's grasp loosened and he turned to face Al-Afdal.

'Al-Afdal ibn Salah ad-Din,' he said eventually, 'like your father, you are an astute man and deserve better from us. Lord Balian told the truth when he requested a prisoner exchange, and that offer still stands. We hoped the man you peak of would be included in such an arrangement but appreciate the fact that his value is far greater than the other prisoners. With that in mind, we are happy to pay you a ransom for his release.

Al-Afdal nodded slightly, acknowledging the openness.

'Thank you,' he said, 'we may be at war, but I think things will go far better for all of us if we are at least truthful in such matters.'

'As do I,' said Cronin.

'With regards to your offer regarding prisoners,' said Al-Afdal, 'alas we are unable to meet your requirements as many of your men are already in chains and on their way to the slave markets. Their lives will be short and painful, but such is the way in war.'

'And the remainder?'

'I think we will keep them to dig our trenches and clean our latrines,' interjected Gokbori. 'Your request is denied.'

Cronin glanced at Balian before turning back to face Al-Afdal.

'And Gerard of Ridefort?'

'Ah, the grandmaster,' said Al-Afdal. 'As you know, my father released him from his imprisonment in return for a vow not to ride against the Ayyubid for a period of ten years. Yet within a few months, he broke his word and led an attack on our lines. Why should we grant such a man a second chance?'

'As you said earlier,' said Balian, 'this is war, and the Holy-land itself is at risk. He did what his conscience told him he should do.'

'At risk? sneered Gokbori. 'It may be at risk to you, Christian, but it is not at risk to us. It is our homeland, and even if it takes a thousand years, we will reclaim every speck of dust ever trodden by the infidels.'

'I meant no insult,' said Balian, 'I was only justifying why a man as honourable as the grandmaster would contemplate breaking such a vow. Whether you agree or not, he sees the Holy-city as belonging to the Christian faith and nothing else matters. Would you not also do the same if the situation were reversed?'

'The question is not relevant,' said Al-Afdal, 'for we are where we are. Your grandmaster chose to break his word and was subsequently captured in battle. He will not be returning with you to the camp of Guy of Lusignan.'

'Why would you be so hasty?' asked Balian. 'He is but one man yet you can name your price.'

'My father already arranged a price for his betrayal,' said Al-Afdal, 'one that has already been paid.'

'What do you mean?' asked Cronin, 'who paid the price?'

'Your grandmaster himself, 'said Al-Afdal, and turned to nod at a guard standing a few paces away. At the signal, the warrior bent down to retrieve something from a sack at his feet and walked forward to place it on the table between the four men. It was the head of Gerard of Ridefort.

Chapter Seventeen

Acre

June - AD 1190
Eight months later

Cronin rode his horse to the shoreline at the southern end of the Christian lines. A small fleet of ships had arrived from Tyre with desperately needed supplies, and Guy had sent him and a squadron of Templar sergeants to ensure there was order as they were unloaded. It had been a hard winter, with hunger and disease picking off the weak and the vulnerable. Every morning, burial details collected those who had died in the night to bury them in mass graves. The stench of death permeated the air, and the army was weak, but with troubles of his own, Saladin was either unable or unwilling to risk an all-out attack.

In Acre, an Egyptian fleet had managed to regain access to the harbour, but there was hardly enough to go around, and the pains of hunger were still a daily companion. The whole situation had gone quiet, and for weeks, hardly a weapon was drawn in anger. Everyone was just concentrating on getting through the winter alive.

Cronin reached the top of the sand dunes and looked along the shore. As far as he could see, the evidence of previous supply fleets lay abandoned along the water's edge, broken crates, empty sacks, and even the skeletal remains of an abandoned ship, its timbers now almost all gone to feed the fires in the freezing camp.

He turned his attention out to see and saw the six ships sent from Tyre, waiting at anchor. One had already sailed as far inshore as possible and had moored onto the temporary jetty.

All along the beach, groups of hungry people gathered to watch the unloading, each desperate to see what had arrived and edging closer by the minute.

Cronin assessed the situation before deploying his men in either direction to form a cordon around the landing area. Once secured, he turned his horse and headed for the jetty before dismounting and walking over to the soldier in command.

'How goes the unloading?' he asked to the man's back.
The soldier turned around and stared at the sergeant.

'Brother Cronin,' he said, breaking into a smile. 'I wondered if they would send you.'

'*Arturas,*' gasped Cronin, recognising the ex-mercenary, 'I thought you were dead.'

'Dead?' replied Arturas. 'Nah, I can't die, there is no place for me in either heaven or hell.' He held out his hand and took Cronin's wrist. 'It's good to see you, my friend, how are you?'

'Exhausted, hungry, aching and cold, but apart from that, absolutely perfect. You?'

'Much the same,' said Arturas. 'The cold is playing havoc with my leg, but that is to be expected.'

'Have you not thought of going back to Tyre?'

'And miss all this,' laughed Cronin, waving an arm towards the sprawling Christian camp, 'not a chance. There is money to be made here, my friend, despite the hardship and I, for one, intend to be rich by the time it all ends.'

'Once a mercenary always a mercenary,' sighed Cronin, 'but it does make me wonder about the decision to put you in charge of the supplies.'

'What are you insinuating?' gasped Arturas with a feigned look of shock upon his face. 'I am the personification of honesty; I'll have you know.'

'I'll believe you,' said Cronin, 'though there are thousands who may not share that view. Just don't let me catch you doing anything that you shouldn't.'

'Ask me no questions, my friend, and I'll tell you no lies.'

'So,' said, Cronin looking around, 'what do we have so far?'

'The first ship has just docked,' said Arturas, 'and we are expecting the ship's master any minute with the manifest.' He looked up. 'In fact, you are just in time. Here he comes now.'

Both men watched as the captain walked along the jetty, holding a rolled parchment.

'Who is in charge here?' he asked.

'I am,' said both men in unison before turning to look at each other in confusion.

'Well,' said the captain, 'who is it?'

Cronin turned back to the captain.

'My friend here is in charge of the unloading,' he said, 'while I am responsible for the security and distribution of the supplies. What have you got for us?'

'On this one,' said the captain, unfurling the scroll, 'mainly flour and a hundred barrels of dried fish. There are some other items on there as well, dates, dried fruit and a few dozen barrels of arrows, but it's all on here.' He handed over the scroll to Arturas.

'What about the other ships?' asked Cronin.

'More of the same, I think,' said the captain, 'I know one is full of livestock, and another carries reinforcements from Tyre.'

'What about that one?' asked Arturas, pointing at the ship furthest away, 'it doesn't look like it is strong enough to sail, let alone carry any cargo.'

'Aye, that one is on its last legs, so to speak, but we have rammed it full of timber and intend to beach it as soon as we have finished unloading.'

'That's a load of firewood,' said Arturas.

'Indeed,' said the captain, 'but the cargo is far more valuable than that. Conrad has sent three trebuchets ready for the next assault. They are in pieces but will take days only to reassemble.'

'A fortuitous addition,' said Cronin. 'Beach it a few hundred paces south, and I'll have our men transfer everything to the camp as soon as we can.'

'Right,' said the captain, 'if everything is fine with you, let's get started.' Without waiting for an answer, he turned away and returned to the ship.

'Get your men ready,' said Cronin, 'we have a long few days ahead of us and remember, I will be checking the cargo in detail against the manifest before taking it back to camp.'

'I would expect nothing less,' said Arturas with a laugh, and turned away to summon the waiting group of workers.

Inside the city, Sumeira waited in the market alongside Shani. In her hands, she held a promissory note for one of the traders who had recently used the cover of darkness to sail a ship full of supplies through the blockade. Several other purchasers also stood in line and beyond them, hundreds of starving civilians, each hoping to beg a coin or a crumb from those with plenty. Slowly the queue advanced until she reached the front and looked down at the man sat behind the table.

'Name,' he said, looking up.

'Sumeira of Greece,' she said.

'You are a westerner,' said the man with a sigh, 'and I do not deal with infidels. Next.'

'The food is not for me,' said Sumeira, 'it is for the hospital situated in the old Templar commandery. Barak el-Sayed said to mention his name and to give you this.' She held out the note which the trader took and read scrupulously before adding some notes on the bottom and handing it back to Sumeira.

'Tell my cousin,' he said, 'that I can supply only half of what he requires. Four barrels of dried fish, four of flour and two of meat.'

'It will have to do,' said Sumeira.

'And also tell him,' added the trader, 'that I would rather deal with someone who speaks our mother tongue, so next time, he should send someone else. Now take this over to the storage area and hand it to the overseer. He will give you what you need.' Without waiting for an answer, he turned his head away and called for the next in line.

Sumeira and Shani made their way over to the side of the market where hundreds of barrels were piled up against a wall. A small man faced away from her, writing on a parchment and she waited patiently until he was finished before speaking up.

'Excuse me, we are here to purchase supplies. I have the necessary documentation here…'

She stopped mid-sentence and stared in astonishment as the man turned around. It looked like Fakhiri the cart-master; the Egyptian who had helped her rescue her son a few years earlier. For a few seconds there was silence, but before Sumeira could speak, the Egyptian snapped at her, cutting short any chance of conversation.

'Well,' he snapped, 'are you going to give me the scroll or not?'

Without waiting for an answer, the man snatched the document and turned away.

'Do you know him?' asked Shani quietly.

'I do,' said Sumeira, 'or at least, I think I do. The man I am thinking of was murdered by a slave trader a few years ago. I even saw his severed head upon the sand.'

'In that case, you must be mistaken,' said Shani, 'for that man's head is still firmly attached to his neck.'

'But he looks exactly the same,' said Sumeira, 'and I swear I saw a look of recognition in his eyes.'

'Even if you did,' said Shani, 'it's obvious he doesn't want to talk with you. Remember, these are dangerous times, and you are a Christian within a city of Muslims. Perhaps he is wary of showing a connection.'

'Maybe,' said Sumeira, 'but I need to talk with him.'

They stopped talking as the Egyptian turned back around to face them.

'Do you have a cart?' asked Fakhiri, this time without the slightest hint of recognition.

'We do not,' said Shani, 'but have the means of paying for the goods to be delivered.'

'It will cost you a silver penny,' said Fakhiri, making a mark on the parchment before looking back into Sumeira's eyes. 'Where should I take it?'

'To the old Templar commandery,' said Sumeira.

'And is that where you live?'

'It is.'

'Then your purchase will be there tomorrow at last light. I will bring the barrels myself.' Without another word, he turned and walked away, leaving Sumeira and Shani staring after him.

'That was strange,' said Shani, 'what trader personally delivers the items when he has an army of beggars desperate for work?'

'The sort that wants privacy,' said Sumeira with a hint of excitement in her voice. 'That was definitely Fakhiri, Shani, and I think he wants to see me in private.'

The following day, to the south of the city, Cronin walked amongst the piles of stores situated along the shore. Hundreds of barrels, crates and sacks lay undisturbed on the beach, and dozens of Templar sergeants guarded it from the many hungry people watching from the dunes. The ship carrying the trebuchets had already been beached and was now swarming with men stripping it of anything that could be put to use. Within days there would be no trace of it ever having existed as every last piece was salvaged to be used for shelters, weapons and fuel.

Five of the ships had already been emptied, and the last was now tethered to the makeshift quay, allowing the troops to disembark before they unloaded the livestock. The resupply was desperately needed, but they knew that far more would be required.

'Cronin,' called a voice, 'look who I found.'

The sergeant turned to see Arturas limping towards him alongside someone he hadn't seen since he had been in Karak castle a few years earlier.

'Hunter,' he said with a grin and walked over to take the scout's forearm in friendship.

'Cronin,' replied Hunter, 'you must be harder to kill than the devil himself. How are you?'

'As well as can be expected,' said Cronin. 'Where have you come from?'

'I found him stowed away amongst the ale barrels,' said Arturas. 'Some men have no shame.'

'I did no such thing,' laughed Hunter, 'I sought passage back in Tyre, and here I am, ready to play my part.'

'You enlisted?' asked Cronin.

'No, for I did not want to be tied down to one master. I bought passage and am free to serve whoever I see fit. I just need to retrieve my horse and find somewhere to sleep.'

'There is much to talk about,' said Cronin. 'I have almost finished here for the day, so why don't you find me later and share some food. There's not much, but we can catch up, and there is a spare tent you can use.'

'Where's your camp?' asked Hunter.

'On the northern quarter of the siege lines. Just ask for me, and someone will point the way. You too, Arturas.'

'I'll see you both there,' said Hunter and turned away to return to the quay.

Later that evening, Hunter handed the reins of his horse to a Templar squire and removed his pack from the back of the saddle. After finding out where he could find Thomas Cronin, he followed a line of weather-worn tents to the far end where he could see several pitched amongst a rocky outcrop. As he approached, one of the Templar chaplains walked towards him.

'Can I help you, friend?' he asked

'I'm looking for Brother Cronin,' said Hunter. 'I believe he is stationed somewhere around here.'

'Indeed he is,' said the chaplain. He pointed to a tent set up against the rocks.

'Thank you,' said Hunter and walked over to the tent. He dropped his pack on the floor and slapped his hand against the oiled linen tent

'Thomas Cronin,' he called, 'are you in there.'

'I am,' came the answer, 'come in.'

Hunter ducked through the flap, and into the gloomy interior where Cronin sat on a makeshift bed, applying a layer of goose-fat to a leather cloak. At the centre of the tent, a small fire glowed under a blackened pot hanging from a tripod.

'Hunter,' said Cronin, putting the cloak to one side and getting to his feet. 'You found me.'

'It seems so,' said Hunter looking around the tent. 'So, this is your home. I have always wondered about how the Templars live.'

'Oh, this is luxury compared to life in a commandery,' laughed Cronin. 'Back there, we have sparse rooms and fixed meal-times. Out here, life can be very difficult so we are allowed to fare the best we can with whatever we have, as long as we observe prayers at the appropriate time.'

Hunter walked over to the fire and looked inside the pot.

'Something smells good,' he said, 'is that meat in there?'

'Aye, I managed to buy a piece of horse-flesh from one of the traders in the camp. It cost me a fortune, but meat is scarce, and I wanted to make you welcome.'

Hunter looked up with surprise.

'You prepared this for me?'

'Not just you,' said Cronin, 'for there are three of us that share this tent, and anything we manage to obtain is divided equally.'

'Where are they?' asked Hunter looking around the tent at the six cots.

'Alas we recently lost two to illness,' said Cronin, 'and one was killed on patrol. The other two have duties elsewhere for a few hours, but I will put their share to one side.'

'Hello in there,' shouted a voice from outside the tent, 'anyone at home?'

Before anyone could answer, Arturas ducked into the tent carrying a water-flask.

'Arturas,' said Cronin, 'perfect timing as usual, we were just talking about food. Are you hungry?'

'Always,' said Arturas, 'and here, I've brought ale.' He handed the flask to Cronin and walked over to sit on one of the stools at a makeshift table.

Cronin looked at the flask in his hand, wondering where the ex-mercenary had obtained such a valued item, but knew he was better off not asking. He placed the flask on the table and rounded up three jacks from around the tent as Hunter joined Arturas.

'So,' said Arturas, looking at Hunter, 'what are you doing here? The last time we met, you were returning to Karak to get your family.'

'I was,' said Hunter, 'but on the way back, we ran into some trouble.'

'What sort of trouble?'

'Wait until Cronin joins us,' said Hunter, 'and I'll tell you everything.'

Several minutes later, all three men were sat at the table, ladling spoons of hot broth into their mouths and braking handfuls of bread from a loaf.

'Do you always eat as good as this?' mumbled Arturas through a mouth full of food.

'Not really,' said Cronin. 'The bread comes from the Templar kitchen tents, as does the broth, but I added the meat earlier.'

'I'll have to come more often,' said Arturas, delving deeper into his bowl.

'So,' said Cronin, turning to Hunter, 'I heard you say something about trouble. What happened, is your family alright?'

'As far as I know,' said Hunter. 'We managed to escape Karak and head for the Salt-sea, but while we were there, my wife and children were captured by a Saracen patrol. I think they were taken to Jerusalem but can't be sure.'

'Did you not follow them?'

'I could not, I still had John-Loxley and his daughter with me.'

'Sumeira's family?' said Cronin with surprise.

'Aye. I persuaded them to come with us to Tyre, but yet again I have let Sumeira down.'

'Why, are they not safe?'

'They are. I took them to Tyre, but her son was also taken by the patrol so finds himself once more a captive. I intended to ride to Jerusalem to search for them, but the countryside is swarming with Saracen patrols, and I would get nowhere near.'

'Even if you did,' said Cronin, 'I can't see how you would even get inside, let alone go unnoticed.'

'Aye, it is a problem,' said Hunter, 'and that is why I came here. I reasoned that the only way to get anywhere near Jerusalem was with Guy's army after he takes Acre.'

Arturas let out a laugh, spurting a shower of ale over the table.

'Did I say something funny?' asked Hunter.

'Aye, you did,' said Arturas wiping the spittle from his mouth. 'I find it amusing that you think Guy of Lusignan is even capable of securing his own saddle, let alone recapturing Jerusalem.'

'Do you not think he will prevail?'

'Look,' said Arturas, placing his jack of ale on the table. 'I know he has a huge army at his disposal, but the man is an imbecile, and as long as he is in charge, the Saracens in Jerusalem can sleep sweetly in their beds knowing they are safe.'

'Is he truly that bad?' asked Hunter turning towards Cronin.

'He means well,' sighed Cronin pouring himself another ale, 'but he swings from hesitancy to impatience, and never seems to have a thought-out plan.'

'Plan?' laughed Arturas, 'he has no idea what one would look like. He has gathered an enormous army to surround Acre, yet our men are perishing for want of food. In my opinion, they would be better off dying on the siege ladders than starving to death.'

'Do not the other commanders have any input?'

'They try,' said Cronin, 'but Guy is fiercely protective of his status, and pay few any heed, especially Conrad.'

'Have they not made a truce regarding the claim to the throne?'

'In a way, yes.'

'When?' asked Arturas looking up. 'I know nothing of this.'

'A few weeks ago,' said Cronin. 'Conrad agreed to recognise Guy as the king, and in return, will govern Tyre, Sidon and Beirut when all this is over. That's why he returned to Tyre, to arrange the resupply convoy we just unloaded.'

'Ha,' snorted Arturas again, 'more men to starve behind the palisades. What a great plan.'

'Actually,' said Hunter, 'it may not matter whether Conrad can recruit more men, for I believe things are about to change greatly.'

'What do you mean?' asked Cronin.

'First of all,' said Hunter, 'Barbarossa and his army are only a few months away, but more importantly, the kings of France and England have ended their feud and have agreed to bring their huge armies to help regain Jerusalem.'

'I have heard such nonsense before,' said Arturas,' and even if you are correct, their arrival could be years away.'

'On the contrary,' said Hunter, 'there are reports that Richard has already sent a great fleet into the Mediterranean Sea. In fact, the last I heard is that they have already raided some Muslim ports in Iberia. Most of his army is already on their way and will take ship in Marseilles.'

'And Phillip?' asked Cronin

'I'm not so sure about him,' said Hunter, 'but I do know that he is also on his way. With Barbarossa's army, that is three huge forces all destined to be here within months, and when they do arrive, there is no way Acre can withstand their combined strength.'

'And your intentions?'

'As soon as Acre falls, I suspect the combined armies will march on Jerusalem, and when they do, I will be in the vanguard.'

'Let's hope you are correct,' said Arturas reaching for the flask, 'another few months in this stinking hellhole is going to make me as mad as a March hare.'

'I suspect we are too late to prevent that,' said Hunter, and both he and Cronin burst into laughter at the hurt look on the mercenary's face.

'Drink,' he said eventually, holding up his jack, 'for who knows when we will next have the chance.'

'So,' said Hunter as Arturas refilled the jacks. 'What about you, Cronin? What has been happening in Acre in my absence?'

'We have attacked the city a few times,' said Cronin, 'with little success as you can see, but when Saladin brought his main army to face us further out, he effectively split our forces in half by forcing us to face in both directions. There have been a few sorties against them, and one full-scale attack, but neither achieved anything except adding to the body count. Now we are at a stalemate until the reinforcements arrive.'

'I hear your grandmaster was killed?'

'Aye, he was. Executed for breaking a vow he gave to Saladin. Alas, he was re-captured, and Saladin made him pay the price.'

'What about supplies?'

'The Saracens control all the routes inland, as well as the coastal roads in both directions. Recently their Egyptian fleet controlled all the sea routes, but we now have our own to protect any are gaining control of the approaches.'

'So, the city is isolated?'

'Not really, they still receive supplies from Egypt. It seems the two fleets often give each other a wide berth and supplies creep in from both sides.'

'So, everything has ground to a halt?'

'It has. The supplies from Tyre may make a difference, but who knows?'

The three comrades drank deep into the night, briefly forgetting their problems, but though they were optimistic about a quick end to the siege, each was blissfully unaware of the hardship that still lay before them.

Inside the city, Sumeira sat alongside a bucket of hot water, stirring a bundle of washed bandages with an iron ladle. Her hair was a mess, and she had to keep pushing it to one side with the back of her hand. The day had been long, and she desperately needed sleep, but she still had to see what she could get from the kitchens to feed the prisoners.

The hospital was half-empty now. Some of the patients had healed and returned to their posts in the city garrison while others hadn't been so lucky and had succumbed to their wounds or infection. Only those with serious injuries still remained, the ones with shattered bones or severed limbs. One had received a serious head wound and just lay in his cot; his mind lost to the world. But Sumeira never gave up and talked to him every day in the hope of reaching him.

Sometimes she thought about Hassan. He had caught a serious infection from the wound in his side and had been at the hospital for three weeks while she fought to save his life, and though he eventually recovered, he didn't once acknowledge her in any way. When he had healed, he left the hospital in the middle of the night and she had not seen him since.

Across the courtyard, one of the guards opened a hatch and talked to someone outside before pulling back a locking bar and opening the gate.

Two men walked through, pulling a hand cart containing several small barrels. The guard closed the gates and talked to one of the men before walking over to Sumeira.

'These men have supplies for the hospital,' he said, 'but need to speak to you about the promissory note.'

'The note?' said Sumeira getting to her feet. 'Is there a problem?

'You will have to speak to him,' said the guard.

Sumeira followed the guard back to the cart. Instantly she could see that one of the men was Fakhiri.

'What's the problem?' she asked.

'There was confusion over the barrels,' said Fakhiri. 'The jailer requested eight, but we could only supply four. My master has since found another two for his cousin, but the note needs altering.'

'I can do that,' said Sumeira, 'for I was authorised to buy eight. Come with me and I will sign the note.'

'Where are you going?' snapped the guard.

'To the hospital,' said Sumeira, 'I will need to read the parchment thoroughly to make sure Barak gets what he has paid for, and it is too dark out here.'

The guard nodded and turned back to look over the cart's contents.

Sumeira and Fakhiri walked through the door into the corridor of the old chapel. As soon as they were out of sight, the physician spun around to face the cart-master.

'Fakhiri, it is you,' she gasped, 'I knew it.'

'Of course it is me,' said Fakhiri.

'But I thought you were dead. I even saw your head.'

'It was the head of my brother,' said Fakhiri. 'Fawzi's men killed the wrong man.'

'I am so sorry,' said Sumeira.

'What is done is done,' said Fakhiri, 'and Fawzi has paid the price. But now we must concentrate on you. I have been searching for you since you disappeared but only found out you were being held here just before Guy's army arrived.'

'That was months ago,' said Sumeira, 'why didn't you come sooner?'

'I didn't expect the siege to last so long,' said Fakhiri, 'and there is no way we can escape the city, so I had to bide my time. I saw you a few times in the market but kept my distance so I did not give you false hope.'

'Yet now you are here. Do you have a plan?'

'Not yet, but after you saw me in the market, I knew I would have to come and explain my manner. I had to pretend I did not know you for both our sakes.'

'I understand,' said Sumeira, 'but what now?'

'I have gained the trust of an important merchant, and there is talk of sending me to Egypt to secure cargo. If that comes to be then perhaps I can smuggle you aboard. It will be risky, but once in Egypt, we can flee the ship and hide in Alexandria before getting you back to Tyre.'

Sumeira's face fell a little as she stared at her friend.

'What's the matter?' he asked, 'is it too dangerous?'

'It's not that,' said Sumeira, 'I would gladly take the risk. '

'Then what is the problem?'

'There are others here,' said Sumeira, 'Christian prisoners and their welfare is in my hands. I can hardly keep them alive as it is, but if I were to flee now, they would certainly die at the hands of the jailer.'

Fakhiri stared at the woman with frustration.

'My lady,' he said, 'I have searched for you for a long time. Many think you are dead, but I never gave up hope. Now you have a chance to be reunited with your family, but to do so, there will have to be sacrifices. You do not know these men and owe them nothing. This city will fall one way or another, and when it does, I don't expect the Saracens to be merciful to any Christian prisoners. If you do not come now, there may never be another chance.'

'Fakhiri,' said Sumeira taking his hands in hers, 'I appreciate everything you have done, I really do, and I am desperate to see my family again, but I cannot condemn these men to die. If I were to escape, Barak would torture them to death, and I cannot have that on my conscience. Perhaps there is a way we could help them too?'

'How many are there?'

'There were fifty, but there are less than half that now.'

'That is still too many,' said Fakhiri, 'I would never be able to get them out without being discovered.'

'Then I cannot leave,' said Sumeira. 'I have to stay for their sakes.'

Fakhiri let out a deep sigh and stared at the woman.

'I do not agree,' he said, 'but I understand. Let me give it some thought, but in the meantime, I will stay in touch.'

'What's going on in there?' shouted the guard from outside.

'I have to go,' said Fakhiri, 'but first, I must give you this.' He produced two leather bags from beneath his cloak and put them on the floor behind the door.

'What is it?' asked Sumeira.

'Food,' said Fakhiri. 'It's not much, but there will be more, I promise.'

'Thank you, Fakhiri,' said Sumeira, 'you are a true friend.'

'There are many hurdles to overcome,' said Fakhiri, 'but I swear, I will do whatever I can to get you out of here. Now, I should go.'

He turned and walked out into the darkness.

'Well,' asked the guard, 'do we unload the cart or not?'

'Aye,' said Fakhiri, 'everything is in order.'

'Take the barrels over to the kitchens,' said the guard, 'I'm not touching them, they stink of fish.'

Fakhiri nodded, and with a final glance towards Sumeira, lifted one of the handles to pull the cart away.

Sumeira watched him go before walking back to the hospital. Her heart was racing for after over almost two years of captivity, there was the slightest sliver of hope.

Chapter Eighteen

Tyre

July - AD 1190

Conrad of Montferrat sat in a hall, surrounded by his advisers. Although his attendance at Acre was intermittent, he still supported the siege by supplying men, arms and supplies whenever he was confident of getting his ships past the ever-present Egyptian fleet. The men surrounding him were the nobles of Tyre who had not gone with the army he had sent and were now busy organising the logistics needed to keep their men at Acre alive. The audience was coming to an end when one of the servants opened the door and walked up to the group of men.

'My lord,' he announced, 'Balian of Ibelin has arrived, and begs an urgent audience.'

Conrad looked around the room.

'Gentlemen,' he said, 'as you can see, my presence is required elsewhere. If there is nothing that will not wait until the morrow, I bid you a good day.'

The men mumbled their agreement and left the room, leaving Conrad and his first knight behind them. Sancho-martin walked over to a table and poured two goblets of watered wine.

'I wonder what he wants,' he said over his shoulder.

'Perhaps Acre has fallen,' said the count, 'and he brings me the news himself.'

'From your lips to God's ears,' said the knight, and brought the two goblets over to where Conrad was sitting. A few minutes later, the doors opened again, and Balian strode in, still wearing his riding cloak.

'Balian,' said the count, seeing the dust of the road covering his clothing, 'your appearance tells me you rode here from Acre. Tell me you did no such foolhardy thing.'

'Indeed I did,' said Balian, 'for what I have to say will wait for no tide or ship.'

'And you met with no resistance from Saladin's men?'

'There was a minor skirmish, but my men distracted them while I ploughed on.'

'Please, sit,' said Conrad indicating one of the several chairs lined up against the walls.

Balian dragged over a chair while Sancho-martin brought him a goblet.

Balian drunk the wine in one draft before handing the goblet back to the knight.

'Another?' asked Sancho-martin

'Please,' said Balian, 'my mouth is as dry as the Negev.'

The Green knight refilled the goblet, and both men of Tyre waited patiently as Balian slaked his thirst.

'So,' said Conrad eventually, 'what is this news that is so important, you risked your life to bring it to me? Please tell me that Acre has fallen.'

'No, it has not,' said Balian, 'and the city stands firm against everything we throw against it, but the news I bring is far more important than the fall of any city.' He looked between the two men before turning his attention back to Conrad. 'My lord,' he said, 'Sibylla, Queen of Jerusalem is dead.'

'What?' gasped Conrad sitting back in his chair. 'Are you sure?'

'I am, my lord. She died yesterday, and I rode here as quickly as I could to bring you the news.'

'What happened?' asked the count. 'Was the camp attacked?'

'Not at all,' she succumbed to the disease that is rampant throughout our positions. What is more, she follows her daughters to the gates of heaven.'

'Her daughters are also dead?' gasped Conrad.

'They are. They also died from the disease. I had arranged to send you a message, but the death of Sibylla changes everything, and I thought you should know as soon as possible.'

'How has Guy taken this news?'

'He is distraught, as you can imagine, but his resolve to capture Acre has not weakened. If anything, there is new steel in his gaze.'

'To lose a wife and children in so short a time would affect any man,' said Conrad, 'even a king.'

'And that leads us on to something far more significant,' said Balian, 'and the main reason I rode here to see you in person.' He looked between the two men before stating what was already forming in Conrad's mind. 'With Sibylla and her heirs dead, can Guy of Lusignan still claim the title of King of Jerusalem?'

Later that evening, all three men sat around a table picking on cold meats and sipping wine. Joining them was the Bishop of Pisa who had arrived at Tyre just a few days earlier.

'So,' said the bishop, 'the facts as I see them are these. Sibylla was crowned as the Queen of Jerusalem in a vote of the Haute Cour, but Guy of Lusignan only gained the crown by marrying her in a ceremony that was opposed by at least half of the council.'

'That is correct,' said Balian. 'I was there, and it was an unpopular union to say the least. He is seen as a weak king and his defeat at Hattin has divided the Outremer as to his suitability to rule. Even now, his continued failure to take Acre casts doubts into the hearts of every man who bears arms on behalf of Jerusalem.'

'That's as may be,' said the bishop, 'but we cannot make decisions on feelings and loyalties. If you want the church involved, we have to deal with facts. Now, tell me about the children that Guy and Sibylla had together.'

'There were only two,' said Balian, 'both girls.'

'The sex of the children is immaterial,' said the bishop, 'I just want to be clear about any succession.'

'The two girls were called Alice and Maria, but they both died a few days ago.'

'And there were no others?'

'No, your Grace, her only other child, Baldwin V of Jerusalem, died a few years ago not long after being crowned king. She leaves no other heir to the throne.'

'So Guy's claim is purely through marriage?'

'A tenuous claim,' said Conrad, 'and in my opinion, one that leaves the unity of Jerusalem in tatters should it go unchallenged.'

'And you wish to claim the throne for yourself?'

'I do, but I also concede that I have no claim by right. This would mean that the throne once again needs to be awarded by the Haute Cour, or in this case, by the assembled Kings of Europe when they all arrive, and I am happy to stand before them to state my case.'

The bishop sat back and stared into his goblet for a few minutes as silence filled the room. Balian and Conrad glanced at each other nervously waiting for the bishop to respond. If Conrad's audacious plan were to succeed, they would need someone of his stature to be on their side.

'Tell me,' said the bishop, suddenly raising his head. 'Who else may have a claim outside of any descendants that Sibylla may have had?'

'Well I suppose Isabella may have a claim,' said Balian, 'she stood against Sibylla when Baldwin died.'

'Do you think she will make a counterclaim?'

'Who knows?' said Balian with a shrug.

'And what of you, Conrad,' asked the bishop turning to the count, 'do you have a wife?'

'There is a woman in Constantinople,' said Conrad, 'but I have not bedded her or even talked to her in many years. For all I know she is already dead.'

The bishop nodded before standing up.

'I think I have all I need,' he said, 'and will give the situation some thought overnight. Let us re-convene tomorrow when I will furnish you with my decision.'

Without waiting for an answer, he walked from the room, leaving the three men staring at his back.

'Well,' said Conrad, 'what do you think?'

'It could go either way,' said Balian, 'but one thing is certain, we need him on our side.'

'There are other bishops.'

'Aye, but this one has the ear of the pope himself.'

'Let's get some sleep,' said Conrad, 'it has been a long day.'

The following morning, all three men met again, this time in Conrad's quarters. The count stood at the window staring out over the city rooftops to the sea while Balian paced the room, nervous about what was about to happen. Eventually, the bishop entered and strode over to a table to lay out a parchment before him. All the other occupants turned to face him.

'Gentlemen,' said the bishop looking up, 'I have given this matter great thought and have come to a decision. It seems to me, and therefore in the eyes of the church, that in these tragic circumstances, Guy's claim to the throne is at the very least, tenuous. Therefore, I am happy to support a challenge to his status.'

Conrad gasped in relief as Balian turned to the count with a smile growing on his face.

'However,' interjected the bishop before any man could speak, 'it is also clear to me that any claim by you, Conrad of Montferrat, is also tenuous and may not gather the support needed to oust a sitting king. Luckily, there are measures we can take to strengthen that claim to ensure you get all the support you need.'

'What are these measures?' asked Conrad.

'It is quite simple,' said the bishop. 'As far as I can see, there is only one other legitimate claim to the throne, and that is from Isabella. What we need is for her to be your wife.'

'But Isabella is already married to Humphrey of Toron.'

'Indeed she is, so we will just have to get her unmarried.'

'And how do we do that? She is fond of him, and it is well known he treats her well.'

'Unless I am mistaken,' replied the bishop, 'I have heard that his gentleness borders on the feminine side. Is this not correct?'

'He is certainly flamboyant in his manner and dress,' said Sancho-martin, 'and the men have many laughs about his masculinity, but I cannot see how that will help.'

'Well,' said the bishop, 'what if someone was to have a private conversation with him about his *alleged* bed preferences? What if he was told there were witnesses threatening to take their accusations to the ears of the holy father himself? Do you not think he may be amenable to stepping aside for the sake of Jerusalem, and in return for a pledge that all such statements would be withdrawn?'

'Are there such witnesses?' asked Balian.

'I do not know,' said the bishop, 'or indeed care. The mere threat of such a thing should be enough. If he is innocent, let him protest, but I suspect he would accept annulment to stop any accusations in its tracks, irrespective of accuracy. When he does, Conrad must marry Isabella with all haste. With both houses united, I see no way any counsel can refute the claim.'

Conrad looked towards Balian.

'What do you think?'

'I feel uncomfortable about the subterfuge, but as the future of Jerusalem is at risk, I think the bishop lays a clear path before you, one that I think you should take with all urgency.'

'And you, Sir Martin?' asked Conrad, turning to the green knight.

'I agree,' said the knight. 'Jerusalem needs a strong king, and there is nobody in the Outremer who has the strength or the ability of you. Pursue your path, my lord, and I will ride at your side avowed to defend your claim to the death.'

Conrad turned to the bishop.

'What about the woman in Constantinople?'

'Leave her to me,' said the bishop. 'All I need from you is the go-ahead, and I will start the process. If God is willing, you can be married to Isabella within months.'

'In that case,' said Conrad, 'do what you have to do. Christendom needs Jerusalem back at its heart, and if I am king, I swear I will recover the city in the name of God or die trying.'

'Amen,' said the bishop.

Chapter Nineteen

Acre

February - AD 1191

The winter months had been particularly hard for the Christians surrounding Acre. Food was scarce, and disease rampaged throughout the camp, devastating the besiegers. The arrival of so many reinforcements, once heralded as a gift from God, was now seen as a curse due to the number of extra mouths to feed. Many starved, forced to scavenge whatever they could, and though the occasional ship managed to land supplies on the beach, it was nowhere near enough, and only those picked by the king benefitted.

The poorest resorted to eating grass in desperation and even the flesh of the dead was not considered a sin to some, always consumed under cover of darkness. Corpses went unburied and poisoned the air with their stench, rats became a valuable trade item, and a horse was worth more dead than alive. The situation was dire, and many men deserted to the enemy after being promised food and shelter.

Inside the city, the situation was no less problematic, and again, hunger and disease worked hand in hand to bring the population to its knees. The garrison of Egyptians suffered just as badly, and their numbers were only a quarter of those that had once ridden so proudly into the city.

Turan-Shah and Salman stood atop the Accursed-Tower on the north-eastern corner of the city, staring out at the Christian positions a few hundred paces away. The sun was setting, and the amongst the smoke of the many campfires they could see individuals walking slowly through the sprawling camp, each wrapped in blankets against the cold as they continued the endless search for food. The smell from the corpses wafted towards the tower, but it was hardly noticed due to the stench of their own dead piled just within the city walls.

'Why do they not attack?' asked Turan-Shah. 'Surely they must know we have suffered many deaths.'

'I suspect they are just as weakened as us,' said Salman, 'and are waiting for the warmer weather so the supply ships can get through.'

'If that happens,' said Turan-Shah, 'then we are destined to lose this battle. We cannot hold out much longer without reinforcements.'

The two men continued to stare out at the Christian camp, both devoid of ideas on how to ease their plight.

'My lord,' said one of the guards, 'look.'

In the distance, they could just about make out four horsemen galloping from the Saracen lines directly towards the northernmost Christian defences.

'Who are they?' asked Turan-Shah.

'I don't know,' said the guard, 'but it looks like they are headed straight for the Templar lines.'

All three stared at the riders. They were getting closer every second, yet still no Christians had raised the alarm.

'What is happening?' asked Turan-Shah, 'why have they not been attacked?'

'I do not think they have been seen,' said Salman, 'they are in a fold in the ground. We can only see them because we are higher up.'

'But why are they attacking the enemy lines with so few men, they will be dead in moments?'

'I don't think they are attacking,' said Salman, 'I believe they are headed for the northern gate.'

'Messengers,' gasped Turan-Shah, and turned to call down to one of his men in the courtyard behind him. 'Sound the alarm,' he shouted, 'and open the gate. We have riders approaching.' He turned to the other guard. 'Alert our archers on the north wall. Tell them to do whatever they can to keep any Christians away.'

He turned back to watch as the Saracen riders got closer to the enemy camp. Within seconds, they broke cover and galloped directly at the nearest palisade. Many of the sentries were so tired that they failed to see the threat, and by the time the alarm was sounded, the four horses had sailed over the first palisades to gallop on towards the city walls.

Over the months the camp had grown much larger, and the Saracen horsemen found themselves riding amongst a village of tents and panicking people.

Crossbow bolts flew through the air, and two of the horses fell to the ground, screaming in pain. Templar sergeants fell upon the riders and dispatched them in short order, but two more continued the charge.

'*Kill them,*' roared a voice and another volley of bolts shot through the darkening sky.

Templar knights ran after them, and when the last horse fell, thought they had killed them all.

For a moment, Turan-Shah stared in horror, realising that whatever their mission had been, he would now never know.

'Close the gates,' he said quietly.

'Wait,' said Salman, 'look.'

Both men stared down and saw the last rider struggle to his feet before staggering onwards towards the northern gate.

'*He is alive,*' gasped Turan-Shah, '*somebody help him.*'

Men ran from the gate towards the injured messenger.

'*Cover them,*' roared Salman, and immediately the night sky filled with Saracen arrows, each headed towards the pursuing Christians. Most fell short, but without their armour, the Templars knew they were running towards certain death. Most pulled up and just stared after their quarry, but one kept running, risking the hail of iron-tipped death that was falling all around him.

'*He is going to reach him,*' shouted Turan-Shah, 'are my archers so useless that they cannot hit one running man?'

'Who is that?' asked a guard, and all heads turned to see a lone figure running out of the shadows at the base of the city walls.

'I have no idea,' said Salman, 'but he wears the black of a Bedouin.'

As they watched, the interloper suddenly came to a stop and notched an arrow into his bow. An arrow sped through the evening air to pierce the pursuing Templar's throat, and the knight fell to the ground, his hands clawing at his neck. Quickly, the Bedouin got to his feet and ran to help the fleeing messenger. Seconds later, the men from the city reached them both and ushered them through the city gates to safety.

'*Lock the gates,*' shouted Turan-Shah, as the first of a mangonel retaliatory strike smashed into the city walls, 'and bring the messenger to me. Bring the Bedouin too, I want to talk to the man who put my best archers to shame.'

Ten minutes later, Turan-Shah stood in the empty dining hall. The doors opened, and one of the guards brought in the messenger. The newcomer had his arm strapped tightly across his chest, and his face was bloody from the fall.

The messenger dropped to his knees and kissed the ground before the Yemeni prince.

'My lord,' he said, 'I have news from Salah ad-Din himself. He said that at midnight tomorrow, you are to send your men against the Christian lines nearest the northern gate.'

'Attack the Templars?' asked Turan-Shah, 'but why? Does he not know we have hardly any horsemen left? If I attack the Christian lines, we will lose the last of them.'

'It is for a diversion only,' said the messenger. 'While you keep the infidels busy, the sultan will send a strong force down the northern coastal path to reinforce the city.'

'The northern road is protected by Christian defences,' said the guard. 'They would be seen before they got anywhere.'

'There will be no defences,' said the messenger, 'at least not at that time.'

'Why not?'

'Because they will all be dead, killed by men of the same faith.'

'What do you mean?'

'Hundreds of Christians have deserted to our side,' said the messenger. 'Many now fight for Salah ad-Din in return for silver and gold.'

'Mercenaries?' asked Turan-Shah

'I believe so,' said the messenger. 'Tomorrow night, they will approach the Christian northern defences and seek shelter, claiming they are a patrol sent from Tyre. Once the camp settles for the night, they will kill as many as possible before sending a signal. When that signal is received, our warriors will ride along the coastal road and into the city. Even as we speak, there are almost a thousand waiting to join you.'

'And that is why we need to attack the Christians,' said Turan-Shah, 'to protect their flanks.'

The messenger nodded in silence.

'So, be it,' said the prince. 'Is there anything else?'

'No, my lord.'

'In that case, get someone to take you to the hospital to set your broken arm. Thank you, my friend, your bravery might just have saved this city.'

'*Allah Akbar,*' said the messenger with a bow before turning and leaving the room. On the way out, he passed Salman on his way in with a worried look upon his face.

'Salman,' said Turan-Shah, looking up. 'Have you brought the Bedouin?'

'I have not, my lord.'

'Why not, did I not make my instructions clear?'

'You did, my lord, but as the gates were closed, the Bedouin fled into the side streets, and could not be caught.'

'Why would he do that? His actions saved the messenger's life, and I would have made sure he was greatly rewarded?'

'I don't know,' said Salman, 'but there is something else you should be aware of, something even more strange.'

'And that is?'

'The Bedouin, my lord. It was not a man; it was a woman.'

The following night, the remainder of Turan-Shah's cavalry lined up just inside the northern gate, accompanied once again by Hassan Malouf, now fully recovered from his wounds. Up on the forbidden tower, all eyes stared northward, looking for the signal. Suddenly, in the distance, a flaming arrow soared skyward leaving a fleeting trail of light behind it like a distant shooting star.

'There it is,' said Turan-Shah, 'open the gates.'

Down below, the cavalry poured out through the defensive walls and turned inland to attack the Christian lines. Almost immediately, the sound of horns filled the air, and defenders ran to their positions, but it was too late, and the Saracen cavalry rode amongst them, creating as much havoc as they could.

Pots of flammable oil shattered amongst the tents, followed by fiery torches. Flames spread everywhere, and as people panicked, the riders pressed through the camp to the open ground beyond. Templars and foot-soldiers alike donned their armour as quickly as they could and faced inland as the Saracen riders re-organised for another attack.

This time, the Saracens sent volleys of arrows into the camp causing further chaos, but the Templars had refocussed, and as half ran to their horses to pursue the Saracens, the rest marched out of the defensive positions in a straight line, protected from the hail of arrows with their shields.

The cavalry officer looked around, knowing they had no chance against the Templar force, but they had to maintain their attention, and could not flee towards the main Saracen army.

'The night is dark he called to his men, and confusion is our ally. Head back into their lines.' As one, the Saracens spurred their horses and galloped towards the oncoming knights. The narrow point of attack rendered the Templar extended line impotent, and despite losing a few riders, the Saracens burst through the line, and back into the Christian defensive positions.

The Templar knights turned inward in confusion; their enemy lost in the darkness. Amongst the tents and makeshift huts, screams of fear and pain once more echoed through the night as the horsemen rendered death and destruction upon anyone within reach.

Another horn rent the air, this time from the city walls and Hassan pulled hard on the reins, turning his horse towards the city. As he broke free from the Christian lines, he saw several more of the Egyptian cavalry also heading for safety, and the tail-end of an Ayyubid relief column galloping through the city gates.

He rode his horse through the wall, and as the last of the original riders followed him through, the giant gates slammed shut behind them. All around him, men and horses were rammed in amongst the narrow streets. Each Ayyubid rider also led a packhorse piled high with supplies and Hassan could see immediately, their arrival was going to make a massive difference.

'Hassan,' called a voice, and the Bedouin looked up to see Salman peering over a parapet.

'Salman,' he shouted back. 'The subterfuge worked.'

'So, I see,' said Salman. 'Are you hurt?'

'Not this time.'

'See to your horse,' said Salman, 'and join me. There is much to discuss.'

'Indeed there is,' said Hassan, and as Salman disappeared from view, dismounted to lead his horse through the growing throng. The plan had succeeded, the city had been reinforced.

The following day in the Christian camp, Guy of Lusignan called the Seneschal of the Templars to an audience, furious that such a large force had managed to relieve Acre. With the death of Gerard, the leadership of the order had temporarily fallen upon the seneschal's shoulders, but he was in no mood to be admonished by so poor a king.

'Who is responsible for this?' demanded Guy. 'Who was in charge of your positions last night?'

'That would be me,' said the seneschal calmly, 'but the attack on our camp was a diversion while the main force rode down the coastal road unopposed.'

'And why was the road not guarded?'

'It was,' said the seneschal, struggling to control his temper, 'but it seems they were tricked and allowed assassins into the camp.'

'Idiots,' shouted the king, slamming his fist onto the map-table.

'Your Grace,' said the Seneschal, 'with respect, what were they to do? The survivors say that the attackers were Christians, deserters from the army you control. Perhaps your ire should fall on the shoulders of those closest to you, rather than seek scapegoats.'

The king stared at the seneschal with shock. Never had anyone stood up to him in such a manner.

'Are you blaming me?' he gasped.

'Your grace. Last night, our positions were attacked, and many knights and civilians were killed. Anyone who still has any strength is currently burying the dead. In the circumstances, we did what we could, but the attack was over before it hardly began. It was well planned and well-executed; my men could not have done more.'

'Yet you suggest the blame lies with me?'

'I am suggesting that if we treated our armies better, and supplied them with more food and cleaner water, then perhaps not so many would be deserting.'

'I give them everything I can,' growled the king, 'the greed of the Pisan merchants limits our options.'

'Yet your table groans with meat,' said the seneschal, 'while our knights' stomachs groan with hunger.'

'I would be careful if I were you, Sir Knight,' said the king, 'you are perilously close to incurring my full wrath. Do not think for one moment that the sight of your head on a pike would cause me any grief.'

'Your Grace,' said the seneschal, 'in the absence of a grandmaster, it falls to me to supply you with the truth of such matters. You are surrounded by flatterers and bootlickers, men who tell you everything you want to hear yet blind you from the truth. Execute me if that is your whim, but know this, if you do, the rest of my brothers will be sleeping safely within the walls of Tyre by tomorrow night, and you will face this campaign without us.'

'You would never do such a thing,' said the king.

'We do not wish to do so, and we are yours to command as you see fit in battle, but we will no longer be held as scapegoats for the failings of others.'

The tent flap opened, and Thomas Cronin entered, much to the annoyance of both men.

'We are in counsel,' roared the king, 'get out.'

'Your Grace,' said Cronin, 'I have news, and thought you would want to hear it immediately.'

'What news?'

'Your Grace, yesterday, twelve ships from France arrived in Tyre. They are the advance ships from Phillip of France, he is only a few days behind with his vast army. What is more, they have confirmed that Richard of England has arrived in Messina along with his army and are currently boarding a fleet to sail here.'

'And you are sure of this?'

'The messages come from the ships themselves. They are loaded with men and provisions, and I am told that as soon as Phillip arrives in Tyre, he will march on Acre forthwith.'

The king fell silent as he took the news in before glancing between the other men in the room.

'Thank you,' he said eventually, 'this is indeed great news.' He turned back to the Templar seneschal. 'I think we have said enough here and need to refocus on what we need to do. I will send men to aid with the burials, but for now, this audience is over.'

The seneschal and Cronin both bowed before leaving the tent, leaving the king and Sir Geraint behind them.

'You should string him up at the first opportunity,' growled Sir Geraint, 'never have I seen so much insolence to a king.'

'Believe me, the idea is appealing,' said the king, 'but he is right, if I were to take out my ire on him, we would lose the Templars.'

'Let them go,' said Geraint, 'they have been nothing but trouble since we arrived yet set themselves above all men. We have more than enough forces with more on their way. We will be better off without them.'

'I'll give it some thought,' said Guy, 'but at the moment, there are other concerns to consider.'

'Which are?'

'The arrival of Phillip.'

'Is this not good news?'

'In essence, yes, but I thought he would land directly onto the southern beaches, not sail to Tyre.'

'Is that problem?'

'Yes, it is. Ever since Conrad married Isabella, he has become more vocal in his claim to the throne of Jerusalem. Our alliance, however threadbare, will only last until such time that the royals of Europe create a new council. After that, we will be bound by the results of a vote.'

'And?'

'Unfortunately, Phillip has great influence amongst all the other countries, and his stay in Tyre gives Conrad a perfect opportunity to push his claim. I fear that by the time he reaches Acre, he will already have decided to support Conrad.'

'Could we not intercept Phillip's ship, and press your own claim before he reaches Tyre?'

'There is no time,' said Guy. 'By the time we find a ship and set sail, Phillip will already be at anchor.'

'There must be something we can do.'

'There is one thing,' said Guy. 'We can petition the King of England for his support. He has just as much influence as Phillip, if not more. If we can press our case to him, we will regain the advantage.'

'So, we sail to Messina?'

'Brother Cronin just said that Richard's army is already embarking the ships, so it is pointless going to Sicily. What we can do is intercept him en-route, then he will hear my case before being poisoned by the lies of Conrad.'

'Do you want me to make the arrangements?'

'Aye, I do,' said Guy. 'Prepare three ships, and have them ready to leave at a moment's notice.'

'As you wish,' said Sir Geraint, and with a bow of his head, left the campaign tent.

Chapter Twenty

The Island of Crete

May - AD 1191

Richard stood on a cliff overlooking the sea on the island of Crete. Tall of stature and strong of limb, he struck an imposing figure and was a much-respected leader throughout Christendom. At six foot four, he was already taller than all of his command, and his fiery red hair made him stand out in whatever situation he found himself, whether that be peace or war.

Richard had left Sicily only weeks earlier with a fleet of over two hundred ships, and seventeen thousand men but a vicious storm had torn the fleet apart, scattering the ships far and wide across the Mediterranean. All the captains had been briefed what to do in such a situation, and over the last few days, the last of those that had survived the storm had limped into the harbours for repair, but twenty-five ships were still missing including the two that had carried his fiancée and his treasury.

'Your Grace,' said one of the knights at his side, 'you have a messenger.'

King Richard turned to look inland where a column of a hundred fully armed knights waited patiently on their destriers for his return. Alongside them, a cloaked figure from the town sat upon a much smaller horse.

Richard nodded, and the knight summoned the messenger.

'Your Grace,' he said with a bow, 'I bring important news. A fisherman has arrived from Cyprus and tells of four ships that were driven to the southern shore during the storm. Three were dashed against the rocks with few survivors, but one remains at anchor off the coast, damaged, but intact.'

'Do you know what ships they were?' asked Richard.

'We do not, but from the fisherman's description, it seems that the one that still floats is that which carries the lady of Thuringia.'

'Is she alive?'

'We have no way of knowing for certain, but he says the ship looks in fair order, so there is every chance that she is. However, the emperor refuses to allow them to land in safety nor supply them with fresh food or water. In addition, the fisherman heard from many people that great treasures have been obtained from the ships and the bodies of those who sailed upon them. Isaac Comnenus himself declared a day of rejoicing.'

'The emperor has always been quick to take advantage,' said the king, 'but I suspect he is premature in his celebrations. Is there anything else?'

'No, your Grace.'

'Then thank the fisherman on my behalf, and make sure he is well rewarded.'

'Yes, your Grace,' said the messenger, and turned his horse to ride back to the dock. As the man rode away, Richard once more turned to stare out to sea.

'Your Grace,' said the knight at his side, 'this is an insult of the most grievous nature. Surely we cannot let it pass without response.'

'We cannot,' said the king, 'yet the Holy-land thirsts for our arrival.'

'What do you want us to do?'

'Have messages sent to Guy of Lusignan at Acre,' replied Richard, 'tell him of what has happened here and that our arrival will be delayed.'

'Delayed?'

'Yes,' said the king, 'make ready the fleet, Sir Crispin, we are going to Cyprus.'

A few days later, Richard stood in the forecastle of his giant warship. The coastal city of Limassol lay before him, and behind him, over a hundred ships spread out as far as the eye could see. Nearer to the shore he could see one of his damaged ships lying at anchor, perilously close to the shore. It had already been established that it did indeed carry his sister Joanna and his fiancée, Berengaria of Navarre, and Richard had already sent a letter to the Isaac Comnenus demanding the ship be allowed to dock in safety but had so far received no reply.

'Your Grace,' said Sir Crispin, climbing a ladder to join him on the forecastle. 'I have received despatches from the fleet, they stand ready and waiting to launch the attack. Shall I give the order?'

'Not yet,' said Richard. 'We will give Isaac a chance to redeem himself, but have water and food sent to my sister's ship.'

'I have already given that order,' said Crispin. 'Perhaps we should bring the ladies back here.'

'They are probably safer where they are for the moment,' said Richard. 'If Isaac Comnenus proves to be a stupid man, then this ship will be a place of war.'

'As you wish,' said Crispin.

The day dragged on until the king's messenger returned with a sealed scroll sent from the emperor himself. Richard broke the seal and read the message in silence before lifting his eyes and staring over the sea towards Limassol.

'Well?' said Sir Crispin, still at his side.

'The man is obviously an imbecile,' said Richard. 'Send the signal, Sir Crispin, Cyprus just made a terrible, terrible mistake.'

Within the hour, dozens of troop-carrying galleys forged through the coastal waters to beach themselves, disgorging thousands of men at arms upon the shore. First to land were the archers, providing a storm of deadly arrows against the defenders while behind them came the foot-soldiers, each fully armed and battle-hardened after the fighting at Messina. Richard was amongst them, his huge figure unmistakeable in the confusion of battle. Fuelled by anger at the insulting letter he had received from the emperor, he led the assault against the defences with no thought of safety or quarter.

Inspired by their leader, his men fought like demons and despite being outnumbered, drove the defenders back from the coast. More men arrived from the ships, and as their number grew, Richard's army rampaged through Limassol before turning their attention on the city's castle.

Alarmed at the ferocity of the attack, Isaac quickly retreated inland along with the bulk of his army leaving his castle poorly defended, and before the day was out, Richard's colours flew from the battlements, the city had fallen.

A few days later, Richard sat in one of the chambers in Limassol Castle, being briefed by his officers. Most of the coast and all the harbours were now in his control, but he knew Isaac still had a substantial army hidden amongst the mountains which posed a considerable risk.'

'Your Grace,' said Sir Crispin. 'We have secured everything you commanded and stand ready to march against Isaac.'

'Excellent said the king, 'but tell your men to wait one more day.'

'Is that wise?' said Sir Crispin. 'Every day we wait allows him to rally more men to his banner.'

'I know,' said Richard, 'but there have been developments.'

'Developments?'

'We have heard that three ships have just arrived from the Holy-land to offer their support.'

'With respect, your Grace, three ships will make no difference, I have more than enough men at my disposal already.'

'Indeed you do, but though this arrival may not provide any military advantage, it will certainly add to our political strength.'

'In what way?'

'I think you are about to find out,' said Richard as a door opened across the hall.

'Your Grace,' announced a herald, 'may I introduce his Grace, the King of Jerusalem, Guy of Lusignan.'

Guy walked across the floor and stood before Richard. Everyone stared, waiting to see how he would greet the monarch. As a king himself, he was entitled to equal status, but to everyone's surprise, he nodded slightly, the faintest semblance of a bow that acknowledged Richard's superior station

The gesture was astonishing, yet carefully calculated, and by the grin on Richard's face, Guy knew he had made the right decision.

'King Guy,' announced Richard, 'welcome to Cyprus. I did not expect your presence.'

'As soon as I heard about the plight of your lady,' said Guy, 'we set out immediately to offer what help we could. Alas, my army is not great for most are camped at the gates of Acre, but those I do have are yours to command.'

'The gesture is well received,' said Richard, 'and we will put them to good use, but first we will celebrate. You and your seconds must join us tonight to toast the safe deliverance of my sister and the lady Berengaria into our hands.'

'We would be honoured,' said Guy.

The following day, Guy of Jerusalem and Sir Geraint made their way down to the docks to return to their ships. The previous night had been spent in deep negotiation with Richard and had ended with a mutually beneficial agreement. Guy would swear fealty to Richard and take his ships to circumnavigate the island to secure any ports or cities still loyal to Isaac. In return, Richard promised to support Guy's claim to the throne of Jerusalem as soon as he reached Acre. It was a fantastic outcome for Guy, and he felt optimistic about his future reign.

'A few more days and we can return to Acre,' said Sir Geraint.

'It may take a little more time than that,' said Guy. 'Once all the ports are secure, Richard still has to prise the emperor from the mountains.'

'I understand that Isaac went back on a pledge,' said Geraint.

'Aye, he did. Some of Richard's men captured him, and he swore fealty in return for his life. He even pledged to lead five hundred men to the Holy land to support the king's crusade, but as soon as he was released, he denounced the agreement and has sworn to fight Richard to regain Cyprus.'

Geraint looked out over the sea to the vast fleet of ships still lying at anchor.

'He can never withstand that,' he said, 'the man is truly an idiot.'

'It would seem so,' said Guy. 'Come, there is a job to be done.'

Just over a week later, Guy was back in Limassol to attend the marriage of Richard of England to Berengaria of Navarre. The marriage had been conducted in the Chapel of St. George, and Berengaria was crowned Queen of England the same day by the Archbishops of Bordeaux, Évreux and Bayonne. A great feast was planned for later in the evening, and Guy was in his quarters getting prepared when a red-faced servant barged into the room without knocking.

'Your Grace,' he said, 'Richard of England is on his way here.'

'Here?'

'Aye, your Grace.'

Guy dismissed the servant and stood facing the door. Moments later, the king strode in followed by his bodyguards.

'King Richard,' said Guy with a nod, 'to what do I owe this honour?'

'I have some time,' replied Richard, 'and thought we could talk about Acre.'

'Of course,' said Guy. 'Can I get you refreshments?'

'There will be plenty of time to eat later,' said Richard and turned to his men. 'You may leave, wait for me outside.'

'Yes, my liege,' said the lead knight and the whole entourage left the room as Richard walked over to the window.

'So,' he said, looking out over the city, 'I hear your men have almost finished securing the coastline.'

'Aye,' said Guy. 'A few more days and the island will be yours.'

'You have done well,' said Richard, 'but there is no need to continue. Send a message to your ships to end their task and return to Limassol.'

Guy looked at Richard with surprise.

'Can I ask why?' he asked eventually. 'Are you not happy with our efforts?'

'Indeed I am, but yesterday I found out that my men have once again caught the emperor and he has agreed to hand over the whole island to my rule. Cyprus is ours, and even as we speak, messages are being sent for all his men to surrender.'

'Well, I can't say I am surprised,' said Guy, 'but I have to admit it has happened far quicker than I anticipated.'

'The man is a coward as well as a fool,' said Richard. 'As soon as he saw the size of the force approaching his hideaway, he laid down his arms and once more pledged his fealty, but this time on one condition.'

'He had the gall to impose conditions?'

'Just the one.'

'And that was?'

'That he be treated like an emperor, and not be cast in iron chains.'

'And did you agree?'

'I did. In fact, I invited him to the wedding feast tonight.'

'After the way he treated the lady Berengaria?'

'I consider myself a just king,' said Richard, 'and as too many men have already died in this unnecessary fight, accepted his terms.'

'Then you are certainly a more forgiving man than I,' said Guy.

'We will see,' said Richard. 'Anyway, I have time, so perhaps some wine would be good while we discuss the situation in Acre.'

'Of course,' said Guy, 'please take a seat.'

Later that evening, all the guests stood behind their seats in a great banquet hall of the castle. The tables groaned under the weight of the food and armies of servants waited to transport as much wine and ale as they could carry to the guests. Richard and his new bride had already entered the room, and after the cheering and clapping had died down, the king invited the guests to all sit.

'My fellow Christians,' he announced, still on his feet, 'I am humbled by your loyalty and love, but before we partake of this magnificent feast, there is one guest missing.'

A murmur of surprise rippled around the room at the mention of the emperor's name, and all eyes turned to the king.

'As you probably know by now,' he continued, 'Cyprus has capitulated and now lies in our hands. The emperor asked only one thing in return for his surrender, and that was that he would never be treated as befitted his station and never be cast in chains of iron. This I agreed and invited him to the wedding.'

Again murmurs rippled around the room, this time in anger.

'Please,' said the king,' raising his voice, 'welcome the Emperor of Cyprus, Isaac Comnenus.'

As he spoke, the far doors opened, and the hall fell into silence. Standing alone, framed between the pillars was the once boastful emperor, dressed in his palace finery. But there was no sign of arrogance or indeed self-respect about him, for around his ankles and wrists, hung heavy chains of silver and gold.

Chapter Twenty-one

Acre

June – AD 1191

King Guy stood atop Mount Toron alongside King Phillip of France. Phillip had arrived from Tyre just a few weeks earlier along with his huge army, and hundreds of carts piled high with supplies. The eastern flanks of the reinforcing column had been protected by Conrad of Montferrat's men, and the sheer strength had meant that any Saracens in their way had fled inland.

Down below the hill, Phillip's army of over ten thousand men had already made themselves busy rebuilding the Christian defences and constructing new siege engines. Mass graves were dug further away from the positions, and any tents once occupied by the diseased were burned to the ground.

For the first time in weeks, squadrons of mounted knights patrolled the outer perimeters of the Christian positions, and smaller patrols harassed the Saracens at every opportunity. Day and night, mangonels, ineffective against the massive outer walls, now hurled rocks into the heart of the city.

Guy was impressed at the organisation but frustrated they had still not launched a full-scale attack.

'Our army grows stronger by the day,' said Phillip.

'Aye, it does,' said Guy, 'and I see no reason why we cannot tear down the walls.'

'I understand your frustration,' said Phillip, 'but it begs the question, why have you not done it before?'

'We have attacked on many occasions,' said Guy, 'but every time we do, the garrison sends a signal to Saladin, and he launches a counterattack from behind, giving the defenders time to reorganise and repair their defences. Until now, we have never had enough men, but with your army, we can face them on both fronts.'

'What happened to Barbarossa's men?'

'His army was reputed to number in the tens of thousands,' said Guy, 'but he drowned in a river on his way here and most returned to Germany. His son, Fredrick of Swabia, continued with those that chose to continue, but they were fewer than seven hundred in number and arrived in a worse state than those already here. To be honest, they were more of a burden than a boon, and when Fredrick died, they also returned to Germany.'

'It sounds like the whole thing has been one disaster after another,' said Phillip.

'With respect,' said Guy, angered at the king's accusatory tone, 'you were not here. We had minimal resources, so I sent pleas for support throughout Christendom, but few answered, and even when they did, their numbers were not enough to make a difference.'

'These things take time,' said Phillip, 'and I had my own affairs to take care of.'

'I hear the main thing was your feud with Richard,' snapped Guy. 'Perhaps if the attention you gave that situation was directed towards saving Jerusalem, we would not now be stood atop this God-forsaken hill.'

'I would soften your tone, Guy of Lusignan,' said Phillip. 'Just remember who is helping who here.'

'I am just as much a king as you,' replied Guy, 'and you are in my kingdom. My opinions are just as valid as anyone else.'

Phillip looked over towards Acre.

'Whatever your opinion,' he said eventually, 'Richard will be here tomorrow, and when he arrives, we will tear down those walls once and for all.'

'That is all I ask,' said Guy. 'Once Acre is in our hands, we will be able to easily resupply our armies and finally march on Jerusalem.'

Over in the city, the Muslim forces were not doing so well. Despite the reinforcements a few months earlier, the garrison was still undermanned, and food was scarce.

The constant barrage from the Christian mangonels meant many of the streets were not much more than piles of rubble, and people lived amongst the devastation like rats, cut down by disease and starvation.

Some of the wealthy occupants fared far better. Out of reach of the mangonels, and protecting their hordes of food with armed men, they hunkered down, waiting for the inevitable.

Up in the commandery, times were even harder for Sumeira and the other prisoners. Many more had died from disease, but still, she would not leave with Fakhiri, knowing that even if she managed to escape, Barak would have the rest of the captives executed. Instead, she ploughed on, doing what she could, not just for the Christian prisoners rotting in their cells, but also for the many sick and injured people of Acre now taking up every inch of space in the makeshift hospital.

Occasionally, whenever a supply ship managed to break through the Christian blockade, Barak's trader cousin would send what he could to the jail, each morsel carefully weighed and recorded for payment at a later date. Whenever this happened, Fakhiri made sure he was the one to accompany the cart, and after so many visits, the guards on the commandery gates were well used to him. At every opportunity, he smuggled in whatever extra food he could get his hands on, but it was never enough, and Sumeira gave every morsel to her fellow prisoners.

'You should get some sleep,' said Shani, seeing her sitting outside the hospital with her head on her raised knees.

'I do not have the time,' said Sumeira, her voice weak with exhaustion. 'There are wounds still to dress.'

'I will take care of those,' said Shani. 'Go to the storeroom and lock the door from the inside. Nobody will seek you there. I will wake you in a few hours.'

Sumeira sighed and looked at her helper. Despite being a Muslim, he had been a great help to her over the past few months, and she knew that many more of her patients would have died had it not been for his help.

'You are a good man, Shani,' she said. 'I couldn't have done this without you.'

'I just did what you directed,' said Shani. 'In the beginning, I had my doubts as your methods were strange to me, but since then, I have come to believe you are the best physician I have ever seen.'

Sumeira smiled and reached out to touch Shani's arm.

'That's a very kind thing to say,' she said,' but it is not enough. Too many have died and will continue to die until this siege is over. I just hope we have the strength to survive.'

'If Turan-Shah prevails,' said Shani, 'I will do everything in my power to secure your release.'

Sumeira smiled, knowing that as a prisoner himself, Shani had little influence at any level within the city.

'Thank you,' she said. 'I think I will get a little sleep but call me the moment you need anything.'

'I will,' said Shani.

Sumeira got to her feet and walked towards the chapel door when someone called her name across the courtyard. She turned around to see the Egyptian walking towards her.

'Fakhiri,' she said, 'I was not expecting you until tomorrow.'

'I know,' said Fakhiri, 'but I came up on the pretence of gifting the jailer with a flask of wine from his cousin. The truth is, I needed to see you urgently.'

'Why?' asked Sumeira, 'I won't be going anywhere soon.'

'On the contrary,' said Fakhiri looking around, 'things are about to get a lot worse.'

'In what way?'

'My sources tell me that the Christian positions have been reinforced by a massive army under Phillip of France. In addition, there are over a hundred ships approaching the coast with another ten-thousand men led by the King of England himself. When he arrives, we can expect a massive assault and the state of the garrison means there is no chance the city will prevail.'

'Is that not good news?' asked Sumeira.

'Overall yes, but until your countrymen march through the gates, you are in terrible danger, not just from Barak, but from any man who serves Saladin within the city walls.'

'But many already know me,' said Sumeira, 'and know I have done nothing but help any sick or wounded who have come before me.'

'Trust me,' said Fakhiri, 'for every man saved, there are a hundred more that hate *all* Christians, and that includes you.'

'And you think they will come here?'

'If it looks like the city is about to fall, which it will, you can wager there will be some who want to exact their revenge upon anyone they can find, and who better than the Christians already being held in the jail?'

'I don't know what to say,' said Sumeira, 'I appreciate you coming, I really do, but I cannot leave, Fakhiri, my place is alongside those who have shared their captivity beside me.

'You are as stubborn as a mule,' said Fakhiri, 'but I suspected that would be your response, so I prepared an alternative.'

'An alternative?'

'Yes, a way to get you, and all your fellows to safety when the city falls. It is dangerous, but if it works, we may just possibly come out of the other side alive.'

'That is good enough for me,' said Sumeira, 'what do I have to do?'

'I'll tell you soon enough,' said Fakhiri, 'but in the meantime, see if you can get whatever food you can to the prisoners. They are going to need all of their strength where they are going.'

In the Templar camp, Thomas Cronin stood outside his tent, washing his face and upper body with water from a wooden bowl. The extra men meant they had far easier access to the various water sources along the coast, and at last, there was enough to be able to keep a semblance of cleanliness throughout the camps.

'Cronin,' shouted a voice, and he turned to see Arturas limping towards him.

'Arturas,' he said, 'what brings you here? You look agitated.'

'Have you heard the news,' gasped Arturas, 'Richard's fleet has been spotted off the coast, dozens of ships each laying heavy in the water. It is being said that the boards of every ship groan under the weight of meat, ale, wine, and whores.'

'Methinks, you are a little optimistic,' laughed Cronin, 'but his arrival is indeed something to celebrate.'

'Either way, it took him long enough,' said Arturas. 'Perhaps we can now finish what we started and get back to Tyre.'

'Isn't there the small matter of Jerusalem to think about?' asked Cronin, pouring away the dirty water.

'I only signed up for Acre,' said Arturas, 'and now we have all these men at arms wandering around without a care in the world, I see no reason to risk my life further. I have salted away enough money to last a year or so in Tripoli so once those walls fall, I will be away from here quicker than a whore divests her garments.'

Cronin laughed and donned his undershirt before picking up his sword belt.

'Come,' he said, 'let's have a look at this fleet.'

A few minutes later they were on top of a nearby hill alongside several other men peering westward. In the distance, ships filled the ocean as far as the eye could see from the majestic, three-masted Dromons, each capable of carrying a thousand men, to the smaller Busses, single-masted ships with thirty oars capable of carrying forty knights and their horses. To the south, oar-driven galleys had already engaged the few remaining Saracen ships and now pursued them along the coast, driving them back towards Egypt.

'Isn't it magnificent,' said one of the men alongside Cronin, 'never have I seen such a sight.'

'Nor I,' said Cronin, 'I just wish they had arrived sooner.'

'I'm just happy they got here at all,' said Arturas. 'I wonder what Richard looks like.'

'I hear he is a giant of a man,' said Cronin, 'and does not suffer fools gladly.'

'Then I expect him to behead Guy of Lusignan at the earliest opportunity,' said Arturas.

'I have to go,' said Cronin and turned to his friend. 'Arturas, we know not what will happen in the next few days, but I suspect our paths may not cross for a while. Try to keep that ugly head as safe as you can, and if we both reach the other side unscathed, perhaps we can share a few more skins of wine from your expertly-hidden hoard of ill-gotten gains.'

'I have no idea what you are talking about,' said Arturas, 'but look forward to being as drunk as any man has ever been, with you at my side.'

Cronin smiled and turned away to return to his tent. He had weapons to sharpen and equipment to clean.

Chapter Twenty-two

Acre

June – AD 1191

King Richard lay on his cot, bathed in sweat. Two physicians sat alongside him, bathing his brow and plying him with Aloe and poppy milk. The first of the ships had landed almost ten days earlier, but despite Richard's eagerness to attack, he had been struck down by a fever and could hardly walk, let alone lead his men into battle. His frustration was only lessened by the fact that he knew Phillip of France had also been struck down and was equally dilapidated.

'Help me up,' he said eventually, grabbing a physician's arm.

'Your Grace, you should rest,' said the physician, 'please lay back down.'

'I have had enough of this nonsense,' growled Richard, 'help me to my chair and summon Sir Crispin.'

'As you wish, your Grace,' sighed the physician, and as he went to find the first knight, his comrade helped the stricken king across the tent. Five minutes later, Sir Crispin entered the tent and walked over to join the king at the table.

'Sit,' said Richard, indicating a chair. 'The rest of you get out.'

Everyone cleared the tent except Crispin, and he waited patiently as the king poured watered wine into two glass goblets.

'I see you are feeling far better today,' said Crispin. 'Have the pains gone?'

'They have not,' said Richard, 'and I am being stabbed by a thousand demons as we speak. But I can no longer rot in my bed when there is a city to take.'

'With respect, your Grace,' said Crispin, 'you can hardly hold a wine jug, let alone a sword. Can I suggest that your physicians are right, and you need a few more days rest?'

'I may not be able to fight,' said Richard, 'at least not with spears and swords, but there are other tactics I can deploy.'

'Such as?'

'As you know,' said the king lowering himself gingerly into his chair, 'it is important to know your enemy and Saladin is no exception. I have travelled halfway across Christendom to face him, and yet feel I know nothing about the man.'

'We have been briefed on several occasions,' said Crispin.

'We have,' said Richard, 'but no sooner are we told that the sultan is a monster with no compassion for man or beast than someone else counsels that he is a man of honour and well-loved by all who meet him. Which is he, Crispin, who is this man who I have come all this way to defeat?'

'I have no answers,' said the knight. 'Only that whatever his true nature, he is the one standing between you and Jerusalem.'

'I agree, but how can I form my strategies when I do not know the true nature of my enemy. Is he a powerful leader to be feared, or a gentle man who only musters such loyalty to his name through respect?'

'Perhaps both,' said Crispin, 'we just do not know.'

'No, we don't,' said Richard, 'but I intend to find out.'

'How?'

'By requesting we meet in person.'

Crispin fell quiet and stared at the king.

'Is that wise?' he asked.

'Not only is it wise,' said Richard, 'it is an essential part of kingship. To reach out to avoid war, yet make it clear the sword of God hangs above them if terms cannot be agreed, is just as potent a weapon as the largest trebuchet. I will suggest we meet alone, man to man without seconds or guards. That way, we can speak truly without the pressure of expectation hanging around our necks like a horse's collar. What do you think?'

'I don't know,' said Crispin. 'It puts you in harm's way for no reason.'

'If he is as honourable as many say, then I will be in no danger.'

'And if he is not?'

'I do not fear any man,' Sir Crispin, 'and Saladin is no exception.'

'Even in your current state?'

'Even in my current state. Send a letter to Saladin suggesting the meeting. Tell him that many men are bound to die over the next few weeks, on both sides, but we have it in our power to stop the bloodshed.'

'And when do you want this meeting to take place?'

'Seven days from now,' said Richard.

'As you wish,' said Crispin, and got to his feet to leave the tent.

'One more thing,' said Richard as he left, 'send in my squires and tell them to bring my armour.'

'Why, your Grace,' said Crispin, 'what gain is there to be had in this madness?'

'There are positions to inspect and men to encourage,' said Richard. 'I may not be able to fight, but I can still lead. I am their king, and they expect it from me.'

'As you wish,' sighed Crispin and left the tent.

A few days later, Guy of Lusignan once again stood atop Mount Toron, frustrated by the lack of movement against the city. The Christian positions had expanded beyond all recognition, but the incapacitation of both kings had ground the whole operation to a halt. Phillip was nearing a full recovery, but Richard was still abed. Sir Geraint pointed down the hillside to where a small column of ten riders was ascending the path.

'That's Conrad,' said Guy, recognising the standard. 'I wonder what he wants?'

'We'll find out soon enough,' said Geraint, 'I'll bring you your cloak.'

Minutes later, Guy of Lusignan stood outside his tent as Conrad dismounted and walked towards him.

'Lord Conrad,' said the king as he approached. 'The hour is late. To what do I owe this visit?'

'King Guy,' said Conrad with a slight nod of the head, 'forgive the hour, but I have been sent by King Phillip to discuss arrangements.'

'What arrangements?'

'Perhaps we can go inside,' asked Conrad, nodding towards the tent.

'Why,' said Guy, 'the night is warm, and the air is fresh. We can discuss what you have to say out here. Perhaps the sight of Acre through the gloom will remind us of why we are all here.'

'As you wish,' said Conrad, and both men walked over to a table at the top of the western slope of the hill. One of Guy's servants poured wine into two crystal goblets before bowing and retreating out of sight.

'This looks very good,' said Conrad, peering into his goblet, 'not like the horse piss we have drunk of late.'

'A gift from Richard,' said Guy. 'I will have some sent over to you on the morrow.'

'A gesture much appreciated,' said Conrad. 'How is the king?'

'Much improved,' said Guy, 'and I expect him to be back amongst the men within days.'

'Really? I hear he is as weak as a mouse and may not survive.'

'Then you need better spies,' said Guy, 'for I talked to him myself this very day. His strength is returning by the hour.'

'I hope you are correct,' said Conrad, 'for if he was to die, then Phillip would take full control of this siege, including Richard's army and if that happens, your claim to the throne of Jerusalem would be untenable.'

'Richard's men would never follow Phillip in a thousand lifetimes, as well you know.'

'Some, perhaps, but men like to be paid, and Phillip is a generous man.'

'What do you want, Conrad?' asked Guy. You haven't come all the way up here to issue idle threats.'

'No, I have not,' said Conrad with a sigh and sat back in his chair. 'I am here at the behest of Phillip himself. He sent me to brief you on a situation you may not be aware of.'

'And that is?'

'Richard has requested a meeting with Saladin, a meeting with no other man in attendance, irrespective of station.'

Guy was surprised at the news but hid it well.

'So?' he said, 'Richard is a king, and has every right to use diplomacy.'

'Aye, he does, but does it not bother you that as a self-declared ally of Richard, you were not even informed of this situation?'

'I expect it slipped his mind,' said Guy, 'and he would have told me soon enough.'

'Yet you told me moments ago, you spoke to him only yesterday. He must be a very forgetful man.'

Guy cursed inwardly at his mistake but continued to project an air of confidence.

'Whatever his reasons, he has my full support,' he said. 'So what are these arrangements you speak of?'

'The day after tomorrow,' said Conrad, 'Phillip intends to launch his attack upon Acre.'

'You are going to attack Acre without Richard's army?'

'Why not? Phillip has come all this way to fight, not to sit in a tent drinking tea and eating dates with the enemy. My army will accompany him on the assault, of course, but we fully expect Saladin to respond with a counterattack from inland. Phillip has requested that in the event of such an attack, he can rely on you and your men to protect our rear.'

Guy stared at Conrad, his pulse racing at the insult.

'Phillip cannot attack Acre on his own,' he said eventually, 'there are leaders here from all over Europe. He should call a council and seek their support.'

'He already has,' said Conrad, 'and most will line up alongside him on the day.'

'There has already been a council?' said Guy, his anger rising. 'Why was I not informed sooner?'

'Alas there was little time, and as you are pledged to Richard, we thought it would be better spent with those of independent mind. But I am here now, and Phillip sees a pivotal role in this attack for you and your men.'

'Protecting the rear?'

'An important role, as well you know.'

'I need to speak to Richard,' said Guy, standing up. 'He needs to know about this plan.'

'Oh he knows already,' said Conrad, getting to his feet, 'and though his men will not be taking part, he is happy for Phillip to proceed. All we need to know now, is will you have our backs?'

Again, it was all Guy could do to contain his anger, but there was no way he would give Conrad the satisfaction of seeing his ire.'

'Tell Phillip,' he said eventually, 'I will send my decision tomorrow. In the meantime, I have things to do so if you don't mind, my men will escort you down.'

'Of course,' said Conrad, and he mounted his horse before turning to face the king one last time.

'I would suggest you do not wait too long, King Guy,' he said, 'for with or without you, Acre is about to fall and as is always the case in such matters, to the victor the spoils.' He kicked his horse and rode down the hill, knowing full well that Guy's eyes were burning into his back.

The following morning, Guy and a bodyguard of twelve, fully armed knights rode to Richard's camp situated just to the south of the Christian siege lines. Above them flew the colours of Jerusalem, and it was obvious to anyone they passed, the king was not in a good mood.

As far as he could see, the shoreline was covered in tents, and battle-worn men sat in groups, sharpening their blades or cleaning their equipment. He approached the centre of the camp and dismounted before Richard's impressive command tent, intent on demanding an explanation.

Two guards approached to block his way with crossed spears while others subconsciously moved their hands to the hilts of their swords, slightly concerned at the strength of the men accompanying the King of Jerusalem.

Guy stared at the guards with astonishment. Not since he had been crowned had any man blocked his way.

'Remove yourself from the king's path,' said Sir Geraint at his side, 'he has business with your master.'

'King Richard is indisposed,' said one of the guards, 'and we have been instructed to prevent all-comers from disturbing his rest.'

'He will see me,' growled Guy, 'for I am no less a king than he. Now get out of my way before my man cuts you down like the dogs you are.'

The two guards stood defiant, but before events could escalate, the tent flap opened, and Sir Crispin emerged to see what was causing the commotion.

'You men stand down,' he said and turned to face Guy. 'Your Grace, please forgive the confusion, but we had no notification of your arrival. What can I do for you?'

'I sent no notice,' said Guy, 'for there was no time, but I am here to see King Richard, and what I have to say will not wait.'

'Alas,' said Geraint, 'the guards were telling the truth, and the king is truly indisposed. Perhaps you could come back this evening.'

Guy seethed at the insult, yet he was surrounded by Richard's men and knew he had no option but to accept. He stared at the knight, calculating how best to remove himself from the embarrassing situation, but before he could say anything, a physician emerged from the tent and walked over to the two men.

'My lord,' he said, facing Sir Crispin, 'King Richard sends message that he will grant an audience with King Guy. I will call you when he is ready.'

'Thank you,' said Crispin and turned back to face Guy. 'It seems you are in luck. Stand your men down, and we will see they get water for your horses.' He turned away and returned to the royal tent, but his place was immediately taken by the two guards.

'What do you want to do?' asked Sir Geraint.

'We are here now,' said Guy, 'so will wait. I will make it plain to Richard that the situation is an insult.'

Ten minutes later, Crispin once more emerged and called across the clearing to Guy.

'King Richard will see you now.'

'At last,' murmured Guy, and walked over to the tent accompanied by Sir Geraint.

'Just the king,' said Crispin, placing his hand on Sir Geraint's chest.

The knight looked down at the hand before looking back up to stare at Sir Crispin.

'Unhand me, sir,' he said calmly, 'I will not ask twice.'

'Geraint,' said Guy, 'stand down. I will be moments only. You can stay out here.'

'As will I,' smiled Sir Crispin, not taking his eyes from his potential adversary.

Geraint waited a moment longer before taking a step back and folding his arms, still staring at Richard's first knight.

Guy entered Richard's tent and looked around. At the far end, a curtain separated the bed space from the main area, and in the centre, a servant added timber to a fire, the smoke rising to escape through the hole at the apex of the roof.

'Please, be seated,' said a steward to one side. 'The king will be with you momentarily. Do you thirst?'

'I do not,' replied Guy and sat at one of the two chairs to either side of the entrance. Moments later, the bed-chamber curtains parted, and Richard emerged fully dressed in heavy dark leggings and an ornate jerkin embroidered with images of hunts amongst the forests of France.

'Your Grace,' said Guy getting to his feet, 'I hope I find you well.'

'You do not,' said Richard, walking over to stand before the rekindled fire, 'but I will receive you, nevertheless. What can I do for you?'

The servant scuttled away as Guy approached the fire, slightly surprised at the reception.

'Your Grace,' said Guy, 'I came to seek an explanation about something that has happened over the past few days.'

'An explanation,' said Richard glancing over to Guy. 'Interesting.'

Guy cringed inside, realising his choice of words had been unfortunate.

'I beg your pardon,' he responded, 'perhaps I should have said enlightenment.'

'Your meaning was clear to me,' said Richard, 'get on with it.'

'Your Grace, I understand that there have been meetings to discuss the attack on Acre, briefings and councils that I have been excluded from. As you know, I swore fealty to you in Cyprus so obviously thought I would be included in all such things.'

'If there have been such meetings,' said Richard, ladling warm wine from a pot hanging over the fire into a wooden tankard, 'then they have taken place without me.' He sipped at the wine before turning to face Guy.

'I don't understand,' said Guy, 'I have been told that you not only know of Phillip's decision to launch a fresh attack on Acre but gave it your full approval.'

'Indeed I did,' said Richard, 'but it was done via messenger, not in person. The sickness returned a few days ago and laid me abed again so I could not venture far. However, the idea to increase the pressure on Acre is sound, and I was happy to agree to the strategy.'

'But do you not think I should have been party to such discussions?'

'You obviously have been,' said Richard, 'else you would not be before me know.'

'I was told only last night by Conrad of Montferrat, whose arrogance was only matched by his barely concealed merriment.'

'King Guy,' said Richard with a sigh, 'I know there is bad blood between the both of you, but you cannot allow the feud to cloud your judgement in these things. There will be accountability in good time, but for the moment we should focus on what is important, and that is combining our strength to capture Acre. With regards to your notification, I was only informed early yesterday morning, and as you can see, I am not yet in full health. If it is an apology you seek, then you have had a wasted journey.'

'Your Grace,' said Guy, 'I seek no apology, just clarification on the whole situation. I have been asked to defend the rear, which I am glad to do, but would ask if it is true that you will not be joining the attack.'

'It is true,' said Richard, 'at least for the time being.'

'Until such time as the fevers pass?'

'My health has no bearing on this decision,' said Richard, 'I am holding back my men as I have requested a meeting with Saladin.'

'You are going to meet the sultan?'

'If he accepts my invitation, yes.'

'To what end, may I ask?'

'To try to save the lives of thousands. It may be a fool's errand, but what sort of king would I be if I did not consider such things before committing many of my men to certain death?'

'Do you think he will cede Acre?'

'Perhaps.'

'And Jerusalem?'

'Surrender may be too much to ask, but there are other options.'

'Such as?'

'King Guy,' said Richard, his voice sharper than it had been only moments earlier, 'I accept that you have a vested interest in all this, but I have already explained the circumstances, and am not inclined to explain my actions further. Be comforted that I am just as committed to recovering the Holy-land as ever I was, and I can assure you that should my negotiations with Saladin fail, then I will attack Acre with every sinew in my body. In the meantime, I suggest you offer King Phillip your full support. Now, if you don't mind, I have things to do.'

'Of course,' said Guy with the slightest of bows, 'please forgive the intrusion.' He turned away and left the tent before striding towards his horse. Sir Geraint joined him as he walked.

'Well,' he asked, 'how did it go?'

'I'm not sure,' said Guy, 'the man is hard to read.'

'So, do we join Phillip or hold back our men?'

'We will join him for now,' said Guy mounting his horse, 'but these situations have a habit of changing quickly.'

Thomas Cronin stood atop the small hill overlooking the Templar lines. Beside him was the new grandmaster of the Templar order, Robert de Sablé, freshly arrived from Europe on Richard's fleet. Robert was an experienced knight and well-used to the ways of war, but he had been a Templar for only a year or so, a fact that cast doubt in many of the order's minds.

'Describe the city to me?' said Robert, staring towards Acre.

'The two outer walls are strong,' said Cronin, 'and mainly built upon solid rock. Each runs in a straight line to the sea from the Accursed-Tower in the north-eastern corner. There are two gates, one in the northern wall, and one in the eastern wall where it meets the sea. Inside the outer wall, there is a second wall no less strong, protecting the city itself. If our forces succeed in breaching the first, they will be caught between the two in a killing zone.'

'And the garrison?'

'It has been relieved several times both from the land and the sea, and we believe it is now several thousand strong. However, we do know they are suffering badly through disease and lack of food.'

'Is there any chance they could receive further reinforcements?'

'No, my lord. With Richard's fleet dominating the sea and Phillip's army strengthening our positions, we now have them completely cut off. It is just a matter of time until the city surrenders.'

'Time which we do not have,' said Robert.

'With respect, my lord,' said Cronin, 'we have been here almost two years. A few more months won't matter.

'We came to return Jerusalem into Christian hands,' said Robert. 'Acre is merely a distraction, albeit a necessary one. We need to secure it quickly while the armies of Richard and Phillip are still strong and healthy. What of our own men?'

'We have about four hundred knights,' said Cronin, 'twice as many sergeants, and two thousand men at arms, including the arbalists.'

'Horses?'

'Not as many as we would like, but enough to keep our knights mounted.'

'It is a fair force,' said Robert, 'though I would have liked more. We must ensure we deploy them carefully, and only when they will have the maximum impact.'

'With respect, my lord,' said Cronin, 'they will not look kindly on being held back from any confrontation purely on the grounds of maintaining our numbers.'

'I care not what they think,' said Robert, we have lost far too many brave knights these past few years. When we attack, it will be to gain the maximum advantage, not at the whim of some glory-hunting monarch with no nose for the ways of war.' He looked left towards Guy's lines in front of the city. 'Tomorrow morning, Phillip of France will unleash his siege engines. Over the next few days, he will maintain the assault with the aim of driving the defenders from the outer walls. Our men will not take part in this attack until such time as we are ready to assault the inner walls. Then, and only then will we once again expose the Saracens to Templar Steel.'

Chapter Twenty-three

Acre

June 17 – AD 1191

Phillip of France sat astride his horse before the battered city walls of Acre. They had suffered a lot of damage but still stood defiant, a testament to the men who had built them so many years earlier. The ballistae of King Guy and his allies were still in place but had been added to by the French king over the previous few days.

Carts of heavy rocks lined up behind the ballistae, and five thousand archers waited to cover the advance as rows of slaves pulled the siege engines into range of the walls.

Over ten thousand foot-soldiers lined up behind the king, though it was anticipated that the barrage would last several days before a large enough breach was created.

Beyond Mount Toron to Phillip's rear, King Guy had amassed his entire army to face inland. It was highly probable that Saladin would attack Phillip's rear to distract them from the assault, and it was Guy's role to repel such an attack, should it occur.

Phillip looked in both directions before lifting his hand for silence. Immediately, any movement or noise along the massed Christian armies died out, and every set of eyes stared towards the city.

Along the battlements, they could see hundreds of Saracen warriors staring back at them, many beneath the yellow standards of the Ayyubid. Every Christian soldier knew the defenders were excellent archers, and would make them pay a heavy price, but never had there been such a strong army ready for the assault, and after almost two years of trying, the feeling was, at last, they had a chance.

'Sir Conrad,' said Phillip, 'give the command.'

Conrad rode a few paces forward so he could be seen by every man.

'Bowmen advance,' he shouted, and the archers ran to the front of the gathered army. Behind them came hundreds of

commoners carrying extra arrows and pots of burning oil, each man having been paid a penny for their service.

When they were just beyond the reach of the defenders' own arrows, the archers came to a stop and formed lines ten deep.

'Nock,' shouted Conrad, 'draw, *loose!* ... Ballistae, *advance.*'

To the sound drums and horns echoing through the morning air, teams of mules drew the ballistae forward into range of the walls, protected by volley after volley of flaming arrows. Up on the walls, the defenders were forced to take cover behind the battlements, as no sooner had one volley of arrows smashed into their positions than it was replaced by another, a constant barrage of death, fired by thousands of disciplined archers.

Within minutes, the ballistae reached their designated positions, and as the commoners ran the animals back to safety, the operators loaded up their siege engines.

'Ballistae,' roared Conrad, lifting his sword high in the air, *'ready?'*

Rows of men held up their arms in acknowledgement, and as Conrad of Montferrat dropped his sword, they hammered the wooden triggers to unleash a deadly rain of death and destruction against the city walls.

At such a close range, and against such a small area, the effect was devastating, and immediately they smashed into the uppermost section, sending dozens of screaming defenders hurtling from the battlements to be dashed against the ground beyond.

Inside the city, the people hid wherever they could. The main assault was focussed on the outer walls, but the larger mangonels hurled their missiles into the heart of the city, killing and destroying everything in their paths. Flaming arrows reached some of the wooden buildings causing panic amongst the population and rows of desperate people formed chains to pass buckets of water from the docks to try to save what they could.

Turan-Shah peered out of one of the arrow slits in one of the lesser towers, staring at the massed Christian armies attacking the central part of the wall.

'Is the signal fire ready?' he asked.

'Yes, my lord,' said one of his men.

'Then put a torch to it,' he said, 'let us see if we can ease this bombardment.'

The man ran from the room and out across the bailey. A few minutes later, he ran up the steps of the forbidden tower, and over to a prepared signal fire.

'Light it,' he shouted, and as he watched, several men applied burning torches to the base of the beacon. Within moments the flames caught, and the messenger walked over to pick up one of the many buckets of seaweed situated along the base of the walls. Others joined him and hurled the contents into the flames.

Within moments the fire changed as the greenery caught alight, sending plumes of black smoke high into the clear morning air.

'That should do it,' said the guard stepping back from the fire. 'All we can do now is wait.'

At the far end of the open plains, Saladin's scouts saw the smoke and turned their horses to ride hard towards his camp. Within minutes they had briefed the sultan, and he turned to face his son.

'Al-Afdal,' he said. 'Muster your forces and ride against the Christians at the base of the king's mountain. Gokbori will attack the northern positions and Beha ad-Din Karakush, the south.'

'My lord,' said Al-Afdal, 'our scouts say the Christians have reinforced their positions facing inland. I suspect they are expecting such a reaction.'

'I'm sure they are,' said Salah ad-Din, 'and our reinforcements will arrive from Damascus within days, but we cannot afford to wait. Our brothers in Acre need us now and we will not be found wanting. We may not be able to defeat them, but every Christian we engage in battle is one less who can turn his attentions upon Acre. Muster the men and prepare to attack.'

'As you wish,' said Al-Afdal

Within the hour, over two thousand warriors rode their horses out onto the plains, followed by as many archers and foot-soldiers. Behind them, Salah ad-Din sat astride his horse, knowing that the next few days would be vital in the struggle for not just Acre, but for Jerusalem itself.

Across the plain, Guy's army poured out of their positions to form defensive lines. Numbers were approximately equal, and the sultan knew that whatever happened, many men were about to lose their lives.

Al-Afdal sat upon his own horse at the Sultan's side, waiting for the signal. Salah ad-Din turned to face him, and with the slightest of nods, gave the command.

'Make the day ours, my son, water the ground with Christian blood.'

Al-Afdal dug his heels into his horse's flanks and galloped out to the front of the Saracen army before drawing his scimitar and holding it high in the air.

'Death to the infidels,' he roared, *'Allah Akbar.'*

'Allah Akbar,' roared the massed ranks of Saracens in response, and as one, raced towards the waiting Christian army.

On the opposite side of Mount Toron, sergeants and officers strode amongst the mangonels and archers, urging them to greater efforts. Seldom a second passed when there were no missiles of some description soaring through the sky, whether it be flaming arrows, stone boulders or clay pots of Greek-fire.

Carts made journey after journey back to the stockpiles of boulders amassed over the previous few months, hardly keeping up with the unceasing rate of fire. Other carts containing barrels of arrows were also brought forward from the camps, the result of tens of thousands of man-hours by the many fletchers brought from Tyre.

Over in the city, Fakhiri ran between the rubble-filled streets. Up above, the sky was filled with black smoke-trails from the constant barrage of arrows, and the occasional boulder whistled over his head to smash into the buildings with devastating effect. People ran everywhere, and the air was full of screaming. The attack was worse than anything they had seen so far, yet Fakhiri knew it was only the beginning of what was yet to come.

He stopped before the house he had shared with the trader for the past year or so. Inside, his master was hiding deep within its cellar, surrounded by his henchmen and enough food and water to last for days. Many of the traders had done the same knowing that whichever side eventually emerged victorious, there would be a profit to be made when the fighting was done.

Fakhiri had no idea where his master had hidden his hoard, but over the past few months had taken measures to ensure his own safety when the inevitable happened. He walked over to a water barrel standing beside the door to the trader's house, and leaning against a wall for leverage, tipped it over, pouring the water into the street. He dropped to his knees and reached inside to retrieve a leather purse containing hundreds of silver coins, the accumulated results of his wheeling and dealing while living within the city.

After hiding the purse about his person, he made his way across the city to the Templar commandery before stopping before the gates and banging on the hatch with his fist.

'Open up,' he said, 'I have a message for the jailer.'

The hatch opened, and Fakhiri was relieved to see the familiar features of the guard commander.

'Ragesh,' he said, 'I am pleased it is you.'

'What do you want, Fakhiri?' replied Ragesh.

'I have come to make you a rich man, open the gate.'

'What do you mean?'

'Let's just say that everything we have done together so far fades into significance when compared to what I have to offer you.'

'I am listening,' said Ragesh.

'Let me in, and we will discuss it,' said Fakhiri, 'unless of course, you are confident that your life will be safe when the infidels arrive, which they will.'

The guard hesitated before closing the hatch and sliding back the bars on the gate.

'Inside,' he said, stepping to one side, 'and go into the gate tower.'

Fakhiri hurried inside and found himself in a circular room occupied by a very young and nervous-looking guard. Ragesh locked the gates and followed him in.

'You, get out,' he said, and the boy ran gladly from the room. When they were alone, he turned to Fakhiri. 'Well, what do you have to say, Fakhiri, and it had better be good?'

'I think it is,' said Fakhiri, 'but first I have a question.'

'Which is?'

'Who do you think will emerge the victor in all this?' He nodded in the direction of the relentless barrage aimed towards the city walls.

'We have been told the Christians waste their time,' said Ragesh, 'the inner walls are unbreachable, and even if they were to fall, our army waits to kill the infidels as soon as they show their faces.'

'And who told you this?'

'Barak himself, and he knows people in high places.'

'And where is your master now?'

'I know not. He left a few days ago but should be back soon.'

'He will not be back,' said Fakhiri, 'for as we speak, I suspect his ship nears the port of Alexandria.'

Ragesh stared at Fakhiri with disbelief.

'You are lying,' he said eventually, 'if he were going to leave, he would have taken me with him.'

'And why would he do that? You are nothing to him except one more servant meant to fulfil his every whim. He is on that ship, Ragesh, along with many other such people. I know for I arranged the passage myself.'

'You did?'

'Aye. He and my master are cousins, and Barak paid a fortune to go back to Egypt before the English king's arrival. I am telling the truth, Ragesh, Barak has left you here to die.'

'You do not know that,' said Ragesh, 'the city could prevail.'

'Ragesh,' said Fakhiri, 'you may not have seen much outside of these prison walls, but I can assure you, I have. For months, I have mingled with the guards along the parapets, supplying whatever they need in return for a crumb of bread or a sip of wine. They thought me a fool and ridiculed my nature, but the ploy worked, and every time I went there, I looked over the wall at the enemy positions.'

'And?'

'For the past few days, I have seen men arriving like never before. Their numbers are vast, and their camps stretch as far as the eyes can see. There are rows upon rows of siege engines, and out at sea, their ships number in the hundreds. We cannot win this battle, Ragesh, it is only a matter of time before the walls fall and they pour in like water through a breached dam.'

The guard fell silent and stared at Fakhiri.

'So, why are you here?' he asked eventually.

'I want to make a trade,' said Fakhiri. 'The lives of the Christian prisoners in return for a purse heavy with silver.'

'How much silver?'

'This much,' said Fakhiri and poured the contents of his purse on the table.

Ragesh stared at the pile of silver. It was enough to set him up for life back in Egypt and an offer to good to refuse.

'It is a fair price,' he said, looking up, 'but I cannot release the prisoners. If Turan-Shah found out, he would have me skinned alive.'

'I don't want you to release them,' said Fakhiri, 'for they are probably safer where they are while this siege is ongoing.'

'So, what would you have me do?'

'I want you to hide them somewhere. Somewhere where they will be safe from any fighting and those who would seek retribution.'

'And where is this place?'

'I do not know, but it has to be within this commandery.'

'Why here, would it not be better to secure them within the city?'

'The streets are full of eyes, Ragesh, and everyone will do whatever they can to save their own lives. To move twenty-five prisoners without being seen is impossible, and their location would be known within minutes. It has to be here, somewhere difficult to find yet big enough for twenty-five men.'

'I know of such a place,' said Ragesh eventually, 'a cellar beneath the floor of a storeroom at the back of the kitchens. It was used to keep food from spoiling in the heat. It is small, but it could work.'

'Then that is where we must take them,' said Fakhiri. 'When the city falls, there will some who will want to exact retribution on any Christians they can find. By doing this, they will be safe, at least for a while, but they will need food and water in case they are down there for any length of time.'

'But if what you say comes to pass and Acre falls, what is to stop them being found and executed?'

'We can only do what we can,' said Fakhiri, 'the rest is up to Allah.'

Out on the plains, the Saracen cavalry raced across the plains towards the Christian lines. Guy's own cavalry were already closing in from the side, but they were moments too late, and the Saracens crashed into the lines of foot-soldiers with devastating effect. Bodies fell everywhere, and in the confusion, the riders took advantage to press home their attack. Once again, the plains surrounding Acre rang with the screams of the dying, and every man fought furiously, desperate to save their own lives.

Despite the initial advantage, the Saracens did not have it all their own way for as soon as the initial impetus had been checked, Guy sent a second wave of foot-soldiers down the slopes to reinforce the lines. Encouraged by the reinforcements, men pulled the riders from their horses before hacking them to death with whatever blade they had to hand.

Within moments, the Saracen foot-soldiers joined the fray, and the fight spread throughout the Christian positions. The Saracen horsemen extricated themselves from the melee, only to find Guy's cavalry waiting for them, and a fully mounted battle broke out over the rest of the field. Men died in their hundreds until again the sound of Saracen horns echoed through the air and Saladin's army retreated.

Nobody on the Christian side took advantage of the withdrawal for every man still standing was just glad to get a momentary respite from the carnage. Bodies lay everywhere, and lakes of glossy blood reflected the afternoon sun.

'We should give chase,' said Sir Geraint on the top of the hill, 'they are in disarray.'

'No,' said Guy, 'that's exactly what they want us to do. Look.' He pointed into the distance where thousands more mounted warriors stood waiting for the command to attack. 'Out in the open, they have the advantage,' he continued, 'and we would lose more men with little gain. Give the order to retreat and rebuild the palisades. Send fresh men to the front lines and position our arbalists on the lower slopes. The next time they come, we will fight them here, where we are strongest.'

'As you wish, my lord,' said Geraint.

Chapter Twenty-four

Acre

July – AD 1191

Day after day, the intense attack on Acre continued. Days turned into weeks and barrage after barrage decimated the outer walls. The allied armies vastly outnumbered those manning the city defences, but every time Phillip committed them to the assault, they were held off by the desperate defenders. After so many attacks, the body count was high, and corpses littered the approach to the city. The smell of death and smoke filled the air, and everyone was exhausted.

Despite this, in some areas, the outer walls were no more than piles of rubble, but the defenders had poured the last of their resources into the weaker areas including filling them with sharpened stakes and flammable oil, ready to be ignited at the first sign of a full-scale assault.

Phillip knew that such things were usual in war, and ordinarily would not have hesitated in committing his men, but the fact remained that there was an even bigger wall a few hundred paces further in, one which had hardly been affected by the barrage from the mangonels. Consequently, he had called a council of all the leaders to agree the next steps and now stood at a table in his campaign tent alongside several other nobles.

'I see no reason to hold back,' said Leopold, Duke of Austria, 'we have fought too hard to get where we are, and every hour we delay is an hour they have to repair their defences. I say we strike now while the men still have fire in their hearts.'

'If we do that,' countered the king of Armenia, 'we would gain the bailey, but the cost in men would be far too high.'

'Then what do you propose we do?' asked Phillip. 'It took weeks just to destroy the outer walls, and even now, we are held back by their fanatical defence. To breach the inner wall could take twice as long, and cost twice the number of men.'

The conversation continued until a knight ducked through the flaps and walked quickly to Phillip, whispering directly in his ear. Phillip's eyes opened wide with surprise and turned to face the other nobles.

'Gentlemen,' he said, 'there has been a development, it seems that King Richard is out of his sickbed and is joining us imminently.'

'Really?' said one of the barons sarcastically, 'I suppose that means he has fallen out with his friend, Saladin.'

'An uncalled-for insult,' snapped Leo of Armenia, 'his diplomacy was aimed at saving lives, nothing more.'

'And where has that got us?' asked Leopold of Austria. As far as I know, he has not even met the sultan yet, and his vast army sits idle amongst the dunes.'

'He has been stricken with the disease,' said Leo, 'as well you know.'

'All I am saying,' said Leopold, 'is that with his men, we can end this siege in days, but without them, all our journeys may have been in vain.'

'Well,' said King Phillip, 'we will find out soon enough. Here he comes.'

Richard ducked into the tent and walked straight up to the campaign table. Some of the occupants bowed in subjugation, while others just nodded politely, unwilling to recognise his greater stature and power.

Richard struck an imposing figure. He was taller by far than any other man in the room, and his chainmail hauberk did little to hide his muscular frame beneath. His tabard was blood red, emblazoned with two lions and around his waist, an oversized sword hung from a tightly fastened leather belt. His legs were encased in chainmail leggings, and if he still bore any weakness from his illness, there was certainly none on display.

'Gentlemen,' he said, 'my apologies for the lateness of my attendance, I had to check something on my way here.'

'No apologies needed,' said Phillip, 'we are just happy you are back on your feet.'

'As am I,' said Richard, 'and there is much time to be made up. My sources have kept me informed of the situation, but perhaps you can tell me of any fresh developments.'

'It will be my pleasure,' said Phillip, 'but first, could I ask how went the parley with Saladin?'

'It did not happen,' said Richard. 'He sent a message that it was not good for kings to converse outside of a treaty, but sent his son, Al-Afdal to negotiate on his behalf. Alas, by then, I was struck down for the second time by the illness and did not attend.'

'So, all negotiations have ended?'

'They have, and I am now focussed on reaching Jerusalem. However, there is this little city to think about first.'

'Indeed there is,' said Conrad of Montferrat, 'and this *'little city,'* as you so quaintly call it, has cost the lives of thousands while your men play dice in the sand.'

'Conrad,' snapped Phillip, 'curb your insolence.'

'No,' said Richard, 'let him speak. We are all men, and if we are hurt by words, what chance do we have against blades?'

'All I am saying,' continued Conrad, 'is we waited a long time for your arrival. When the sails of your fleet were first seen on the horizon, grown men shed tears of relief, yet here we are, almost a month later with not a single blade blooded amongst your men. Can you wonder why there is frustration amongst your allies?'

'I accept your criticisms,' said Richard, 'but was not able to lead my men for reasons you all know. Now those reasons have gone, and I am here at your side, ready to be counted.'

'And you are welcome,' interjected King Guy, cutting off any further negative conversation. 'Perhaps we can all now turn to the matter in hand.'

For the next few minutes, Phillip recounted the situation to Richard, with the latter just listening in silence.

'There is no doubt that our progress has been hard-fought,' said Richard eventually, 'and every man here has played his part, but I agree that to pause now invites even more hardship. I understand that even if we were to get past the first wall, we would be caught in a killing zone so we must ensure that does not happen.'

'And how do we do that?' asked Leo.

'By immediately creating a secondary breach in the inner walls. That way, our impetus will continue into the city. My men will be at the forefront of the assault, as will I, and I swear that I will not rest until Acre is ours.'

'That is all very well,' said Conrad, 'but how do you intend forging this second breach?'

'Lord Conrad,' said Richard, 'there may be those amongst you that think my men have been idle these past few weeks, but I assure you nothing could be further from the truth. While we were waiting, they have been building two siege engines, capable of demolishing the stoutest of walls.'

'I heard rumours of these machines,' said Guy. 'Our patrols say they saw them a league to the south, but they were being disassembled.'

'They were but have now been brought here ready to use. It will take two days to put them back together, and when done, I assure you they will bring this siege to a swift and decisive end.'

He looked around the tent. Everyman was staring at him, some with doubt, but most with respect. Richard had a fearsome reputation, and they knew that if anyone could bring the siege to an end, it was him.

'So,' he continued, 'if there are no more questions, what I propose is this. Today, we will task as many men as we can spare to bring larger boulders from the cliffs. The day after tomorrow, the trebuchets will open the barrage at dawn, but it is imperative we keep them well-fed. If we target the same area, the walls will be breached within days and we will go on the attack.' He turned to the new grandmaster. 'Sir Robert, your order has borne the brunt of Saladin's wrath these past few years, so it is to you I turn to offer you the chance of retribution.'

'Just name the task,' said the grandmaster, 'and we will embrace it with all our hearts.'

'I expected as much, so once the second wall is breached, you will have the honour of taking the city.'

'Thank you, your Grace,' said Robert.

Richard looked around the tent again.

'Now, we have wasted enough time so unless there are any other questions, let us all go back to our men and make ready. At dawn, the day after tomorrow, we will throw everything we have against Acre and will not stop until it is in our hands or we have died trying. Agreed?'

'Agreed,' said the assembled nobles, and Richard turned away to leave the tent, leaving them staring after him.

'You have to admit,' said Conrad, 'the man is full of self-confidence.'

'He has the heart of a lion,' said Leopold of Austria, 'and will not be found wanting.'

'Richard the Lion-hearted,' said one of the nobles. 'It would make a good epitaph for any man.'

'Only time will tell,' said Phillip, 'but in the meantime, I propose we give him our full support. It is time to bring this debacle to an end.'

Chapter Twenty-five

Acre

July – AD 1191

Two days later, tens of thousands of men formed up before the ravaged outer walls of Acre, shivering in the early-morning air. Dozens of mangonels could be seen in the gloom before them, temporarily silenced as the Christian forces moved into position.

Behind them, rising high above their heads loomed the two huge trebuchets Richard had brought from England. Named Bad Neighbour and God's Own Catapult respectively, each was a devastating weapon of war and took many men to operate. The rate of fire was relatively slow compared to the smaller mangonels, but the huge payloads meant the effect was devastating.

Gradually the sky lightened, and every man fell silent in anticipation. Behind them, a solitary drum started beating, joined every few seconds by another until the air throbbed to the sound of the war drums. Archers strung their bows while men at arms checked their equipment for what seemed like the hundredth time. Belts were tightened, ties slackened on scabbards and riders leaned forward to tap gently on their horses' necks. Richard himself sat upon his horse to the front of everyone. He knew there was little he could do until the last of the walls fell, but he also knew it was important for the besiegers to see him to the fore. The morning got even lighter, but still he waited for the right moment to unleash the attack.

When it seemed he would wait forever, the sun finally cleared the mountains and the first rays hit the topmost part of the Forbidden-tower. It was the moment he had been waiting for, and as the battlements lit up in the sun's light, he drew his sword and held it high in the air.

'*Men of Christendom,*' he roared through the morning air, 'in the name of God almighty, *let battle commence.*'

He dropped his sword sharply, and thousands of men watched in awe as a huge boulder, engulfed in the flames of Greek oil, flew above their heads, to smash into the inner wall with devastating effect. A huge chunk of the battlements immediately disintegrated sending rubble and screaming men into the city. A second massive boulder flew through the morning air to smash against the inner wall, and as the effectiveness of the huge machines became clear, the cold soldiers forgot what lay before them and broke into sustained cheering.

Richard smiled inwardly. He had deliberately engineered this moment for maximum effect and as the roars of approval echoed in his ears, his sword dropped again, unleashing his smaller mangonels against what remained of the outer wall.

The Christians watched the heavy and sustained attack in awe. Saracens died all along the wall, and there was seldom a second when there were no boulders flying through the air. The siege-engine operators worked harder than they ever had before, each team being offered a purse of silver if they outperformed the one alongside them.

Every few minutes, another giant missile soared above them all, their target the inner walls and though there was little that fire could do against solid stone defences, Richard had ordered that each was to be set alight to create fear in the hearts of the defenders. Hour after hour the barrage continued until eventually there were dozens of fresh breaches all along the perimeter.

Eventually, all the mangonels fell silent, getting ready for the next part of Richard's plan. Behind them, the trebuchets continued their deadly barrage against the inner wall, but the English king had a new task for the smaller siege engines.

'*Reload,*' roared one of the commanders, and the mangonel operators placed new missiles into their weapons, clay pots filled with Greek-fire. '*Ready,*' roared the commander, '*release!*'

Again, fiery missiles flew through the air, this time smashing into the already destroyed outer walls. The liquid fire covered everything in reach, but more importantly, set light to the pools of oil strategically placed by the Saracens to repel the attack when it came. Within minutes the whole of the wall was engulfed in flames, overwhelming any timber defences as well as anyone not quick enough to escape the rain of death.

Richard rode to the front of his army, knowing that the moment of assault was quickly approaching. Alongside him were the generals and nobles who were going to lead the assault on either side.

'In a few minutes,' he said, 'I want every mangonel dragged a hundred paces forward. Once there, tell them to open fire at the inner battlements with Greek-fire. Follow them up with our archers. Once we have achieved dominance, upon my signal, I want you all to attack the walls with everything you have.'

'Should we not create more breaches?' asked one of the nobles, 'the southern part of the wall is well defended.'

'It is but I need you to keep the Saracens occupied while we attack the breach. The same thing goes for the northern segment. He turned to Sir Guy, sitting on his own horse a few paces away. 'King Guy, how is our rear?'

'My army is on alert,' said Guy, 'but Saladin's main force has moved southward so does not appear to pose any further risk.'

'Tell your men to stay wary,' said Richard. 'Saladin's army is vast, and there could still be many warriors hidden amongst the hills.' He looked over towards the city, seeing the flames beginning to die down. 'Prepare to move the mangonels,' he said, 'and muster the men.'

Minutes later, the battle drums once again echoed throughout the Christian positions, and as thousands of arrows darkened the sky, the massed ranks started running towards Acre. The final assault had begun.

In the city, Turan-Shah was surrounded by his commanders just inside the inner walls. The stench of smoke filled the air, and the noise of the terrible bombardment caused the very ground to shake.

'I want every man we can spare onto the battlements,' shouted the prince, 'we have to hold the breach at all costs.'

'We have no more men,' replied one of his officers, 'they are all either dead or fighting as we speak.'

'Then drag the civilians up there,' said Turan-Shah. 'Any man, woman or child capable of bearing a knife or hurling a rock needs to be on those walls.'

'Why?' asked one of his men, 'there is no way we can withstand that army.'

'To buy us time until the reinforcements come. Last night we sent six messengers out of the city under cover of darkness to let Salah ad-Din know the seriousness of the situation.'

'My lord,' said another officer, 'the messengers did not get through. 'Every one of them was captured and killed. The Christians hung their bodies from gibbets outside the northern gate.'

The prince thought furiously. Unless Salah ad-Din sent reinforcements, they were doomed to lose the city and probably every Muslim still inside it.

'We have to get a message to the Sultan,' he said. 'Is there any way of getting through their lines?'

'The port has been blockaded,' said one of the men, 'and the city is surrounded with Christians. We could try again tonight, but they will be expecting us. They have eyes on every stone in every wall, and nobody can get out without being seen. We are trapped like rats in a barrel.'

'There is a way,' said a voice and all eyes turned to see Hassan Malouf standing to one side.

'If you have any ideas, Hassan,' said Turan-Shah, 'then now is the time to share them.'

'My lord,' said Hassan, 'I think I can get past the guards without being seen and pass any messages on to Salah ad-Din.'

'And how do you intend to do that? The men we sent last night were the best we had yet even they were caught. They must have every path and every track covered.'

'Then I will use no paths, but go the same way that I arrived, via the sea.'

'You just heard that the port is blockaded, they will sink any boat on sight, no matter how small.'

'My lord,' said Hassan, 'if you recall, I reached Acre by swimming from the southern dunes and back into the port around the harbour walls. I see no reason why my journey cannot be reversed. If I go when it is dark, I should be able to reach the shore within an hour.

'Even if you do, I'm sure there are hundreds of Christians along the dunes. They would see you in moments, even in the dark.'

'Not if I stay in the water as long as possible and make my way southward with only my head exposed. Nobody will expect anyone to come that way, and I can be beyond their positions by dawn. After that, I can make my way to Salah ad-Din's camp and pass on your message.'

Turan-Shah turned to Salman.

'You know this man better than most. What do you think?'

'As usual, it is an idea born of madness, but if anyone can do it, he can.'

The prince nodded and turned back to face Hassan.

'Hassan Malouf,' he said, 'it seems like whenever there is a dire need, it is to you we turn for deliverance. Yet again, the fate of this city lays in your hands, but if you think this can be done, then go with my blessing.'

'What is the message, my lord?' asked Hassan.

'Tell the Sultan of our situation. Beg of him the support of his entire army with all haste. Tell him without it, we will surely fall within days.' He removed a ring from his finger and gave it to Hassan. 'Give him this so he knows your words are mine.'

'As you wish,' said Hassan, and left the courtyard closely followed by Salman.

'Hassan,' said Salman, 'wait.'

The Bedouin stopped and turned to the warrior who had become his friend.

'Are you sure about this?' asked Salman. 'You got away with it once, but you may not be so lucky a second time.'

'What other option is there?' asked Hassan. 'The city is surrounded, and this is the only way to get help. At least this way we have a chance and as you said, I have done it before.'

'Yes, but this time you will have to stay in the water a lot longer. You were freezing last time; the cold could take you as surely as any blade.'

'I will take my chances,' said Hassan, 'and don't forget, I am fluent in their language, so when I do go inland, I can pretend to be one of them. It is the only way, Salman, it is something I have to do.'

Salman placed his hand on Hassan's shoulder.

'In that case, do what you have to do, and if it is Allah's will that we both survive, I will ensure the Sultan knows of what you did here today.'

'Thank you,' said Hassan, 'but it is almost dark, so I must go.'

'Do you want me to come down to the harbour with you?'

'No, it is better if I go alone.'

'Then be safe, my friend. I will pray for you.'

Hassan nodded and watched as Salman walked away, not knowing it was the last time they would ever speak.

Chapter Twenty-six

Acre

July – AD 1191

For days, the massed Christian armies had thrown everything they had against the inner walls. As far as the eye could see in both directions, desperate men scaled the elongated ladders to reach the battlements, while equally terrified defenders did everything they could to send them crashing back to earth. Arrows flew in both directions, and the cries of dying men echoed through the air.

Everything seemed to be ablaze, and the screams of men being burned alive were the most heart-wrenching of all. Those unable to help themselves were dragged free from the chaos by civilians risking their own lives, all thoughts of payment discarded in the dire need to save lives.

Despite the frantic and determined defence, some of the besiegers made it to the top and flew at the nearest guards, knowing they only needed to last a few seconds to allow their comrades to join them. Battle-hardened Saracens threw themselves at the attackers, just as experienced and just as brutal. Once again, steel hacked through human flesh and blood fell from the parapets like scarlet rain. The battle was brutal, relentless and unforgiving.

'*Your Grace,*' shouted a voice, 'you have to attack now, we cannot keep this up much longer.'

'Not yet,' said King Richard holding up his hand. He looked around him. To either side stood a long line of Templars, each afoot with blades drawn, and all staring towards the wall just a few hundred paces away. Some he had brought with him from England, but the majority were those who had been at the siege since day one.

He turned his attention back towards Acre. The boulders from the mangonels and the two giant trebuchets were still smashing into the walls either side of the largest breach, and the city itself could clearly be seen through the rubble and smoke. Despite this, the king knew the breach had to be as wide as possible to avoid his men becoming forced into a deadly bottleneck. Several more boulders smashed into the defences until, with a terrifying roar and a massive cloud of dust, a huge section collapsed in on itself, unable to hold its own weight after the incessant battering.

It was the moment Richard had been waiting for, and as the surviving defenders desperately sought to recover, the king roared out the command everyone had been waiting for.

'Men of Christendom,' he roared, 'for God and for Jerusalem, *attaaack!'*

As one, the remaining assault troops started to run across the bailey between the two walls. At their head were almost two hundred Templar knights, led by the unmistakable figure of the king. His stature meant he stood out above them all, and many archers on the wall singled him out as a target, but despite their arrows thudding into the ground around him, fate was on his side and he advanced unhurt.

The sight of Richard leading from the front forged great courage in the hearts of every man that followed, and they ran towards the second breach with little thought of their own safety.

Arrows rained down from the walls to either side, and men fell in their hundreds, but they forged ahead and charged through the dying flames towards the waiting enemy.

With almighty roars of anger, the knights waded into the defenders, their heavy blades cutting through leather armour into the flesh beyond. Years of frustration and the desperate need for revenge poured from their hearts into their swords, and they marched forward, unleashing their fury upon the terrified Muslims.

More and more followed them through the breach, desperate to help their comrades and behind them, hundreds of black-clad sergeants brought up the rear. Saracen reinforcements ran from the city to force them back, and the fighting spread from the walls into the surrounding streets. Men on both sides fought desperately, each knowing that they had to kill or be killed. There was no thought of quarter and the sound of steel on steel mixed with the roars of the enraged and the cries of the dying.

Amongst them all, untouched yet covered in the blood of his enemies stood the figure of King Richard, his blade no less active, his fury no less fervent. Any man who could see him couldn't help but be impressed as he led from the front, cutting down men with unfettered brutality administered with unforgiving rage.

Inside the city, the overwhelming barrage had wreaked devastation, and people scrambled to find a place to hide from the Christian foot-soldiers.

Fears of anticipated Christian brutality swept through the population, increasing in intensity until the thought of surviving to face their tormentors was almost worse than the thought of a bloody death at the end of a sword. Gangs of criminals grouped together to take advantage of the confusion and preyed upon the weak, robbing them of whatever they could to buy their lives when the city fell.

Panic reigned, and people ran everywhere, many wounded from the flying shards of rock or burned from the fires that blazed throughout Acre. Wooden buildings collapsed in flames, and women clung desperately to their children, preying to their deities to spare their lives.

Amongst the devastation, Fakhiri clambered amongst the rubble. He knew that when the soldiers came, they would see him only as a Saracen and there would be little chance for explanation. Desperately he made his way across the city, twice having to defend himself from the brigands taking advantage of the panic. Against all the odds, he arrived at the commandery and hammered on the gates.

'*Ragesh, open up!*'

Eventually, the gates creaked open just enough for Fakhiri to squeeze through before being slammed behind him. Ragesh slid the bolts across and turned to face the Egyptian.

'I thought you were surely dead,' said the guard.

'Well, I am not,' snapped Fakhiri. 'Have you made the arrangements?'

'It depends,' said Ragesh. 'Do you have the silver?'

'I do,' said the Egyptian, 'but we have to move the prisoners *now.*'

'Come with me,' said the guard and led Fakhiri to the hospital to find Sumeira.

'Sumeira,' said Fakhiri seeing her sitting on a cot at the far end of the room, 'come, we have to go.'

'Go where?' asked Sumeira getting to her feet.

'I'll explain as we go,' said Fakhiri, 'but we have to leave now. Are there any Christian patients in this room?'

'One,' said Sumeira.

'Can he walk?'

'Yes.'

'Then bring him with you but do it quickly. There is little time.'

'Wait,' said Sumeira, 'you know I will not abandon these people so where are you taking me?'

'Sumeira,' gasped Fakhiri, 'these men are Muslim and will not be harmed if the citadel is overrun. The Christian prisoners, however, are in danger and even now there are gangs of men roaming the streets killing anyone of a different faith. If you stay here, you could be dead within hours along with all those you have kept alive in the cells.'

'What about Shani?'

'I will stay here,' said Shani from behind her, 'and continue to look after the sick.'

Sumeira spun around and stared at the orderly who had become her close friend.

'You can't,' she said. 'You would be in too much danger.'

'I have to,' said Shani. 'My people will not harm their own, and when the Christians come, if they have hearts even a quarter of the size of yours, they will not harm the sick or those who care for them. Now hurry, you must go.'

Sumeira paused before walking over to the orderly and embracing him.

'Stay safe,' she said, 'and I'll see you soon.'

'Sumeira,' snapped Fakhiri, 'we have to go, *now!*'

The physician turned and walked over to a cot.

'David,' she said, 'come with us. We have to go.' She helped the fellow prisoner to his feet and walked slowly over to the door. Outside, Ragesh was waiting impatiently.

'Hurry,' he said, 'before I change my mind.'

'He is weak,' said Sumeira, 'and can hardly walk.'

Ragesh mumbled something under his breath before pushing the physician out of the way and throwing the prisoner over his shoulder. The man cried out in pain but the guard ignored him and strode across the courtyard.

'Careful,' shouted Sumeira, running after him, 'his ribs are broken.'

They headed through the doorway and into the commandery. Halfway along the corridor, two more guards were leading the prisoners further down the corridor.

'Can these men be trusted?' asked Fakhiri quietly.

'They can,' said Ragesh, 'and have been paid well.'

'Where are we going?' asked Sumeira.

'Ask your friend there,' said Ragesh and pushed past the prisoners.

'Fakhiri,' said Sumeira, turning to the cart-master, 'I thought we were getting out of here. Where are you taking us?'

'The streets are not safe,' said the Egyptian, 'so we are hiding you somewhere where they will not be able to find you.'

'And where is that?'

'You will see soon enough.'

At the far end of the corridor, a doorway led into a smaller passageway and down a staircase into a kitchen. At the far end, Ragesh entered a storeroom and sat the injured prisoner on the floor before lifting the trap door and standing to one side.

'Get in,' he said.

The prisoner walked down the steps into the darkness, followed by the others until there was only Ragesh, Fakhiri and Sumeira left above. The physician crouched down and peered down the steps. The room was windowless but lit with a single candle, and she could see the frightened faces of the prisoners staring back up at her. Against the far wall, there was half a sack of food scraps and a small barrel of water.

'I don't understand,' said Sumeira, standing up and turning to face the two men. 'You were supposed to take them to safety, but instead, you are locking them in a place even worse than the one they came from.'

'This *is* a place of safety,' said Fakhiri, 'and it won't be for long. The room is an old storage cellar and unknown to anyone except those who used to live in the commandery. There is enough food and water for a few days, but you will be out long before that.'

'But what if they find it?' asked Sumeira, 'we will have no way of getting out.'

'I am hoping that nobody will seek you here,' said Fakhiri, 'If anyone comes, Ragesh and his men will show them the empty cells and say you all escaped. That should be enough to send them searching in the city.'

'I don't know,' said Sumeira, 'there must be a better place.'

'Sumeira,' said Fakhiri, 'listen to me. There are hundreds of angry people out there, all facing up to the fact that this city is about to fall. Many have already taken out their ire on the innocent, and they seek them out like dogs after rats. I won't tell you what they are doing to them but let's just say, none survive. This is your only chance, and I swear that once the fury had subsided, I will come and get you myself.'

Sumeira looked between the two men before turning away and climbing down the stairway. She crawled over and sat amongst the emaciated prisoners, glaring back up the stairs towards Fakhiri.

'Be patient, my lady,' said Fakhiri peering down. 'This will go quicker than you think.'

He slammed the hatch and locked it in place, before placing the key beneath his jerkin.

'Why do you lock the door?' asked Ragesh. 'They cannot go anywhere.'

'I know,' said Fakhiri, 'but if anyone finds the room before the fighting is done, I want to delay them as long as I can. Now, help me find a rug to cover the trap door. We have to hide its existence.'

Ten minutes later, both men peered into the storeroom from the doorway. The trapdoor was covered with a threadbare rug and the floor covered with various empty sacks and crates, giving the impression the room had already been ransacked.

'It will have to do,' said Fakhiri.

'In that case, there is a certain purse of silver we need to discuss.'

'Don't worry, Ragesh,' said Fakhiri, 'I have your money. Now let's get out of here.'

Chapter Twenty-seven

Acre

July – AD 1191

Down in the harbour, Hassan sat on a step, watching the sun sink towards the western horizon. The water lapped gently against the pontoons as if waiting for his foolhardy mission to begin. Something moved in the shadows, and his hand sought the hilt of the knife hanging from his belt.

'Who's there?' he said, getting to his feet, 'show yourself.'

'Hassan,' said a quiet voice. 'It is good to see you again.'

A shadow emerged to stand just outside the circle of light thrown by one of the harbour torches.

'Step forward,' said Hassan, 'so I can see who you are.'

The person took another step towards him, and he could see they were dressed in the black thawb of the Bedouin.

'Do I know you?' he asked.

'You should do,' said the voice, 'you once saved my life.'

The figure lifted a hand to remove their hood and Hassan gasped when he realised he was talking to a young woman.

'Jahara,' he asked, 'is that you?'

'Hello, Hassan,' she said, 'it has been a long time.'

Hassan stared at the girl, hardly knowing what to say. She was the only other person to have survived when his tribe had been slaughtered by Raynald of Chatillon and his men a few years earlier.

'What are you doing here?' he asked, 'you should be with Yousef's cousin in his goam?'

'I was,' said Jahara, 'but I came here to fulfil a promise.'

'What promise?'

'Not here,' said Jahara, 'there are too many eyes. Follow me.'

She ducked back into the shadows and headed across the jetty towards the remains of half-sunken hulk near the far jetty. She climbed down a rope and crawled through a hole in the deck, closely followed by Hassan.

Inside, the tiny cabin was illuminated by a solitary candle, shielded from the outside by a carefully placed planks. A blanket and a water-skin lay in the corner and the whole place stank of rotting fish.

'It is safe, and it is dry,' said Jahara, seeing his disapproving gaze, 'that is enough.' She pointed towards an empty box against a wall. 'Please sit.'

'So,' he said, looking around the tiny room, 'how and why are you here? I thought you would be somewhere in the depths of the Negev.'

'I was,' said Jahara. 'When you left me with Youssef Bin-Khouri, I did what you suggested and travelled to his cousin's goam. I met the man we talked about, and I spent every day learning the skills of the Fedayeen. He treated me like a daughter, yet never forgot what it was I wanted the most.'

'Every day, he showed me how to move and live as a Hashashin. From sunrise to sunset, he taught me things that no man or woman should ever learn, how to mix the plants of the desert to make a poison that would kill in minutes, or days depending on your whim. He taught me how to nick the veins of domestic animals without them making a sound and drink their blood to stay alive yet leave them unmarked and unharmed amongst my enemies. But most importantly, he taught me how to use a knife and how to use a bow.'

'We practised without rest until my arms ached and my fingers bled. I doubted my own commitment, but he would not let me rest until eventually, I became so skilled in both, there was no man in the goam who could match me.'

'I don't understand,' said Hassan, 'it takes a lifetime to become Hashashin, yet you had only a few years.'

'I know, and there is a lifetime of learning that I do not have, but I have enough to do what I must do.'

'And what is that?'

'You know my pledge,' said Jahara, 'I have sworn to kill the man responsible for slaughtering our people, a vow that is as alive in my heart today as it was on the day I made it.'

'Jahara,' said Hassan, 'you are too late. That man was called Raynald of Chatillon, and he was killed at Hattin.'

'I know of his fate,' said Jahara, 'and at first, I thought my quest had been in vain, but now I know different.'

'What do you mean?'

'The Templar castellan may have given the orders,' said Jahara, 'and it was his men that bore the blades, but when you want to kill a snake, you must always go for the head.'

'Are you talking about the grandmaster?'

'Oh no, Hassan,' said Jahara, 'I don't want part of the beast, I want it all. I want the person responsible for the slaughter of not only our tribe but of every other Arab who has ever suffered at the hands of the Christians. I want the head of the serpent, Hassan, I am going to kill the King of Jerusalem.'

'That is ridiculous,' said Hassan, 'you will never get close to him. He has too many guards, and you are just a ...' He stopped suddenly, staring at the young woman who had helped him bury his wife.

'A girl?' said Jahara, finishing his sentence. 'The girl you once knew is long dead, Hassan, and in her place lives one that only exists to avenge her people. I am still young, that much is true, but it is not a weakness, it is a strength. Who would suspect someone as young as I of being a risk? All I need to do is get within range of the king, and I can do what I came to do.'

'You will be caught and killed,' said Hassan.

'I care not about my own life,' said Jahara, only in gaining revenge.'

'Even if it was possible,' said Hassan, 'why have you come here, to Acre?'

'Because you are correct, it is impossible to get anywhere near the king amongst his defences and his own people. But if Acre falls and the Christians come, confusion will reign, and nobody will worry about a beggar girl walking amongst the carnage. It is then that I will have my chance, it is then that I will strike.'

Hassan's eyes widened as he suddenly realised something.

'It was you,' he said quietly. 'When that messenger from Salah ad-Din was being run down by the Templars outside the city walls, it was your arrow that struck the Christian down.'

'It was,' said Jahara.

'Your intervention saved the messenger's life,' said Hassan, 'yet you disappeared as soon as they brought you inside. Why was that?'

'The situation was not planned,' said Jahara. 'I had infiltrated the Christian lines and lived amongst them for many days, hiding amongst the destitute. When I could not get near their king, I knew my only chance was to get inside the city and await his arrival but had no way to get in. Allah himself intervened when he sent those messengers, and I was able to take advantage. Once inside the walls I knew there would be too many questions and the Christians have spies everywhere so I had to hide. Now the time is almost here, and I intend to do what I came to do or die trying.'

Hassan shook his head but knew he would not be able to talk her out of it.

'Jahara,' he said, 'I know not what to say. My heart bleeds that your path has brought you to this, but I know any words of discouragement will fall on deaf ears.'

'They will,' said Jahara, 'so do not waste them. I am only telling you so that in the event that I die, you would not be left wondering what happened to me.'

'How did you find me?'

'I saw you in the street a few days ago and have followed you ever since. There was no opportunity to talk to you alone until now. But why are you down here?'

Hassan told her of his plan to swim out past the harbour walls to get a message to Salah ad-Din.

'It seems that Allah has set us both paths of great danger,' she said eventually.

'It seems so,' said Hassan, 'but I have to go. The task will get no easier the longer I wait.'

'I'll come with you,' said Jahara, and together they crept out of the wrecked boat and along a wooden jetty stretching out into the harbour. Hassan removed his thawb and handed it to the girl before sitting on the edge of the jetty and lowering himself into the cold water.

'Be safe, Hassan,' said Jahara, and watched as he pushed himself away from the jetty to start his swim.

On the outer edge of the city, the battle had ground to a halt with many of the Christians taking shelter amongst the rubble and the few houses that still stood. Exhausted Saracens stayed in their positions behind hastily erected palisades, knowing that it was only a matter of time before they were overrun.

Further into the city, people of many faiths were dragged screaming from their hiding places and put to the blade or beaten to death by the mob. The blood-lust surged through angry veins, and throughout the night, hundreds of innocent people died. As anticipated, some raced to the commandery, knowing full well that there were Christian prisoners inside but after being refused access by the guards, joined forces to break down the gates.

Inside the storeroom, the terrified prisoners heard the commotion and pressed themselves even harder against the walls, as if by doing so, their chances of discovery were lessened. Without any windows, and only a tiny airbrick for ventilation, the room was thick with the smell of the unwashed prisoners and it was all Sumeira could do not to gag.

'They're going to find us,' whimpered one of the men, 'we're going to die.'

Robin the blacksmith reached over and forced him to the floor, placing his hand over his mouth.

'Shut up, you fool,' he hissed.

The voices came closer, and they heard the sound of men searching the kitchen above.

'What are they saying?' whispered one of the men.

'One of them is asking one of the guards what happened?' said Sumeira. 'He's told them we all escaped and ransacked the kitchens to find food before escaping into the city.'

'So why are they still looking?'

'They are starving said Sumeira, 'and are looking for food.'

'Sumeira,' said Robin, 'if they find us, we will all be killed, but you will suffer something far worse.' He paused before continuing. 'If you wish, I can make sure that never happens.'

'How?' asked Sumeira.

'I still have that knife you brought me. It grieves me greatly to say this, but if we are captured, and if it is your will, I can send you to live in God's grace unsullied.'

Sumeira turned to stare towards the man in the darkness.

'You would kill me?' she asked quietly.

'Only if that was your wish. I will make it quick and as painless as I can, but if they take you alive, I believe your fate will be far, far worse.'

Sumeira turned away, unwilling to consider his suggestion until there was no other option.

The sound of men searching the kitchen got even closer, and the prisoners fell deathly silent, knowing their fate would be decided in the next few minutes. Everyone held their breath, waiting for someone to discover the hatchway and moments later, a voice rang out with excitement.

'They've found us,' groaned one of the prisoners. 'We are dead men.'

'No,' hissed Sumeira. *'Be quiet.'*

More excited shouts followed, and they heard the sound of the nearby searchers scrambling to get back to the main courtyard.

'What's happening?' whispered Robin.

They've found something' said Sumeira, straining to hear the excited conversation outside. *'It sounds like...'* She turned to face the terrified prisoners. *'They've found a purse of silver.'*

The men stared back with astonishment. They could hardly have wished for a timelier intervention, and everyone realised that they were safe, at least for the time being.

'What now?' asked one of the prisoners.

'Now,' said Sumeira, *'we wait.'*

Chapter Twenty-eight

Acre

July – AD 1191

Turan-Shah stood on the roof of one of the buildings overlooking the breach in the inner wall. Night had fallen, and he could see dozens of lights as many of the attackers lit fires amongst the devastation. As he watched, more men moved up to reinforce the Christians, ready for the final attack at first light.

He knew that there was no way the remnants of his army could ever hold them back and wanted to attack the new Christian positions with every fibre in his body, but to do so would be committing his men to certain death. All he could hope for was that the few warriors he had left could defend the narrow streets long enough for Hassan to reach Salah ad-Din. One of his men came out of the stairwell door and ran across to kneel in front of him, offering up a parchment.

'My lord,' he said between breaths, 'I have been tasked with bringing this message from the Christians. It was brought to us under a flag of truce only moments ago.'

Turan-Shah opened the scroll, struggling to read it in the dim light of the moon. A few moments later, he lowered his arms and stared out over the city towards the breach in the wall.

'My lord,' said Salman at his side. 'You look concerned. May I be as bold as to enquire about the message?'

'It is from the one they call Richard of England.' He turned to face Salman. 'He invites me to discuss terms for the surrender of Acre.'

'What are you going to do?'

'I will engage with him,' said the prince, 'and give him false hope that I am indeed considering surrender, but I will include terms that I know will not be accepted. If nothing else, it will give Hassan extra time to reach Salah ad-Din.'

'And if he does not make it?'

'He has to, Salman,' said Turan-Shah, 'or this city will be in Christian hands by nightfall the day after tomorrow.

Just offshore to the west, Hassan swam southward keeping far enough offshore to not be seen by the many men camped on the beaches.

Eventually, his progress waned, and he turned towards the beach. To his dismay, there were still Christian tents as far as the eye could see, but he had no other option. He swam into the shallows and as soon as he could feel the gravelly stones beneath his feet, turned southward again, making good distance until he finally passed the last of the tents and crawled out onto the beach, exhausted.

For what seemed an age, he just lay on the sand, letting the small waves crash over his body. He felt like he had no strength to stand, let alone walk, and the cold was now seeping into the core of his body. Shivering badly and hardly able to move, he desperately wanted to just curl up into a ball and hope that sleep took him away from his discomfort, but deep down inside he knew that to falter was to die and he slowly dragged himself to his feet.

The cold night air cut him like a knife, and he knew the first thing he had to do was to find some clothes. He made his way further up the beach and keeping close to the eroding cliff edge, made his way back northward towards the nearest Christian position. Within minutes he could see the last tents of the Christian camp, but more importantly, the position of their sentry post situated amongst a grove of olive trees. Dropping to his knees, he crawled closer and saw two men talking quietly between themselves.

Hassan's heart dropped. In his current state, one would have been hard enough, but against two, he knew he had no chance. He watched for ten minutes or so and was about to move on when one of the men stood up and walked a few paces into the undergrowth to relieve himself. Hassan had little time to think and knowing he may not get another chance, got to his feet to follow the guard through the shadows. As soon as his quarry stopped, Hassan ran the last few paces and grabbed him from behind, his arm wrapping around the Christian's throat to stifle any scream.

The guard struggled violently, trying to dislodge his attacker and hurled himself to the floor to try to knock Hassan free, but the Bedouin clung on for dear life, using every last ounce of strength in his body until eventually the struggling eased and the soldier breathed his last.

Hassan released his victim and scrambled to his knees. Gradually his breath returned, and he looked down at the body. His urge was to take what he needed and disappear into the night, but he knew that the man's comrade would raise the alarm in minutes.

He reached down and retrieved the dead man's knife before standing up and walking back to the sentry post. The second guard was sat on a log, stirring the contents of an iron pot hanging from a tripod over the fire. Behind him was a makeshift wooden wall made from ship's timbers and driftwood, erected to reflect what little heat there was down onto the two bed spaces at its base.

Having manned many a lookout post during his time with the Templars, Hassan knew that they would have taken it in turns to sleep, while the other looked over the wall, but circumstances meant that the surviving guard was more interested in his supper than any imminent danger.

'It's nearly ready, Karl,' said the guard as Hassan approached out of the shadows. He looked up and stared in horror as Hassan ran the last few steps and launched himself over the fire to plunge a knife deep into his throat.

Both men sprawled onto the floor and the guard tried to call out, but the initial strike had done its job, and all that came out of the guard's mouth were gurgles of blood and saliva. Hassan pulled his knife free before plunging it into his victim's heart.

For several minutes he lay there, hardly able to move. At any moment he expected more guards to arrive, but even if they did, he knew he would not be able to fight them off. Gradually, some of his strength returned, and he picked himself up to strip his victim of his leggings, jerkin and waist belt before helping himself to what was left in the spilt cooking pot. Feeling renewed strength flowing through his veins, he drank as much water as he could from the water-skin hanging on the palisade before tucking the knife under his belt and disappearing into the darkness. All he had to do now was find Salah ad-Din.

In the Christian forward positions, Richard had made his command post in one of the few buildings still standing. Inside they had pushed everything to one side and laid timbers across two trestles to make a table. A large map of the city lay on the surface, and one of Richard's men was busy making amendments to show the up-to-date situation.

Richard watched him work, asking questions as more and more information came in. The local battle had died down, and everyone sought to strengthen their positions in case of a counterattack in the night.

Besides Richard stood the Templar grandmaster as well as several of his best generals.

'What is this?' asked Richard, pointing to a small circle on the map.

'That is another breach, your Grace,' said the mapmaker, 'it was forced by Leo of Armenia.'

'How far did he get?'

'Not far and he has had to withdraw his men to the outer wall, but the breach has been made and offers us another option.'

'How many casualties have we taken?'

'It's hard to say, your Grace. Many are still unaccounted for but at a guess. I would say well over five thousand dead and at least as many wounded. We will know more tomorrow.'

'It could be worse,' said Richard. 'What news from the Saracens?'

'They have answered the message, your Grace, and have sent a list of requirements including high reparations and a demand that Jerusalem remains in the hands of the Muslims. They also say they will relinquish Acre only when Saladin himself instructs them to.'

Some of the men gasped at the audacity of the demands.

'Is he mad?' asked one. 'Surely he knows we can never accept such idiocy.'

'Oh he knows,' said Richard, 'and I suspect he is playing for time. Is there any sign of Saladin's army to the east?'

'Guy of Lusignan reports that he repels counter-attacks on a daily basis, but they are from Saladin's allied tribes. There is no sign of the main Ayyubid army.'

'I hear he has gone south,' said another general, 'to prepare for our march on Jerusalem.'

'He will never stop us,' said Guy, 'we are now too strong.'

'Strike Jerusalem from your minds,' said Richard, 'for there is still a city to take, and without Acre, there can be no march south. Now, someone brief me about the garrison. Do we have any updates?'

'Your Grace,' said Sir Crispin, 'we have had many men deserting from the Saracens. The story they tell is much as we expected, their numbers are low, and most are weak through exhaustion and hunger. We should break through tomorrow.'

'There will be no attack tomorrow,' said Richard, 'for I gave my word to Turan-Shah that he has a full day to negotiate. Send him another message declining his offer and remind him of the consequences.'

'Your Grace,' said another knight, 'there is another situation you should be aware of.'

'And that is?'

'There is a faction within the city that have sworn to fight to the death. They are fanatics who's aim is to continue killing Christians, no matter what the odds.'

'And how do you know this?'

'We were told by some of the deserters. They said they were approached by men unhappy with the way Turan-Shah has led the city. Now they have formed their own group and intend to fight to the last man.'

'Even if the city cedes?'

'Especially if the city cedes,' said the knight. 'They intend to create positions and take as many of us to hell alongside them.'

'Do you know where this pathetic action will take place?'

'There are several, your Grace,' said the knight, but one, in particular, gives us great cause for concern.' He turned to face Robert de Sablé. 'My lord,' he continued, 'they are going to use the Templar commandery.'

An hour later, the grandmaster called the seneschal and his senior knights to a briefing. With them, as senior sergeant of the Templars was Thomas Cronin. Robert de Sablé recounted the briefing he had had with the king and told them of the faction's aim to fight to the death from the Templar's own citadel. Every man in the room was horrified, and voices rose in anger.

'Silence,' said the grandmaster, holding up his hand. 'I am as angry as you and knew you would not want to stand back while these heathen sully our name. That is why I asked the king to be allowed to reclaim the citadel.'

'And so we should,' said one of the knights. 'It is ours by right, and we must never allow it to be used in any way against Christendom.'

'Aye,' shouted the remaining men.

'The time will come,' said the grandmaster raising his voice, 'but first there is work to be done.' He looked around the room. 'It has been four years since any Templar set foot in the citadel, and most of those died at Cresson and Hattin. None of us even knows the layout so we have to be careful.'

'I do,' said a voice and they all turned to face Thomas Cronin standing at the back.

'Step forward, Brother Cronin,' said the grandmaster, 'and tell us what you know.'

Cronin walked to the table and looked down at a rough sketch of the city.

'The Templar quarter is here,' said Cronin pointing to the small spur of land edging out into the inner harbour. It is as far away from the breach as it can be, and we will have to cross the city to reach it. Once there, we will find an outer wall separating it from the rest of the city. During the day, people were allowed to come and go to trade their wares, but at night, it was secured by several gates. I would expect this wall to be the first line of their defences. Inside the wall, we will find a courtyard and on the far side, the commandery itself. There is one gate, but it is much stronger than the others. The walls are higher, but again, I cannot see any problems in gaining access.'

'Will we need mangonels?' asked the grandmaster.

'No, my lord, there is little room, and if we want to reclaim our citadel intact, I suggest we do so by using rams and Templar steel. A surprise attack should find them unprepared, and I know where the weak points are.'

The grandmaster looked around the room.

'Well,' he asked, 'what say you?'

'I say we do it,' said the seneschal. 'They sully the ground upon which our brothers prayed, and that is unforgivable.'

'Aye,' shouted the rest of the men again, and Robert de Sablé turned back to Cronin.

'Brother Cronin,' he said. 'I find myself in the strange position of asking a sergeant to lead an assault. Your reputation goes before you like a banner, but it would be unfair for me to place such a burden on your shoulders.'

'The burden is light,' said Cronin. 'I know the place well and am just as angered by the desecration as you. I am happy to lead, my lord. Just say when.'

The grandmaster looked out of the window to see the faintest rays of light rising over the eastern walls.

'It is nearly dawn,' he said, 'so the Yemeni prince has until midday tomorrow to make his decision. Unfortunately, he has the word of the king that there will be no attack before then. What we can do, however, is prepare. Tell me what we need.'

On the far side of the city, Fakhiri hid amongst a pile of rubble, watching with dismay as dozens of men headed into the Templar citadel. Any intention of releasing the prisoners as soon as the city fell dwindled away and he knew that their fate was now completely out of his hands. As he watched the activity continue, the guard commander hurried past his hiding place, looking for somewhere to hide.

'*Ragesh,*' hissed Fakhiri, '*wait.*'

The guard stopped and looked around.

'*Over here,*' said Fakhiri and waited as the Saracen joined him in the shadows.

'*What is happening?*' hissed Fakhiri, '*who are these men?*'

'Most I do not know,' said Ragesh quietly, 'though I recognise one as a manipulator who tries to recruit others into his fanatical ways. They talk of the final sacrifice and aim to fight to the end. What are you doing here?'

'I was going to check on the Christians,' said Fakhiri, 'but can get nowhere near.'

'The last time I checked, they were fine,' said Ragesh.

'When was that?'

'Yesterday. The citadel was overrun by those seeking revenge, and the hiding place was almost discovered, but I distracted them.'

'How?'

'By placing my purse of silver somewhere, it would be easily found. Their greed drew them away, but I am now as poor as the day I agreed the subterfuge.'

'I will pay you back, Ragesh, I swear it.'

'I am more interested in securing my life,' said Ragesh.

'How are they?' asked Fakhiri

'They are afraid and cramped, but they still have some water. How long they will last, I do not know, but the commandery is now in the hands of the fanatics, and there is little you or anyone else can do.'

Fakhiri thought furiously, knowing full well that it was unlikely the prisoners would be spared should they be found.

'I have an idea,' he said, 'one that may be doomed to fail, but I cannot stand by and see them all die.'

'What idea?' asked Ragesh.

'It does not concern you,' said Fakhiri, 'but you have my gratitude. Hide yourself away, Ragesh and do not emerge until the city surrenders.' He looked at the guard's clothing before adding, 'and if I were you, I would find some different clothes. I suspect any Christian seeing a Saracen jailer walking the streets will not wait for an explanation.'

'Where would I find a change of clothes amongst all this?' asked Ragesh.

'Look around you, my friend, 'said Fakhiri, 'the streets are full of corpses. Never has any man had such a choice. Now I have to go. If Allah sees fit to merge our paths again, I will see you are suitably recompensed for your help.'

Ragesh nodded and watched as the diminutive Egyptian scrambled away over the rubble.

'Stay safe, Fakhiri,' he said quietly, 'and may Allah go with you.'

Chapter Twenty-nine

Acre

July – AD 1191

A few hours later, Fakhiri stood in a doorway to the rear of one of the palisades blocking the streets to the city. With no way past, he was growing frustrated, knowing he was running out of time.

He looked around, desperate for inspiration, and his gaze fell on a nearby house. The house had been damaged and one of the shutters hung by only one hinge, but the building was still intact, and he could see it overlooked the perimeter walls beyond the palisade. He hurried over and pulled the shutter aside before climbing into a dust-filled room. Searching the ground floor for an exit to the front of the house, he found only a terrified woman and two children crouched into a corner.

'Please,' gasped the woman, pulling her children closer towards her, *'do not hurt us.'*

'I'm not here to hurt you,' said Fakhiri walking over, 'but I need to get to the Christian army. Is there a door or a window that faces east?'

The woman pointed towards the ceiling.

'In the room above.'

Fakhiri left the family and run up the stairs to find another shuttered window in the eastern wall. He peered through the wooden slats and could see dozens of Christian soldiers hiding amongst the rubble. He stepped back to consider his options. If he opened the shutter, the chances were that he could be cut down by the Christian archers but seeing no other option, decided it was a risk he had to take.

He searched for a white cloth, but finding nothing, he returned to the room with the family and approached the scared mother.

'Please,' he said, 'I need your scarf.'

The woman's hand lifted to her head; her eyes filled with confusion.

'There is no time to explain,' said Fakhiri, 'but someone's life depends on it.'

The scared woman pulled the scarf free and handed it over.

'Thank you,' said the Egyptian and ran back up the stairs. Taking a deep breath, he opened the shutters slightly and reached out, waving the white scarf as a flag of truce.

'*Hold your arrows,*' he shouted, '*I have important information for your masters.*'

Down below, some of the arbalists jumped to their feet and aimed their crossbows at the first-floor window.

'Hold,' shouted one of the knights, 'let us see what he has to say.'

Fakhiri held his breath, waiting for the hail of death to begin, but nothing happened, and he risked taking another look. Down below, several men had their crossbows aimed directly at him, but none had yet loosed their bolts.

'Who are you?' shouted a voice.

Fakhiri looked out to see a Templar knight standing behind the arbalists.

'My name is Fakhiri,' he shouted, 'and I am a cart-master from Egypt. I have important information for your masters.'

'What is this information?'

'I cannot shout it,' said Fakhiri, 'for if I were to be heard by your enemy, it could cost the lives of some of your comrades.'

'That sounds like a threat,' said the knight, 'and we do not respond to threats.'

'Please,' shouted Fakhiri, 'it is no threat, my choice of words is poor. But if I cannot speak to your masters, then more Christians will undoubtedly die and amongst them, a lady. Allow me to descend and if you find my message to be false, then do with me what you will.'

'What weapons do you have?'

'Just a knife.'

'Then throw it down. For all we know you could be an assassin.'

Fakhiri did as requested while staying hidden behind the partially opened shutters.

'Now show yourself,' said the knight.

'Do you swear not to kill me?' replied Fakhiri.

The knight turned and bellowed across the Christian positions.

'Everybody lower your weapons.' He turned back to face the window. 'Now, get on with it, Saracen, or we will fill that building with Greek-fire.'

Fakhiri took a deep breath and nervously opened the shutters. He climbed down to a ledge before lowering himself the last few feet to the floor.

Two soldiers walked over to search him before taking an arm each and dragging him over to face the knight.

'So,' said the knight, 'what is all this about.'

'I need to see the one called Thomas Cronin,' said Fakhiri.

'Thomas Cronin?' replied the knight, 'I do not know the name.'

'I do,' said a voice from behind, 'he is a senior sergeant with the Templars. He's with the grandmaster in a briefing.'

The knight turned to see one of the arbalists standing behind him.

'Even so,' he replied, turning back to face the Egyptian, 'you can tell me what it is you have to say. I will make sure he gets to hear it.'

'No,' said Fakhiri, 'I have to tell him. Only he will understand the seriousness of the situation.'

'You are beginning to anger me,' said the knight coldly, 'tell me what it is you know, or I will have you whipped.'

'Do what you must,' said Fakhiri, 'but I stand by what I say. There are many lives at stake, including a Christian woman, a physician who has tended many of your own men. Do you want that on your conscience?'

The knight stared at Fakhiri, struggling to control his anger.

'Tie his hands,' he said eventually, 'and take him to the grandmaster but if it turns out he is wasting our time, string him up.' The knight turned away as Fakhiri was bound and led over to the damaged building used by the Templar commanders.

Inside, Thomas Cronin was briefing the officers about the layout of the citadel, and everyone looked up as two foot-soldiers dragged in the Egyptian.

'Who is this?' asked the seneschal.

'I forget his name,' said one of the soldiers, 'but he says he has important information for Thomas Cronin.'

All eyes turned to look at the sergeant who walked over to stare at the prisoner.

'Your face is familiar to me,' he said. 'Where have I seen you before?'

'In Karak,' replied Fakhiri. 'I was taken prisoner by Raynald of Chatillon on the road to Damascus but managed to escape when a woman called Sumeira left the fortress to find her son in the town of Segor.'

'Yes, I remember now,' said Cronin. 'Hunter told me that when she was betrayed by a slave-trader, you set out to find her. That was almost two years ago.'

'It was, and I searched for many months until I found out she had been brought here to Acre. I came as quickly as I could and entered the city just before the city was besieged. Since then, I have lived amongst the shadows waiting for an opportunity to free her.'

'Sumeira is alive?' gasped Cronin.

'She is,' said Fakhiri, 'but she is in terrible danger and needs your help.'

For the next ten minutes, Fakhiri told the sergeant about the peril Sumeira and the other prisoners were in. Everyone listened in silence before Cronin turned to the guards.

'Take him outside,' he said, 'and wait for me there.' As the three men left the building, Cronin turned back to face the other Templars.

'The man is nothing but a spy,' said one before he could speak, 'either that or he is mad.'

'I don't believe him,' said another. 'He obviously knows about the fanatics in the citadel and has been sent here to sell us a fabricated story.'

'To what end?' asked the seneschal.

'It's simple. If we were to believe him, then we might hold back the attack, which gives them more time to bolster their defences. I say cut off his head and send it back to those who sent him.'

'Thomas Cronin,' said the grandmaster. 'What say you?'

'My lord,' replied Cronin, 'the woman he speaks of was a good friend of mine, as is the scout he mentioned. His tale contains enough information that only Sumeira would know, which makes me believe he is telling the truth.'

'So you think she, and many other Christians are now holed up in a cell beneath the very citadel we intend to strike tomorrow?'

'Yes, my lord, I do.'

'And what are your thoughts on this?'

'I need to talk more to the Egyptian,' said Cronin, 'but if he is indeed telling the truth, then these people have already suffered years of imprisonment and need our help. I accept that we need to attack the citadel, but my gut tells me we should also do whatever we can to secure their release.'

Robert de Sablé stared at the sergeant, his mind racing.

'Brother Cronin,' he said eventually. 'I understand that this news must have brought doubt to your heart, as it has mine. The thought of any Christians being so close to death at the hands of the godless is enough to make any man fall to his knees and wail. But this operation is too important for us to falter. If we hold back, even for an instant, then we hand the advantage to those who would see us dead. Whether the man is telling the truth or not is irrelevant, I cannot delay the attack nor soften the blows we intend to land.'

'My lord,' said Cronin, 'if I may…'

'Brother Cronin,' interrupted the seneschal, 'you heard the grandmaster. We cannot risk the success of this mission for the sake of a few individuals. Once we secure the citadel, you are welcome to do what you can for these people, and I suggest you interrogate this Egyptian further to find out where they are incarcerated, but more than that we cannot do.'

Cronin stared around the room, his heart racing. His desperation to do something to save Sumeira was almost overwhelming, but he knew the seneschal was right. They were at war, and in war, people died.

'I understand,' he said eventually. 'May I leave to question him further?'

'You may,' said the Seneschal and turned back to the city map.

Outside, the two foot-soldiers were tormenting the prisoner, holding him against a wall while stroking his throat with a dagger.

'Leave him be,' said Cronin walking over, 'and untie him.'

'Are you sure?' asked one of the men, 'he may be an assassin.'

'I can take care of myself,' said Cronin, staring into the Egyptian's eyes. 'Cut his binds and leave him with me.'

A few seconds later, Fakhiri rubbed his wrists as the two men returned to their positions amongst the smoky ruins.

'You had better be telling the truth,' said Cronin when they had gone, 'or I swear I'll cut your throat myself.'

'Every word of it is true,' said Fakhiri. 'I have known of her whereabouts for many months and have tried to help whenever I can.'

'If you have known where she is for all that time,' said Cronin, 'why have you not freed her?'

'Believe me, I tried,' said Fakhiri, 'but the woman is as stubborn as a camel and would not leave the others. In the end, I realised that she was safer where she was so just tried to aid wherever I could.' He paused and stared at Cronin with expectation. 'So,' he said eventually, 'are you going to help or not?'

'There is much you do not know,' said Cronin. 'It may be of help, or it may make the situation worse.'

'What are you talking about?'

Cronin looked around before grabbing the Egyptian by the arm and dragging him behind a wall.

'I am about to tell you something,' he said quietly, 'but I swear that if you share this information, I will hunt you to the ends of the earth.'

'My loyalty is with Sumeira,' said Fakhiri, 'and I will do nothing that puts her further at risk.'

Cronin looked around again to make sure they were not overheard.

'Listen,' he said, turning back to Fakhiri, 'tomorrow at noon, I am to lead an attack upon the very citadel about which you speak.'

'You are going to attack the commandery?'

'We are. The thought of fanatics despoiling our holy places is more that we can countenance and we intend to wrest it free from their hands before they do too much damage.'

'Thomas Cronin,' said Fakhiri quietly, 'if you do this, the prisoners may not survive.'

'Did you not say that they were secure within a hidden stone room?'

'They are, but if the defenders fire the commandery, as they surely will, Sumeira and the rest of the prisoners will be baked alive. You have to stop this attack.'

'I cannot,' said Cronin, 'nor do I wish to. But I agree we cannot allow our comrades to die in such a manner. We have to get them out before the attack begins.'

'And how do you intend to do this?' asked the Egyptian. 'You just said you will be at the head of the Templar army.'

'And I will be,' replied Cronin, 'but that does not mean there is nothing I can do. Follow me.'

The two men left the bailey and headed out through the Christian lines. Fakhiri looked around with wonder. He had known the infidel army was vast but never had he seen so many men at arms.

'Where are we going?' he asked.

'You will see soon enough,' said Cronin and made his way towards the tented camp at the base of Mount Toron. As they approached, one of a group of men turned slightly and watched as they approached.

'Cronin,' said Arturas, 'I thought you would be up to your neck killing Saracens. What brings you here?'

'I have news,' said Cronin, 'a problem that we need to solve.' He turned to Fakhiri. 'Tell him what you told me.'

Fakhiri looked up at the mercenary. They had met once before, but it had been a long time ago, and it had been dark.

'You may not remember me,' said Fakhiri, 'but I was the slave you allowed to go free through the gates of Karak with Sumeira of Greece.'

'I remember,' said Arturas slowly. 'You hid in the dark and heard us planning.'

'I did,' said Fakhiri. 'And after that, I accompanied Sumeira to Segor, but alas, she was betrayed and taken into slavery by a man called Fawzi.'

'What is all this about?' asked Arturas, looking over to Cronin. 'This was a long time ago, and Sumeira is probably long dead.'

'She is not dead,' snapped Fakhiri, 'she is very much alive, but she is in trouble, and if we don't do something soon, that situation will only change for the worst.'

'Wait,' said Arturas, 'before you say another word, there is someone else who needs to hear this.' He turned and shouted towards one of the nearby tents. 'Hunter, we need you out here.'

A few seconds later, Hunter ducked out of the tent and walked over towards the men standing by the fire.

'Cronin,' he said, recognising the sergeant, but before he could continue, he stopped dead in his tracks and stared at the Egyptian. *'Fakhiri,'* he gasped, 'what are you doing here?'

'It seems he has found Sumeira,' said Arturas, 'but if I'm not mistaken, she is in the city and needs our help.' He turned towards the Egyptian. 'Does that sum it up?'

'It does,' interjected Cronin, 'but it is far more complicated than that. Is there somewhere we can talk, just the four of us?'

Arturas nodded.

'Come with me,' he said, and they headed away from the tents to an unmanned palisade at the foot of the hill. 'So,' he said, 'tell us everything you know.'

For the next ten minutes, Fakhiri and Cronin briefed the two men including the whereabouts of the prisoners and the plans to attack the citadel. Hunter and Arturas listened carefully until they all fell silent and stared at each other.

'So in essence,' said Arturas, looking at Cronin, 'if you and your comrades are attacking the citadel tomorrow, Sumeira and the prisoners are likely to die in the onslaught.'

'That's about it,' said Cronin.

'And you can do nothing about it so came to us.'

'I cannot stop the attack, Arturas, you were the only other options I could think of.'

'No, you did right,' said Arturas, 'for the answer is plain to see.'

'It is?'

'Aye,' said Arturas. 'Tonight, I and a handful of my men will pay the citadel a little visit. '

'I will come with you,' said Hunter

'You have a family to find,' said Arturas, 'and this may be a one-way trip. We can manage alone.'

'Sumeira is as much family as anyone,' said Hunter, 'and besides, I owe her that much.' He looked over at Cronin. 'Leave it to us, my friend, we will get her out. Now you should go, you have an assault to plan.'

Cronin nodded and turned to leave, but Fakhiri stayed where he was.

'What are you waiting for?' asked Arturas. 'Get out of here.'

'I wish to come with you,' said Fakhiri.

'Forget it,' said Arturas. 'For all I know you are no more than a Saracen spy and will lead us into a trap.'

'He is no spy,' said Hunter. 'I will vouch for him.'

'Even so, he is still a Saracen, and I don't trust them.'

'The streets are complicated,' interjected Fakhiri, 'and many are blocked with rubble. The night will be dark, and you will never get across the city on your own, but I know the alleyways and streets frequented by murderers and thieves. If we go that way, you will have a better chance of getting through alive but alone, you are already dead men.'

'So be it,' said Arturas eventually, 'but the moment he puts a foot out of place, he will feel my dagger in his back, agreed?'

'Agreed,' said Hunter and turned to Fakhiri. 'Come, I have food, and while we eat, you can fill us in on what exactly awaits us in Acre.'

Fakhiri turned back to Cronin.

'You have my gratitude,' he said. 'There is now hope where there was none, but I implore you, in case we do not make it, take care when you assault the citadel. Her life and those of your fellow Christians depend on it.'

Chapter Thirty

Acre

July – AD 1191

Turan-Shah once more sat amongst his generals and advisors in one of Acre's many halls. He had received Richard's refusal regarding terms of surrender and having heard nothing from Salah ad-Din, was beginning to think that Hassan had failed in his task.

'My lord,' said one of his men, 'to hold out further will only delay the inevitable and cost the lives of the last of our men. I suggest that you agree terms while you have this chance and lead our men out of Acre with their heads held high.'

'I disagree,' said Salman from across the room. 'The Christians will never allow the full garrison to just leave, they will want to retain some bargaining power to recover any prisoners that Salah ad-Din has taken. We should treat them with the contempt they deserve and fight to the last man.'

'Brave words from someone whom I have not seen wield a sword in anger since he has been here,' said one of the warriors.

'I was sent by the sultan himself,' said Salman, 'and ordered to stay at Turan-Shah's side. I have spilt my fair share of Christian blood and will spill much more these next few days.'

'To do so will result in many more Muslim deaths,' said the officer. 'Have not enough already died?'

'Give Hassan a chance,' said Salman. 'He has not let us down yet, and there are still several hours until dawn. When the sun rises, our lookouts will be able to see any movement out on the eastern plains, and if that is the case, all we have to do is hold out the infidels for a few more hours.'

'They are like ants upon the ground,' said another officer, 'never have I seen so many Franks.'

'Numbers are of little use when the battlefield is narrow,' said Salman. 'A few men can hold back an army when penned in between two buildings. I say we refuse to negotiate further and make them pay dearly for every step they take.'

Turan-Shah had held his tongue throughout the meeting but now held up his hand to demand silence.

'I have listened,' he said, 'and I have considered all options. I value the input of every man in this room, and I know that if ordered, all would lay down their lives in the name of the sultan.' He looked around the room. 'We all know that without Salah ad-Din we cannot win this battle, but I still have faith that he will deliver us from the hands of the infidels, so this is what we will do. I will set out new terms for the surrender of Acre, terms that will be more palatable to the Christians. Amongst them, I will demand that our men be granted safe access from the city and allowed to return to Egypt as free men. I will also demand the word of the Christian king that once we leave, any Muslims remaining in Acre will be treated fairly. They are no less casualties of war than those who died upon the walls.'

'And when will these terms be requested?' asked one of the officers.

'We will wait until first light tomorrow,' said Turan-Shah, 'and if Salah ad-Din has not responded by then, the message will be delivered. If the terms are accepted, we will cede the city at noon.'

'With respect, my lord,' said Salman, 'to even suggest surrendering the city is an insult to the sultan and to Allah himself. If this treachery goes ahead, then I will not be at your side.'

'Curb your tongue, Salman,' said one of the officers, his hand moving to the hilt of his scimitar, 'else I will remove it from your head.'

'Enough,' shouted Turan-Shah. 'The Christians are more than happy to spill our blood, and we will not aid them by fighting amongst ourselves.' He turned to Salman. 'I think you are wrong to discount these options,' he said, 'but I respect your choice. You must do what you have to do, but unless we have any hope of relief from Salah ad-Din, then I will not stand by and watch the last of my men die for no reason. Now you should go, Salman, and it would be better if you did not seek the company of my men or me again.'

'As you wish,' said Salman coldly. 'I shall pray for you, Turan-Shah, and hope Allah enlightens your path before it is too late.' He bowed slightly and turned away to leave the room. When he had gone, Turan-Shah turned his attention back to his officers.

'Bring me a scribe,' he said, 'and share any food we have left amongst the men. Whatever happens tomorrow, this is the last night they will be manning the barricades.'

South of the city, Hassan Malouf travelled as fast as he could through the darkness. Since killing the two guards he had made good progress, but when the bodies had been found, the Christians had deployed mounted Turcopole patrols to search for the perpetrator. In desperation, Hassan had been forced to hide for most of the day, deep within a thicket of scrub and thorns. The seekers had come close and even tried to search the thicket, but it was too dense, and they turned their attention elsewhere. As soon as they had gone, Hassan had left the safety of the bushes and continued his journey, but he had lost a lot of time, and he had still found no trace of the Ayyubid positions.

Within the hour, he emerged from the rocky landscape out onto a plain. With little time remaining, he broke into a run, knowing that the defence of Acre and consequently, that of Jerusalem was in his hands.

In the citadel, Sumeira huddled amongst her fellow prisoners. The night was cold, but there was nothing any of them could do. Water was running out, what little food they had was already gone, and some of the men had curled up on the floor, certain they were going to die. At first, Sumeira had done everything she could to encourage hope, but as the days had passed, even her faith had been tested.

For the past few hours, the sound of many men shouting and chanting echoed around the citadel, their main message being what they were going to do to the infidels when they arrived. At first, Sumeira hoped it was just bravado, a hope that was dashed when she heard some poor soul being dragged into the citadel from wherever they had been hiding, only to be hacked to death by the die-hard fanatics.

'We have to surrender,' moaned one of the men, 'we cannot go on like this. I would rather die at the end of a sword than endure another day in this hell.'

'We cannot,' said Sumeira, 'at least not yet. Fakhiri promised he would be here and I still have faith in him.'

'Your friend is Muslim,' replied the prisoner, 'and is probably laughing at our fate as we speak.'

'He said he will come, and he will,' said Sumeira.

The cell fell quiet once more but despite her assurances, deep down inside Sumeira feared the worse.

'Come on, Fakhiri,' she said quietly to herself, 'don't let us down now.'

Out on the plains, Hassan stumbled on. His body was exhausted and his thirst unbearable, but still he walked. In the distance, he could see hundreds of tiny lights on a distant mountainside and knew that this far south it could only be the Saracen camp. Encouraged, he pushed harder, but his strength was gone, and he managed only a few hundred more paces before collapsing to the ground, all hope of reaching the sultan gone.

Slipping in and out of consciousness, Hassan had no idea how long he was there, but he gasped aloud as a trickle of cold water splashed over his face.

'He lives,' said a voice. 'I was right.'

'Just as well,' said a second voice, 'or I would have wasted water for no reason.'

Hassan looked up to see two men standing above him. To his relief, they were Ayyubid scouts, no doubt from the camp of Salah ad-Din.

'Who are you,' asked one of the men, 'and why are you out here in the middle of nowhere?'

'My name is not important,' said Hassan, 'but I have an important message for the sultan.'

'A message for the sultan,' laughed the first rider. 'And what makes you so important that you believe Salah ad-Din would grant you an audience?'

'I have a message from Prince Turan-Shah,' said Hassan, 'the garrison commander at Acre, and if I do not get to the sultan quickly, the city could fall within days.'

The first warrior looked at his comrade before reaching down and taking Hassan's arm. He pulled him to his feet and stared into his eyes.

'You had better not be lying,' he said, 'or I will kill you myself.'

'I swear I am telling the truth,' said Hassan, 'look, I bear the ring of the prince to prove it was he that sent me.' He removed Turan-Shah's ring and gave it to the first guard. The two men looked at it before turning back to face Hassan.

'This is your lucky night,' said the one. 'Come, we have horses.'

Inside the city, Fakhiri hid amongst the darkest shadows. The air stank of burning and smouldering fires cast eerie shadows dancing upon damaged walls. Taking advantage of the lull in the bombardment, people started to emerge from the ruins in search of food and water.

Behind him, hidden in the alley were another five men including Arturas and Hunter. They had bypassed the barricades an hour earlier by retracing the Egyptian's route up through the window and through the house into one of the inner streets. At first, they had made good time as there were few people remaining so close to the beleaguered city walls, but as they got nearer the centre, the busier the city became. Satisfied that it was safe to move, Fakhiri retreated down the alleyway and crouched to speak to Hunter.

'I think it is as good as it is going to be,' he said, 'and we can wait no longer. The streets will contain people, but they will have other things on their minds. Keep your hoods up and move quickly. If you are challenged, do not stop just plough on as fast as you can.'

'Will that not raise suspicion?'

'With any luck, they will think us no more than brigands, the city is crawling with them, so we will not be pursued. If we get split up, just keep heading east as far as you can go. Eventually, your path will be blocked by the citadel walls, and I will be waiting inside a nearby church. You can't miss it, even in the dark. The spire has been demolished.'

Hunter turned around to face the other four men.

'Did everyone hear that?'

'Aye,' came the response.

'In that case,' said Hunter, getting to his feet, 'let's go.'

He followed Fakhiri out of the alley and into the main street, his face hidden beneath the deep hood of his cloak. For several minutes they made good headway. Many people stared as they passed, but nobody challenged them and they reached the central square with no incident.

'The going should be easier from here,' whispered Fakhiri as they regathered in another alleyway. 'The next quarter is populated by the poor and the destitute. They will have no interest in who you are or what you fight for, only if you are likely to have something of value and trust me, they will not think twice about slitting your throat to get it. Move fast but keep your wits about you.' He headed out of the alley and into the poorer quarter of the city, half walking and half running to make the best time possible.

Arturas brought up the rear, his damaged leg preventing him from running any faster. Gradually he fell further behind until he suddenly found himself alone in a pitch-black alleyway having missed a turning that his comrades had taken.

'*Shit,*' he mumbled to himself and turned around to retrace his steps, only to be confronted by three men looming out of the shadows.

One of them said something and drew a knife, and though Arturas could not understand the dialect, it was obvious they wanted him to hand over anything of value. He searched within his cloak, finding nothing but a small flask of wine and a single coin. He threw them over, and the first man handed them to his comrades before turning back to face the mercenary.

'*Sayf,*' he said, pointing at the hilt of the sword visible beneath the open cape, '*sayf.*'

'You are not having my sword, my friend,' said Arturas menacingly, 'now get out of my way.'

All three men stared at him with surprise, realising he was not an easterner.

'*Infidel,*' spat one of the men and drew a large knife from his belt.

'*Allah Akbar,*' said another and drawing his own knife, rushed towards Arturas.

The experienced soldier quickly ducked to one side and grabbed his attacker before hurling him against a wall and plunging his own blade into the back of the man's neck. He immediately turned and ducked under the second man's awkward attack before thrusting his knife up under the attacker's ribs and into his heart. He spun around, expecting to fight the third man but the attacker had seen enough and turned to flee into a side street.

'Arturas,' said Hunter appearing out of the gloom, 'what's going on?'

'I had a little problem,' said Arturas, 'but it's all sorted now.'

'So I can see,' said Hunter, 'come on, let's get out of here.'

The two men retraced their steps and within minutes, rejoined Fakhiri and the others outside the damaged church.

'Is this it?' asked Arturas, looking at the wall looming above them.

'That is the citadel,' said Fakhiri, 'but the commandery is on the far side. What we need to do now is get inside.'

'And how do we do that?'

'I will try to get in and open one of the lesser gates, but how to get into the commandery itself, I have no idea.'

'Let's get inside the citadel first and worry about that later,' said Hunter. 'Show us where to go. '

'Follow me,' said Fakhiri and once again set off into the darkness.

'He needs hamstringing,' grumbled Arturas as the rest of the men followed the Egyptian.

'You don't fool me,' said Hunter, taking a drink from his waterskin, 'you are enjoying every moment of this.'

'I have to admit, the blood hasn't raced through my veins like this for many a year,' said Arturas, 'I just wish we could do it a bit slower.' With a deep breath, he pushed himself off the wall and followed the rest of them along the citadel wall.

Half an hour later, with the five Christians hidden outside one of the lesser gates, Fakhiri returned to the main entrance and waited in the shadows for an opportunity to get inside. Eventually, a group of men approached the gates, and Fakhiri stepped out of the shadows into their path.

'My friends,' he said with a bow, 'I assume you are going into the citadel. Will you allow me to accompany you?'

'Who are you,' asked one, 'and why can you not just ask at the gate?'

'Alas, I am no warrior,' said Fakhiri,' just a man who fears the infidels more than death itself. I think I will be safer inside, but if I go alone, they may think I have nothing to offer and turn me away. But I am a man of many talents, my lords, and will serve you well.'

'We need fighting men, not beggars,' said the warrior, 'get out of my way.'

'Wait,' said a voice and another warrior stepped forward to stare at Fakhiri. 'I know this man, he served us well on the battlements.'

'Master Salman,' said Fakhiri, recognising the Saracen officer, 'it is good to see you again.'

Salman turned to the group leader.

'I will vouch for him,' he said, 'he comes with us.'

'As you wish,' said the Saracen and continued towards the gate. Fakhiri followed, hardly believing his luck. He would soon be inside the citadel which meant he was one step closer to freeing Sumeira.

Chapter Thirty-one

Acre

July – AD 1191

The sun was well above the horizon when the message finally reached Richard from Turan-Shah. The rest of the nobles in the tent waited in silence as he read it silently, knowing that the fate of the city depended on what was on the scroll. Eventually, Richard looked up and faced the men.

'The prince has offered favourable conditions,' he said, 'and wants to discuss terms in person. Sir Crispin, tell the siege-engines to stop the barrage and inform the men they are to cease all hostilities immediately.'

'Can I tell them why?'

'Aye, you can but warn them against complacency. The city is not ours until the document is signed and Saracens march out of those gates.'

'Yes, your Grace,' said Crispin.

Richard turned to the rest of the occupants of the tent.

'Sir Robert,' said Richard, seeing the worried expression on the grandmaster's face. 'Are you not pleased?'

'Of course I am,' said the grandmaster, 'but my job is not yet done. There is still the matter of the citadel to sort out.'

'You could wait until the details of the surrender are finalised. I suspect it will be no more than a few days.'

'I would rather not,' said the grandmaster, 'every moment wasted allows more desecration to take place, there are still Christian prisoners hidden amongst the ruins. Despite the possibility of the city's surrender, I request permission to march on the citadel at the earliest opportunity.'

'Turan-Shah is coming to meet with me at noon,' said the king, 'and I will express my anger at the situation. Prepare your men, and if the prince refuses to do anything about the fanatics in the commandery, then you are free to do what needs to be done.'

'Thank you, your Grace,' said the grandmaster and left the tent to make the final arrangements.

To the south, Hassan Malouf waited near the sultan's compound. The scouts had brought him to see Salah ad-Din, but this was as close as he was allowed to get.

A group of men emerged from the central tent and walked towards him. Hassan immediately recognised Salah ad-Din's son, and his heart lifted. Of all people, he would be the one most likely to believe him.

'Hassan Malouf,' said Al-Afdal, 'you are alive I see.'

'I am, my lord,' said Hassan, 'and I come bearing grave news.'

Al-Afdal and looked down at the ring in the palm of his hand.

'This ring was given to you by Turan-Shah?'

'It was, my lord, to ensure the message was taken seriously.'

'And what does the prince have to say?'

'My lord,' said Hassan, 'the walls of Acre are crumbling. When I left, the outer defences were already breached, and the Christians swarm like flies upon a rotting corpse. If we do not do something straight away, the city will fall. They need reinforcements, my lord, or Acre will not last another day.'

'And you think that another assault on their rear will stop the attack?'

'I am not versed in the ways of generals,' said Hassan, 'but if the attacking force is strong enough and makes its focus the eastern side of Mount Toron, the Christians will have no choice but to turn and defend their positions. At the same time, a column of warriors could access the northern gate to reinforce the city. We have to do something, my lord, or Acre will fall.'

'I have heeded the message,' said Al-Afdal, 'and because of your bravery, we will send every warrior we can spare against the infidels. You have done well, Hassan, and have our gratitude.' He held out his hand. 'This ring is now yours to keep. Wear it well and if you ever need to see me, use it as a message.'

'Thank you, my lord,' said Hassan, 'I just hope we are in time.'

In the commandery, Arturas, Hunter and the other three men had been let into the bailey by Fakhiri through the side gate and just before dawn, had managed to scramble up a damaged wall to access the commandery compound itself. With the sun rising, they were at severe risk of being seen and had been forced to hide in one of the unused lookout towers.

'Where is the storeroom?' asked Hunter quietly.

'In there,' said Fakhiri, pointing at a building. The only way in is on the far side.'

'I can't see any way of getting closer without being seen,' said Hunter, 'they outnumber us fifty to one, and we would be overwhelmed before we got anywhere near.'

'So what do we do?'

'All we can do is get into position and wait,' said Hunter. 'Once the Templars attack, we may be able to take advantage of the confusion, but until then, there is nothing we can do.'

'And if the attack doesn't come?'

'Then, as soon as it is dark, we will take our chances.' He looked up at the sky. 'It's almost midday,' he said, 'so I reckon we have still got a few hours. I'll take the first watch, the rest of you get some rest.'

Unaware that help was so close, the prisoners in the storeroom were close to breaking. Each knew they could not go on much longer, and with only a few mouthfuls of water left in the barrel, it was only a matter of time until they succumbed. Sumeira had taken every opportunity to encourage her fellow prisoners, knowing that if they called out to beg for mercy, the chances were they would all be dead within minutes.

'We are almost out of water,' said one of the prisoners. 'Once that is gone, there is no sense in going on.'

'I understand,' said Sumeira, 'and I thirst as much as you, but the barrage has stopped, which means they must be talking terms.'

'Or our allies have retreated and given up,' said Robin.

'No,' said Sumeira. 'Fakhiri told me the army is as big as any he has seen, and two great kings have come from France and England. I think they may be discussing terms of surrender.'

'Even if they are,' replied Robin, 'the handover could take days, and we would be long dead from thirst by the time they arrived.'

'If we are careful, the water will last until nightfall, and by then the heat will have subsided.'

'And if nobody comes?'

'If nobody is here by dawn tomorrow, then I will call out myself.'

'Dawn it is,' said Robin, 'I just hope we can last that long.'

On the eastern edge of the city, Richard's men had made a clearing in the midst of the rubble and erected a shelter as protection from the heat of the midday sun.

On the one side, Richard of England and Guy of Lusignan sat alongside Phillip of France, all three wearing their full royal regalia. Behind them were the many nobles from the countries throughout Christendom who had brought their armies to fight in the crusade.

Each waited patiently for the Saracen deposition to arrive. All eyes were focussed on the main street leading from the walls into the heart of the city. The barricade had been removed by the Saracens an hour or so earlier and it was obvious this was the way they would come.

The sound of horses echoed down the street, and every Christian stared as the Saracen negotiators emerged into the clearing. At their head, was Turan-Shah, adorned in his Yemeni finery and sat astride a magnificent white horse. Behind him came his generals on their equally magnificent horses followed by a hundred warriors, each bedecked with gleaming metal armour, and carrying stringed recurved bows and quivers packed with arrows with snow-white feathers.

'It looks like they are out to impress,' said Phillip.

'It does,' said Richard, 'though I suspect that is all that is left of their army.'

As the column approached, the three kings got to their feet and waited as Turan-Shah and two of his generals dismounted before walking over to the shelter.

'Prince Turan-Shah,' said Richard, 'welcome.' He pointed to the three seats on the opposite side of the table. 'Please be seated.'

All six men sat down and waited as servants brought trays of chilled water and fresh fruit. Each man took a sip of water, and once the formalities were over, Richard turned to face the prince.

'Turan-Shah,' he said, 'I have heard much about you, and if truth be told, I am impressed at the way you have repelled our forces for so long.'

'Allah is always with us,' said Turan-Shah, 'and it was his hand that kept you away.'

'You speak our language,' said Richard with surprise.

'I speak many languages,' said Turan-Shah. 'It is the way of civilised people, is it not?'

'Indeed,' said Richard, 'but to my shame, I have not yet had the chance to learn yours. Perhaps I will do so these next few months.'

'If you wish, I will send a teacher,' said Turan-Shah.

'You have my gratitude,' said the king and looked down at the scroll before him on the table.

'Turan-Shah,' he said, 'I have read your counteroffer, and the terms are mostly agreeable to me. There are some minor things that our people can sort out over the next few days, but alas, I have two conditions that must be adhered to before I can add my signature to this document.'

'There was no discussion about conditions.'

'We are having it now,' interjected Guy of Lusignan.

'And what are these conditions?' asked the prince.

'The first is straightforward,' said Richard. 'I realise it will take a day or so to muster your people to leave the city, but as soon as I sign this parchment, my men must be given immediate access to fly our banners from the walls of Acre.'

'Agreed,' said Turan-Shah. 'and the second condition?'

'I understand there are several Christian prisoners being held in the western quarter of the city,' said Richard. 'They need urgent medical attention, and we want them released immediately.'

'I am not aware of these people,' said Turan-Shah.

'No, you wouldn't be. It seems they are in hiding and are surrounded by armed men.'

'Where are they being held?'

'In the old Templar commandery.'

Turan-Shah stared at the king before turning to the man at his side and talking quietly in Egyptian. When he was finished, he turned back to King Richard.

'The place you speak of is not manned by any of my men. It is occupied by those who believe it is better to die than surrender.'

'Fanatics,' said Richard.

'Name them what you will. I do not agree with their calling but accept that Allah's hand guides each of us in different ways.'

'So they will not be surrendering?'

'As they no longer answer to me, I do not know.'

'Yet if you ordered them to surrender, they would?'

'As I said, they no longer answer to me. Only to themselves and to Allah.'

'If they intend to resist us, Turan-Shah, I will have no option but to kill them all, treaty or no treaty. To do so puts our own people at risk, so I ask you again, can you not get the prisoners released into your custody?'

'I suspect the knowledge of Christian prisoners hidden within their reach would be seen as a great asset to those who fight on, and I see no possibility that the prisoners will be released unharmed. There is nothing I can do.'

'Can you not have your men force them out?'

'King Richard,' said Turan-Shah. 'I am willing to cede the city, besmirch my name and face the wrath of my sultan. One thing I will not do is turn Muslim against Muslim. I disagree with what they are doing but will not stand in their way. If they are a problem, then it is one for you to sort out, not me.'

'So,' said King Richard, 'if I understand you correctly, you are happy to cede the city but accept there is more fighting to be done.'

Turan-Shah stared at the king before giving a single nod.

'That is correct.'

King Richard looked at the monarchs on either side of him before turning back to the prince.

'In that case,' he said, my additional terms are these. 'I need you to allow my men to pass your defences without retaliation. We will do what has to be done to rescue the prisoners and if that means the deaths of those responsible, then so be it. You will not retaliate.'

'This can all be done at a later date when we have gone,' said Turan-Shah

'Our information says they may not last that long,' replied the king, 'I need to move today and no later.'

Turan-Shah talked to both of his generals before facing the king once again.

'If these are the limits of the extra conditions, then I agree to the terms. The city and the prisoners are yours, Sir Richard, now let there be a sheathing of swords.'

The three kings got to their feet as did the Saracens and as Turan-Shah and Richard reached across the table to grab each other's hand, a massive roar of approval echoed around the encampment. The surrender had been accepted, and after being under siege for almost two years, Acre had finally fallen.

Out on the eastern plain, Hassan Malouf rode his newly-acquired horse along the front of the largest Ayyubid army he had ever seen. As far as he could see, row after row of Saracen cavalry sat upon their horses waiting for the order to attack. Thousands of foot-soldiers stood behind them, knowing that this time there would be no withdrawal and they would not stop until they relieved their brothers in Acre. At the front of the army, Al-Afdal and Gokbori both sat upon their own horses, ready to lead the charge.

'My lord,' said Hassan, reining in his horse. 'May I be blessed with riding alongside you?'

'As you wish,' said Al-Afdal, 'but do not expect to be kept from the fighting. This time we lead our men from the front.'

'I would have it no other way,' said Hassan and turned his horse to face Acre.

'Ready the men,' roared Gokbori and as signal horns echoed across the plain, thousands of Saracen warriors prepared to advance.

Hassan swallowed hard knowing that this battle was going to be unforgiving and with the Christian army stronger than he had ever seen before, one that he knew he would likely not survive.

Gokbori drew his scimitar and raised it in the air. Riders tightened their grip in anticipation, and horses strained against their reins. The emir looked towards Salah ad-Din's son for the final command but paused as he saw the look on Al-Afdal's face change from determination to confusion.

'My lord,' said Gokbori, 'we await your command.'

Al-Afdal continued staring at the part of the city that could be seen to the left of Mount Toron before turning to face Gokbori.

'Call off the attack,' he said, 'and return to camp.'

Gokbori stared in amazement, not sure what to do.

'My lord,' he said eventually, 'our forces are straining at the bit. We are stronger than we have ever been and our brothers in Acre have begged for our intervention. To hold back now is a betrayal.'

'Is it?' asked Al-Afdal, 'or is it a sensible decision to keep our men for the defence of Jerusalem?

'Deny the Christians Acre,' said Gokbori, 'and there will be no need to protect Jerusalem.'

'It is too late for that,' said Al-Afdal, 'look again at the city.'

Gokbori and Hassan turned to stare towards Acre. At first, all they could see was that the battlements were now adorned with many flags, but as realisation dawned, Hassan's heart sunk. They were the banners of the Christians.

'The city is already lost, Gokbori,' said Al-Afdal, 'the garrison has surrendered. Stand down the men.'

Chapter Thirty-two

Acre

July – AD 1191

Deep in the heart of the city, men and women alike fled for their lives, seeking safety wherever they could amongst the ruins. The streets echoed to the sound of a thousand marching men, and many of Acre's population thought that it was only a matter of time before they were slaughtered. But there was no need for such fear, for the mighty military machine that was the Templar brotherhood only had thoughts for one target, the citadel.

Onward they marched through the streets, almost two hundred Templar knights accompanied by four hundred sergeants and four hundred archers. Behind them came the horse-drawn wagon holding the battering ram needed to break down any gates.

The column was packed tightly with the outer ranks facing their shields outwards against any potential attack, but apart from one man who was trampled underfoot after hurling himself at the front of the column, there were no incidents to deal with, and they quickly reached the far side of the city.

Thomas Cronin led the way alongside Robert de Sablé and the seneschal, and as they neared the citadel, Cronin held up his hand to bring the Templar column to a halt.

'Why are we stopping?' asked the grandmaster.

'The citadel is just beyond the next row of buildings,' said Cronin, 'if we split the column here, there are streets to either side of us so we can spread the attack.'

'And the gates?'

'They are just before us. As they only lead into the outer courtyard, they may not be barricaded, but even so, they will slow us down. I suggest a sudden attack may gain us access, but we must waste no time.'

'So be it,' said Robert and turned to the seneschal.

'Bring up the ram,' he said, 'and deploy our men to protect them. Tell the archers that if as much as a bird shows their head above the walls, I want a dozen arrows in it before it knows what is happening.'

'As you wish,' said the knight and turned away to organise the attack.

'You have done well,' said the grandmaster turning to face Cronin. 'If you wish, you can stay with me during the attack.'

'With the greatest of respect, my lord,' said Cronin, 'my place is amongst my fellow sergeants. With your permission, I will fight amongst my brothers.'

'I understand,' said the grandmaster. 'I would do the same. Now be gone Brother Cronin, we will speak again when the task is done.'

'Of course,' said Cronin and turned to find his fellow sergeants.

Within a few minutes, the Templar army had spread out throughout the streets just out of sight of the citadel. Battle-hardened men rested their hands on the hilts of bloodied swords, banishing all thoughts of mercy from their minds. The fortress belonged to them and one way or another, they were going to get it back.

Robert de Sablé turned to the signaller at his side.

'You know what to do,' he said, 'sound the attack.'

The horn blower sent the signal echoing through the streets, and as Acre resounded with the sound of Templar horns, a thousand men burst forth to attack the citadel, each with the same battle cry roaring from their throats. '*À moi, beau sire! Beauséant à la rescousse!*'

Inside the disused watchtower, Arturas's eyes sprung open and he leapt to his feet. The three other men in the room did the same and rushed to the tiny window that looked inward over the commandery.

'I'd recognise that battle-cry anywhere,' gasped the mercenary, the Templars are here.'

Everyone stared over to the main building. Saracens poured from inside to join the defences in the front courtyard.

Hunter ran into the room and looked towards the others.

'Grab your weapons,' he said, 'and get ready to move.'

On the eastern side of the citadel, the sudden attack had caught the defenders by surprise, and after a brief but brutal battle at the gates, the Templars forced themselves into the outer bailey before spreading out to form a shield wall. Behind them came the rest of the assault force as well as the cart pulling the battering ram.

'*Archers,*' roared the seneschal, 'target the walls. The rest of you, upon my command, *advaaance.*'

Protected by their shields, the Templars marched towards the large gates into the commandery compound. Up on the battlements, hundreds of men did what they could to repel the assault, sending volley after volley of their own arrows against the Templars.

In the courtyard, the cart holding the ram had been unhitched from the horses, and dozens of foot-soldiers ran to take their positions at the timber crossbars fixed across the armoured tree trunk.

'*Ready,*' roared the seneschal as soon as they were in place, '*advaaance!*'

The men leaned into the task, and within seconds, the heavy battering ram smashed into the timber gate, sending it creaking inward.

'*Again,*' roared the seneschal and the men turned to return the cart to its original position. Several were cut down by arrows but were quickly dragged away and replaced by others.

'*Ready,*' roared the seneschal again, '*advaaance!*'

Over and over again they repeated the operation and over and over again the gates held until, with over twenty Templar foot-soldiers dead or wounded, they managed to send the ram crashing through into the commandery courtyard.

With an almighty roar, the knights followed it through, smashing into the defenders with their heavy shields and huge swords. Behind them came the sergeants, spreading out to assault the flanks, but despite their strength, the fanatical defenders were just as determined, and the fight became a storm of blood and pain.

On the far side of the commandery, Hunter and his comrades raced across the courtyard and edged their way around the building. Hidden from sight behind a wall, they watched as the Saracens swarmed over the battlements to repel the attackers.

'I smell fire,' said Fakhiri and looked upward to see smoke coming from one of the upper windows.

'They know their time has come, said Hunter and have fired the buildings. We have to get our people out of there.'

They emerged from behind the wall and crept around to the entrance. Hunter and Arturas managed to get inside unseen, but as the rest followed, one of the Saracens on the battlements saw him and sounded the alarm.

Immediately, dozens of Saracens turned and ran across the courtyard to cut them down.

'We've been seen,' shouted Arturas, drawing his sword, 'you keep going, we'll hold them off.'

Hunter and Fakhiri continued down the corridor as the mercenary, and the other three men formed a line at the door. Within moments, one of the Saracen warriors crashed into them with little thought for his own safety. Arturas's sword cut him down, but the impetus had forced them back, and the warrior was quickly replaced by two more.

The fight intensified, but the narrowness of the corridor meant only a few Saracens could approach at any one time. Arturas and his men fought furiously, killing anyone who came against them but the Saracen numbers were just too great, and they forced the Christians further back along the corridor. One of Arturas's men suddenly fell with a spear through the throat, and the mercenary knew, they could not hold them back much longer.

In the eastern half of the commandery, the skill and discipline of the Templars meant they had made short work of the defenders, and they spread out to kill anyone hiding within the buildings, fighting through the smoke and flames as the remaining fanatics set light to anything that would burn.

Smaller battles continued throughout the compound with the Templar sergeants mopping up the last of the resistance. Thomas Cronin was to the fore, his blade dripping with Saracen blood as he led his men from engagement to engagement. Slowly and surely, he made his way throughout the commandery, focussing on the bloody task in hand but always aware that Sumeira and the prisoners were still out of his reach.

In the cellar, Sumeira and the prisoners sat in the dark listening to every shout and every scream.

'What was that?' asked one of the prisoners,

'Shh,' said Sumeira, holding up a hand, *'listen,'*
The sounds continued, but she had no idea if the people responsible were Christian or Saracen. Suddenly someone banged hard on the hatch, and with a gasp of relief, she heard the sound of Fakhiri's voice.

'Sumeira, are you there?'

'It's Fakhiri,' shouted Sumeira, getting to her feet. She climbed the stairs and banged on the hatch with her fist. 'Fakhiri,' she shouted, 'yes, we are still here. Can you get us out?'

Fakhiri unlocked the hatch and pushed it up against the wall. Sumeira ran up the last few steps and into Fakhiri's arms, crying with relief.

'You did it,' she gasped, 'you came back.'

'I said I would,' said Fakhiri, 'but I was not alone.' He glanced over to the scout guarding the kitchen door.

'Is that *Hunter?*' she gasped.

'It is,' said Fakhiri, 'but there will be time for reunions later, we have to get you out of here. How are the rest of the prisoners?'

'Too weak to move,' said Sumeira. 'Are we not safer here until the fighting is over?'

'No,' said Fakhiri, 'the building is ablaze, and the fires are spreading. We'll just have to carry them one by one. Is there another way out?'

Before Sumeira could answer, Arturas burst into the kitchen, followed by his remaining two men.

'There are too many of them,' he shouted, barricade the door, but it was too late, and the pursuing Saracens poured into the kitchens. Fakhiri pushed Sumeira back against the wall before drawing his knife and joining the fight. The Christians fought furiously but were outnumbered and knew it was only a matter of time before they were overwhelmed.

One of the warriors saw Sumeira and ran towards her with a bloody scimitar, but Arturas saw the danger and launched himself at the Saracen, knocking him off his feet before cutting his throat. Blood spurted everywhere, and Arturas pushed his victim away before turning to face Sumeira. His face was ashen, and as the physician watched, he fell into her arms, clutching at a deep wound in his side.

'Arturas,' she gasped and lowered him to the floor.

He rolled onto his back, gasping in pain and Sumeira lifted his hauberk to see a sword wound beneath his ribs. She placed both of her hands over the wound and pressed as hard as she could. Arturas cried out in pain, but she knew she had to stop the bleeding.

A few paces away, Hunter, Fakhiri and the last remaining mercenary fought for their lives. Dead and dying Saracens littered the kitchen floor, but there was at least a dozen more spread out throughout the room.

A voice called out above the noise of the fight, and the Saracens withdrew a few paces, leaving the Christians gasping for breath.

'What's going on,' asked Hunter, 'what are they doing?'

As if in answer to his question, a bloodied Saracen warrior entered the room and stared at the exhausted defenders. In his hand, he held a scimitar, saturated with Christian blood. He looked around the room before settling his gaze on Fakhiri.

'You,' he snarled. 'All this time, you have been nothing but a traitor to Islam.'

'Think what you will, Salman,' said Fakhiri, 'I only ever wished to right an injustice and never betrayed Allah.'

'I should have listened to my men and killed you at the gate,' said Salman.

'Why not try now, Salman?' said Fakhiri, his eyes never leaving the Saracen, 'you, me and two knives. Let us see who the greatest warrior is.'

Salman returned the stare before reaching down and picking up a fallen spear from the floor.

'I am no fool, Egyptian,' he said, 'and pick my fights carefully, but know this. After I have cut your heart in two, I will burn your comrades alive and give the woman to my men.' He lifted the weapon to shoulder height and braced to hurl it into Fakhiri's chest.

Sumeira screamed with fear, but before the Saracen officer could launch the spear, his face suddenly changed, and he looked down at his own chest in confusion. Sticking out between his ribs, was the blade of a Templar sword.

Everyone stared in shock as the Saracen fell to his knees. Behind him, standing in the smoke-filled doorway, was Thomas Cronin, his black tabard saturated with Saracen blood.

Before anyone could react, more Templar sergeants pushed past Cronin and fell upon the remaining Saracens. As they fought, Cronin pulled his sword out of Salman's back and walked over to Sumeira, now sitting with Arturas's head cradled in her lap.

'Is he dead?' he asked.

'No, but I need to get him to the hospital as quickly as I can. Is it safe out there?'

'Almost,' said Cronin. 'I'll get my men to clear the way.'

'Here,' said Hunter walking over with Fakhiri, 'we'll take him.'

'Where are the prisoners?' asked Cronin.

'In there,' said Sumeira, nodding towards the storeroom. 'They will need help.'

With all the remaining Saracens now dead or dying, the rest of the sergeants climbed down into the cellar and carried the prisoners out and away to safety. Sumeira followed Hunter and Fakhiri outside and across the body-strewn courtyard to the chapel.

Inside, the hospital had been wrecked, but she quickly made space and waited as Hunter and Fakhiri laid Arturas carefully on a horsehair mattress. The two men removed the mercenary's upper clothing and watched as Sumeira tried desperately to stem the bleeding.

'It's no good, she said, wiping her eyes with the back of her hand, 'I need my medical equipment. Without it, I am useless.'

Before anyone could answer, a man forced his way past Hunter and dropped to his knees alongside Sumeira.

'*Shani,*' she gasped, looking up, 'Thank God you are alive. What happened here.'

'After you left,' said Shani, 'Turan-Shah sent men to collect all the wounded, but I stayed and hid amongst the rafters. I suspected that you would return and if you did, you might need these. He turned away and retrieved a linen bag containing rolls of clean bandages and every missing piece of Sumeira's equipment.'

'Shani,' said Sumeira, 'you are truly an angel, and just might have saved this man's life.'

'Perhaps, but by the look of him, we need to act quickly.'

'We do,' said Sumeira, 'and you know what we have to do.' She turned to the men who had just saved her life. 'My friends,' she said, 'there are no words to thank you for what you have done, but for now you should leave us to get on with our work. Your friend is in good hands.'

Chapter Thirty-three

Acre

July – AD 1191

The following day, Hunter walked back into the chapel in the Templar commandery. The last of the defenders had all been killed and all the fires extinguished, but the buildings themselves were severely damaged.

The timely arrival of the Templar sergeants the previous day had ensured every prisoner was rescued and Sumeira had quickly taken them to what remained of the makeshift hospital.

With access to fresh water and food gifted from the Templar soldiers, she made them as comfortable as possible and at last, knew they were going to be safe.

'Sumeira,' said Hunter from the chapel doorway, 'there's someone who wants to see you.' The scout stood to one side, and Sumeira saw Cronin standing in the doorway.

'Cronin,' she said, standing up and walking across the room. 'I was hoping I would see you again before you re-joined your brotherhood. I just wanted to say thank you for what you did.'

'There are others who played a far bigger part than me,' said Cronin, 'most of whom are in this room.'

Sumeira looked across to Hunter, now sat on the far side of Arturas's bed. In the corner, Fakhiri was talking to Shani, trying to sell him some herbs he had stolen from one of the many prisoners.

'They are,' said Sumeira, 'but nevertheless, you still have my gratitude. Without your intervention yesterday, who knows what would have happened?'

'You are safe now,' said Cronin, 'that's all that matters.'

'So do you have to leave?'

'On the contrary, I have come to tell you the king is creating a hospital nearer the city centre. You will have much more room and access to whatever you need. We will wait until the sick are able to be moved, but our order wants to return the chapel to a place of worship as soon as possible.'

'I understand,' said Sumeira, 'give me a few days, and we will be out of your way.''

'How is Arturas?' asked Cronin.

'It's all down to infection,' said Sumeira, glancing towards the unconscious mercenary. 'We have stopped the bleeding and cleaned the wound, but the rest is up to him.'

'He'll make it,' said Cronin, 'just tell him there is free ale in the new hospital and he will drag his cot there himself.'

'I'm sure he will,' laughed Sumeira and took the sergeant's hand gently in hers.

Cronin looked down with surprise before looking into Sumeira's eyes.

'Cronin,' she said, 'during my captivity, I had time to think and realised that life is but a fleeting moment. I also realised that it is our own responsibility to do everything we can to make ourselves as happy as we can be. With that in mind, I have to be true to myself and say something to you, something that may make you uncomfortable.'

Cronin sighed deeply and stared at the physician. His feelings for the woman had long been buried but were now forcing themselves to the surface, a situation that was not tenable in times of war.

'Sumeira,' he said, cutting her short, 'perhaps one day, God willing, there will be time for such conversations, but that day has not yet come. We are still at war, and there is the small matter of Jerusalem to consider. If I return from there alive, then perhaps we will talk of such matters. Until then, such things should be kept private so as not to hurt others.'

'I understand,' said Sumeira, releasing his hand, 'but that day may come sooner than you think.'

'What do you mean?'

'I am going to Jerusalem,' she said, 'I still need to find my son.'

'Discard the idea, Sumeira,' said Cronin,' you will never get into the Holy-city alone.'

'I will not be alone,' said Sumeira, 'for if what I am hearing is correct, there will be at least forty thousand other Christian souls alongside me.'

'We managed to take Acre,' said Cronin, 'but paid a high price in human lives. The siege of Acre will pale into insignificance compared to an assault on Jerusalem. I suspect that death and disease will plague us every step of the way, and even if we make it, there is no way that Saladin will let the Holy-city go without fighting to the last man.'

'That may be so,' said Sumeira, 'but my son is within those walls, and as long as there is the slightest chance that he is alive, then I will go to the ends of the earth to find him. And besides, if it is going to be as bad as you say, you will need every physician you can get. Get used to the idea, Cronin, I am going to Jerusalem, and nothing you can say will stop me.'

To the south, part of the Christian army formed up on either side of the southern road, a show of strength to the Muslim occupation forces now leaving the city. Despite the relief of every Christian witnessing the withdrawal, there was no celebrating or humiliating insults. Too many of their comrades had died, and every man was just relieved it was over.

At the head of the column rode Turan-Shah on his magnificent white horse, followed by his ceremonial bodyguards and what was left of his army. Behind them came a bedraggled column of Muslim civilians, all released as part of the deal made with King Richard.

The Christians watched them pass in silence, shocked at how few warriors actually remained and with growing admiration at how such a small force had managed to keep them out for so long.

Up on the top of Mount Toron, King Richard stood alongside King Phillip of France and King Guy of Jerusalem, watching the procession snake towards the south. Behind them, spread across the open plain, the rest of the Christian army waited for the signal to move, tens of thousands of tired and hungry people, each waiting to enter Acre.

Out at sea, supply ships edged closer to the harbour, each weighed down with the supplies and equipment that would be needed to feed and rebuild the city.

'Well,' said Phillip, 'we did it. Acre is ours.'

'Aye, we did,' said Richard, 'but the city is in ruins.'

'Work for the masses,' said Guy of Lusignan. 'Give me five years and the city will be as great as ever it was.'

'A long-term vision,' said Richard, 'but one of secondary importance.'

'What do you mean?'

'The hard part has been done,' said Richard, 'but we need to open urgent negotiations for an exchange of prisoners as well as the return of the true cross.'

'And after that?'

'After that,' said King Richard as Turan-Shah's army disappeared into the distance, 'we do what we came here to do. We march on Jerusalem.'

Epilogue

Acre

Two weeks later

Following the surrender of the city, it had taken several days for the Christian army and its thousands of followers to feel safe amongst the streets and buildings. Some fanatics still formed minor pockets of opposition, but with the blood lust of the templars still high, their resistance was short-lived, and peace soon descended like a comforting blanket.

Many of those who had barely survived since the siege began now walked freely about their business and traders set up stalls in the marketplaces and along the city walls. Anyone who had no means to pay for food was put to work rebuilding the walls, welcome employment that put at least one hot meal in their bellies each night.

Supply ships started arriving from Cyprus, and in Acre's smaller harbour, men and women alike worked hard unloading them for a promise of a meal.

Amongst them was a simple Bedouin girl. Quiet in deed and manner, she laboured from dawn till dusk, and most days went unnoticed by all except those who worked alongside her. By night she slept in the corner a tiny room at the back of a cellar in one of the dock houses.

It was dark, and it was dirty, but it was also warm and very private, which suited her needs perfectly. After all, it wasn't every day that you got to kill a king, and with so many lining up to claim Acre as their own, all she had to do now was decide which one.

The End

Templar Glory

With Acre secured and Richard commanding the combined Christian army, there was only one thing more to do, and that was to reclaim Jerusalem. But Saladin also commanded a united army, one that was greater than any led by Richard, and though he may not have been able to stop the advance, one thing was certain …

He would fight the Lionheart every step of the way!

Coming Soon - Templar Glory, the exciting fifth book in The Brotherhood series.

The Brotherhood Book V

Author's Notes

As usual in these sorts of books, historical facts have been intertwined with fiction, enabling a much easier read around the reality of the battles, and the events leading up to pivotal points in history. Wherever possible, I have stuck to the facts, but allowance must be made for artistic license. In the notes below, I have tried to highlight the more important information, separating fact from fiction.

Terminology

The term *'Saracen,'* was a general derogatory name often used for any Arab person at the time. It did not refer to any one tribe or religion and was considered offensive by many of the indigenous cultures.

Similarly, the term *'Crusader'* was never used in the twelfth century as a reference to the Christian forces. They were usually referred to as the *'Franks or Kafirs'* by the Saracens.

The *'Outremer,'* was a generic name used for the Crusader states, especially the County of Edessa, the Principality of Antioch, the County of Tripoli, and the Kingdom of Jerusalem.

The Knights Templar

The order of the poor fellow-soldiers of Christ, and of the Temple of Solomon was formed in or around AD 1119 in Jerusalem by a French knight, Hugues de Payens. They were granted a headquarters in a captured Mosque on the Temple Mount in Jerusalem by King Baldwin II.

At first, they were impoverished, focusing only on protecting the weak on the road to Jerusalem, but after being supported by a powerful French Abbot, Bernard of Clairvaux, the order was officially recognised by the church at the Council of Troyes in AD 1129. From there they went from strength to strength, and soon became the main monastic order of knights in the Holy-land. Their influence grew across the known world, not just for their deeds of bravery, but because of their business acumen, and the order went on to become very wealthy, and immensely powerful.

The Emblems of the Templars

The Templar seal was a picture of two men riding a single horse. This is thought to depict the order's initial poverty when it was first formed though conversely, one of the rules of the order was that two knights could not ride one horse. Another explanation talks about the representation of 'true' brotherhood, wherein one knight rescues the other knight whose horse is probably injured. Intriguingly enough, there is a plausible commentary regarding two soldiers on a single horse, written by Saladin's chronicler Bahaed-Din Ibn Shaddad (referenced from Knight Templar 1120 – 1312 By Helen Nicholson)

"On June 7, 1192, the Crusader army marched to attack the Holy-city, (then occupied by Saladin). Richard's spies reported a long-awaited supply train coming from Egypt to relieve Saladin's army...when Richard received information that the caravan was close at hand...a thousand horsemen set out, each of whom took a foot soldier (on his horse) in front of him...At daybreak, he took the caravan unawares. Islam had suffered a serious disaster...The spoils were three thousand camels, three thousand horses, five hundred prisoners, and a mountain of military supplies. Never was Saladin more grieved, or more anxious."

When travelling or going to war, they rode under a white flag emblazoned with a red cross. Some historians believe it was in honour of St George, who's spirit many soldiers believed was seen at the battle of Antioch in AD 1098 during the first crusade.

The image of the cross was also used on other items of clothing, and equipment by the Templars, and indeed other orders of warrior monks (though not in red.) However, research shows that the red cross was not officially adopted until it was awarded by Pope Eugene III in AD 1147. Before this time, the knights wore only a plain white coat.

Conrad of Montferrat

Conrad of Montferrat was an Italian nobleman who arrived in that Holy-land just after the battle of Hattin. Upon reaching Acre, the captain of the fleet realised it was already in the hands of the Saracens and diverted to Tyre. Conrad quickly assumed command of the city from Reginald of Sidon and cast the Ayyubid banners into a ditch.

"Conrad was vigorous in arms, extremely clever both in natural mental ability, and by learning, amiable in character, and deed, endowed with all the human virtues, supreme in every council, the fair hope of his own side, and a blazing lightning-bolt to the foe, capable of pretence, and dissimulation in politics, educated in every language, in respect of which he was regarded by the less articulate to be extremely fluent."
Brevis Historia Occupationis et Amissionis Terræ Sanctæ ("A Short History of the Occupation, and Loss of the Holy Land")

Conrad's father, William V of Montferrat, had been captured at Hattin, and when Saladin attacked the city on the second occasion, he produced Conrad's father and offered to release him in return for the city. It is said that Conrad refused point-blank and aimed a crossbow at his father's heart saying he had lived a good life and would die in the cause of Christianity rather than see Tyre surrendered. It is also claimed that his father was supportive of his stance. Saladin eventually released William anyway, and he returned to his son in 1188.

Conrad began circulating his own claim to the throne, a claim that was divisive amongst the Christians all across the Outremer. His claim gathered strength with the support of his cousins, Leopold V of Austria, and Philip II, King of France, while Richard the Lionheart supported Guy of Lusignan. Saladin realised the conflicting positions could be the catalyst for division amongst the Christians, and in late 1188, released Guy of Lusignan in the knowledge that it would seed discontent amongst the two factions.

Conrad successfully defended Tyre from the Saracens on at least two occasions and went on to support the siege of Acre.

The Green Knight

Sancho-martin is actually a real character from the time. He gained his nickname from the colour of his weapons and armament. He is reputed to have been a formidable fighter and gained the admiration of Christian and Saracen alike. It is said that Saladin was so impressed, he offered the Green knight untold riches to fight in the Saracen cause, an offer that Sancho-martin refused. His death is unrecorded, but some say it was his efforts that inspired the tales of the Green Knight in the stories of Camelot.

Turan-Shah

Although there was indeed a Yemeni prince called Turan-Shah, (who, incidentally, was Saladin's older brother,) there is no record of the name of Acre's Muslim commander at the time of the siege.

Balian of Ibelin

Balian was one of the few nobles to escape Hattin with his life. He fled to Tyre before heading to Jerusalem to retrieve his wife and children. While there he became involved in the negotiations with Saladin for the surrender of the city, and eventually handed over the keys to the Tower of David on October 2, 1187, but only after paying approximately 30,000 dinars from his own treasury for the release of 7,000 prisoners who did not have enough money to buy their own freedom.

There is little evidence that he fought at the siege of Tyre, but it is evident that he swore fealty to Conrad of Montferrat and was alongside him at the siege of Acre.

The Siege of Acre

In 1189, Guy of Lusignan, King of Jerusalem, led his army to Acre. He immediately attacked the city but was unsuccessful, so put it under siege. Hearing about this, Saladin surrounded the Christian positions with his own army, cutting off any access to reinforcements or supplies. On October 4th, 1189, the Christians attacked Saladin's positions with the Templars on the left flank making great inroads into the Muslim lines. Saladin was quick to react, and when the Christian army split up to plunder the dead, the sultan launched a counterattack to great effect.

At the same time, a Saracen sortie from the north gate of Acre fell upon the Templar positions from behind, forcing them to retreat to defend their own lines. During the battle, Conrad of Montferrat was surrounded, and it was only the intervention of Guy that saved him from probable death. When the battle was over, both sides claimed victory, but Gerard of Ridefort, the Templar grandmaster, was captured and executed.

Over the next eighteen months, the siege of Acre continued with little effect. The Christian army received many reinforcements from all across Europe, and the Muslim garrison was reinforced, first by a fleet of Egyptian ships, and then by an army, helped by deserters from the Christian camp.

The lack of food and poor sanitary conditions meant that disease was rife amongst the besieging army, and many died, including Sibylla, the Queen of Jerusalem, and her two daughters. Upon their death, Conrad of Montferrat took advantage of Guy's weak claim to the throne and orchestrated his marriage to Isabella to mount a claim of his own, a declaration supported by Archbishop Ubaldo Lanfranchi of Pisa.

Cyprus

After conquering Messina in Sicily, Richard sailed for the Holy-land but encountered a massive storm. Some of his shops reached Cyprus, including the treasure ship. The one carrying his sister, and his fiancée limped towards Limassol and remained at anchor until the king arrived.

The Emperor of Cyprus refused to return any treasure or prisoners along with refusing to supply the damaged ship with any fresh water. When Richard arrived, he tried to reason with Isaac, but when he received dismissive messages in return, attacked the island and drove the emperor inland.

Isaac agreed to surrender, but soon went back on his word, and regathered his army in the mountains. Richard was joined by Guy of Lusignan along with other nobles from the Holy-land, and once again defeated Isaac. Upon capture, the emperor begged Richard not to place him in chains of steel, so Richard had him bound in fetters of gold and silver.

The Fall of Acre

In the spring of 1191, after conquering Cyprus, Richard of England arrived in Acre. At first, both he and Phillip succumbed to the disease ravaging the Christian camp, and the final assault was delayed.

Phillip recovered quicker and assaulted the city without Richard, but the English king did not lay idle. Instead, he tried to negotiate with Saladin, requesting that they meet in person, but Saladin was reluctant and sent his son instead. Richard's illness meant that he could not attend the meeting, so finally, on June 7, AD 1191, he joined forces with the rest of the besiegers and attacked Acre. With him he had two enormous trebuchets called God's Own Catapult and Bad Neighbor, both essential in breaching the city walls.

When it was obvious that the city would soon fall without reinforcements, a swimmer left the harbour to warn Saladin, but it was too late, and on July 12, 1191, Acre surrendered to the Christians.

More books by K M Ashman

The India Summers Mysteries
The Vestal Conspiracy
The Treasures of Suleiman
The Mummies of the Reich
The Tomb Builders

The Roman Chronicles
The Fall of Britannia
The Rise of Caratacus
The Wrath of Boudicca

The Medieval Sagas
Blood of the Cross
In Shadows of Kings
Sword of Liberty
Ring of Steel

The Blood of Kings
A Land Divided
A Wounded Realm
Rebellion's Forge
Warrior Princess
The Blade Bearer

The Brotherhood
Templar Steel – The Battle of Montgisard
Templar Stone – The Siege of Jacob's Ford
Templar Blood – The Battle of Hattin
Templar Fury – The Siege of Acre
Templar Glory – The Road to Jerusalem

Standalone Novels

Savage Eden
The Last Citadel
The Legacy Protocol
The Seventh God

Audio Books
Blood of the Cross
The Last Citadel
A Land Divided
A Wounded Realm
Rebellion's Forge
The Warrior Princess
The Vestal Conspiracies
The Tomb Builders
The Mummies of the Reich

Contact Kevin at:

Website - **KMAshman.com**

Facebook - **www.facebook.com/KMAshman**

Email – **Silverbackbooks1@gmail.com**

Printed in Great Britain
by Amazon